# on the precipice

## Book 3 of the Trailblazer series

### Robin Reardon

IAM Books
www.robinreardon.com

Many thanks to my friend Jean who, calling on her years of experience living on Mount Desert Island and her wonderful attention to detail, helped to make sure my main character Nathan didn't get lost on any of the beautiful trails in Acadia National Park.

You are not in the mountains. The mountains are in you.
— John Muir


There is a crack in everything. That's how the light gets in.
— Leonard Cohen

# FOREWORD

By
Stevie M. Jonak

"No one can make you feel inferior without your consent."
~ Eleanor Roosevelt

As I began composing the foreword for *On The Precipice*, I realized how well the quote above applies to the story. Eleanor Roosevelt was married to the only U.S. president to date who was a wheelchair user. When in 1921, after sixteen years of marriage, polio left her husband Franklin Delano Roosevelt in need of a wheelchair, Eleanor stayed with him. In a time when most disabled individuals were institutionalized, her decision— and, frankly, his family's decision—to support him in his bid to win the presidency was radical.

In *On The Precipice*, the main character (Nathan Bartlett) is attracted to Drew Madden, who uses a wheelchair. However, Nathan struggles with the idea of having a romantic relationship with Drew because of his disability. This reluctance is something wheelchair users almost always face in their relationships.

Most people who use wheelchairs want a life that includes dating, desire, love, and sexual intimacy as much as anyone without a disability does. In depicting the progress of Nathan's and Drew's relationship, Reardon does a wonderful job of showing all aspects of life for someone who uses a wheelchair, both in terms of romance and in terms of life in general.

Another way in which Eleanor Roosevelt's quote applies is that Drew doesn't allow anyone to make him feel inferior, whether it's Nathan or society in general. Society tends to look upon people with disabilities as "less-than," and Drew does not let anyone make him feel like he is anything other than a complete person. *On The Precipice* depicts this concept in a way that should help many non-disabled readers challenge their assumptions and change their outlook on the disabled community.

The character of Drew Madden has enough money to buy any medical device he needs or wants, which makes it possible for him to remain active and productive. But that is not true for far too many in the disabled community. For example, in 2016 the poverty rate for disabled individuals was 21%, compared to 13% for non-disabled people. This means the disabled must rely on the approval of various health insurance companies if they need to acquire expensive mobility aids.

Powered chairs can cost several thousand dollars, and manual chairs cost between $500 and $2,000, depending on what customizations the individual needs, and there are some specifications that push the cost far higher. The high cost of chairs places the disabled who need them at the mercy of their health insurance policies' rules. This always means that someone who needs a wheelchair could not receive financial support for more than one chair at a time, forcing the individual to choose either a powered or a manual chair.

In addition, if the individual has a manual wheelchair, insurance companies will not pay for a powered chair, provided the user can push a manual chair indoors, regardless of whether a powered chair would be necessary for outdoor use. And if, because of exceptions, an individual manages to procure a powered chair through insurance and the original manual chair (still a necessary item) needs repair, insurance will not cover it. Anything like vehicle accommodations are completely beyond the scope of insurance, as are special-use chairs like all-terrain chairs and easily-collapsible powered chairs.

In this story, most of what the character Drew can purchase for himself—aids that help him live a better quality of life—are considered luxuries in reality. These "luxuries" significantly improve his mobility in general and enhance his access to locations outside his home. In the real world, however, these mobility aids are financially beyond the reach of the vast majority of the people who would benefit from them.

While the limitations of insurance coverage are problematic, the single biggest reason many people with disabilities live in poverty is the set of regulations and requirements of the Social Security Administration.

The 2020 maximum for Social Security Income (SSI) is $783 a month. Minimum wage is roughly $1,100 a month. That's a negative monthly delta of $317.

There are extremely complex regulations regarding how SSI applies in the case where the individual's assets are concerned. The agency monitors the individual's bank accounts closely, and it performs extensive annual interviews to determine whether the benefit will be continued. In many cases, acquiring an asset worth over $2,000 will eliminate SSI.

If disabled people marry, they run the risk of losing their income and Medicaid insurance, placing many in a position where they cannot afford to marry. With most welfare benefits, the income of the entire household is taken into account. This means that if the newly-married individuals' combined income is greater than regulations allow ($3,000 as of this writing), the disabled person(s) will lose both SSI and Medicaid benefits. The result is that many people with disabilities are forced to remain "roommates" with the person they want to marry.

Disabled individuals in the workforce face financial discrimination as well. It's legal in most states for an employer to pay disabled individuals well below the federal minimum wage of $7.25 an hour. Wages for the disabled are sometimes as low as $2.15 an hour, far below the poverty line.

This practice conceals an ugly reality. Welfare benefits—benefits that the disabled could not afford without significant earnings—have a value assigned to them. That value is added to whatever the individuals earn. If this total exceeds a certain limit, the benefits are removed. As long as their earnings are low enough, they continue to receive the benefits they need. Because most disabled individuals are not in higher earnings brackets, they can't afford to pay for the benefits they would lose. The result is very low pay, and even with welfare benefits in place these individuals remain in financial poverty. This situation is improving slowly but is still problematic as of this writing.

Ironically, individuals with disability almost always have living expenses above and beyond non-disabled citizens, which exacerbates the already profoundly unfair financial situation most will find themselves in.

As if the financial hardships and limitations were not enough, the disabled are often accused of fraud—that is, of pretending that they are disabled in order to receive government benefits, to avoid having to work, and even to be sure of having "the best parking spaces."

Society appears not to realize or believe that most people with disabilities would prefer not to have them, even without the benefits that come with them.

I hope that readers will see in the lives of Drew and Nathan some of the challenges disabled people in the U.S. have faced for decades and continue to face today. Drew is very honest about his experiences and about how he lives as a disabled man in contemporary society. Nathan is honest about his concerns when it comes to the idea of dating someone in a wheelchair. Some of his concerns might sound harsh, but they are valid. They are real. Anyone in his position would have to face them.

Above all, what I most want non-disabled people to absorb from the character of Nathan is that he is willing to ask questions, to learn from Drew, and ultimately to change his views on the disabled. From Drew, I want readers to see that being disabled does not define the person. Drew has many attributes that define who he is as an individual: Confident. Smart. Sexual. Strong. Independent. A multi-dimensional personality is true for most of the disabled. You will see this, if you will let them show you. But first you must see them.

In *On The Precipice*, Reardon shows with great detail what disabled people live with and what non-disabled people think of them. I'm hoping readers will recognize these things as they witness them in society and in their own perceptions and behavior.

I am also hoping readers see in Drew a regular, average guy and not just some inspirational trope—something we see all too often in entertainment. He is a person just like anyone else, and he represents disabled people as they can be seen every day. Roughly 25% of the U.S. population is disabled in some way—one of the largest minorities in this country. They are everywhere, for everyone to see during everyday interactions, maybe even next door. They are deserving of the same regard and respect as anyone else.

This book is beautifully written and shows disabled people in a way that most stories do not. This is the story we need now. This is the story disabled people deserve now.

My name is Stevie M. Jonak, and I am a full-time wheelchair user. I have never been able to walk. I was born with a birth defect called spina bifida and also have several other conditions related to it, so I have no mobility and no feeling from the hips down. I rely on Social Security and other welfare services in order to live. Without these services I would not be able to live independently. I live alone with my cat Lillium, and I consider myself lucky to be able to do so—luckier than many people with disabilities.

I provided advice and guidance concerning the character of Drew as much as I could, but ultimately it was Reardon's words that made Drew who he is. I hope other wheelchair users in the disabled community relate to and agree with this story. I hope I've done them proud.

Stevie M. Jona
Louisville, Kentucky
July 2020

ROBIN REARDON

# CHAPTER ONE

The woman was talking to herself. At first I was sure it had to be that she was wearing an earpiece, and her conversation was with someone on the other end of a phone line. I figured that as we got closer to each other on the sidewalk, I'd be able to see what device she was using.

But no.

Maybe it was the amount of gesticulating she was doing with her hands that gave it away. Maybe it was the wild nest of her dirty blond hair, dirty in more ways than one. Maybe it was the disheveled appearance of her mismatched clothing, or the way she would shout every third or fourth word. Whatever the clue was, I finally realized that if she was talking to someone, it was someone in her own head.

Just another day in New York City, I told myself—silently—as I tried to tear my gaze away from her. And I was so focused on what I was trying not to see that I didn't see what I should have seen, and before I knew it I'd been pushed into the narrow space between two buildings.

My back hit the brick wall with a painful thud, and the dirty white face of some guy in a dark blue hoodie was inches from mine. Between our faces was the blade of the knife he held. I barely registered that behind this guy was another guy.

No one said anything. The second guy moved forward and fished through my pockets. He took my phone and my wallet. He lifted the key ring attached to a tiny replica of the Eiffel Tower, which held the keys to Nina's loft, but there was nothing on it to indicate what it opened, so he threw it aside. Then he forced my left wrist against the bricks behind me so he could take my watch, the Garmin Forerunner hiker's watch that Gram had given me for my birthday during my junior year at college.

My mind must have been desperate for something rational in the midst of this chaos, because I remember thinking, *I'll have to buy another watch.*

I felt all this rather than saw it, because my eyes weren't sure whether to focus on the knife or the face of the guy threatening to cut off my nose. And it all happened so fast—and I know this will sound crazy—that I didn't have time to be scared. There was adrenaline, yeah, big time, and I could feel my heart pounding, but my brain didn't register anything until the two thieves dashed out of the alley, my possessions now theirs.

At that point my knees buckled a little, and I leaned against the brick wall as I slid down a few inches and then bent at the waist, hands clinging to my knees for support, my breath coming in harsh gasps. It was probably about two minutes, maybe more, before I had the strength and the stability to look for the key ring.

As I picked it up, the pointy bits of the tower pressing reassuringly into my clenched hand, I thought, *It's a good thing I back up my phone to my laptop frequently.* Looking back, I suspect my frazzled brain was still seeking desperately for an anchor, for something that was normal and predictable and safe. Like buying a new watch.

Key ring in hand, I looked toward the street to make sure my assailants weren't there, but one step forward told me I needed support. I leaned my right hand against the bricks and moved slowly toward the lightness of the street I had so recently been following, a street that had seemed like a normal city street just a few minutes ago and that now seemed like a war zone.

I managed to stand unsupported where the alley opened onto the sidewalk, and my eyes darted in a frenzy in one direction and then another. There was no sign of the thieves, but—hell, there'd been no sign of them before the attack.

I stood rooted to the cement for some amount of time I

couldn't have gauged. I must have looked a little wild, because people walking by were giving me odd looks.

Aloud, I said to myself, "They're gonna think you're like that woman."

That irony was enough to make me rub my face and move forward in the direction I'd been going before I'd been nabbed. I'd gone a block and a half before I could wrap my terrified brain around where I was and where I was going and how to get from where I was to where I'd been going before the sky fell.

Half of my brain wanted to scream, to release the massive lump of pain in my chest that came from the absolute helplessness I'd felt when all that had existed in the world was that shiny knife blade and what it had threatened: the end of me, the end of my life, the end of everything I wanted to be and do and experience, forever and ever.

The other half of my brain was working like mad to control all emotion—whether it was grief or fear or regret or anything else—and just get me back to Nina's Broome Street loft. A voice in my head, which I managed to keep from speaking aloud, said, *Just keep walking. In fifteen minutes, you can collapse and scream all you want.*

I fixed my eyes straight ahead, focusing on nothing, and I kept walking.


It was maybe four o'clock by the time I fumbled my way into Nina's building, up the elevator to her sixth floor loft, and into the foyer, where I sat heavily on the bench to my left. It was an odd piece, made of some kind of wood I didn't recognize. Wood, of course, lends itself to being carved and shaped, but this bench was so unembellished as to be austere, devoid of any characteristic that would allow me to connect with it. Even the grain of the wood was featureless.

I rubbed my hand gently along the edge, glad of something solid beneath me, even this empty thing, and thought—not for the first time—how well it fit into the rest of the loft.

This loft was not really my sister Nina's. It belonged to her boyfriend, Luc Beaumont, a French fashion photographer who, I suspected, wasn't famous enough to have the wealth necessary to underwrite this blandly but expensively appointed space. It seemed likely his family had had something to do with it. And it seemed likely that the blandness would mean the place could be ready quickly to go on the market, if it came to that.

I hadn't met Luc yet, though. When I'd arrived about ten days ago, on August twelfth, he had already left on a trip to visit his family in Normandy and, as Nina had put it, "to rest up before the madness of Fashion Week in New York and then Milan, both in September."

"Visit his family." That phrase seemed to echo through the empty loft. It implied home, which included people who cared about you, people you could rely on—such a long way from this sterile environment my only surviving family member now inhabited.

Where I wanted to be, at that moment, was back in New Hampshire, back in the large colonial-style house where I'd grown up, that house full of memories and comfort, that house that had sheltered and nourished the life I'd lived with my sister Nina, and my brother Neil, and my Gram. I felt a new lump rising in my throat, a lump made of the profound sadness of knowing I could never be in that house again. Nina and I had sold it just last week to a young family from Cincinnati. There was a Mom and a Dad and two boys and a girl. Just like my family had been. Just like my family had stopped being, first because my parents and Gramps had died in a car wreck when I was all of one year old, and then, second, after Neil had been burned to death in a forest fire only a few years ago, and third after Gram had died of a stroke just last March.

Even the Subaru Forester Gram had bought a few years

ago, mine after her death, wasn't here with me; it was tucked into the back of the driveway at a friend's house in Concord.

I had no more home.

I stood, still a little shaky, and moved forward into my very temporary home, a place to stay for a few weeks while I sorted myself out. Nina called this a loft, but someone's money had restructured it so that there were distinct rooms. The foyer led into the living room, where a huge circle of thin metal, stuck with flame-shaped bulbs, hung over the couch and two chairs. All three of those pieces were covered with leather of a mottled pale brown, all with low backs and arms, all equally without personality or warmth. To my left, facing the couch, was a fireplace. Inside it was a wrought-iron—what, candelabra, maybe?—that held several fat, grey candles. The fireplace gave off the air of something that was ornamental rather than functional, but it was summer—hardly the season for fires—so perhaps I was being ungenerous. But it was so different from the fireplace at my real home, which was sometimes stacked with wood and sometimes was in need of cleaning out from having hosted several glowing fires.

I moved across the room to the windows overlooking Broome Street and gazed sightlessly at the building across the way. The fingers of my right hand wrapped around my left wrist before I realized why. Those fingers were feeling the skin where my watch had been, the watch Gram had given me as though it had been a token of acknowledgement that I had successfully followed in Neil's footsteps, that I had figuratively stepped into the hiking boots the fire had burned from his feet. Getting that watch from her was as though she was saying, "Neil would be so proud of you, Nathan. You've become the mountain man he was meant to be."

I could buy another watch. Gram's inheritance—which had come as a complete surprise to Nina and me, given Gram's history of thrift—meant I could buy almost any watch I wanted. But it would never be the same. It wouldn't be a watch on which Gram had asked the jeweler to inscribe "NCB." Nathan Cassidy Bartlett.

Sometime around seven o'clock I heard the lock turn in the door to the hall, and Nina came in. Rustling noises indicated that she was carrying some number of bags. She came into the living room and saw me sitting on the unwelcoming couch, staring at the useless fireplace, a glass of scotch—raided from Luc's collection of beverages—on the glass-and-chrome coffee table in front of me. The scotch was a single-malt, The Glenlivet XXV, which I'd priced online at around four hundred dollars a bottle. The glass Nina saw had been filled twice before, and there was not much left of my third pour. I didn't look away from the grey candles.

"Nathan? What on earth are you doing, sitting here in the dark?"

"It's not quite dark."

She dropped rather than set her bags on the dining table, which was several feet behind the couch. "It's dark enough." She moved toward the couch, stood behind me for a few seconds, and then walked around where she could face me. "What's going on?"

I looked up at her, struck yet again (perhaps partly because of my inebriated state) at her exotic beauty, an artifact of our vague, somewhat remote Chinese heritage. It had been evident in her teen years, but now that she was in her early twenties she was stunning. The effect was, no doubt, enhanced by her talent at her chosen career in the world of fashion, but she needed little makeup for the clear skin surrounded in a perfect heart shape by her straight, nearly-black hair.

When I didn't speak, she prompted, "This isn't like you, sitting in the dark, getting drunk on scotch. What's going on?"

She was right. It wasn't like me, though I had

developed a taste for single malts earlier in the summer, at a hotel in San Francisco, after a spiritual quest on the island of Kaua'i, and after that nearly dying in an airplane when it lost cabin pressure over the Pacific, on its way back to the mainland.

I leaned forward, took another sip, and set the glass down heavily.

"I got jumped. One of them had a knife."

"What? Are you all right?"

I nodded. "On the outside, yeah." I didn't know where to go from there.

"Where were you?"

"Houston Street. I'd just come from visiting that methadone clinic to see how it operates. I was on my way home...." Home. "I was on my way back here when two guys hauled me into an alley." I stared around Nina at the grey candles. My voice sounded flat, but I figured it was better that way than shouting and yelling, an urge the scotch had helped me quell. "They took my phone, my wallet, and—" I almost lost it here. I closed my eyes and took a deep breath. "And my watch."

"The watch Gram gave you?"

"The same."

She moved around the coffee table and sat beside me on the couch, partially facing me. "But you're all right? They didn't cut you, did they?"

I shook my head. "No physical damage."

She stood, went to the wall and flipped the switch that sent light into that overhead wheel of faux flames, and sat down again.

"Did you tell the police?"

I looked at her. "Why? What on earth good would that do?"

"Nathan, snap out of it. The watch might be in a pawn shop right now. Your wallet, or what's left of it, might be in a trash bin very near where this happened. And dealing with your phone might be more trouble for them than it's worth, so it could be in the same bin." She got up again and fetched her cell phone.

"I understand they took your phone, but you probably walked right past a police station on your way home." I knew she was dialing nine-one-one.

I started to shake my head, but her attention went to the conversation she was having on the phone. When she hung up, she was all business. She took away my glass and the bottle I'd brought to the couch with me. She made a mug of coffee on the Keurig in the kitchen and brought it to me.

"Drink this. They'll be here in a few minutes. What bank was your credit card from?"

I told her, and she searched on her phone for a contact number. She dialed and handed the phone to me. I had just finished reporting the theft and was beginning to be able to focus on things when the police arrived, a man and a woman.

I don't remember much of the conversation. After they left, Nina surprised the hell out of me. She hugged me.

Over the Thai dinner that Nina had brought home in the bags, she apologized more than once as though the attack had been her fault. She had, in fact, been the one to suggest that I see how a recovery clinic operated, given my intended career in addiction recovery, after I had added an advanced degree to my undergraduate psychology education.

"I'm so sorry I sent you over there, Nathan. I just thought it would be a good idea for you to see how a clinic like that works. Honestly, in all the time I've lived in New York I've never felt threatened by anyone like that. Nothing like this has ever happened to me, or to Luc."

"I hope it never does. Seriously. It's—it makes you feel useless. I keep thinking I should have fought back."

"No, you should not! A knife, Nathan? No. You did the right thing."

I took what reassurance I could from Nina's comments. It wasn't enough, though, to take away that helpless feeling, that worthless feeling.

Since Neil had died, in the spring of my freshman year at college, I'd worked hard at reinventing myself. I mean, I was no wimp before, but picking up Neil's mountaineering baton had meant that I'd gained a lot of muscle, a lot of strength, and a lot of self-confidence. I'd scaled mountains alone that most people wouldn't hike with help. I'd braved the death-defying Crawler's Ledge on the Kalalau Trail on Kaua'i, helping to save another hiker who had fallen over the edge. And afterward, on that plane? Flying to San Francisco? When the cabin pressure had plunged and those masks had dropped on their snake-like tubing all over the cabin, I'd helped other people. Like the little girl next to me, whose panicked mother had two other children to take care of in the row behind me. Like the people who—for reasons I can't fathom—didn't put their masks on and dropped like flies in the aisle. I hadn't hesitated. I'd held my breath and helped get some of those people back into their seats and masked before returning to the mask I'd left, so that I could save their lives.

The one glass of scotch, which I'd ordered at the hotel after that, had been celebratory. The scotch I'd drunk tonight had been to escape.

I was not like that. I didn't try to escape difficult things, dangerous things. Maybe my inaction had been sensible, but—shit. Why hadn't I at least tried to defend myself?

And then there was the career I wanted, the career that would put me in direct contact with people who were addicted to things like opioid pills and heroin and crack and fentanyl. People who frequented clinics like the one I'd visited earlier today. And, very probably, people like the two guys who'd jumped me.

I was going to have to develop a very different kind of balls from the ones that made it possible for me to rescue fallen hikers or save unconscious airplane passengers.

Nina had been right. The very next afternoon, while I was hanging around that sterile loft, trying to distract myself by using my laptop to explore graduate programs, Nina called from her office. The police had called her to say they had found my watch, and my wallet, with only the cash missing from it. The phone didn't show up. And the police couldn't return the watch or the wallet until they'd finished processing them, which I took to mean fingerprinting, maybe lifting touch DNA, whatever.

Some of the funk that had settled over me after the attack lifted. But only some of it. Because when I considered going out to get a new phone, I came to a frozen stop inside the main door of Nina's building, unable to step out onto the sidewalk. I stood there, staring through the metal grating embedded in the glass door, at the action on the street outside. Cars drove by, and trucks. The occasional pedestrian passed along the sidewalk. At one point, a teenager—no doubt deaf to the world because of music pumping through his earbuds—happened to glance at me. Maybe it was my profound stillness that affected him, maybe the blank look on my face, but his whole body shrank suddenly, and he nearly tripped as he took a frantic step sideways.

I let out a barking laugh. And I was just about to open the door and brave the world when I realized that I couldn't get a new phone. Not today. I had no cash, no credit card, no way to prove who I was so I couldn't even write a check. The sudden return of this profound helplessness, this overwhelming sense of inadequacy, brought impotent tears to my eyes. I turned around and headed back up to Nina's loft.

I was curled into a ball on the spare-room bed, feeling profoundly sorry for myself, when I heard the door to the loft open. I glanced at the clock beside the bed: four o'clock.

Wait; four o'clock? Nina had been early last night, arriving at seven. I knew work was crazy busy at the fashion magazine where she worked, as everyone was preparing for Fashion Week. So what was she doing home at this hour?

"Nathan?"

I uncurled slowly. "In here."

By the time Nina came into my room I had managed to sit up. She was all smiles.

"Present!" she announced as she tossed a bag onto the bed. It was a white plastic bag with the silver Apple logo on it.

My eyes went wide and I grabbed it. A phone! Nina had bought me a new phone!

I nearly tore the box open, which is pretty impossible; Apple sends its technical offspring into the world packaged in seriously hard cardboard, pure white.

"I got you the same color you had before. Hope that was okay."

I nodded, my eyes glued to the device. "Perfect." I glanced up at my sister. "Thank you."

"They need to hear from you about replacing the number on it with the number you had before, if you still want it. Now I have to get back to work. Not sure what time I'll be home, and I'll probably have dinner in the office. But now you can order yourself something, right?"

I grinned at her. "Right."

"And you can busy yourself setting that thing up."

"Thanks, Nina. Really."

"Have fun!"

And she was gone.

A new phone. Nina had taken time out of her frenetic day to go out and buy me a phone. Or maybe she had an assistant who could do that for her. It didn't matter. She had done it. My eyes watered for the second time that day, this time for a good reason.

It did take me a little effort to get my old phone number

assigned to the new phone, but I managed to get the thing set up and restored with data from my laptop by the time my order of tacos with extra guacamole and an order of flan arrived. I sat at the dining table and streamed a *Simpsons* rerun on my computer while I ate. I had almost finished my flan when I heard a key turning in the door. My assumption—that it was Nina returning home a little sooner than expected—was confounded by what sounded like luggage being wheeled in. My last spoonful of flan was frozen in the air halfway to my face as I watched a man walk into the living room.

I knew from a photo Nina had shown me that this was Luc. Luc Beaumont, fashion photographer and world traveler, moderately tall and slender, dark brown hair cut in stylish waves. His shirt, tucked into medium grey slacks, was an artful blend of stripes and accents in hues of blue ranging from dark to nearly white. Draped over his luggage was a jacket in a slightly lighter grey than the slacks.

Instantly I felt like a cliché, the kid brother shoving take-out Mexican food into his face while watching cartoons on a computer screen. My jeans and red-dirt T-shirt with the pale brown stylized gecko on the front, which I'd bought in Hanalei, were not doing nearly enough to sustain the feelings of existentialism and self-confidence I'd brought home with me after the death-defying hike I'd undertaken on the island of Kaua'i in July.

I set the spoon down.

Luc flicked on the switch for that huge circle of bulbs overhead and then glanced at me, not in alarm, but appearing puzzled over who I was and what I was doing at his dining table. I got off my chair and moved toward him.

"Luc?" I walked with my right hand held out, doing my best to appear confident and deferential at the same time. He extended his hand, and as we shook I added, "I'm Nathan. Nina's brother."

He reclaimed his hand and waved it over his head as if

to acknowledge a recovered memory. "Of course. Of course. She said." His accent was not heavy but it was definitely French. "Forgive me while I...."

I stepped aside so he could pull his luggage past me and toward the bedroom he shared with Nina.

As I swallowed the last of my flan and hurried to get the table cleared off and the detritus of my meal dealt with and out of sight, I tried to remember when Nina had said Luc would return. Wasn't he, like, ten days ahead of schedule, something like that? It was August twenty-third, and he wasn't due back until Monday, September second. New York Fashion Week started on the sixth, and Nina was sure Luc wouldn't want me hanging around (she didn't put it like that) while both of them were gearing up for that event, so I'd agreed on that time for a visit with my college roommate and best friend El Speed (Larry Speed) and his new bride Ellie, in Orono, Maine, where they were enrolled in graduate programs.

I had been researching graduate programs for myself, taking a gap year for now, for about the last three weeks, and I had some good candidates. I wanted a psychology program where I could specialize in addiction treatment and recovery, and these days—what with the opioid crisis being what it was—a lot of institutions were offering some very tempting programs. So I was having a hard time deciding on my top choices. One of them, no doubt, would be the University of Maine, in Orono. El Speed and Ellie had both encouraged me to apply there, and I would, but I couldn't apply to just one program.

So what was Luc doing back here already? And would his presence here mean I had to pack my bags and high-tail it out before I'd planned to? Should I text Nina and let her know he was here? Because, surely, if she'd known he'd arrive today she would have told me. But would that make her crazy work day even crazier? I decided not to text.

I was almost done cleaning up in the kitchen when Luc

reappeared, now in jeans. He opened the fridge, and grabbed a small bottle of San Pellegrino sparkling water. He leaned against the island behind him and took a swig.

He asked, "Did Nina happen to say when she'd be back?"

"Late. She said she might be having dinner at work."

"Ah, good. So you and I can have a chat."

I glanced at his almost-handsome face, clear of any facial hair below his eyes. Nina had said he was divorced with a five-year-old daughter living with his ex in New Jersey, I think. She'd said he was, what, thirty-two? Thirty-five? His half-smile was impossible to interpret. Was it an offer of friendship, or did the other half of that smile hide a threat?

He turned toward the living room. I grabbed another bottle of the microbrew I'd had with dinner and followed him. He sat in the chair that faced away from the window, and I settled into the corner of the couch nearest him.

"How is the, uh, the search going? For school?"

So he must be trying to find out when I'll be leaving. Nina and I had already established that once I had a first choice of schools, I'd move to be close to it. "Good. Too many choices, actually."

"So no decisions yet. You should take your time."

Okay, so I did not know how to interpret this guy.

"Nina tells me you were hiking in Hawai'i." I was about to respond when he added, "A spiritual quest, she called it."

Okay. Wow. Thanks for nothing, Nina. How the hell was I supposed to reply to that?

Again, before I could respond, he spoke. "Did you find what you sought?"

Solid ground, now. "I did. Yes."

"And what was that?"

Several different phrases flashed through my brain. Like, *Who wants to know?* Like, *Why do you ask?* Like, *What, Nina didn't tell you?* What I finally said was, "Connection. Family connection."

He looked confused. "But your family is only Nina, correct? And she was here."

"That's why it was a spiritual quest."

"Ah. So, with your dead family. I see."

He drank from his bottle. I drank from mine. I decided to go on the offensive. "You were just with your family, I understand. In Bernay. France."

He took another swig and then nodded. And then said nothing.

So I prompted. "You left there a little earlier than you planned, I think."

He waved a hand near his head, and somehow the meaning was different from what it had been the first time he'd done it. This time there was something dismissive in it.

"I had enough family time. Maybe too much."

Too much. He'd had too much family time, while I mourned my two family members who had died in the past few years, wishing like hell I had more time with them, embarking on an exotic excursion to try and reconnect with them.

"Interesting. I went all the way to Kaua'i to connect with mine."

He nodded as he gazed at his water bottle. "I think we want what we don't have and aren't satisfied with what we do have. Do you agree?" He looked at me as he lifted the bottle and drained the last of the bubbly water into his mouth.

I'd forgotten that the French are known for their own brand of existentialism. I responded with something Gram used to say. "Happiness isn't getting what you want. It's wanting what you have."

Luc chuckled and gazed back at his bottle. "I wouldn't know."

Dark. Again, I was at a loss with this guy.

He set the empty bottle on the coffee table, crossed one ankle on the opposite knee, and folded his fingers together.

15

"Still," he said, picking up on a previous thread, "I support your effort. I told Nina, 'Let him do this quest.'" He chuckled. "'Even if you don't like this Conroy.' That's what I told her."

He grinned at me as I struggled to think what to say. I came up empty.

"Conroy was a lover, no?" Nina had clearly told him quite a bit.

Lover. Ha! Conroy would have shuddered at the idea. "That's too elegant a word." I gave him an assessing glance. I doubted I could shock him, but—let's see. "He was the trip leader. He and I—we were more like fuck buddies."

Luc laughed. "I have not heard this term. It's very descriptive." He lifted a hand, not quite repeating his waving gesture. "This hike. It was dangerous?"

Had I told Nina that? I couldn't recall. "Part of it, yes."

"This 'Crawler's Ledge.' It sounds ominous."

And just like that, something opened up. Something made me trust this guy enough to describe just how ominous it had been, and just how important a role I had played. I told him about Margot, the only woman on that strenuous hike, and what a trooper she was—never complaining, never asking for help, determined to hold her own.

I told him about being on that "ominous" part of the trail, where the rock face goes nearly straight up to your left while your boots struggle to fit onto the narrow red dirt track, the other side of which is a precipitous plunge hundreds of feet to massive waves crashing against volcanic rock.

I repeated Conroy's warning for Luc: "There's nothing but empty space between you and a fall that will last only until your body smashes onto the rocks below. It might be carried out to sea in pieces, or it might lie there until it's picked apart by sea birds."

Luc's expression changed from sincere interest to the kind of fascination that says, *Tell me the worst. Don't hold back.*

"Margot was in front of me when this blast of wind came from nowhere. A piece of canvas flew off the pack of the guy in front of her. She lost her balance." I paused for a sip of beer. Luc said nothing, just watched me, waiting for the story to continue.

"She fell over the edge."

"My God."

"It was surreal. It was like the world stood still. Conroy and I dropped to the ground and peered over the edge. I was sure I would see something like what he'd told us about. But instead, there she was, lying on an outcropping maybe eight feet down."

Luc was riveted. He shook his head a couple of times, not quite in disbelief. So I went on with the steps Conroy and I had taken to get her, and then her pack, back up onto the trail.

"She wasn't hurt?" Luc wanted to know.

"She said only her pride. But the fall did a bit of a number on her shoulder."

"A number?"

"Sorry. It was sore where she landed on it."

Margot had sat with her back against the rock face and sobbed for some minutes, Conroy holding her shoulders and just letting her cry. And when she was able to stand, she'd said she couldn't keep going. At that point, we were maybe half-way through the really dangerous part of the trail, but the next day we'd have to come back over it. The Kalalau Trail is not a loop; it's one way in, and the same way out.

I told Luc, "I left with her."

Luc's foot dropped to the floor and he leaned in my direction, his right hand extended. I gave him mine, and we shook again. "You are a noble fellow," he told me. He sat back in his chair and added, "I think you did not tell Nina this story."

I laughed as I realized he was correct. "I don't know why not. I'm sure she could handle it."

"You protect your sister. This is good, I think."

I laughed again. "Or maybe I just didn't want her to think she'd been right about not wanting me to go."

Luc smiled at me and then stood. "I will make some dinner. You have eaten?"

"Yeah."

"Come entertain me while I cook."

I watched from across the island as Luc did marvelous things with eggs and some cheese and linguine. I think parsley was involved. Or maybe it was tarragon? I almost regretted being full of tacos. While he worked, and then as we sat on stools at the island and he ate his dinner, I told him about El Speed, and about Ellie, and about how I was going to visit them in their rented house in Orono. I described how Nina had been the one to come up with the name El Speed, based on the "L. Speed" in the return address of a letter he'd sent me before we even met, after we'd been assigned as roommates by the university. I told Luc about a few of my hiking adventures, including the day I'd met Conroy half-way up Cannon Mountain in New Hampshire. I considered telling Luc how Conroy and I had fucked on the summit of South Kinsman, but before I could make up my mind, I heard Nina's voice.

"Luc? You're home?"

He didn't call out. He waited until she came into view, when he stood and gave her a quick hug and a quicker kiss. "I had enough of France. And enough of the Beaumonts."

"You probably scared the hell out of Nathan."

"I don't think Nathan scares easily."

# CHAPTER TWO

If he'd been happier to see Nina, I would have really liked the guy. But who am I to judge anyone else's relationship? I decided to make my exit so they could talk or whatever.

Alone in my room, I put in my earbuds and let the sounds of Keola Beamer's Hawai'ian slack key guitar music carry me back to the trade winds and the crashing waves and the feeling of infinity that had changed me. Infinity is different from eternity. It has no beginning and no end. It just is. That's what I'd felt on Kaua'i.

I'd been playing this very album the night Margot and I had camped out on our way back to the Kalalau trailhead. The music had attracted the attention of a guy named Wayland who had come to the Na Pali Coast, Kaua'i's eastern shore, a few years ago and had never left. It was illegal to live in the forest there, but he was not the only one. There were quite a few "Kalalau Outlaws."

Wayland had given Margot and me what he called Kalalau names. He'd dubbed her "Intrepid" because of her determination and tenacity on that rugged trail, and because of her bravery in climbing off the ledge she'd fallen onto. And he gave me a name I will never forget: "Trailblazer." He'd said I was seeking myself in the wilderness and that I would lead the way for others. I was still trying to understand what he'd meant, but I sure liked the sound of it.

I let my mind drift back over my experiences on Kaua'i as the music played. When the album ended, an idea came suddenly into my mind, the kind of suddenness that has a sharp point to it. I'd heard Nina playing a song more than once in the evenings, alone in her bedroom, one I didn't recognize. But I'd caught enough of it to find it.

I remembered the line: *I hope I'll know him if he's ever near.*

Nina had told me she and Luc were not in a serious relationship. I think her words had been, "It's not like I'm going to marry him." That was last May. So when I heard that song, the sadness and the near-hopelessness of it struck me. If Nina had been playing a whole album, that one song wouldn't have felt significant. But she'd played just that one song.

So I searched for the lyrics. It turned out to be a song by Karla Bonoff, "If He's Ever Near." And one line in particular hit me: "I thought you were the one." It goes on from there about not seeing the lies in his eyes, and about giving up trying to see love, and how hard it is to see love when it's right in front of us, so how do we know when it's there?

I pulled my earbuds away from my head and sat on my bed in a kind of stunned silence, unable to reconcile what I knew of my sister with a woman whose search for love was bringing her down. And now her words, "not like I'm going to marry him," rang hollow.


When someone makes a decision, it's usually based more on emotion than facts. And it wasn't just in my study of psychology that I've seen this born out. It has worked that way in my life and in the lives of people I've known.

The idea for some time had been that I'd take this gap year to apply to some number of schools, and after a short stay with Nina, a visit to Maine to see El Speed, and then maybe a little more time with Nina, I'd move close to my top choice of schools in the hope that I'd get accepted there. So when the time came for me to pick a top choice for my master's degree program, although I planned to apply to a few different schools, I followed my heart. I decided to move to Maine and hope Orono wanted me as much as I wanted to be there.

A huge part of the draw was El Speed, no question. But there was something else that influenced me. It was a call from Margot.

On our trip without the other hikers back to Ke'e Beach, where the Kalalau Trail started, Margot and I had confided in each other about a number of things. Her story was that the inappropriate interest her father was taking in her wasn't discouraged by her alcoholic mother or her unsympathetic brothers. She'd started hiking years ago as a means of escape, and now that she had her Master's in Social Work she was ready to leave all that far behind. Since hugging each other farewell at the airport on Kaua'i, we'd exchanged a few texts. She'd told me she was actively looking for work.

Luc had arrived on a Friday, and on Saturday evening, while I was cleaning up after another of Luc's French-themed dinners that Nina and I shared with him, my phone rang. I saw that it was Margot. To no one in particular I said, "I'll call her back later." No one offered to step in and take over the clean-up job for me, so it was another half hour before I shut the door to my room and called her back.

"Hey, Intrepid," I greeted her with the name our Kalalau outlaw had given her.

"Hey back, Trailblazer." I could hear the grin in her tone, and I answered it with one of my own. I could still see the look she had given me over dinner at the lodge where we'd stayed our last night on Kaua'i. She'd leveled those green eyes at me, and she'd smiled a smile that had appeared innocent, and she'd said, "So Conroy is bi? But not you?"

Unsure where she was going, determined not to assume anything, all I'd said was, "Uh, no."

The smile had taken on new meaning. "Too bad."

Conroy was bi. He'd made that abundantly clear, along with the fact that he was putting down roots nowhere and for no one. That wasn't me. I'd decided I was ready for a real relationship, one in which neither of us would cringe if the other said *I love you*. But it would not be with a woman—not even Margot, as compatible as we seemed to be. Still, she was dear to me. I'd helped save her life, and she'd rewarded me with a level of trust she gave to few other people.

Over the phone line, I heard the excitement in her voice. "Nathan, I have such news! Maybe for both of us." She paused, perhaps waiting to test my enthusiasm.

"Spill, Margot."

"Okay. Here's the thing. I got a job! And it's kind of in your neck of the woods. I'll be working for a recovery clinic in Maine, doing school outreach and a few other things. Isn't that great? Addiction recovery! Right up your alley!"

That *was* great news. She'd be far away from Idaho and her poor excuse for a family. "Congratulations! What part of Maine?"

"The clinic is just outside of Bar Harbor. So, Mount Desert Island. I've never been there—I did my interview on Skype—but online the area looks absolutely gorgeous. Rocky coastline, pine trees, wildlife—and Nathan, mountains! Okay, they're not very big mountains, but they're supposed to be great fun to hike. So that's right up your alley, too!"

"I'm sensing a pattern."

She laughed her honest, musical laugh. In my mind I saw her toss her long, strawberry blond hair over a shoulder. "Smart man. Yes. Not only is there a pattern, but listen to this. They have another opening. It's an administrative post, but wouldn't it be a great introduction for you? I know you want to work in addiction recovery. Wouldn't this be a good place to get your feet wet while you figure out your next move?"

I was trying to take in all the information she was throwing at me, thinking how I'd just recovered from the aftermath of visiting a methadone clinic, when she added, "So during the week you'd have this job in a recovery clinic, and on weekends you could hike! *We* could hike! I mean, of course we wouldn't always have to hike together, but—oh, hell, Nathan, say something!"

"Okay, um… wow? Sorry if that's not what you were hoping for, but—Jesus, Margot, I need to take this in. I mean…. Okay, so I was kinda sorta thinking I might move to Maine anyway, because I've decided—and this is only in the last couple of days—that U of Maine Orono is my first choice."

"But that's perfect! Didn't you tell me your best bud is there?"

"He is. And I haven't even told him yet."

"So, listen, how about if I send you information about the clinic, and you can check it out. If you decide it looks good and you want to contact them, you can say I told you about the job. Maybe they'd even have something else, something more along the lines of what you want to do for this year."

I barked out a short laugh. "As if I had any idea what I want to do 'for this year.'"

"So I'll send it?"

I took in a deep breath. "Sure. Why not?"


I'd never been to the Maine coast. And I'd certainly never been to Bar Harbor, the largest town on Mount Desert Island. When I looked up images of the area on the internet, I was hooked. Maybe it wasn't Kaua'i, but Margot had been right; it was gorgeous.

I sent a text to El Speed. *Can you imagine me living on Mount Desert Island?*

Maybe ninety seconds later I saw, *Hell yeah. Is that an option?*

*Maybe. We'll see. I'll get back to you.* I got a thumbs-up icon in reply.


Nina spent most of Sunday at work, while Luc went to meet friends for brunch. I was not invited, but that was fine by me;

I had work to do.

First, for some fun and maybe to whet my appetite for the place, I perused scenes of Acadia National Park. Even though it was not Kaua'i, it offered its own majesty, its own mystery. The mountains, as Margot had said, were not high. But—hell, that just meant I could take an afternoon hike, or spend a weekend day and claim a few peaks at once. And in different seasons, which Maine offered in a way Hawai'i did not, the same hike would look different. I knew from hiking in New Hampshire's White Mountains that a vista full of green leaves looks almost entirely different when the leaves are crimson and gold, and different still when the dark green of pines shows through bare branches.

Another appeal was that with small peaks, I might once again be able to do some winter hiking. My very first climb, up Mount Chocorua in New Hampshire, in a friggin' snowstorm, had nearly been my last. The effects of the frostbite my feet had suffered would be with me for the rest of my life, so vulnerability to cold severely limited what outdoor activities I could do in winter. But a short hike? That seemed do-able.

Next I looked into the clinic where Margot would be, Bar Harbor Recovery Center. They had a number of outreach programs, which made sense; her job seemed like it fit into that category. They had a staff of several people, some with professional-sounding titles, and a front desk receptionist. The open position was for an administrative assistant, supporting the counselors as well as the executive staff. It required typing skills, which I had, and experience with a couple of standard computer-based applications, another couple of checkmarks for me. One thing it said made me wonder whether Margot was right, whether it really would be a good starting point for me. That one thing was this statement: "Minimal contact with clients." I knew "clients" meant addicts. If I had minimal contact with the people who needed help, people whose treatment and recovery I wanted to focus on when I was ready, why couldn't I just as well be on the sales floor of a hiking goods store?

I had just sat back in my chair at the dining table, staring at my computer screen, when I heard the lock turn in the door, and then Nina came in. I turned just my head toward her.

"My god, girl, you look done in." And she did. Her hair was not its usual sleek self, her skin looked almost blotchy (which just didn't happen to Nina), and her typical proud posture had slumped.

She stood still and closed her eyes briefly. "You have no idea." She sighed. "Luc still out?"

"Haven't seen him since maybe eleven or so."

"Good. I'm taking a long, hot bath. See you in a few hours."

I knew she was exaggerating. And in fact, she was back out in about forty-five minutes, looking much more like her usual self. She sat in the chair across from me at the table and grinned. "I'm not good at relaxing."

I laughed. "Tell me something I don't know."

"What have you been up to?"

"Well," I opened, my tone implying there was actually something to tell her, "I've made a few decisions. Though there might be a fly in the proverbial ointment."

I glanced at her; did she really want to hear about my day? She tilted her head slightly and raised an eyebrow. So I decided she did.

"A woman I met on my hike last summer is moving to Bar Harbor. In Maine. She's in social work, and she's got a job at a recovery clinic there. She called last night to tell me about it. They have an opening in the clinic that I'm considering applying for." I paused to see where Nina's thoughts were.

"Maine? Are you applying to schools in Maine?"

"Yeah. El Speed is there, at Orono. They have a decent program."

25

"I thought you were leaning more toward urban areas, urban clinics."

I shrugged. "I could still end up anywhere. The job isn't what I want to be doing for long. It might let me see the workings of the clinic, though."

"And the fly?"

I let out a breath. "It's an administrative job. The online description says I would have minimal contact with clients."

"Clients. Addicts?"

"Yeah."

She nodded slowly, thoughtfully. "As I recall, the only jobs you've held in the past were true temp positions. The dining hall at college. The ice cream parlor in the summers and weekends at home. So you haven't really gone through an interview process. Right?"

"Right. So?"

"So here are a couple of pieces of advice that you might find useful. One, don't assume that the job description is cast in stone. If you want some responsibility it doesn't mention, be ready to state clearly what else you'd like to do, why, and why you're qualified for it. And two, the interview is a two-way street. They're interviewing you to see if they think you're a good fit, and you're interviewing them to see if they can offer you what you want in an environment you think you'll like."

All I could do was stare at my sister. Nina was all of one year and a couple of months older than me. Where the hell did she learn all the stuff she knew? I mean, sure, she'd always been a little—scratch that—very precocious. And she'd always seemed more mature than I ever felt. But... wow.

"Thanks." It was all I could think of to say. "And I like the look of the area."

"Lots of mountains? Trees? Rocks?"

I laughed again. "How did you guess?"

She grinned. "Mountain man Nathan." She stood,

looking tired again. "I'm gonna go lie down for a bit. Then we'll see whether we're up for going out to dinner, with or without Luc. Sound good?"

It did.

We did go out later. Luc had not returned, and as far as I knew he had not contacted Nina. She treated me to a truly gourmet meal at a restaurant in midtown, the name of which escapes me now. I had an appetizer of quail drumsticks on something called micro greens, filet mignon with a truffle wine sauce, and molten chocolate cake, which was a mound of chocolate cake that oozed liquid chocolate when you cut into it. Nina ordered a bottle of wine that cost about a hundred and fifty dollars, and we finished it. We took a cab each way and didn't get home until eleven-thirty. It felt sophisticated in a way I had experienced only once before—that one meal I'd had in San Francisco, when I'd stayed there for a night on my return flight from Kaua'i.

Luc was home when we got there, in one of the living room chairs, reading a printed book, a glass of scotch in one hand.

Nina blew him a kiss. "Simply knackered," she said, which I took to mean exhausted. Was that fashion industry lingo? I had no idea. "Going to bed."

I followed her through the dining room toward the bedrooms. At my door, which was the first, she turned to me and leaned against the other side of the hall.

"If you go to the wilds of Maine for now," she said, "keep in mind that civilization offers things you can't get there." She smiled and reached a hand toward my face. She didn't quite touch me before she dropped her arm and headed toward her room.

As I watched her go, I wondered whether she wished I were staying closer to New York. I thought to myself, *And there are things that civilization has forgotten about. Things that are pure, and tangible, and that don't cost a hundred and fifty dollars a bottle.*


Monday morning I called the clinic. The young-ish sounding woman who answered the phone transferred me to a woman named Jennifer Baker, the center's administrative director.

"Oh, yes, Margot Truman," she said, her tone cheerful and friendly. "You're a friend of hers, you say?"

"That's right." I decided against saying I'd met Margot in July, just a few weeks ago. "She said there was an opening I might be interested in."

I expected Jennifer (she told me to call her by her first name) would tell me about the position, or say she'd send me an application, or something like that. But instead she asked me questions. It was an impromptu interview, and I'm grateful now that I realized that immediately.

"What's your interest in addiction recovery, Nathan?"

"My undergraduate degree is in psychology. UNH. University of New Hampshire. I'll be applying to a few schools this year for an advanced degree, including the University of Maine, in Orono. I want to focus on treatment and recovery as a career."

"Why?"

Wow. Okay. Well, the first question had been easy to answer. Frantically, I debated inside my head for how much information to give this woman I'd never met.

*Because my first boyfriend, who was in recovery when I met him, disappeared suddenly and completely from my life just as I was falling in love with him. It had felt as though fentanyl meant more to him than I did. It broke my heart.*

No, Nathan. Don't say that.

*Because a dear friend of my best friend's wife got addicted as the result of fraternity hazing, and he's been in and out of recovery ever since.*

Closer.

This is what I said, finally. "People I care about have suffered from opioid addiction. I've done a lot of thinking about what it is they're really searching for. The substances they can't get enough of are a substitute. That's why they can't get enough of them. I want to help people find their way back to a place where life has enough meaning to help them recover."

She paused long enough to make me wonder if I'd said something wrong. Then, "Where are you right now, Nathan?"

"New York. City, I mean. New York City."

"Are you planning to be in Maine any time soon?"

"Yes. Very soon."

"Good. Because I'd like to meet with you. Can we set a time?"

*They're interviewing me. But I'm interviewing them, too. Thanks, Nina.* "Before we do that, I have a question."

"Yes?"

"Online it says this position has minimal contact with clients. Is that cast in stone?"

Another pause. "Well, as you know, the job is administrative. We put that description in there so if someone were concerned about meeting with people who had been abusing substances, the applicant would know they wouldn't need to have much contact with them. That—correct me if I'm wrong, here, but that doesn't sound like you."

"No. You're right." And she *was* right. As long as none of them would wave knives in my face.


Nina gave me a big hug as I was leaving the loft, bright and early Wednesday morning. "You can come back any time," she told me. "I mean, if you don't like the job, or if you want to stay here to look at schools in the city." She waved a hand that looked not at all like Luc's hand waves. "You know what I mean."

I was off to Maine, leaving the sterile Manhattan loft

and the dirty city streets behind me. The car Nina had ordered for me arrived only a few minutes late, according to my reclaimed Garmin Forerunner hiker's watch. From my position just inside the building's front door, sheltered from the light rain that was falling, I saw the car pull up.

The ride to LaGuardia Airport, especially that early in the morning, was dull and grey, making the dirty parts of Manhattan and Queens look even dirtier and making the mental images I had of mountains and blue seas and rocky hillsides seem more appealing than ever. Waiting for my flight to Manchester, New Hampshire, I pretended to read news on my phone while going over in my mind what I wanted to say to Jennifer Baker during my interview with her, tomorrow morning. I wondered whether she'd have me take a typing test or demonstrate my familiarity with PowerPoint and Excel. Before long, though, my thoughts turned to other aspects of this trip.

Margot's job wouldn't start until next Tuesday, the day after Labor Day. She'd told me she'd rented a two-bedroom flat in a house for a couple of weeks, through Airbnb.

"One hundred ninety a night!" she had told me last night, when I'd called to tell her I was headed to Maine. "But it's less than most places, given that not much was available this time of year. And I'll need to be able to cook and stuff, so I wanted a kitchen. Jennifer said she'd help me find something more permanent once I get there."

She chatted for a minute or two about her job and my interview. Then: "Oh my god, Nathan! You should stay with me! Provided you get the job, of course. It would be so much less expensive and so much more fun! What do you say?"

"I'll be there Thursday, staying at an inn for a few nights. You aren't arriving until Saturday. I'm heading to Orono Saturday to see El Speed and Ellie for a few days."

"Okay, that works. And if you do get the job, maybe we could find a place to rent together. What do you think?"

It wasn't a bad idea. I was pretty sure we'd get along

well enough as roommates, and it did seem less lonely. But everything was happening so fast. And I'd be living and working with the same person, though it wasn't clear how much our jobs would intersect.

"It's worth considering. Can we wait until I see what happens with the job?"

"Of course. But they'll love you!"

I chuckled, remembering Nina's advice. "*I* might not love *them*."

"Oh, pish. You will. But fine, let's talk more when you know."


From Manchester, I had arranged for another limo to get me to Concord. It was extravagant, but I was going to have to drive Gram's car—I mean, my car—almost five hours to Bar Harbor, and having left New York so early, even a rest of only half an hour seemed worthwhile.

It was already early afternoon when my car dropped me off at Mrs. Ford's house in Concord. It was her driveway where Gram's car had been waiting for me. Her only child, Jeremy, had been Neil's hiking buddy since they'd begun claiming peaks as teenagers. They'd died together in that fire.

Mrs. Ford wrapped me in a long, hard hug. She'd hugged me the day before I'd left Concord for New York, when I'd dropped the car off. That day, she'd released me from the hug but had kept her hands on my shoulders. She'd said, "My goodness, Nathan. You have become quite the gorgeous young man. And so strong! Your Gram was so proud of you. I hope you know that."

Today she just hugged me and then smiled. "It's so good to see you again, Nathan. I've got some lunch ready for you."

I hadn't expected lunch, but I was glad of it; I'd figured I would just stop someplace after I left Concord, but this was better. I'd adored Jeremy, and Mrs. Ford was a sweetheart.

I'd been the one to tell her that her son was dead, and how he had died. I never want to have to tell anyone anything like that again. To this day, I don't know whether she ever knew that Jeremy was gay. To me he'd been almost like a second big brother. He'd been the one to offer me the best advice after that nearly deadly winter climb up Mount Chocorua.

"You should climb it again," he'd told me. "Kind of like getting back on a horse after you've been thrown."

I'd shrugged. "I don't know whether hiking is going to be my thing."

"Honey, I ain't talkin' about hiking. I'm talkin' about self-respect. I'm talkin' about self-worth. Look, you'll do it or not, but I highly recommend it. And if I were you, I'd do it alone."

"Why?"

"You're the only one you need to prove something to."

So I'd hiked it alone, at the end of that summer. And it had been exactly the right thing to do.

It took me nearly hour to drive from Ellsworth on the mainland into Bar Harbor itself. There was a lot of traffic; I figured it was due to the Labor Day weekend coming up. With grey skies overhead and the occasional drop of rain hitting my windshield, I drove over low bridges across salt marshes, past some touristy places, and just after entering a wooded area I turned onto Paradise Hill Road, where my phone told me I'd encounter the visitors center for Acadia National Park.

Inside the rustic-looking building was a 3-D miniature re-creation of the park in the center of a large room, and bookshelves all around offered maps and information about the area. I bought a book about the park and a large folding map.

Back on the road I passed more heavily-wooded areas,

then small, single houses set among the trees, and then more motels and touristy kinds of places as I got close to town.

As a special good-luck gift to me, Nina had procured and paid for a room for tonight, and Thursday and Friday, at an award-winning inn near the water, the Ullikana.

"The name has something to do with Hawai'i," Nina told me. "It's kind of unclear what, exactly, but I figured I was on the right track."

As I pulled into the white gravel parking area around seven o'clock, I saw that Nina had chosen well, or at least beautifully. One look inside the front door made me feel like it was a little too grand for me. The building had that kind of ancient elegance that has an aroma as much as an appearance: old wood, well-worn carpets from foreign lands, and dusty, hard-cover books from decades past, waiting on dark wooden bookshelves. The front room was massive, with a huge oriental rug on the floor. Across from the heavy, wooden front door was the kind of staircase that a gorgeously-gowned woman might descend slowly toward a cluster of admirers.

My room was on the third floor, so I got to climb not only those stairs but also the less impressive flight above them. I was in a room that had two names: Lilac, and Audrey. I couldn't make any sense out of the explanation, except that once upon a time, when the place had been a private home, a girl named Audrey had used the room. There was no view from it, really, but it was large and airy and painted in a delightful pattern of several colors.

I stood staring at the few pieces of luggage I'd brought up from the car and assessed my state of mind—and my body, too, because I was physically tired after all the traveling. But even though I was tired, static electricity ran through me. I lay down on the bed for a minute or two, which my body seemed to appreciate, but almost before I knew it my hyperactive brain had pulled me to my feet again.

Was I nervous about my interview tomorrow? Well, yes, of course. It would be the first time I'd had to represent myself to anyone outside of family and school, and tomorrow I'd have to do it in a way that would get me something I wanted. I felt prepared, given the wealth of material I'd sent to Jennifer. But there seemed to be a lot riding on this. If I didn't get this job, I wasn't sure what else this area could offer me over the winter by way of employment; so many things here would shut down once the summer vacation season ended.

I decided I had to go out and walk around. Besides, I was hungry.

I ended up in a pub where they served all kinds of micro brews. I sat at the bar and figured, you know, I was in Maine, so I ordered fish and chips and a flight of brews. I suppose lobster would have been more iconic, but I didn't care for it.

The bartender was a young guy with a buzz cut and a number of piercings. We got to talking hiking, and I happened to mention that I wanted to do a hike tomorrow afternoon, after my interview.

"Oh, man, you gotta do the Precipice."

"Sounds challenging."

"It's the best fucking climb on the island, hands down. You earn every view. And there are a lot of them. So you do a lot of earning. It's the only trail on the island with real bragging rights."

Back at my room, I looked the trail up in my new book and on the map. It went nearly straight up the eastern side of Champlain Mountain. I watched a couple of Youtube vids where hikers had worn GoPros or something like that. The trail was every bit as rugged as I'd been told: sheer cliffs you had to scale on iron rungs that had been pounded into the granite by somebody; parts of the path that were a little over a foot wide on smooth rock that sloped down sideways; fields of boulders that must be the results of incredible rock slides.

One thing I noticed was that the hikers who seemed to be the most proficient wore gloves. A quick search revealed

34

them to be something called crag gloves—one article of climbing gear I'd never felt the need to purchase. I'd have to check them out. And I'd do it before making plans to hike the Precipice Trail.

# CHAPTER THREE

At precisely nine twenty-five Thursday morning, I parked in the small lot at the Bar Harbor Recovery Center. It was a short distance south of the town center in what must once have been someone's house, though clearly the original building had been expanded quite a bit. Something caught my attention right away: the thick, black bars covering the windows on the ground floor. I had a bit of a flashback to my attack in New York, but I put it aside. I knew this clinic dispensed meds, and I figured that's why the bars were there. They seemed a little extreme, but they were part of the package, and I'd better get used to that.

Inside the front door was a hallway that led past several rooms. Motivational posters covered most of the wall space. One in particular caught my eye. An image of a mountainous landscape was done in a soft wash of lavender. Superimposed over that was a quote: "The opposite of addiction is not sobriety. It is connection." It was credited to Johann Hari.

Interesting. Connection was what I'd told Luc I'd been seeking on Kaua'i. My spiritual quest.

The first door on the right was a reception area with two desks in it. The one on the right, near one of the windows with bars, was occupied by a young woman with hair so black it must have been dyed. Her cluttered desk had a sign on it that identified her as Katie Tollman. She looked up as I entered the room.

"Nathan?"

"That's right."

She stood and held her right hand toward me. I gave her mine. "I'm Katie. Jennifer asked me to have you wait just a few minutes while she deals with something."

It was tempting to ask what that meant, but it was not my place to ask. I was not an employee. Yet. Instead, I looked around the office space, but there were no chairs.

Katie must have noticed me looking for one. "Oh, sorry. Yeah, we don't like to encourage people to hang out in here. You can sit there." She pointed to the other desk, several feet from hers. "That will be your desk, anyway." Her eyes widened and she added, "Oh, I mean, you know, if you get the job."

I smiled, inwardly thinking, *And if I* want *the job*.

I sat at "my" desk, which did not face Katie's. Both desks more or less faced the door to the hall. There was another door, closed, just to the right of where I sat. I found out later that it led into a storage room with a photocopier in it.

To Katie I said, "I hope there's nothing here I shouldn't see."

"Nope. All client files are locked away." Her eyes went to a tall filing cabinet to the left of the hall doorway.

A desktop computer sat sleeping in front of me. I gazed at it.

"And you won't be able to see anything there, either," Katie told me, as if I'd been trying to snoop. "It's all passworded. You'll get your own logon. You know, if...."

I nodded. "Um, what can you tell me about the bars on the windows?"

She chuckled. "Let's hope you never have to find out." She grinned almost conspiratorially at me. "Seriously, though, there are meds on the dispensary side of the clinic. Serious meds."

"Got it." As I had figured. Though that didn't explain the first part of her reply.

I pulled out the folder I'd brought. I'd sent Jennifer a completed application and scans of everything else via email, but I'd also brought a copy of all of it. There was a copy of my UNH transcript, and a résumé. I'd also sent other material

I'd collected in the process of applying for graduate programs: references (which consisted of a mix of Gram's friends from Concord and my psych professors), and a short essay about my personal and career goals.

By the time Jennifer came to let me know she was ready to see me, I'd used my phone to identify a few options for places to live if everything worked out here. Margot said she'd rented her apartment for two weeks, through September fourteen. She could cancel part of it with forty-eight hours' notice, or if necessary she might be able to extend it, but ideally I/we should find a more permanent place.

"Nathan?" I stood, and Jennifer and I shook hands. She was tall, forty-ish, and her dark gold hair fell in waves onto her shoulders. "I'm so glad you could come in person. I'm not a big fan of Skype for important meetings."

"So I guess Margot was so impressive that Skype didn't get in the way."

Jennifer laughed. "Well, as her friend, you would know. She'll be starting on Tuesday."

Jennifer's office was all the way in the back on the right side of this part of the building. It was a large corner room, and it would have been brighter if there hadn't been so many trees just outside the windows—and, maybe, if there hadn't been bars on the windows. She gestured toward a pair of chairs facing her desk.

Jennifer picked up her own paper copies of everything I had sent her electronically. She asked me a bunch of questions that seemed pro forma; in fact, a lot of the answers were right there in the paperwork. I felt like a suspect in a criminal case who says, *I've already been over this with three other cops*, and who is then told, *But we want to hear it in your own words*.

I guess all the boring stuff was just to get me comfortable. Or maybe she needed to verify that I knew what was in the documents, in case I'd had someone else prepare them. Then she looked up from the paperwork and said, "I know you've had some personal experience in which people close to you have been in recovery. Could I ask you to talk about them in a little more detail?"

I hoped my frozen stare didn't look like a frozen stare. But I needed to think. Finally I said, "I don't mind telling you about someone I'll call John. I knew him when we were freshmen at UNH. He decided to pledge a fraternity, and it happened to be one known for hazing. One of these stunts had to do with beer and fentanyl."

I took a breath; not too much detail, I told myself. Jennifer doesn't need to know that "John"—Gordon—was a close friend of Ellie's, or that Ellie is now my college roommate's wife.

"Anyway, my roommate and I reported the hazing to campus police, and they cracked down on the frat. Unfortunately, John was already addicted. He left school after midterms his first year. I'm not in close touch with him, but I know he's been in and out of recovery since then. I don't know his current status."

"Thank you for that confidence, Nathan. It sounds as though you didn't have a lot of contact with him in terms of his struggle. Is that fair to say?"

"I guess. I mean, yes."

"I believe you said there were other people you knew." She waited without directly asking me for details. Clearly, she wanted me to talk about this.

"One other person, actually." I stopped.

"And who was that?"

I felt my breathing grow shallow and quick. Jennifer must have seen that.

"I don't mean to pry, Nathan. Perhaps you could just draw me a few rough lines around the situation."

I took a deep, shaky breath. "It was a very close friend." Friend. Alden had been a friend, sure. But I'd loved him. I'd thought he'd loved me. He'd made love to me, that much was sure. "I guess what I can tell you is that it was very painful for

39

me. In the end, I was left feeling as though fentanyl had meant more to my friend than I had." I waved a hand as if to say, *That's not really the point.* "I know that's a selfish way to look at it. I know it wasn't about me. But that's how it felt at the time."

"Are they in recovery now?"

"I have no idea. They cut me out of their life." It felt odd to refer to Alden as "they," but I preferred to reveal as little personal information as possible, not only about him but also about my personal life, at least for now.

Jennifer's eyes closed just long enough to be more than a blink. "I'm so sorry, Nathan. Thank you for telling me. Now, considering substance abuse in general, you said on the phone that you thought abusers were looking for something— something that the substances they use are substitutes for. What do you think that is?"

I'd actually given this some thought. It didn't surprise me that Jennifer asked this question. I was ready.

"It seems to me they don't know where they belong. And the places where they'd like to belong seem to the abusers like something they aren't worthy of. So I think they feel a kind of worthlessness. And once someone becomes an addict, that's validation that they aren't worth anything. So it feeds into itself. It makes believing that they're worthy of happiness, and worthy of love, impossible. So I think it's a substitute for what they want to feel about themselves and can't."

Jennifer's eyes were on me, but she seemed to be seeing something else. The only sound for several seconds was the tapping noise made by the pen in her right hand.

Finally she spoke. Quietly. "That's very insightful. And it leads to an important question I'm required to ask you."

I wasn't sure how much more intensity I wanted to deal with, but I sat still.

"Are you now using, or have you ever used an illegal or addictive substance?"

I relaxed, and I think she noticed that. "I like beer. I had a few beers before I was legally allowed to drink. And last summer, I decided I like single malt scotch. Other than that, no."

Jennifer laughed, and I heard relief in it. "In my experience, alcoholics don't generally scruple regarding the brewing techniques of their scotch. It does happen, of course, but it's rare." Then she added, "We accept federal funds here, so I have to ask about marijuana."

I think I blushed. "Sorry. I genuinely forgot about that. But it didn't happen often, and I haven't had any in several months. I won't be using if I work here." I smiled, hoping that would help. Then I said, "Why did you ask? And what significance would it have had if I'd said yes to more than that?"

"That's an excellent question, and I appreciate that you're brave enough to ask it. The answer is that I need to know whether you are in recovery before I consider you for a job in a clinic such as this. We prescribe substances such as methadone, which takes the edge off of the cravings for some addicts, and they can come to rely on it—crave it, if you will—as they progress in their recovery. If you'd said you were in recovery and clean, it would not have disqualified you. In fact, several of us here—myself included—are in recovery. If you'd said yes, it would have led to more questions. That's all."

Wow. She was so forthright about herself, I was a little stunned. I nodded. "That makes sense."

"And I have another question for you. Would you be willing, both before you begin this job if we go that far, and also at random intervals while you're here, to subject yourself to testing?"

"That makes sense, too. I have no objection."

"Would you be willing to have our doctor examine you, at our expense, if we offer you the job?"

"Yes." Looking for track marks, perhaps? I had debated

what to wear and had decided on a light blue shirt with long sleeves, khaki slacks, and a tie in patterns of beige. She couldn't see my arms—or between my toes, an injection site I'd heard some addicts use, though the idea made me shiver.

"Excellent. Now, tell me more, if you would, about your career goals."

We talked for about an hour altogether. It wasn't a problem for Jennifer that there was a good chance I wouldn't be in Bar Harbor next year. It wasn't a problem for me that the position didn't pay especially well.

"Now, about the question you asked me on the phone regarding contact with clients. Despite your degree in psychology, Nathan, you are in fact not a therapist or a counselor. Not yet, anyway. So we would never put you in the position of counseling a client. But if you're interested, and if your work allows time or you're willing to use your personal time, you would be welcome at group sessions, at my invitation. You would not participate, of course. It would be like auditing a class."

"There wouldn't be an issue around confidentiality? I mean, just knowing who's in the program?"

"Oh, working here, you'd see them, one way or another. And in your work, you'd have access to their personal files. All employees need to sign a contract that includes a very strict, very legal confidentiality section. So this would not be a bridge too far, in my opinion. Would you be interested?"

"Yes. Very."

"I've already reached almost everyone on your reference list."

Wow. I'd only sent it to her on Monday afternoon. She must have been busy. She stood, and so did I. The interview was over.

"I'm not an impulsive person, Nathan, and you don't seem to me to be one, either. Just the same, barring any problems that arise from the final reference or from the doctor's examination, I would love to offer you the position, right here, right now. Do you need time to consider things?"

I did not. I liked Jennifer, Katie might be a treat (I hoped), and Margot had been right; this would be a great jumping off place for me. Plus, it might be just for this year, so how bad could it be?

I smiled. "When do I start?"

"How about the same day as Margot? Next Tuesday?"

We shook on it.

Jennifer walked me back out to the reception area and asked Katie to give me a copy of the contract I needed to sign.

"Got it all ready for him," Katie said. She handed it to me, a grin on her face. My name was already typed into the appropriate places. "I had a good feeling."

Jennifer asked Katie to add an addendum about getting a pass from the doctor. She told me the doctor appointment could wait until next week as long as I stopped by his office before noon today to pee in a cup.

"Where are you staying, Nathan?" Jennifer wanted to know.

"The Ullikana." She looked impressed. I added, "A gift from my sister. It's just for a few days."

"She has good taste."

"She does, actually. She's in fashion."

"I see. Still, that's a temporary place to stay. Katie, could you give Nathan the sheet of contacts—"

She didn't finish her sentence before Katie handed me another piece of paper with rental contacts and information.

"If it's all right with you, Nathan, we'll wait on a tour of the facility until Tuesday. That way I can take you and Margot around at the same time."


The doctor's office was close enough for me to walk. I didn't see him, but a nurse gave me a cup. I gave it back, full enough of the required liquid. And then I was free.

The day was brighter than yesterday had been, and I was determined to get some hiking in. My sights were set on Gorham Mountain, which seemed just large enough to be satisfying. Clothes changed into hiking gear, bagged lunch (courtesy of the Ullikana) in my pack, I headed for the Park Look Road.

Ocean on my left, rocky mountainous land on my right, I was ogling the scenery and almost missed a sign on my right that pointed toward the trailhead for the Precipice Trail. On a whim I pulled into the parking lot.

There were maybe three other vehicles there, and a few people were standing around, gazing up in the direction of the trail, up the nearly vertical rock face that loomed ahead of them. One of them took a couple of photos with a phone.

I left my pack in the car and walked toward the trailhead, where there were large warning signs—complete with pictures—about the dangers of the trail, stating the recommended age for hikers, their physical stamina, and the relative comfort they should have with heights. The signs offered dire reports of injury and death that can befall unwary hikers. A set of long granite slabs, set horizontally into the hillside like a rustic staircase, led up from the parking area. At the top was a metal gate, open at the moment, that could be closed and locked as someone, presumably a park ranger, deemed necessary. Nighttime, maybe? Stormy weather? It wouldn't have surprised me if the gate had held another sign: Abandon all hope, ye who enter.

I stood at the base of the stairs and gazed into the relative darkness of the trail on the other side of that gate. Tumbles of craggy rocks disappeared up into the trees. If not for the warning signs, and the comments of the bartender last night, it wouldn't have looked like much more than a steep initial beginning to almost any New England mountain trail.

All those warnings would, I expected, discourage many

people. They should. To me, however, they were the opposite of frightening. They were compelling. But I was not doing this trail today.

As I turned back toward my car I saw someone I hadn't noticed before. He was maybe twenty feet to the right of the warning signs. He was in a wheelchair. And he was looking right at me.

I took in the longish light brown hair, brushed off his forehead; the full, neatly-copped beard and mustache; the somewhat heavy eyebrows that extended past the outside edges of his eyes; and the handsome ruggedness of his face. Something about his eyes held me in place. They were intense, and yet there was a gentleness about them.

Slowly, still watching me, he reached for something beside his chair. It was kind of a placard, maybe eighteen inches high and two feet across. It was bright yellow with bold, black lettering. I dropped my eyes to it.

**I GOT THIS CHAIR HERE.**
**ASK ME HOW.**

So he'd been one of the hikers who should have taken the warnings seriously. He must have fallen. He should have stayed away from this trail. I'm ashamed of the thoughts that shot through my head more quickly than I could have spoken them. *Not a real hiker. He's no mountain man.*

Quickly I turned away from him and headed to my car.

As I continued along the road toward the Gorham Mountain trailhead, images came to me from El Speed and Ellie's wedding, which I'd attended at the end of July, under a huge white tent in the park where they'd had their first date. I was in a folding chair beside Mrs. Speed, and I had asked her about the planks of plywood that led from the parking area to the front of the tent. Mrs. Speed had pointed toward the far left side of the front row.

"Ellie's best friend Laura uses a wheelchair," Mrs. Speed had told me.

There had been a young man sitting beside Laura, not

in a wheelchair, talking with her. Mrs. Speed had said he was Laura's boyfriend. "I think they'll be engaged before the summer is out. Maybe today! Weddings are great for that."

In the short time between Mrs. Speed's explanation and Ellie's entrance into the tent, I barely had time to realize that I had no concept of what Laura's life would be like. I also realized that the measures by which I had come to assess people were useless when it came to Laura. I didn't know how to see a disabled person rather than their disability. My standards had come to be all about physical vigor, strength, and stamina. And I felt shame again about the thoughts that had come into my mind about the man who'd fallen from the Precipice.


With Gorham still ahead of me, I couldn't resist stopping at a place where I could park the car and wander down close to the water over massive rock formations. I found a spot that wasn't a bad place to sit, wrapped my arms around my knees, and let myself sink into the environment as the lonely sounds from a buoy in the water came to me, carried on the light wind.

Kaua'i was the first place I'd ever been where I'd experienced the vastness of the ocean. This was the second. In some directions, across expanses of water, I could see land that looked much like what was behind me: dark evergreens, leaves just beginning to change from summer to autumn colors, huge granite boulders tumbled like so many stones from a giant's hand. But in other directions, there was nothing but ocean.

The Pacific Ocean had been massive, with a pull that was deep and powerful beyond anything I'd felt before. Standing on a tiny volcanic island, I had felt that power from my feet to the crown of my head, and I'd known in my very gut that it cared nothing about me one way or another.

The power of the Atlantic Ocean, though still

impressive and not to be trifled with, seemed... well, not superficial, I would never say that. But the personality of it seemed more accessible.

I don't know what I'm talking about. All I know is that it felt very different to me.


Gorham Mountain was the perfect climb for me that day. My boots landed with satisfying solidity on the many rocks, some flat and some in piles, that occasionally made way for earth or tree roots. As the trail got steeper, there was the familiar, validating burn of muscles in my legs. I kept up a steady, fairly quick pace, not allowing myself to slow down for the steeper sections, and my lungs got a real workout. At one point, the trail led beneath the huge extended ledge of a boulder the size of a garage. I had to lean forward as I passed beneath it.

From the summit, I could turn in various directions and see endless forests carpeting hill after hill, or endless ocean, or a complex pattern of rocky fingers of land reaching out to deep blue depths.

I sat on a ledge of granite with a view of the rugged Maine shoreline. Scraggly blueberry bushes with no more fruit, their leaves turning bright crimson, clung to what crevices they could find in the rock. I allowed my mind to wander.

I loved hiking alone. There was no conversation, no music, no accommodation for someone else's needs or shortcomings, no concerns that someone else would notice mine. There was no one to compare myself to. It was just me and the mountain.

What I was doing today was testing this part of the world. I knew better than to expect the same physical challenge New Hampshire offered. I wasn't looking for the stunning experience of being in some kind of nexus between life and death, the breathless mixture of paradise and hell that

Kaua'i had given me. What I wanted to know was what lessons these mountains, this landscape held for me.

The sky overhead was that invigorating combination of bright blue and scattered clouds, some small and blindingly bright, some large and menacingly dark underneath. It was a little too warm for my liking; I prefer to feel cool breezes when I stop moving. And there were a few too many bugs. But that was the weather's fault, not the mountain's.

I pulled out my lunch and ate it, chewing slowly, thoughtfully. Once or twice a small group of hikers passed by behind me, their friendly chatter growing louder as they approached and quieter as they passed. I sat where I was, facing away from them, and let them be.

Just before heading back down, I texted Margot.

*Got the job. Starting the same day as you.*

Within a minute, I saw, *YES! Want to room together after that week?*

*One condition. You let me pick the place. You can have right of refusal.*

No response for almost a minute. Then, *Why?*

*Tell you when I see you. Meanwhile, what's your monthly rental limit?*

After another pause: *I know what you're doing.*

I shot back a laughing emoji. *Are you gonna let me do it?*

*If I don't, you'll just rent an exorbitant palace all by yourself, won't you?*

*Not exorbitant. But come stay in a nice place with me. Yeah?*

*kk* with a smiley face emoji followed by a red heart, and a dollar amount.

Truth be told, I had an ulterior motive. It's true we'd gotten along really, really well for the few days we were alone on our return to the Kalalau trailhead, but living with someone is a risk. So I wanted a place I'd be happy living in if we decided to part ways.

I was back at the Ullikana before five. After a quick shower I sent text messages to Nina and to El Speed letting them know I got the job and would be staying on the island, at least through the winter. Then I decided to walk through the town of Bar Harbor, maybe browse in a few of the less touristy shops.

I decided there was not much on Main Street that offered anything I wanted, other than a restaurant or two and a couple of shops with genuinely nice things in them. It was just after six o'clock when I turned off the main drag and onto a small side street to see what was there. Maybe fifty feet ahead, a couple of young guys—teens, by the look of them—approached someone on the sidewalk. They didn't seem friendly. And in fact, the person they were approaching was in a wheelchair. At first I thought, *Second one today*. But then I realized it wasn't a second one. It was the same one.

Unfriendly was an understatement. The wheelchair guy was at an ATM, and there was no doubt in my mind that he was about to be robbed.

Memories of my own recent brush with street thugs were still fresh and painful, but they weren't as painful as the regret at my lack of resistance. I ran toward the ATM.

By the time I'd covered half the distance, it was evident my help wasn't needed. Moving so fast my eyes couldn't quite follow, wheelchair guy had grabbed one thief in a vice grip by one shoulder near his neck, and the look on the thief's face said he was in agony. Wheelchair guy's other hand grabbed the waistband of the second thief's jeans, and the muscles of his arm bulged beneath the short sleeve of his dark green knit shirt as he lifted the punk off the ground and actually threw him down onto the pavement.

My pace slowed as I watched this incredible scene play out, but I kept moving forward. Who knew what would happen next?

What happened next was that one of the two punks saw me and grabbed his friend, and they high-tailed it off in a hurry. But there were bills, wheelchair guy's money, fluttering all around him. Maybe he had a way of retrieving them, but I figured he wouldn't turn down some friendly assistance.

He turned toward me as I approached, those gentle eyes not looking so gentle now.

I came to a stop maybe five feet from him. "Looks like you didn't need any help with those guys," I said. "But can I help with the clean-up effort?"

"I would appreciate that. Yes."

His voice was deep and resonant, and it pulled at something deep inside me. *Careful, Nathan,* I told myself. *You've fallen for one straight guy already at least in part because of his voice, and another guy who was bi and the wrong guy for you. It's just a voice.*

It was true. One of the first things that had attracted me to Daniel (the guy who'd led me up Mount Chocorua) and then to Conroy (who stayed in one place for no one) had been the quality of their voices.

I busied myself scurrying after the money, which seemed to be playing a game of tag in the light breeze.

As I handed the retrieved bills to him, wheelchair guy said, "Thanks. Usually I go into the bank. Makes me less of a target. But it was so pleasant outside today, and I stayed at my post too long. So the bank's closed."

"Your post?"

He gave me an assessing glance. "I believe you saw me at the Precipice trailhead earlier." He held his right hand out. "Drew Madden."

His hand dwarfed mine, not just in size but also in raw power. I did my best to return the grip. "Nathan Bartlett."

My mind was scrambling for a jumping off place to ask him about his "post," and I almost missed what he said next. "The least I can do is buy you a beer. Do you know

50

the Lompoc?"

I shook my head, wondering if I could find a way to decline. I mean, the guy was in a wheelchair. How would he take it if I said no thanks? He didn't give me much time to make up my mind.

"Walk with me." And with what looked like a flick of a couple of fingers, he turned his chair and headed off. There didn't seem to be a way to decline at this point, so I kept up with him.

People coming toward us on the sidewalk made way when they saw the chair, and Drew did a couple of interesting maneuvers if he wanted to overtake someone in front of us. We rounded a couple of corners and headed up a slight incline, which seemed to slow Drew down very little, and he turned toward the doorway of The Lompoc Cafe.

"An open table! We're in luck!" Drew announced as he passed through a gate covered in greenery. I looked closely; there was a tree on either side, maybe beeches or poplars, and the branches of the two trees had been trained to wrap around each other, forming a canopy over the gate.

Drew wheeled over to the one unclaimed patio table. "Outside okay with you?"

"Great. Sure." Even though he asked, I couldn't help feeling like I was in tow. If I'd said, *Gee, no, I'd rather go inside,* he would probably have done it, and yet—maybe it was the chair. Maybe something in me said he should have his way because he was in a wheelchair. Or maybe he was exuding a particular type of entitlement because of his disability. Whatever. Outside was my preference, anyway.

With his left arm he pushed one of the metal wire chairs aside so he could wheel himself up to the table. I sat in the chair across from him. I tried to assess his age. Thirty, maybe? With that full beard it was hard to tell. Before I had time to wonder what on earth we'd talk about, Drew spoke.

"You're probably wondering why I was there. At the Precipice trailhead." He didn't wait for me to respond. "Or maybe you've already guessed that I got hurt falling from a ledge. There's a bit of a story behind it, but I don't know that I want to go into it just now. I already explained it to several people today."

I had opened my mouth to respond even though I didn't yet know what I was going to say, but I was saved from whatever that would have been when a waiter approached.

"Hey, Drew! How's it goin'? Who's your friend?"

"This here's Nathan Bartlett. He just rescued the money that the wind tried to take from me at the ATM."

"What?"

Drew laughed, low and honest. "Those punks got me again."

"Second time now, right? You'd think they'd learn."

"Maybe they have. I gave 'em a whopping. Anyway, the bills went all over the place. Nathan collected them, so I'm buying him a beer for his trouble. Nathan? This is Lonny."

I nodded at Lonny, who handed us menus. He didn't leave.

Drew wasn't reading his menu. "What style beer do you prefer, Nathan?"

"I usually like pilsners and IPAs best."

He lifted his chin and pointed it in the general direction of my menu. "I highly recommend the Mason's Liquid Rapture Double IPA."

I glanced down at that one. The menu said it was from Brewer, Maine. "Can't go wrong with a brew from Brewer, I suppose."

Drew told Lonny, "I'll have my usual." We handed the menus back to Lonny, and to me Drew said, "Strong Black Velvet Stout."

I sat back in my chair, hands resting on the table edge, and wondered—again—what to say to this guy. And again, he took the lead.

"You looked like you were ready for a hike, when I saw

you earlier. Not the Precipice, though?"

I shook my head. "Gorham. I just pulled in at the Precipice because the bartender at the Beer Works last night mentioned it."

"How did you like Gorham?"

"It was the right climb for the afternoon." I wasn't sure how much to say about my experience. I didn't want to brag, but I kind of wanted this guy who could thwart two thieves from the seat of a wheelchair to know I had some hiking chops. "This is my first full day on the island. I got here yesterday afternoon."

"From?"

What to say? I gave him the easy answer. "Most directly, New York City. I was visiting my sister."

"Where's home?"

Lonny set our drinks down, and I waited for Drew to take a sip, which left a little foam on his mustache before he licked it off. I lifted my glass, said, "Maybe here," and took a sip.

Drew threw me a deliberately puzzled look. "Gonna have to give me a little more than that."

I chuckled. "I'll give you the abridged version. I grew up in Concord, New Hampshire. Through a series of unfortunately accidents, which I won't go into, there's only two of us left in the family. My sister Nina, and me. We just sold the house in Concord. She's been living in New York for a couple of years. Fashion industry. I'm taking some time between my undergrad years and starting on an advanced degree. I just took a job, starting next Tuesday. So I'll be here for the year, most likely, until I figure out which school I'll go to."

One side of Drew's mouth lifted in amusement. "Excellent job on the condensed summary. You could write for *Reader's Digest*."

I gave a slight shrug and drank some more of my brew. "This is great, by the way. Good recommendation." I glanced around at the next table as a young couple, a guy and a girl, got up and left. A couple of young women moved toward the table immediately. They passed right behind Drew, and one of them stared down at his chair as she passed. I couldn't read the expression on her face.

Aware of Drew's eyes on me, I figured it was my turn to ask a question. "And you? Where's home?"

"Grew up right here on the island. I went to school in Boston, undergrad and grad, and came back when my parents died. Which *I* won't go into. Now I live in the house I grew up in, in the village of Hall Quarry."

Wow. So we had something in common in terms of family tragedy. "What's your subject?" I asked. "Of study, I mean."

"Creative writing. I write mystery stories."

"Really? Anything I might have read?"

He eyed me a little oddly. "Lots of people ask that. The answer never seems to be 'yes.'" I felt like squirming, but I didn't. I held his gaze and waited. He asked, "Do you read mysteries?"

I chuckled a little nervously. "Busted. No."

He nodded. "And you? What are you aiming for?"

"Psychology. But not the standard shingle-on-the-sidewalk therapy business. I want to specialize in addiction treatment and recovery."

I'd hit a nerve. I recognized it, because I'd seen it once before. The start of my freshman year at UNH, over my very first restaurant dinner with Alden, I'd mentioned Gordon and the frat hazing that had involved fentanyl. At the mention of that opioid substance, Alden had frozen, very much like Drew just now. I hadn't known then that Alden was in recovery.

Was Drew? Had some accident—like falling off the Precipice—injured him so that he'd needed opioids for the pain, and he'd had trouble getting off them again?

Uncomfortable, I dropped my gaze to my beer glass, wrapping both hands around it as the only form of security available to me at the moment.

Drew was silent for maybe five seconds, and then, his voice quiet but with an edge, he said, "Why that specialty?"

I looked up. What was it I had said to Jennifer just this morning? She was in recovery, though I hadn't known it at the time. Saying the same things to someone who probably had been—Jesus, or maybe still was—addicted, felt frighteningly different. So I didn't mention any of what I understood addiction to be like.

"I was close to two people who were addicted to fentanyl. One has been in and out of recovery for a few years now. The other had been in recovery before I met him. We were—very close, and I knew him only a few months before he relapsed." I let a few beats go by. "There has to be some way to help people stay sober."

The edge in Drew's voice was sharper now. "And you think you can find it?"

My tone wasn't entirely soft, either. Who was he to challenge me? "I think I can help. I don't expect to come up with some miraculous cure for addiction. But I want to be involved in the attempt."

He was watching me closely. This time I didn't drop my eyes. We held each other's gaze for several seconds, and then he dropped his eyes to the table. When he looked up again, his gaze was gentle once more.

"Change of topic." He let a couple of beats go by. "What kind of a hiker are you?"

"Avid." I chuckled. "Sorry; that's not very descriptive. I love to hike alone, but I don't always. I've done eleven of the four-thousand-footers in the Whites, and a few of the smaller peaks. And I've hiked in Hawai'i."

Drew blinked. "What's there to hike in Hawai'i? Volcanos?"

"I was on the island of Kaua'i. The Kalalau Trail. It's not a peak, but it's very challenging in parts. Especially along Crawler's Ledge." With a start, which I hoped was not evident to Drew, it hit me that I couldn't claim the Kalalau among my completed trails. I'd turned back with Margot after she'd fallen.

Just then someone who was leaving another table, talking to his friend and not watching where he was going, tripped over one of the wheels on Drew's chair and nearly fell.

Instead of apologizing, the asshole said, "What the fuck, man?"

Drew had been holding his beer glass, about to drink, and the jolt sent some of his beer sloshing over the glass rim. He closed his eyes and ground his jaw, but otherwise gave no indication that anything had happened.

I wasn't sure what to do. Drew must have heard my chair scape backward as I prepared to get up and—I don't know, defend him or something, because he glanced at me and, just slightly, shook his head.

Drew's refusal to confront the asshole brought me up short. Why hadn't he said something? Why had he stopped me? It couldn't be a lack of courage, and it certainly wasn't a lack of confidence.

Neither of us spoke until the jerk and his friend were gone. Then Drew said, "In case you're wondering, I generally try to ignore shit like that. It happens all the time. I'd be confronting people constantly."

I wasn't sure how to respond to that, so I lifted my glass and drained the little that was left in it.

"But, hey," Drew said, his voice friendly and open again, "let's not allow that to spoil this gorgeous evening. How do you feel about ordering some food?" He drained what was left in his own glass after the recent spillage and smiled.

I'd known I was gay since high school. I'd been out since early in my freshmen year at college. My ability to sense when another guy is gay had gotten pretty good. And I saw something in Drew's smile. I heard something in his tone. I felt something coming from his eyes.

Up to this point, maybe because of my own discomfort about the chair, I'd neglected my usual habit of assessing a guy's looks, his facial features, his muscle tone, his overall attractiveness. This process didn't depend on whether I thought the guy was gay or was someone I might be interested in. It was a habit, really. Drew's ability to dispatch those hoodlums at the ATM had made an impression, but since then I hadn't given much thought to whether he was attractive.

Now, with his suggestion that we spend more time together, I took a good look. He was attractive. Very attractive. So, was the wheelchair interfering with my assessment of whether I'd like get to know him any better than sharing a beer? And a question I hadn't yet considered flashed through my mind: If this guy is gay, and he likes me, and I like him, would there be any question of consummation? That is, sex? Was that even possible?

But whatever it was that his eyes were sending me, it held me. And wheelchair or no wheelchair, sex or no sex, I heard myself say, "Why not?"

We were still locked on each other's eyes, with me trying to appear very casual about it and probably failing, when Lonny reappeared and broke the spell, if that's what it was. "I saw that jerk. Sorry I couldn't get here sooner to clean up the spill." He wiped up the puddle of beer and pulled two menus from where he'd pinned them to his side with an elbow. "Can I interest you guys in dinner?"


By the time I'd finished my appetizer—something called the Beehive, with garlic and goat cheese and honey on toasted bread—I'd learned that Drew's hiking chops exceeded mine. Or, they used to. He'd hiked Kilimanjaro and Denali and even Mont Blanc, and he'd once considered joining a team to climb K2. Somehow he managed to relay all this information without sounding like he was bragging, or trying to impress me. It could have been that when he spoke about these climbs, it was from the perspective of having been hiking with someone more experienced, more athletic, more prepared.

Lonny took our appetizer plates and set our dinners down. Drew had ordered a burrito dinner that hadn't seemed as attractive on the menu as it looked on a plate. I'd ordered a pizza with some unusual toppings, including something called harissa, which Lonny had described as a spicy mixture of garlic, roasted peppers, cumin, and a couple of other things I don't remember.

As soon as Lonny was gone, Drew pointed toward a nearby audio speaker, which was playing some folksy song featuring a female singer.

"Love her."

"And she would be...?"

"Molly Tuttle." He smiled as a he listened for several seconds. Then he picked up his fork and asked, "Why do you hike, Nathan?"

It was one thing to describe our respective summits. It was another to dive into the philosophical reasons behind the activity. Did I want to get into that with this guy? Or was this conversation getting a little too intense for people who'd just met? I stalled for time. "How much time do you have?"

"I have all night."

I wasn't sure how to take that. *Was* he gay? Did he think I was? Was there a subtext in those four words? I decided to take them at face value. And, vaguely aware that I was going along with this line of questioning because I was influenced by his disability—another of those he's-disabled-so-he-should-get-what-he-wants moments—I answered him.

I borrowed some of what Neil would have said in answer to that question. Neil was always so clear about everything he did, and his reasons for hiking were no exception. They had become my reasons. So I decided to risk telling Drew something that might turn him off, or it might turn him on, and in either case his response would tell me a lot about him. And anyway, it was my turn to show off a little.

"Hiking a mountain…. It's kind of a metaphor for life, I think. While you're climbing, you have to pay attention to a lot of details. Like not putting your weight onto a rock that isn't steady. Or finding the best way to cross a stream. Not tripping on tree roots. And whether the trail is exhausting or dangerous or even boring, you have to keep going. That's the daily life part, the little-picture things.

"But then," I leaned back, lifted what I think was my third glass of beer, and took a sip. "Then you hit the summit. Then it isn't about all those details any more. It's about the realization that you are infinitesimally small. And at the same time, you're massively huge. You're a tiny speck on an infinite landscape, and yet you're an integral part of everything that is. And the way you got there was by going through all those details that you might have been tempted to dismiss as unimportant. But they're the stuff of life. They're what got you to the summit."

I watched Drew's face for a reaction. His head was slightly tilted, his eyes on mine. He'd been listening, not even once looking like he wished he hadn't asked, or like he wished I'd get to the point. So even though it took him several seconds to say something, it didn't feel like an uncomfortable silence.

"That is probably the most philosophical description of hiking I've ever heard. But I have to ask, is that something you need to be reminded of? I mean, once you've hiked one mountain, once you've experienced that metaphor, why hike again?"

I gave him a half smile, again stalling for time. It was a great question, but it led to yet more intensity. Drew's questions made me think in a way that conversations with most people didn't. They didn't feel like challenges, exactly, and yet there was something subtly invasive about them. And as for this question, he'd hiked quite a few mountains, himself; maybe he was playing devil's advocate.

Finally I landed on this: "Perspective isn't something we gain once and don't need again. You can't stay on the summit. So there's always another wobbly stone underfoot, always another tangle of roots to navigate. I need the promise of more summits to help me keep working through all those pesky details."

*How many beers had I had? Was it really three? Or had I lost count? And did I ever talk like this when I wasn't drunk? And by the way, was this guy always this intense?*

"Why did *you* keep hiking?" I asked, the beer probably speaking at this point. "And why did you start?" If I hadn't been at least a little drunk, I would never have asked those questions. On the surface, they were fair game; he'd been asking me the same things. But my questions were about the past. By implication, they pointed right at the fact that he'd hike no more.

He tilted his head to the other side and looked at me closely. "Before I tell you," he said, forming his words slowly, "let me ask you one more thing." He paused, and I tried to appear as though I wasn't nervous. "What does this chair say to you about me?"

I shook my head. "Not a fair question. I don't know you well enough to say."

"If we were to leave here and go down a couple of streets, do you think people would be looking at me? At us?"

"Of course they would. Some of them, anyway. Though they probably would try not to let either of us see that. I'd guess it would be like it was on the way here from the bank."

"How much did that bother you?"

Our eyes locked together yet again, and something hit me. "Are you testing me?"

He looked down briefly and then up again. "Maybe a little."

I blinked. *Testing me?* That pissed me off. "Is this something you often do with strangers who help you out of awkward situations?"

"No. Just the ones I think I like. That's not a lot of people. So I'm sorry if I seem a little...."

"Intense?"

He chuckled. "Yeah. That's one word. But I like to know when someone feels like this chair," and he slapped the side of one wheel, "makes them see me in a certain way. A way I don't like." His smile seemed a little apprehensive.

*Testing me....* I might have scowled at him. Or glared. I'm not sure. "Y'know, I'm not in the habit of diving into heavy conversations with people I don't know. I don't usually mention family tragedy to complete strangers. And since this might be important to you, I'm not even sure I'd have come with you for a beer if you hadn't been in a wheelchair."

His face looked like granite, it was that hard. In a way, I'd just told him I pitied him. I reached into my pocket for my wallet and pulled several bills out, more than enough for my share of dinner and a tip, and I dropped them onto the table. "Maybe I wasn't the only one being tested."

I stood and walked toward that gate with the tree branches entwined into each other's space, now even more noticeable because of the strings of lights woven through them, shining in the dark.

Drew didn't call out to me. He didn't say anything. He just let me walk away.

# CHAPTER FOUR

Friday was my day for practical arrangements. First I used the rental information Katie had given me, went to see a few places, and signed up for a really nice condo in Southwest Harbor that Margot and I could move into the following Saturday. It was a little pricey for the first few weeks, but after mid-October the price went down enough to be reasonable for me. Then I hired a mover to fetch my worldly effects, currently stashed in a storage unit in Concord, and bring them to Bar Harbor.

This was ignoring my promise of giving Margot the right of refusal, but I had no doubts about this place. It was in a gorgeous setting. Weathered board exterior gave the place a natural look, and it was directly across the road from the actual harbor. Our place had views of the water. And the village of Southwest Harbor was charming—just enough stores to be useful, not enough to get super fancy or crowded. I knew she'd love it.

I felt very grown up.


I checked out of the Ullikana around nine thirty the next morning and texted El Speed to let him know what time I was leaving. I knew that as I drove away from Bar Harbor, Margot was on her way to the island.

On a whim Friday night, I'd downloaded a couple of Molly Tuttle's recordings. I'd kind of liked the sound of her voice when I'd heard her at the Lompoc, and I didn't want to let that odd confrontation with Drew ruin anything musical. As soon as I had driven clear of town I selected them to play. I liked the first tune, which seemed basically like folk music.

It was lilting and a little nostalgic with sweet, clear guitar work. Then the second song started, and immediately something inside me pulled back. I kind of liked the tune, but this was more bluegrass than folk—lots of twangy banjo sounds. And someone played a country fiddle in that slightly frenetic, wailing tone that sounds like widows keening.

I was still trying to decide how I felt about bluegrass. There was a decidedly bittersweet taste to it for me, heavy emphasis on "bitter." In his role as my father figure, Neil had taken care of me, stood up for me, guided me, loved me, made me feel like I had a family despite having no parents. I had adored him. And I had thought I knew him.

But at the church gathering after his funeral, the woman he would probably have married played a song she declared had been his favorite, a song she said was how he lived his life. One line in particular seemed to stand out: "Go grab your life and live it." It was by a bluegrass band, Cherryholmes.

It had stunned me that Neil would have been into bluegrass at all, let alone that his favorite song—at least according to Miss Cotton Hazard—was in this category. And the fact that I hadn't known, and Cotton had, added to the resentment I'd felt that he'd spent his last free time before that fateful hike— the one that had killed him—with her, when he had originally intended to spend it at home. With me.

Then there was the guilt. Obviously I hadn't known Neil as well as I'd thought. As well as I should have.

And there was more. More of the bitter. Because after Gram had died last March, a line from deep inside my memory had declared: "Gravestones cheer the living, dear. They're no use to the dead." It had stuck in my brain like a piece of grit you can't locate and remove from your irritated eye. So I'd searched the internet. It turned out to be the last line of the song "Buy For Me the Rain" by yet another bluegrass group, the Nitty Gritty Dirt Band. It was deep in my memory because the teenaged Neil had played the song so often.

So, you see, I should have known this about Neil. I should have known that of the various types of music he liked, bluegrass was high on the list.

I wanted to give bluegrass a chance. Neil had obviously liked it. At the same time, I hated it, because it had revealed so starkly how one-sided my relationship with him had been. How self-centered *I* had been.

I switched the music to Ed Sheeran's *No.6 Collaborations Project* album. Much better.


I hadn't seen El Speed since his wedding at the end of July, and I was a little anxious about what our relationship would be like now. We'd been college roommates and best friends for four years, and although I liked Ellie well enough, there was no reason to think things between me and El Speed would be the same, and every reason to expect some differences. In fact, after they'd gotten engaged part-way through senior year, El Speed and I had drifted a little apart. He'd spent nearly every weekend in Maine with Ellie, and when she'd visited UNH I'd felt like a third wheel.

Now they were in their own home. A married couple. I did my best to keep my mind on the journey to avoid creating unpleasant scenarios that almost certainly wouldn't happen.

All I had for information about El Speed's rented house was an address. Following my car's GPS, I drove through landscape that changed from lots of trees and hills and lakes to commercial strips to houses to commercial strips and back to trees, only to do it all again. As I got closer to Bangor the trees thinned out but never disappeared. Then the part-green, part-autumn gold took over again and never let up until I turned off of Route 2 onto a smaller road. Two more turns brought me into open land with trees and hills in the distance.

I turned into a driveway that was an opening between two sections of rough-hewn fencing. It led a couple of hundred feet toward a detached garage painted the same soft yellow as the house to the left of it. There was a window in the garage framed by dark green shutters like those on the sides of the house's windows. A tool shed to the right of the garage was also pale yellow. Every building had a dark green roof and shutters, and bright white trim.

I hadn't even turned off the engine when the door in the middle of this side of the house opened, and El Speed and Ellie both stepped out onto the small porch. Ellie stayed there while El Speed nearly jumped the five steps down from the porch and ran over to me. As soon as I'd stepped out of the car I was wrapped in a bear hug by the guy who'd felt like a brother for four years.

This warm greeting was more than I probably deserved. I'd nearly missed his wedding. In my defense, he'd changed the date from June to the end of July, in direct conflict with my planned trip to Kaua'i, and I'd gone on that trip despite the conflict. If it hadn't been for Margot nearly falling into oblivion and then wanting to turn back before the hike was over, I would have missed El Speed's big day altogether.

El Speed released the hug and held my shoulders with his hands. He looked down from his six-foot-plus height, a smile lighting his whole face and causing his blue eyes to sparkle. He wrapped one arm around my shoulder and led me to the house.

"Say hello to my wife, and then we'll give you a tour."

Ellie and I smiled at each other. My smile was sincere; I think hers was.

"Larry," she said, "let's sit for a couple of minutes. Otherwise, why did I bother to make lemonade? Fresh lemons and everything!"

I was going to have to get over my mild surprise whenever I heard El Speed referred to as Larry. He was El Speed to me, maybe to Nina, and—really—to no one else. I refused to give up the nickname, but I had to let other people call him Larry.

I watched Ellie as she moved around her kitchen, the long strawberry-blond hair—so like Margot's—in its usual high ponytail that swayed with her motions as it cascaded from a head nearly as high off the ground as her tall husband's. She seemed genuinely happy. I couldn't help smiling at the way she seemed to be glowing.

El Speed brought a plate of sugar cookies to the table. "I made these, I'll have you know. Sit, Nathan."

"Yes, sir! But I'm not so sure about the cookies."

Ellie said, "You'll be surprised! I've been teaching him how to cook."

"Like hell!" El Speed protested. "I'm the food chemist, remember? You've just been making me follow your recipes."

Ellie turned toward him, hands on hips and a teasing gleam in her eyes. "I think that's what I just said."

The banter went on like that as we sipped glasses of lemonade between bites of what were very good cookies. Then I got a tour of the house. I knew they'd rented a place in Orono while they worked toward their respective masters degrees, El Speed's in food chemistry and Ellie's in elementary education, but I'd pictured something cramped and semi-urban. This was much nicer than that, if still what a realtor might call "cozy."

My room was upstairs, tucked under the slope of the roof in the back, a small but charming space with a single bed, a wooden chair, and a small bureau—perfect for my needs while I was here. Their room was on the other side of the upstairs, under a broad dormer with windows that looked out across fields and toward woods and a pond. I dropped off my bag and we all headed back downstairs for a tour of the grounds.

"This is a great place," I said to no one in particular as we stood behind the house and gazed off across the fields and into the forested distance.

Ellie nodded. "We were beyond lucky to find it. The

owner built a bigger house a couple of miles north of here and wasn't quite ready to sell this one. I gather it's been in the family for some time."

Dinner was a simple affair, but that's not a complaint. Grilled salmon (El Speed at the grill), steamed asparagus, and saffron rice with bits of red bell pepper scattered through it.

We ate outdoors. There was a small patio set of table and chairs, left there by the previous owners along with a huge tent-like net thing that fit over the large umbrella, which was on a post inserted into the middle of the table. So, no bugs. I wondered if Ellie would refer to the time I'd gone with her and El Speed to stay at his family's rustic cabin on a lake. I'd complained about the whining and biting of mosquitoes that had plagued me all night, and she'd said, "What's a little blood? You won't miss it."

For a variety of reasons, Ellie and I had gotten along terribly well on that trip—which was the first time I'd met her—and this dismissal of my woes had not sat well with me.

After El Speed and I helped bring used dinner dishes into the kitchen, Ellie handed El Speed clean plates and forks and shooed us back outside. When she rejoined us, she brought out dessert, which she said was her signature "three-berry pie." It was absolutely delicious, and I praised it accordingly.

When we'd finished our respective pieces of pie (El Speed had two), Ellie opened a new topic: the reason I'd nearly missed her wedding.

"So, Nathan, what can you tell us about this spiritual quest you were on?"

I wasn't sure where to start, and in fact I was trying to assess how pointed her tone sounded. When I didn't speak right away, El Speed clarified.

"You remember. The one that was more important than our wedding." There was no mistaking *his* tone.

67

I let out a long breath. "I promised you an explanation. So here goes."

It was not an easy thing to talk about. As I'd told Luc, it was about family. I went into much greater depth with El Speed and Ellie. I owed them that. I told them how truly horrible it had made me feel that I hadn't known my brother or my grandmother nearly as well as I should have. I said how guilty I'd felt that I hadn't asked Gram more questions about her life, and that I'd taken Neil's love, his support, and the sense of belonging he'd given me for granted.

"That's all well and good," Ellie said, sounding almost like when she'd told me I wouldn't miss a little blood, "but what's it got to do with Hawai'i?"

"I'm getting to that." I was debating in my mind how much to say about Conroy, the handsome, sexy, charismatic leader for that hike who'd seduced me in more ways than one. I decided they needed to know about only one of those ways.

"I'd met this guy Conroy when I was hiking Cannon Mountain."

El Speed interrupted. "The one you fucked on the summit?"

Crap. I'd forgotten I'd already told him about that. "Yeah, but that's not relevant.

Ellie wanted to know, "Why not?"

"Because that's not why I went on the hike. We weren't—well, we weren't together that way by the time I went on the trip." Never mind that we had been fucking right up until a few weeks before it. "On the hike, I was just another hiker. Anyway," I looked at each of them in turn with a glance that said *Let me finish,* hoping they'd see that despite in the dimming light.

"Conroy knew I was feeling really shitty about myself. He said he was leading a hike to a place where there is no bridge between the physical and the spiritual, because there's no need for one. They exist together."

I could tell from the look on Ellie's face that there was

about to be some comment along the same lines as the mosquito shaming, so I glared at her and kept talking.

"This might sound like a lot of mumbo-jumbo to some people. But it isn't. There is something special there." I'd stopped just in time before saying "magic" instead, because I was afraid Ellie would have labeled me as a nut job. "I spent a couple of days on my own before the hike started, and I did a lot of deep thinking during that time."

Ellie wasn't patient. "You still haven't said why this was a spiritual quest."

"You haven't given me much of a chance." I drained the last of the wine from my glass and set it down firmly. Ellie sat back in her chair and folded her arms in front of her.

"Like I've said, I took Neil for granted. Gram, too. She went to the same church all her life, and because she never pestered any of us kids to go with her, I assumed it was more for company than anything else. But planning her funeral, and at the ceremony, I realized I hadn't understood at all. She was deeply religious. When I told Conroy this, he said his impression of her was that she was spiritual, that it went deeper than religious tradition. He reminded me that when he'd talked about Kaua'i to her once, in decidedly spiritual terms, she'd been fascinated. So Conroy suggested that I should do something spiritual, to honor her and reconnect with her and with Neil."

I tilted my wine glass just to make sure it was empty.

"I was just hanging around that big old house, all by myself, after school let out. It felt like it was haunted. Conroy pointed out that I couldn't exactly come to a good emotional place about my family in that house where all the memories were, where I felt bad about myself. So I signed up for the hike." This was a little out of order, but too bad. "And then you needed to change the date for your wedding." That much was true.

I leaned my head back and closed my eyes for a few seconds before going on. No one interrupted me.

"Conroy had been right. The time I spent alone on the north shore of that island was like preparation for the hike itself. And on that hike," I sat forward, hands gripped between my knees, "I helped save someone's life. One of the hikers fell over the edge of the trail at Crawler's Ledge. Conroy and I saved her. At one point, I had to climb down a rope onto a ledge several feet below the trail. And I had to wait there, alone, for a few minutes while Conroy prepared something on the trail above. There was nothing but a few feet of red dirt," and I paused for second in respect for the place, "between me and all the strength of the Pacific Ocean pounding on volcanic rock a few hundred feet below me."

Through the darkening air I looked first at Ellie and then and El Speed and decided to tell them what had happened next. "And while I waited there, staring off into nothing but vastness, I felt both Gram and Neil with me. I can't tell you how, and I can't tell you why. But it was undeniable. It felt like they were forgiving me. And I realized that was what I'd gone there to find. So when Margot, the woman who had fallen, said she didn't feel she could go on, I volunteered to return with her."

I paused, a little surprised at how much I'd revealed, and glad no one had interrupted me.

El Speed said, "So you didn't finish the hike?" He sounded gentle, even sympathetic.

"I did not. I can't claim the Kalalau Trail among my completed hikes. It will always be the one that got away. And yet, it delivered in a way no other hike ever could."

"Would you ever go back?" Ellie wanted to know.

"I doubt it. It was such a magical experience," I was now unafraid to use that word, "that I'd be disappointed if a second trip didn't quite measure up. But I learned things about myself, and about life, that will stay with me."

There was a quiet moment while we listened to the crickets in the grass, and I heard the distinct whine of a mosquito from the other side of that wonderful net.

Ellie said, "So we owe the fact that you were at our wedding to this woman. Margot. If she hadn't needed to turn back...."

"Yeah," I said, hoping I didn't hear accusation in her voice.

"Do we get to meet her?"

I chuckled. "Funny you should ask. I haven't told you all my news."

El Speed thought he could guess. "We know you got that job you were applying for in Bar Harbor."

"Not only that, but I found out about it through Margot, because she had taken a job at the same clinic. We're both starting on Tuesday. And we decided to room together. So, yeah, you probably will meet her at some point."

It was getting dark, and they didn't have anything to light the table, which gave me an idea for a housewarming gift. We made it back inside without, I think, bringing any bugs with us. I offered to wash or dry dishes, but I was deemed the guest, at least for tonight.

"Maybe tomorrow," Ellie said.

We sat for a while in the living room and discussed what movie to watch. While El Speed was getting it queued up, Ellie asked, "Anyone special in your life right now, Nathan?"

As I shook my head, an image of Drew Madden flew into my brain. I assured myself that was because he was the only person outside of the clinic I'd met since arriving in Bar Harbor. And it seemed unlikely we'd have any more philosophical dinners together.


The last night I was there, Sunday, the three of us grabbed our beverage of choice, braved the mosquitos, and dashed under the net umbrella after the dinner dishes were washed and put away. The day before, I'd found a package store and procured a nice single malt, so El Speed and I each had a glass of that.

Ellie had rated it "Eeeewwwww" after her taste in the kitchen and had wine instead.

We sat quietly for maybe five minutes, listening to the crickets and the whine of frustrated mosquitos and the whispering of distant traffic. Out of that dark a thought jumped into my brain, and before I could assess the wisdom of saying it aloud, it escaped through my mouth.

"Ellie, your friend Laura. Did she and Tim get engaged? Mrs. Speed suspected it was imminent."

El Speed and Ellie both turned to look at me, but that's all I could tell in the dark; their expressions were unreadable.

After a short pause, Ellie replied, "As a matter of fact, they did. They're getting married in late October. Did you speak with them at our wedding?"

"No. I might not have noticed them, but I asked Mrs. Speed about the plywood path that led to the tent. That's when she pointed Laura out to me."

"What made you think of that just now?"

I shrugged, more for my benefit than anyone else's as they probably couldn't see it. "Thursday afternoon I was on my way to a mountain for a short hike, and I passed the trailhead for this trail that's supposed to be pretty rugged. Deadly, even, it seems. At least at times."

"Precipice," El Speed said. "I've done it."

"Me too," added Ellie.

I was glad they couldn't see the surprise on my face. From their tone, it didn't seem as though either of them had thought it was especially brag-worthy, as the bartender had indicated, and yet Drew Madden, hiker extraordinaire and wheelchair martial artist, had nearly died on it.

"So is it a big deal, or not?" I asked.

"Depends," El Speed said. "Partly it depends on the weather. Or if there's ice on anything. Or if you're not as ready for it as you think you are." He took a sip of scotch. "You could do it easily. Just choose the right day. And not between late March and mid-August, because falcons nest there, and hikers would disturb them. The park closes the trail for that."

"So… anyway, I pulled into the parking area. And there was this guy—"

El Speed interrupted me. "Wheelchair? Beard? Warning sign?"

I could almost hear myself blink. "Yeah."

"Drew Madden. He's kind of famous."

A sort of chuffing noise escaped me. "Go on."

"I don't have the whole story, but I'm sure if you searched the internet you'd find it. A few years ago, if memory serves, he was hiking on his own—which you're kind of not supposed to do on that trail. But anyway, he was, and ahead of him was this couple with a kid, maybe ten? Something like that."

"An eleven-year-old boy. Darren." Evidently Ellie's memory was a little better than her husband's. "They also strongly discourage hiking that trail with children."

El Speed picked up the story again. "Right. So Darren was having some trouble on one of the ladders. There are these iron rungs pounded into the granite in lots of places, and some of them go straight up. Darren's dad was behind him, and when the kid fell his dad tried to catch him, but the kid went kind of sideways. Toward Drew. Unfortunately there was a ledge falloff right behind him. So Drew didn't try to grab the kid. Instead, he reached out and pushed the kid away from him and onto another part of the ledge. He saved the boy. But that sent Drew flying backward."

I sat in stunned silence while El Speed twirled his glass without drinking.

Ellie said, "I think a tree broke his fall to some extent. But he'll never walk again."

"So Drew is a hero? What's the sign for, then?" I almost added, *So he can brag?*

"I think he wants to talk people out of taking their kids on the trail," was El Speed's assumption.

"I think he wants everyone to be sure they're ready for everything the trail throws at you," Ellie added. "Did you talk to him?"

How much to tell them? *No* was a lie. *Not at the trail* would just lead to more questions.

"I saw him later. He was thrashing two young punks who were trying to rob him at an outdoor ATM."

"What?"

"He sent them packing. It was amazing. But his money went flying, so I gathered it up. We went for a beer at the Lompoc."

"I love the Lompoc," was El Speed's reaction.

"You did?" Ellie was more interested in the man. "What's he like?"

"Well… for one thing, he's done a lot of hiking. Serious hiking. Denali serious. So I guess if anyone is going to hike the Precipice alone, it would be him. And he grew up on Mount Desert Island. Lives in the house he grew up in. His parents are dead."

"So he lives alone?"

Good question. "I, uh, I didn't ask."

"Well, it's a small island. You're bound to run into him again."

Just what I was afraid of.

# CHAPTER FIVE

Monday afternoon, I'd barely pulled into the driveway of Margot's Airbnb rental when she came dancing out to greet me. Her hug was fierce.

"Nathan! Oh, I'm so glad you're here! Is this exciting or what?"

The place was what realtors might advertise as "charming" and "intimate." But it would suit for the week.

She had rented a car when she'd landed on the mainland and had already gone grocery shopping, which I really appreciated. "I'll have to buy a car soon. Used, probably."

We walked into town and stopped for a drink before dinner in the place where the bartender had told me about the Precipice. The Lompoc might have been more fun, but I wasn't going to chance running into Drew. Not yet, anyway.

Sitting at the bar, we ordered beers and raised our glasses to each other.

"Now, don't be mad, Margot, but I've already rented a place. We can move in this coming Saturday."

Margot had a pretty scowl, made even less ferocious by the freckles and by the fact that she wasn't actually mad. "Tell me."

So I did. "We can drive out there after work tomorrow so you can see it. But I did take pictures." I handed my phone to her.

She scrolled through, eyes wide and a smile on her face. "Furious, Nathan. I'm furious. Because you managed to find this place so quickly!"

"Well, you found me the job."

She laughed. "True enough." She took a sip of beer. "I

don't suppose you've heard from Conroy."

"And I don't suppose I ever will."

"I got an e-post-card from Erik. He wanted to know if I was okay."

I pictured Erik Buxton, the tall New Zealander who'd been my favorite person on the Kalalau hike, before Margot and I got to know each other better. Forty-ish airline pilot, thinning light brown hair, blue eyes with squint lines around them as though he looked into the distance a lot. He'd had a wry sense of humor and a delightful accent.

"That was nice of him. I didn't!"

"Maybe if you'd fallen over the edge of the world, he would have sent something to you, too."

"I liked Erik. He sure had a way of putting that humorless Owen in his place." Owen had been all about expensive clothes and equipment, and Erik had quietly inserted verbal pin pricks into the guy's ego at strategic times.

"Yeah," Margot almost sighed. "I liked Erik a lot."

Margot and I chatted about nothing much for a bit, and then the bartender came by to see if we wanted a refill.

"Say," he said to me, "did you make it to the Precipice?"

I shook my head. "Not yet. Drove by the trailhead, though."

"Did you see Drew?"

"I did, yes."

"Nut job, if you ask me." And he left to get our second round before I could decide what, if anything, I should say in response.

"Who's Drew?" Margot wanted to know.

I gave her a thumbnail sketch of the story El Speed had told me. I said nothing about dinner at the Lompoc.

"He sounds like a hero. Why is he a nut job?"

"No idea."

We decided to drive by our condominium complex before dinner instead of waiting until tomorrow. We couldn't go in yet of course, but Margot was impressed.

"I can't believe I'm going to live here! Nathan, if you could see the place where I grew up...." She shook her head slowly.

"I didn't grow up in luxury, myself. Gram was very thrifty. Which is why I can do this now."


Rather than go back and cook dinner, we treated ourselves to dinner at a restaurant in Southwest Harbor, not far from what would be our home. Afterward, back at the rental, I called Nina. Even though it was Labor Day, she was at the office.

"I have just a couple of minutes, Nathan. You can imagine...."

"Yeah, I know, Fashion Week starts Friday. Just wanted to let you know I found a place here. I'll text you the address."

"New job is tomorrow, yeah?"

"It is."

"Are you nervous?"

*Why would I be nervous?* "Not so far."

"I was thinking about those two thugs who attacked you. They were probably...."

"Yeah, I suppose they probably were using. Still, that was New York City."

"Druggies are druggies, Nathan. They have no geography and no scruples."

"Um, Nina, have you ever known anyone who was in recovery?"

Momentary silence. "Well, no. Still. Be careful."

It was not like my big sister to be solicitous of me. Or of anyone, really.

"Not to worry," I told her. "I'll let you get back to it. Break a leg, and all that. I don't suppose you could have Luc send me some of the photos he takes?"

She laughed. "Doubt it. Take care, Nathan."


Tuesday was a bit of a whirlwind. After Katie gave Margot and me a printed orientation package ("It's all in your email as well"), we got a tour of the facility by one of the counselors, Kenneth "Call me Ken" Lane. He was a pretty nondescript kind of guy, the type that makes detectives wince when you try to describe them: "Medium height, medium build, light brown hair."

"I'm in recovery," he informed us, almost as though it were part of his title.

Ken seemed quite taken with Margot. She saw that too, and at one point whispered to me, "Gonna have to watch this one. I'm telling him you're my boyfriend." And she winked at me, by which I hoped she meant "Psyche!"

The facility was divided into two separate sections. My desk was in the administrative building, where the group sessions and other meetings and interviews were held. The other section, which Ken showed us only from the outside, was the dispensary.

"Twice a day," he told us, "at nine and again at five-thirty, clinic members who are prescribed methadone or buprenorphine come here according to their schedule with us."

I looked at my watch: nine forty-five.

Ken saw me. "Yeah, they leave pretty quickly. They start queueing up a little after eight, but they don't hang around once they get their meds."

"What's the difference between the two drugs?" Margot asked. I knew, but I let Ken answer.

"They both replicate the effects of opioids to reduce cravings and give members a chance to reduce their addiction gradually. Methadone is a stronger drug, but it can have some of the same side effects as opioids, and it can also be addictive. Buprenorphine is less powerful, less addictive, and has fewer side effects."

Margot asked, "So someone might graduate from methadone to buprenorphine?"

"Sure, but we tailor the treatment to the member's needs and response."

I asked, "How often do you test for drug use?"

"Urine tests? That's random, so no member knows when it will be their turn. Helps keep them on target."

"What happens if they fail?"

"Again, it kind of depends on a number of factors, but… I'll just say it's a big deal."

Ken talked us through a lot of protocol, stuff that was already in our intro packets, but I figured the clinic would want it stressed; a lot of it had to do with confidentiality and client privacy. We had a short break for lunch, which was sandwiches brought in for us from a place in town. Ken warned us, "This won't happen again. You should probably bring lunch most days."

Jennifer appeared at the end of our meal and took Margot away to meet people she'd be working closely with, while Katie claimed me and gave me a thorough explanation of the front room protocol, file cabinets, and computer usage. She was favorably impressed with my competence in basic office programs, and she introduced me to the custom program the center used. That was a little idiosyncratic, but it wasn't so complex that I expected to have trouble using it.


The week went on kind of like that. Margot and I would have breakfast, pack our lunches, and Margot would drive us to the center. It was a fifteen minute walk, so if I'd had to get back on my own, I could. Margot's job included working with schools, so she needed a car. Once we moved to Southwest Harbor, though, we wouldn't be able to carpool any longer.

Over dinners, which we took turns making (though

Margot was by far the superior cook), we compared notes and gossiped about people at the center. We decided we really liked Jennifer and Katie. Ken was an open question. There was another counselor there I thought was interesting, not because he was attractive (though he was), or because he might be gay (despite what Margot had to say about it), but because he seemed very intense and kind of dark. He was also very nicely put together, in a compact package that appeared powerful. Juan Diego.

I was a little disappointed that I didn't get to sit in on any of the group sessions that week. Jennifer said, "Maybe next week. We'll see."

Saturday was a big day: the move to our new digs. Neither bedroom had a water view, but one was bigger, and Margot insisted I take that one. The moving van with my things arrived mid-afternoon, and that meant we had some furniture. Nina and I had donated the furniture from all the bedrooms except mine, so Margot was on an air mattress for now, with suitcases standing in for a bureau.

Rather than cook dinner in our new kitchen, exhausted as we were, we decided to eat out, Margot's treat.

"Ken told me about this great place," she said as we were discussing options. "It's called the Lompoc Cafe."

I tried not to flinch. I figured I might as well get it over with; it was a small town, and I couldn't avoid it—or Drew, probably—forever. "I've been there. It's good."

"When did you have time to do that?"

"I was here a few days ahead of you, remember." Should I tell her more about Drew? What if he were there? Might as well bite the bullet. So I told her, with as little embellishment as possible, the story of Drew's fall, of the ATM, and of how Drew and I had gone to the Lompoc afterward.

"That's so cool! D'you think we might see him there?"

"Honestly, Margot, how would I know? He likes the place, but whether he goes there once a week or once a month...."

"I hope he is. I mean, maybe I didn't end up in a wheelchair, but I could have! Falling off Crawler's Ledge and all." She smiled at me, saw the horrified expression I must have had on my face, and added, "Oh, don't worry. I wouldn't go up to him and tell him how much we have in common. But really, Nathan, you're a bit of a hero, too. You and Conroy."

"Whatever. Let's go."

So we did.

And Drew was there, alone at a table outdoors, a beer in front of him and an e-reader in his hand. He glanced up as Margot and I came in through that leafy canopy. He looked at me, then at her, then more intently at me as if trying to decide whether to speak.

I guess this was my night for taking bulls by their proverbial horns. I walked over to him.

"Drew. How are you?"

He looked almost amused. "Good, all things considered. Who's your friend?"

"This is my roommate, Margot Truman. Margot, Drew Madden."

He extended his right hand toward her. "Forgive me if I don't stand." It was hard to read the grin on his face.

Margot let out one of her musical laughs as she shook his hand. "You are forgiven."

"Join me?"

Despite the cooler weather that evening, there were no other open tables on the patio. I looked at Margot. She definitely wanted to sit with him.

"Sure," I said. "Thanks. Are you having dinner or just a beer?"

"Just placed my order."

It wasn't Lonny tonight, but a woman whose name I don't recall. She came by pretty quickly, and after Margot and

I had ordered, Drew glanced at Margot. "So did you two meet here on the island? Is there a roommates app?"

Margot really did have a very nice laugh. "Nathan and I were both on a hike in July. The Kalalau Trail, on Kaua'i."

"Ah, yes," he said, eyes toward me for a few seconds. "I've heard about this Crawler's Ledge. Does one actually have to crawl?"

Margot was enthusiastic. "Oh, thereon hangs a tale!" I didn't interrupt, and I didn't contribute. I let Margot tell Drew the whole story. Well, I didn't interrupt until she wildly overstated my part in her rescue.

"Margot exaggerates," I said.

"Oh, no," she insisted. "Conroy was the one with the rope, and he knew about tying knots in it to help me grip, but both of you pulled me up. And then," and here she looked intently at Drew, "Nathan volunteered to climb down to that ledge and retrieve my pack."

"Did he." Not a question.

"And when I realized I'd be a total drain on the group if I tried to go on from there—I mean, I was in a state—Nathan said he'd go back with me."

Drew glanced at me. "So you didn't finish the trail."

I felt my back stiffen.

Drew chuckled. "No criticism. In fact, you go up in my estimation. I get the sense that you pride yourself on your mountaineering skills, and I'm sure you were looking forward to the challenge." To Margot he said, "I'm very glad you had such gallant company on your return journey."

Our food arrived at that moment, which filled the awkward pause it felt like to me.

Lifting his napkin, Drew said, "And now you're friends for life. I like that story." If he thought we might be more than friends, he gave no clue.

Perhaps Margot felt the need to return some of the praise Drew had offered me. In any event, she said, "Nathan told me about how you chased off those two thugs at the

ATM. I can imagine propelling your wheelchair would increase your arm strength. But that much? Really?"

I cringed, but Drew laughed. "Nathan, I like your friend. And Margot, you are correct. I do quite a few things, beyond wheeling myself around, to increase my upper body strength. I don't know whether Nathan told you, but I'm a bit of a mountaineer myself, so when I fell and found myself in this chair, I decided to become a different kind of athlete."

He took a mouthful of food and chewed slowly. I was dying to ask what that meant. Margot was braver than I was.

"Do you mean like the Paralympics?"

"I don't go that far. But one of my favorite ways to maintain strength is the climbing wall at this gym I go to sometimes."

That was too much for me; I couldn't stay silent. "You climb up those molded hand-bolds, straight up a vertical wall?"

"Yup. You should come with me sometime. Ever done that?"

I shook my head, trying hard not to look as overwhelmingly impressed as I was.

Margot put my own thoughts into words. "That's amazing! I wouldn't have thought it was possible to do that with just your arms."

Drew took a sip of his beer, eyes on her as he set it down. "Did you hear about the wheelchair team who towed a Boeing 787 one hundred and six meters?"

Again, I couldn't help myself. "Are you fucking kidding me?"

Drew threw back his head and laughed. "Ninety-eight of them. November, I think, last year. It was at Heathrow. The plane weighed over a hundred and twenty tons."

"Why would they do that?" Margot's eyes were wide.

"A fundraiser for Aerobility. A UK charity. They help people with disabilities learn to fly."

I felt my head nod.

"Nathan, you look as though you understand."

"I guess if I were to become disabled, something like that would help me get my confidence back."

"That's exactly right."

Up to this point I would have guessed that Drew was taken with Margot, as would have been perfectly reasonable; she's adorable, and she was obviously not at all put off by the chair. But suddenly it felt different. After his last comment, Drew's eyes held mine with an intensity that even Margot noticed. In my side vision I saw her look from one of us to the other a couple of times before I finally dropped my gaze.

By the time the meal was over, Drew had asked Margot about her job, and she'd revealed that both she and I were at the Bar Harbor Recovery Center. So now he knew where I worked. At least no one talked about living quarters, so our condo complex wasn't mentioned. For whatever it was worth, he didn't know where I lived.


She'd noticed, all right. On the drive home, she made that clear.

"He likes you, Nathan. I think he's gay."

"Don't be ridiculous. He hardly knows me." I was tempted to describe how my first dinner with Drew had ended, but I wasn't sure it would show me in a good light.

"Maybe, but I think he wants to. You'll notice he didn't invite *me* to go wall-climbing with him. Or *us*. Just you."


That night, after apologizing to Margot for the noise I was about to make, I hung a tapestry in my bedroom. Partly it was to take my mind off of Drew Madden, whose face somehow kept appearing in my mind's eye. But mostly it was because this particular tapestry meant so much to me.

It had been Alden's. It had hung in his living room in the house he rented off campus when he and I were students at UNH. Slightly abstract, it showed sharp mountain slopes in autumn colors descending from all directions, some overlapping others, all essentially leading down to a pristine mountain lake. Alden had said it was by "Sarah Warren," a weaver who lived in northern New Hampshire. After Alden disappeared, his mother had given that tapestry to me. And after Neil died, it had inspired me to follow in his bootsteps, up mountain trails, across high ridges, claiming peaks more or less in his name.

Several times, while hiking in New Hampshire's White Mountains, I had come across vistas very much like that tapestry. Those times felt like signs that I was on the right trail, in every way. I was doing what I was meant to do.


Monday, Jennifer invited me to sit in on an afternoon session. It was scheduled late enough for teens to attend after school, and in fact it was all teens. I did my best to hide my dismay that on this small island, with a population well below fifteen thousand and only one high school, there would be enough kids who not only had substance abuse problems, but there were enough of them that seven would be willing to show up at a group meeting in a recovery center.

Jennifer introduced me to the group and added that I was an observer only. "Nathan will be working in the front office."

One girl, slouched in her chair, bright pink streaks in hair that had obviously had the life bleached out of it, challenged me. "What's your stuff?"

Jennifer interrupted before I could ask what she meant. "Nathan isn't here to discuss anything about himself, or anything at all. So whether he has a preferred substance or not is irrelevant to the group."

So the girl had assumed I was in recovery. Not sure how I felt about that, so I filed it away to consider later.

I guess it should not have surprised me that it was so

hard to get teens to talk about... well, anything. There was one kid, though—oversized jeans, ratty maroon T-shirt, dark unwashed hair falling onto his forehead—who kept looking at me. I couldn't figure out why, so whenever I looked his way, I kept my eyes moving as though I'd barely noticed him. Oddly, I felt as though I'd seem him before, but I couldn't for the life of me have said where.

The kids who did say something had comments that didn't surprise me. Jennifer did what she could to help bolster the kids' resolve, but what I heard made my heart ache.

"I figured, you know, nobody cared anyway, so what the fuck?"

"Sometimes it calls to me so loud I can't hear anything else."

"I cry every day. I'm running out of tears. But the world's not running out of oxy."

"In here? Sure, I wanna stay clean. I wanna live! But I know that before I even get home, somewhere someone is gonna be there with this stuff that will kill me. I wanna care. I wanna say no way José. But I don't know if I'll be able to."

"Yeah. Right. In here it's all, 'You're doin' great, Jimmy!' In here I get all pumped up, and I feel strong enough to do what I have to. But out there?" Jimmy's voice faltered. "Out there I know heroin's been doing friggin' squat-thrust exercises. It's been pumping' iron. Its muscles are bulging. It's half again as tall as me. I can't fight that."

These kids sounded so discouraged. They needed hope.

About half-way through the session, Jennifer looked at the kid who'd been staring at me. He hadn't spoken so far. "Emmett? How have you been feeling?"

His slouch was so complete I wondered if he'd melt onto the floor. He glanced from her to me. "Who's the chink?"

Before Jennifer could respond, I leveled my gaze at him, my glance as soft as I could make it. With words that came from someplace in the universe I'd never been before, I heard my voice say, "When you get to the bottom of that Pandora's box with all the world's evils in it, I'll be part of the hope you find there."

Everyone stared at me. I knew the next move was mine. I stood. "You're not ready for me yet, though. I'll be back another day to see if anything has changed." And I left the room.

The walk from the session room to the reception area was a blur. I sat down at my desk and logged onto the computer, doing my best to look carefree and busy.

Katie could tell something was up. "What's going on? I thought you were in the session."

"I was." I took a deep breath and rested my hands on the edge of my desk. "I'm *so* fired."

"What? Why?"

"I dropped a bomb in the teen session and walked out."

"What did you say?"

Before I could decide how to reply, Emmett appeared in the open doorway.

"What the fuck was that?"

I glared at him. "Who wants to know?"

"Me! *I* want to know!"

"Next time, don't call me names, and maybe I'll tell you."

"You're—you're just a fucking secretary!"

"No reason secretaries can't fuck. They have the same rights as anybody."

Emmett had no response to that. He stood there for another ten seconds or so and left the building as noisily as he could.

The next thing I knew, Katie was laughing. She was still laughing when Juan Diego's head appeared in the doorway, followed slowly by the rest of him.

Juan asked, "What did you do?"

"Something dreadful, clearly."

"Well, you got that kid to speak. If that's dreadful, too

bad. See if you can do it again." And he disappeared.

Katie's laughter had calmed to giggles. "That's why I'm laughing. I don't think I've ever heard Emmett's voice before. Most of us haven't." She grinned at me. "What name did he call you?"

"It was a slur on my partially-Chinese heritage."

"And what did you say?" She was still chuckling.

I found myself chuckling, too. "I told him I was the hope at the bottom of Pandora's box, or words to that effect."

Her mouth dropped open. "Did Jennifer tell you to leave?"

"No. I told myself to leave."

Not long after that, the other kids who had been in the session started filing out past the reception office door and into the daylight of the late afternoon, some of them staring at me as they passed. I expected to see Jennifer at any moment, summoning me to her office. That happened, but not until nearly closing time.

She appeared suddenly, startling both Katie and me. "Nathan?" As I looked up, Jennifer turned and walked toward her office. Obviously I was supposed to follow her.

I didn't wait to be told to close the door. I figured, *This job was worth a try.*

She got right down to business. "I'm not going to tell you that I'm happy with what happened in session this afternoon."

I waited, ready for the worst.

"But I hear that when you left the room, Emmett followed you and confronted you."

She waited until I said, "That's right."

"Juan overheard the exchange. He told me what each of you said." I sat silently as she took a breath. "Emmett almost never speaks. I was surprised when he spoke to you in session. But I'm flabbergasted that he confronted you afterward."

She stood, walked to the window behind her desk, and

gazed out between the bars for a moment. Then she turned to face me.

"My undergraduate degree was in education and counseling," she said. "During my last year, I had to do an internship at a middle school. There was one girl who was extremely religious. Christian. And for some reason, she had become catatonic, though no underlying causes were diagnosed. She just refused to speak. I decided to... well, take her on."

Jennifer's smile seemed to be at herself, like when a memory makes you say, *What a fool I was*.

"So I did. It was painful. I would ask a question, she would sit there. I would ask another, and she would sit there. And one day, from out of the blue I guess, it occurred to me to talk about scripture. And immediately, she started to pay attention. But she still wouldn't speak. So I started deliberately misquoting famous passages. I'm no biblical scholar, but I could sure misremember a number of things. And that got her going."

She sat at her desk again. "Today, you did something like that for Emmett. He responded to you. Granted, it was confrontational, and I don't think he sees you as a friend. But it was a start."

She paused, partly—I suspected—to see if I had anything to say. So I said, "And how bad was it? Am I fired?"

Jennifer started to laugh and then did her best to stifle the impulse. For a few seconds, she regarded me. "Where did that come from? That bit about Pandora's box?"

"Honestly, I have no idea. But there was no way I could respond to what he said, so I guess I responded to where it came from."

"And that was?"

"His pain. His hopelessness. And I really do want to help in that way. Give people hope, I mean."

She gave me a sideways glance, like she was contemplating something. "Would you come to the Thursday session and see how he responds to you?"

Whew. Not fired. I grinned. "If I say yes, do I get to keep the job?"

"Nathan, I was never going to fire you. So, yes. Of course. But I am going to caution you to tread lightly. It's discouragingly easy to push these kids just a little too far, and they fall over some edge."

Falling off of edges—first Margot, then Drew—was becoming a pattern. I would avoid any other falls if I could. Mine or someone else's.

Katie was still in the front office when I got back to my desk, even though it was after five.

She was ready to leave, leaning against the front of her desk. "So?"

"Not fired after all."

"Cool." And she smiled and left.

I told Margot all about my adventure in teen confrontation over dinner.

"You are a character, Nathan. And speaking of characters…."

"You have a story about your day, too?"

"Better. I looked Drew Madden up. Got his address. He wasn't home, so I left my phone number in a note at his house and invited him to dinner tomorrow night. He texted and said he'd be delighted."

"You—*what did you say?*"

"You heard me." She sounded pleased with herself. "He likes you, Nathan. I'm sure you know that. Maybe you like him too, maybe you'll just like him for a friend. But he's a cool guy. And I, for one, would like to get to know him better."

*This is what happens,* I told myself in my head, *when I*

*keep things from Margot. I should have told her how dreadfully my first meeting with him ended.* But the only thing she had to go on was how friendly things had been with the three of us, Saturday evening. It was too late to say anything now.

Margot wasn't done. "And you should see his house! There's money there."

Like I cared. But I did help Margot move a few things in our apartment around to be sure there would be no obstacles for the wheelchair.

I dreamed about Drew that night. There wasn't much of a plot. Nothing much happened. I just kept seeing his brown eyes, with that gentle expression in them. Somehow, in the way of dreams, I could tell he was smiling, even though I didn't actually see anything but his eyes.

Around four o'clock I woke up. There was a little bit of a breeze coming in through my partially-open window. The bed was warm, the air was cool, and all through my body I felt a deep, profound sense of peace.

# CHAPTER SIX

It had taken no time at all for me to become convinced that although I would gladly help Margot with grocery and cooking chores, she was the chef, not I. So far in our roommate experience, she had wowed me with her roast chicken, her ginger-turkey meatballs, her salmon in some kind of concoction of onions and red bell peppers that had been cooked until they were silky—the list was long.

"I did most of the cooking at home, back in Idaho," she told me when I waxed enthusiastic. "Who else? Mom would have burned the place down, she was that drunk most of the time. And my brothers were useless. Plus, it was a kind of offering to my dad. You know, like, 'Leave me alone and I'll make really good meals for you.'"

"Did that work?"

"Mostly. Whenever he tried anything, the next couple of meals would be lousy." She laughed, but I heard pain in it.

She planned what sounded like a simple meal for Drew, which surprised me a little. She called it a Mexican salad. It was a warm day, so at least salad was appropriate.

She had made the rather intricate dressing the night before, as well as the ground beef, which she'd cooked with spices and chopped tomatoes. When we got home from work, she had me chop jalapeños for the guacamole and shred some Monterey jack cheese for the salad. It no longer seemed so simple. But it did promise to be delicious.

Margot had bought pilsner glasses for the beer we'd have with the meal, though when she'd had time to do that, I couldn't have said. By the time Drew was supposed to arrive, everything was ready. Everything but me.

"What about the chair?" I nearly shouted at Margot.

"What about it?"

"How will he get up here? Should one of us wait downstairs?"

"Nathan, calm down. There's a ramp up to the door, and our buzzer is low enough for him to reach. We'll buzz him in, and he'll come up on the elevator. How do you think he gets around without you everywhere else he goes?"

She was right. Even so, I watched out the window, so I saw the dark grey van Drew drove. I watched as it pulled into a handicap spot. I couldn't see what was happening very well, but it looked like something extended out of the back end of the van. Tinted side windows kept me from seeing more than general movement inside. Then I saw Drew, in a different wheelchair from the one I'd seen him in before. This one was powered, and the thing rolled out of the back of the van like that was the most natural thing in the world. Drew pressed something that must have been a remote control and the van closed itself up, smooth as you please.

The chair rolled up the ramp and into the building, and our buzzer sounded.

Margot pressed the intercom button. "Hey, Drew. I'll leave the buzzer on for twenty seconds. Will that be enough time?"

"More than."

As we waited for Drew to appear in our open doorway, I gazed at Margot with new respect. It was like the chair, to her, was as natural as a pair of working legs, and she already knew how to accommodate the differences.

I had to ask. "Have you known someone else who uses a wheelchair?"

"Sure. In my internship, I worked with two clients who used them."

Social work. Right. That made a certain amount of sense.

Drew's chair rolled into the apartment as though it already knew the way. I have to say, it looked like quite the chair, and I wondered how much it had cost him. It had three sets of wheels: medium size in the front, larger ones under the seat, and two small wheels behind. The base of the thing under the seat was bright shiny blue, and matte chrome-like piping that started in the front came to a downward point at the back. It seemed to take up more room than the chair I'd seen him in at the Lompoc, which he'd had to wheel, himself; no power.

I wondered why he didn't use this fancy chair when he sat there waiting for unsuspecting hikers. Maybe he wanted using a wheelchair to look as unglamorous as possible? More likely, I was sure the powered version would prefer not to be rained on, if the weather changed.

Drew and Margot exchanged greetings, he handed her a bouquet of purple iris and white daisies, and then he nodded toward me. "Nathan."

"Glad you could come." How stupid was that? Suddenly I felt almost violently self-conscious, as though something huge hung in the balance, something that depended on Drew's approval.

He looked around. "Did this place come furnished?"

"No. This stuff was all from my Gram's house. She died last March."

He nodded, and it was impossible for me to tell what he thought, or why he had asked. To be fair, it was all stuff that Gram had had for decades; not only was it old, but also it was a little beaten up.

Margot hadn't planned on appetizers. I hadn't thought to ask her about that, but now I wondered whether it would be more challenging for Drew to manage that kind of finger food in the living room. So we all gathered around the dining table, which was at one end of the long living room.

Neil had encouraged Gram to update the sound system at home about five years ago, and I'd kept it. So I was able to play background music from my phone. I had selected a few albums from Neil's old collection I thought Drew would probably not know, just because they seemed a little obscure to me. Each of them featured Charlie Hayden, playing jazz double bass with different musicians on other instruments, primarily piano. It was all very mellow.

Obscure, it might have been. To me. But not to Drew. He commented on the first selection. "Wow. Is that Charlie Hayden? Who's at the piano?"

I had to look it up. "Kenny Barron."

"Nice." He picked up a corn chip, scooped some guacamole with it, and popped it into his mouth. "Margot Truman, did you make this?"

"Nathan helped."

"You could sell it. Best guac I've had in a while."

He had compliments for the beer, the salad, and the apartment. "How did you guys find this place?"

I let Margot answer. "Nathan found it."

"I love the setting."

"Your house isn't exactly in a bad spot, either." Margot must have taken a good look around.

Drew chuckled. "Somes Sound is lovely. Sometimes I just gaze across the water and stare at the rocky cliffs on the other side."

So far, Drew had focused primarily on Margot. I told myself that was fine. As the meal continued, even though he would acknowledge me if I said something, he continued to direct his attention toward Margot. And it began to bother me. But then there was an exchange in which I didn't want his attention.

Margot asked, "Do you live in that big house all by yourself?"

"I do now," Drew said, "ever since Ned moved out, just over a year ago now."

"Ned?"

"My ex-partner. I'd hoped he would be my husband one day, but…." His voice trailed off.

"I'm sorry," Margot said. "I shouldn't have asked."

ROBIN REARDON

I did my best to focus on my plate, or at least to be seen as focusing on my plate. Drew had let that cat out of the proverbial bag so smoothly, as though no one in the world would even flinch at the implication. Was he trying to make some kind of point? And would Margot, in her matchmaking enthusiasm, tell Drew that I was gay?

He moved on to other things. "My parents left me the house when they died. Five years ago. They were flying a Piper cub, headed for a private airfield up the coast. It was just foggy enough that they shouldn't have gone." He gazed out of the window. "They're essentially buried at sea."

Margot said, "Oh, Drew—"

He shook his head. "No, it's probably the way they would have chosen, if given a choice. They died together. And they loved the sea." He stretched his shoulders backward. "But let's talk about something else."

"Oh, well," Margot's face lit up, "I could tell you how invaluable Nathan was when I went to buy a car."

Still, he didn't glance at me. "Please."

"Sunday we went to this dealership in Ellsworth. We were looking around the lot at the used cars, and this guy named Freddie came up. He really looked the part, you know? Cheap suit, scuffed shoes, all that. He said to come into the office, so we did, and he asked about my budget, financing, that sort of thing."

Drew drained the last of his beer, and I took his glass into the kitchen to refill it, listening carefully to Margot's story.

"So Freddie goes into some office to talk to someone, the manager I guess. I couldn't really hear them for about a minute, and then their voices got louder. Freddie said, 'Oh, that one. That's out of her price range.' Right away I saw Nathan's face change. He knew what was going on, but I was clueless." She deepened her voice. "'Maybe we could make an exception for her,' he says. They went back and forth like that, talking loudly enough to be sure I'd hear them. And

96

I *still* didn't know what was going on."

Drew said, "But Nathan did." He glanced at me as I set the refilled glass down.

Margot laughed. "He sure did! He said, 'They're trying to fleece you. Let's get out of here.' And he stood up and headed for the door, me at his heels. Freddie comes out of the office and says, 'Margot? Where are you going?' We're at the door by now. Nathan holds it open for me, and as I'm going out he says to Freddie, 'Nice try.'" She laughed again. "Anyway, we went to another place and got what I think is a good deal on a Honda CRV. Red! Just like I wanted."

Drew turned to me, his glass raised. "To Nathan, guarding against his roommate's financial ruin."

Though not entirely sure I liked that toast, I raised my glass and touched his with it. It was harmless, right? Margot, too, lifted her glass and touched it to ours.

It occurred to me that he had referred to Margot as my roommate, not even my friend, let alone my girlfriend. And as Drew's eyes stayed on me, I felt an intensity that was nothing like the peace my dream about him had brought me. And this intensity… there was something carnal, something physical about it.

My heart was racing, and I was having a little trouble getting a full breath. Somehow I knew he could tell. What the hell was going on? Was I really turned on by a guy in a fucking wheelchair? And if I was, what would that even mean?

Over ice cream topped with her home-made fudge sauce, Margot started up another conversational topic while I sat there, stewing in my mixed emotions.

One voice in my head said, *He had a partner, boyfriend, whatever. It's not like he's completely out of the running for relationships.*

*He was testing me!* I told the voice. *He led me on with talk about hiking, and then challenged me to criticize him for being disabled!*

*Okay,* the first voice spoke up, *But he can climb walls. And he fought off two delinquents at once. And for most of the time, didn't you really enjoy his company?*

*Conversation,* sure, my more confused self said. *Talking is one thing. Hiking together, though, that's out of the question. And it's really important to me. There's all kinds of things we couldn't do together. And how difficult would sex be? He's in a frigging wheelchair!*

*Thousands of couples manage with one partner who uses a chair, just fine,* turned-on me said. *And he's already got it figured out. You wouldn't be starting from zero.*

*But—*

*He's strong. Very strong. He could probably lift you over his head and suck our dick from there.*

That made me have to clear my throat rather awkwardly.

"Nathan?" Margot said, her head tilted.

"I'm okay. Just swallowed wrong."

"Right, but Drew asked if you'd like to see his van. You know, with the wheelchair fittings and all that."

I'd heard nothing of what he'd said. Nothing.

I looked at Drew. The amused expression I saw there was almost annoying enough to make me ask why I would want to see his stupid van. In my head, I heard Gram's voice: *Don't be petulant, Nathan.* Whatever. I pushed my chair back. As I followed Drew out of the apartment I called back to Margot. "Don't wash up. I'll do that."

Our short trip down the elevator was silent. I couldn't think what to say, and I was afraid I might say something I'd regret. We were out of the building before Drew spoke.

"I hope this wasn't awkward for you. My coming here. I almost declined Margot's invitation."

So, as it turned out, he didn't care that it might be "awkward" for me? "Why did you decide to come?"

We were at the van by now. It was dark enough outside that I couldn't have said what color the vehicle was if I hadn't seen it earlier. Drew moved to the back of the van and stopped, facing me.

"I wanted to see you again. So much of our first conversation was really enjoyable, and I was sorry that I spoiled it."

I nodded. "You mean with that test."

"Yes. Ordinarily I wouldn't presume to ask about that, not after just meeting someone. So it's kind of a testament to the effect you had on me that I jumped the gun, as it were."

I crossed my arms over my chest. It was the only protection I had. "What effect was that?"

Drew waited until I looked at him. "I really like you, Nathan. I loved what you said about hiking. You're not just doing it to prove what a man you are. There's real meaning there. There was real meaning for me, something I didn't get a chance to tell you before I ruined things."

I looked down at my feet and scuffed one toe on the pavement. "I don't think all the ruination was yours."

When I looked back at him he was smiling. "So have I guessed right? Would it be fair to say that you're attracted to men?"

I glanced sideways and back at Drew. "Wow. You don't waste time."

"Correct. I don't."

What the hell. "Yes, it would be fair to say that."

"Just so you know, I'm not gay. I'm bi."

So the looks he'd been giving Margot…. "Are you telling me you're attracted to my roommate?"

"No. I like Margot very much. But when I've been attracted to a woman, it's been to a very earthy type of woman. Margot is adorable and a sweetheart, but she's not earthy." He let a few beats go by. "What I'm telling you is that I'm very, very attracted to you."

He could have put me on the spot and asked if I was attracted to him. He could have asked, again, if the chair bothered me. He didn't. He didn't wait for me to say anything. He backed the chair away from the van a little distance and said, "Watch this."

He pressed a button on his remote control. The back panel of the van lifted, and then a metal ramp unfolded and settled onto the pavement. I could barely see inside, but it looked like there were two seats behind the driver area that had been folded up to the sides. Drew rolled up the ramp into the van, and he did something to make the driver's bucket seat rotate to face right. Then, somehow, he anchored the chair, maneuvered himself from the chair onto the seat, and rotated the seat to the front again.

He called, "Stand back, Nathan." The ramp folded up into the back, and the back panel lowered into place with an efficient, quiet thunk. He was ready to go.

I heard the engine start, and Drew lowered his window. I moved toward it.

"I just want you to know," he said, "that I'm not expecting anything. I hope you'll think about what I said, and—well, all right, I hope you think about me. I'll be in touch soon, and we'll see what happens next. Is that all right with you?"

He looked so—God, so *normal* sitting there in the van. There was no chair visible, nothing to reveal his disability, noting unusual about him at all. Unless, of course, you considered how gorgeous he was, how powerful he was, how intelligent he appeared, how worldly he seemed… yeah, nothing unusual at all.

"Sure. That works." That was all I could think of to say, though I almost added, *I've been so dull the last couple of times I've seen you. Why are you attracted to me?* So I added, "I, uh, I really liked that first conversation, too."

He smiled again and nodded. "See you."

As I watched the van drive off, some of Drew's words echoed in my brain: *You're not just doing it to prove what a man you are.*

Was that entirely true?

My very first hike, the one that had nearly been my last, was—surely—my effort to prove something. I'd wanted to prove something to Daniel. To Neil. Maybe even to myself. But had it been all about being a man?

And after that, all the peaks I'd claimed—had I claimed them for the joy of it? Partly. Yes. But wasn't it also because it was what Neil would have done? Wasn't I trying to prove... well, *something?*

I'd met Conroy Finnegan, a professional hike leader, while climbing Cannon Mountain. I'd felt like I had to prove that I could keep up with him. But was I trying to prove that to him, or to me? And did it make me a man?

And if I had come to judge someone's worth, their value to me at least, according to physical vigor, where did Drew fall in that assessment? Was he a man? No question. Was he vigorous? No doubt. But could he hike?


Emmett didn't show up at the Thursday teen session. I wasn't sure whether to be disappointed or relieved. Maybe both. Afterward, Jennifer told me not to worry about it.

"He's still meeting with Juan for his counseling appointments and showing up for his meds. He'll be back. And chances are he wouldn't have given you very much in the way of engagement today, anyway. These things take time, Nathan."

When I got back to the office, Katie had a knowing, or maybe conspiratorial look on her face. She handed me a piece of paper. It was folded in half, but not very tightly, and I was sure she had read it.

*Let's go for a hike. Give me a call. DM*
There was a phone number below that.
A hike.... A hike?

"He stopped by to leave this for you," Katie said, obviously wanting more information. "I didn't know you knew Drew."

It took me a second to register what she was implying. "I didn't know *you* knew Drew."

She waved a dismissive hand. "Oh, sure. He used to come in here all the time. He wasn't a counselor, but he used to do things with one of our teen clients. Johnny Crosby. Johnny was in a wheelchair, too."

"Really. Wait—'was?' Where's Johnny now?"

It was like a fog gathered around Katie's face. "He's... um... he's not with us anymore." Not knowing what that might mean, I shrugged and shook my head. "He died. Last year. Heroin laced with fentanyl."

Wow. Was that the reason for Drew's reaction over our first dinner? When I'd mentioned my career goal, he'd drawn back almost physically, and I'd wondered if he might be in recovery. But had it really been about Johnny?

Katie brightened. "So how *do* you know Drew?"

I told her the story of helping him recover his wind-blown money, adding that we'd gone for a beer after. This time I didn't omit that the drinks had been followed by dinner. I could tell Katie would love to have asked questions about whether there might be more to this connection, but I just smiled and sat at my desk. I hadn't told her that I was gay, but it was possible she had guessed—especially if she knew that Drew was bi.

Maybe half an hour later, I took a break. It was drizzling out, but I walked around to the clinic side; no one was there right now, and there was an overhang to keep the rain off me.

I stared at Drew's note. I pulled out my phone. I stared at the note again without really seeing it.

"Damn it." The sound of my own voice startled me. But I knew it was time I stopped learning about Drew from other people. I called.

He answered on the third ring. "Nathan. Hey. I take it Katie gave you my note."

"She did. Um... I'm a little confused, though."

He laughed. "Yeah, I'd say sorry about that, but I'm not sorry about that. I'm not talking about hiking the Canon Brook Trail up Cadillac Mountain. But have you seen much of the carriage road system?"

I had noticed it on maps. It had seemed too tame for my attention. "Not yet, no."

"It's not exactly mountain trails, but I bet you'd get a good workout. Are you up for it? Weather Saturday is supposed to be great. Mixed sun and clouds, chilly wind, perfect for physical exertion."

Would he be using his powered chair, I wondered? And just how fast could it go? But no; he'd mentioned physical exertion. Or was that just *my* exertion?

Fuck it. Whatever.

"Sure. What time, and where?"

"Meet me at the parking lot at the northwest point of Eagle Lake at ten. Depending on how long we want to go for, we can get lunch after. Sound good?"

"Great. See you then." Lunch. That was good. I wasn't ready for another dinner, especially if it was just the two of us.


That evening, there was an envelope in the mail with the return address of a "D. Madden," addressed to Margot. She tore it open.

"What a gentleman!" She waved a greeting card in my general direction and then read the inside aloud. "Dear Margot, thank you for a delicious dinner and for your delightful company. One day soon, I'll return the favor. All my best, D."

She handed me the card. The front was a watercolor drawing of bright blue sea rolling in white curls to meet a rocky coastline. On the back of the card, it identified Otter Creek as the location. Right here on the island.

As I handed it back to her, she said, "I hope you

noticed—and I hope you appreciated—that I didn't pester you about what you and Drew talked about when you went down to the van after dinner."

"I described the mechanism to you. Remember?"

"Ah, yes, but you repeated none of your conversation. I'm just sayin'."

I hadn't felt under any obligation to repeat what we'd said. However, by now I knew that hiding things altogether from Margot wasn't going to work. Still....

I said, "So, look, I don't want you to make too much of this. If you go pushing the guy at me, I'll be less inclined to want to see him at all. You get that, right?"

She sounded a little annoyed. "Why do you think I didn't pester you for details?"

"Okay, fine. What I want to tell you now is that we're going—well, Drew and I are going for an outing," I couldn't bring myself to repeat what he'd called it—a hike—"on the carriage roads on Saturday. In the morning. But, really, I don't know that it will mean anything along the lines of what you keep insinuating."

"For God's sake, Nathan, all I did was tell you he likes you."

"And invite him to dinner. And give me meaningful glances anytime his name comes up."

She grinned. "Okay, but let me just ask—without pushing! I'm not pushing. Is there a particular reason why you would *not* want to consider a relationship with him? Something beyond friendship, I mean."

My eyes narrowed. "Are you challenging me about the wheelchair?"

"Maybe. Do you *feel* challenged about the wheelchair?"

I let out an irritated breath through my nose. "You remember Conroy?"

That obviously confused her. "What about him?"

"Conroy and I saw each other—and you know what that means—on and off for nearly a year, up to just before the

Kalalau trip. He made it very clear he wasn't looking for anything long-lasting. *Very* clear."

I waited to be sure that had sunk in.

"Got it. So?"

"What Conroy made me realize was that I'm ready— maybe even looking—for something that *does* last." I repeated for her something I'd said to myself just a few months ago. "I want a partner, not a fuck buddy."

If that last phrase shocked her, she didn't let on. "So what's your point?"

I rubbed my face. "All right, so there is an issue with the wheelchair. Look, Margot, you know how important physical activity is to me. Hiking mountains is at the center of that."

"Why?"

She was right. She wouldn't have a clue. "Let's have a drink. I'll tell you why."

We sat in our living room, her with a glass of red wine, me with a bottle of beer, and I told her about Neil. I told her about how many times he'd asked me to hike with him, and I told her I'd refused for many reasons. Like I didn't want to look like a novice compared to his expertise. Like I was afraid I'd really love it and want to keep hiking with him, and he wouldn't always want a little brother hanging on. And, possibly most important, Neil had given me so much, not just in terms of making me feel safe and loved, but also in terms of things like his baseball glove, his teddy bear, and the model of the Messerschmitt that he'd saved up his money for, constructed lovingly, and had then given to me after I broke—and he repaired—the propeller.

"Hiking was his thing. And downhill skiing. I chose to ski Nordic. So maybe part of it, too, is that I wanted to be my own person, my own athlete. But when he died—"

I stopped talking and gazed at Margot's face for a few seconds. I'd told her a little about Neil during our return to the Kalalau trailhead, just the two of us, after her fall. So she knew that he had died. But what I'd told her had been limited to why his death, and Gram's, had brought me to Kaua'i.

I decided to give her a bigger picture. "You've shared so much with me. I guess it's my turn. Neil and his friend Jeremy were hiking in the Priest Wilderness, in Virginia. It's extremely remote. They'd taken all kinds of precautions. But it didn't help. They got caught in the kind of forest fire that's called a fire tornado, because it moves so fast and so unpredictably, and it burns so hot."

I had to stop for a minute. I gazed down at my beer to regain the composure I'd been about to lose. Margot waited patiently.

I took a sip of beer. "The park rangers identified them by their location and a couple of items that didn't burn beyond recognition. Even dental records didn't help." I didn't tell her his last act had been to call me. I didn't mention the screams that had seared my ear over the phone as the fire overtook him. I didn't tell her I'd heard my brother die.

Margot's voice was quiet, tender. "Oh, Nathan. I'm so sorry."

I took a stabilizing breath. "The spring before he died, I nearly died, myself, hiking up a mountain in the winter. In a snowstorm. Mount Chocorua. I was a stupid idiot, and I did it because I wanted to impress the guy who'd invited me. The whole thing was his idea. And he—well, let's just say he wasn't especially prepared, and he didn't prepare me well, at all. And here's the really stupid part. He wasn't even gay, and I knew that. So it wasn't like I hoped to impress him in a way that would make him want a relationship with me."

I watched as Margot poured herself a little more wine.

"Neil had been planning to climb all the peaks in New Hampshire over four thousand feet. Forty-eight of them. You get a special membership in a mountaineers' club if you do that. So after he died, I used some of the insurance money for the policy he'd taken out on himself to get some serious hiking gear. I went back up Chocorua that fall, alone. And after that, I started hiking for real. I've got several of those forty-eight peaks so far, and I don't intend to stop."

"And Drew can't hike with you."

"Drew can't do a lot of things with me."

"I get that Neil was very important to you. But it almost sounds like hiking has taken his place. What will it prove if you get all those big peaks to your credit?"

Her words stunned me. Hiking had taken Neil's place? *Nothing* could take Neil's place! Had I been treating it as though it could? But as for the peaks…. "It just feels important."

"So you've never asked yourself what you'd do next. Once you belong to that club."

"Next?"

"Well, again, does it prove anything? I assumed you hiked because you love it. So why do all those particular peaks matter so much?"

I didn't want to voice the reason. It was that Neil had wanted them. "I—it's not a question I've ever asked myself, okay?"

"Okay. That's fine. I'm not the one who needs an answer, anyway. That would be you."

The ghost of Jeremy Ford whispered in my ear: *You're the only one you need to prove something to.*

Margot stood. "Ready for dinner?"

# CHAPTER SEVEN

When I pulled into the Eagle Lake parking lot Saturday, Drew's van was already there. He was out of the van, in a chair I hadn't seen before. Made me wonder just how many chairs he had. This one looked special, though, I have to say. Instead of arm rests, it had long handles with bright blue casings. The back wheels were large, and they had what looked like mountain bike tires on them. The spokes were the same bright blue as the handle casings, giving the whole thing a very cool, racy look. There was only one front wheel, small, extended fairly far out in front of the seat.

Drew himself looked ready for anything in khaki slacks, a red windbreaker, and a navy cap. He smiled broadly as I approached him.

"Ready for a workout?" he asked, his deep voice big and booming even in this outdoor setting. "I see you've worn the correct shoes."

I had considered my shoes carefully, actually. For easier trails, my usual outfit would include a pair of low hikers—different from my hiking boots, which were higher than my ankles. But I'd looked into the carriage roads, and they seemed to be mostly paved or graded with crushed gravel. Not exactly challenging terrain. So I'd worn running shoes. But as for his comment....

"The correct shoes for what, exactly?"

"Running! Come on." He wheeled the chair away from the parking lot and, gripping the lower part of the long handles, he pushed them forward and back. The chair moved smoothly along a pathway and onto a gravel road. He turned left, and we went under a stone-arched bridge, the paved road that cars used above us. Once we were past the bridge, the intense blue of the lake was in front of us almost immediately.

Drew paused at a particularly good viewing spot. A breeze lifted a few locks of my hair.

"You can see a lot from here. For example," he pointed directly across the lake to the south, "there's Pemetic Mountain. Just over twelve hundred feet. It's the fourth highest peak on the island."

He swiveled slightly to his left and pointed southeast. "Cadillac Mountain is the island's tallest peak at fifteen three, give or take."

He gave me a minute to take in the view before turning slightly south.

"Over on the west side of the lake you can see Conner's Nubble, a baby at five-eighty-something. And beyond that is the somewhat taller North Bubble, and then South Bubble beyond that."

Again he paused while I silently admired the vista. Autumn colors were just getting going, so most leaves were still on the trees.

"Enough sight-seeing," Drew declared. "Let's go!"

He pumped the levers, holding them from the upper part now, and off he went, heading south along the wide, groomed gravel path, the lake on his left.

If I had thought this was going to be a stroll in the park for me, I would have been wrong. I had to jog to keep up with Drew in that fancy chair.

My research had told me that this carriage road, which goes all the way around Eagle Lake, was about six miles long. I began to wonder if Drew was going to make me jog the whole way.

We passed a middle-aged couple walking a dog. We passed another couple, younger, with a baby carriage. People on bikes came toward us from the opposite direction. At one point, three bicycles came from behind and passed us.

Finally Drew pulled over to the right. He was a little

winded. I was outright panting. He either didn't notice my condition, or he ignored it.

"This trail here," and he pointed to the right, "leads up Conner's Nubble, and then to both Bubbles." He looked at me and smiled. "Let's take a short break and admire the water. You can see Cadillac really well from here, too."

Hands on my hips, lungs still pulling in air greedily, I faced the mountain. It was small by my standards, of course, but it was an attractive peak. It seemed everything around here was gorgeous.

The breeze wafting toward me over the water, stiff enough to ruffle up a bit of churn in the lake, was refreshing and invigorating.

"Have a seat, Nathan." Drew gestured toward a fallen tree, the thick trunk solidly on the ground. I sat.

I took a closer look at the chair. "What kind of chair is that?"

"It's called a Freedom Chair. Made by GRIT. How much do you want to know about it?"

"Tell me."

"The drive train is composed mostly of mountain bike parts. These are mountain bike tires. That means repair parts are easy to come by." He grinned. "I like blue. You could get yellow, red, purple—lots of different colors."

"Can it go anywhere a mountain bike can go?"

He tilted his head and nodded. "It can, at least in terms of topography. Going uphill is different, though, because on a bike, you use your legs. I have to propel this with my arms, so it's less efficient. But I can take this baby over curbs, over rocky trails that aren't steep, over granite ledges, over low rock formations—though that kind of surface does slow me down quite a bit. And on flat surfaces, I can go faster than I was going just now."

He'd mentioned everything except a true mountain trail. I asked, "How steep a grade can you climb?"

"The chair has no limits. So it depends on the rider.

That would be me. And I have to admit I can't do a truly steep incline, or even a moderate one for very long. And a lot of the trails here on the island include long stretches of granite steps, which is more than I can handle. But I can do lots more rugged stuff than this carriage road."

I couldn't help grinning, though I did my best to restrict it to one side of my mouth. "So you just wanted to make me work for it today. To keep up with you, I mean."

He laughed. "You've got it." He looked toward the lake and back at me. "I don't suppose you have a mountain bike?"

"No."

"Roller blades?"

I shook my head.

"Well then, Nathan, you're never gonna be able to keep up with me."

He took about one second to turn the chair and head back out onto the carriage road at a pace as fast as my run, no longer jogging. Full tilt. And he was right. He was going faster.

I let myself drop behind and slow to a walk, watching as Drew also slowed, turned, and waited for me to catch up to him. By now we were close to the opposite end of the lake from the parking area.

"Enough of me showing off," he said. "Let's just walk for a bit."

I kept pace with him easily as we moved along, the wind stronger now as it came at us across the full length of the oblong lake. We stopped at the southernmost point and admired the view silently, the occasional walker or bicycle passing behind us, until Drew broke the silence.

"So I didn't tell you why I hiked."

"No. You didn't get a chance." We both gazed north across the water.

"Hiking was my way of reaching out to the universe. I preferred to hike alone, in case the universe had anything to say to me. I knew I could hear it better without anyone else around, because most people feel the need to fill silence with talk. But communication is so much more than the spoken word."

"What kinds of things did the universe tell you?"

Drew chuckled. "I can't tell you how many times it reminded me that it was not all about me."

I looked at him. "What wasn't all about you?"

"Anything, really. I once sprained my ankle, badly, on puny little Parkman Mountain." He pointed southwest. "Had to hobble down on my own, cursing, yelling at the mountain. And you know what?"

I did know. "It didn't care."

Drew turned to look at me, and he threw back his head and laughed. "Yes! That's exactly it! The magnificent indifference of nature."

"My brother used to say that. I mean, that the mountain doesn't care. And once I started hiking, I knew he'd been right."

"Your brother." He paused again, but I said nothing, trying to decide whether to speak or not. "You've told me it's now just you and Nina." He'd remembered her name. "That means your brother was included in the tragedies you mentioned."

When I still didn't speak, he didn't pry. He turned the chair back onto the carriage road and moved forward at a walking pace. I followed.

We moved along in silence for a bit, until Drew asked, "How are you liking your work at the clinic?"

I'm not sure what made me want to talk about Emmett, except that some combination of the exercise, the sweetness of the air, and Drew's silent compassion had opened something in me.

"There's this kid," I opened. "Okay, bad start. Trying again."

I took in a long breath and reminded myself that I couldn't mention Emmett's name.

"My job is in the front office, executive support. So a glorified secretary, I suppose. I knew that going in, but this is my gap year, and Margot talked me into coming here. My boss, Jennifer, knows I'm interested in treatment and recovery, so she let me sit in on a teen session Monday on the condition that I don't speak."

Drew chuckled. "And you spoke."

"Oh, I spoke, all right." I told him what "this kid" had said to me, what I had said to him, and how he had come to find me later for that confrontation. "Jennifer wasn't altogether fine with what I did, but she said no one else had gotten the kid to speak. So she asked me to sit in again on Thursday. But—well, he didn't show up."

"I hope you don't think his absence was in any way your fault."

I glanced at him and grinned. "This isn't about me."

He came to a full stop, surprising a bicycle rider who was coming up from behind us. He looked directly at me.

I watched him and waited. It was at least ten seconds before he spoke.

"This is not a test. I'm going to ask you something outright. But first, I'm going to be bold. I'm going to tell you something. Like I've already told you, I don't like to waste anything, including time. So I'm going to take a risk I did not intend to take today. Not yet. But here it is."

He looked down at the gravel for a second and back up at me. "I like you, Nathan. I more than like you. I respect you. I enjoy you. I feel at home with you in a way I haven't felt with anyone in a long time. It seems to me that we communicate well, and not just in words. You have an intensity that I find compelling, and it comes through in how honest and direct you are. I want to spend time with you. As much time as you'd be willing to spend with me. So now the question."

He bit his lip and let it go. "Does the fact that I'm in this chair mean that you would not be interested in seeing where time spent with me might lead?"

I felt the need to stall. His question was something that had been bouncing around in my head since Margot's dinner. Maybe the bouncing had started before that. And he'd just asked a question I had yet to answer for myself.

"I need a minute. Let's keep walking." He'd used the term walk, so I felt I could, too.

He moved forward again, me at his side. He didn't speak; he let me think.

As I walked, I stole sideways looks at him, and each time I did that, I felt a pull somewhere deep inside me. I just couldn't quite figure out if it was coming from him, which might have implied that he had a strong effect on me, or if it came from me, which would have meant—what?

He was right about some things. I was kind of intense. I had none of Conroy's devil-may-care attitude toward life, bouncing around from house sitting job to house sitting job, setting down roots nowhere. I didn't have the cavalier attitude of Daniel, who had led me into the wilderness and nearly to my death after the throwaway line, "It's a good day to die." I wasn't good at sarcasm or comedic humor. But was I honest?

My brain skittered away from that question, a smooth stone skimming across open water in no particular direction. I wasn't even sure I was honest with myself.

What was Drew asking me? Where things might lead, he'd said. That was almost like saying that someday he wanted to be married, and it might be to me if things went well. I mean, he'd already said he'd been thinking of marriage a year ago.

Did I want marriage? Yes. Did I want marriage to someone in a wheelchair, no matter how powerful he was otherwise? Or did I want a marriage in which my husband and I would hike together, scale peaks, challenge each other to new feats of mountaineering achievement?

Margot's question haunted me. What *was* the point of claiming forty-eight New Hampshire peaks? Was it really just because Neil had wanted to do it? What would that particular achievement do for me? Would it bring Neil back? Would it somehow make me worthy of Neil?

Okay, that last one stung. And maybe that was the problem. Something in me was convinced I'd never be worthy of Neil. And the fact that he was dead meant any progress in that direction was hopeless, because he was now a ghost. You can't be worthy of a ghost.

Fuck it. What did I have to lose, here? It wasn't like Drew had actually proposed marriage. And things might lead absolutely nowhere. We both knew that.

I stepped over to the left, the side of the road toward the lake, and stopped. We were most of the way back to the parking lot, and I didn't want to have this conversation there.

Drew pulled in to face me and waited.

"Here's the thing," I opened, knowing that was lame and not caring. "I can't give you an honest answer right now, because I don't know what it would mean. I don't know enough about your life, about what it would mean to spend that time with you. I don't know anything about the challenges you face, and some of them would become mine as well."

I stopped for a breath, and Drew stayed silent. His face was unreadable.

"Last time I saw you," I said, "you told me I wasn't trying to prove something by hiking. But you're wrong. I'm not sure what I'm trying to prove or who needs to see it. I love hiking, but there's baggage there. So I don't yet know how important it would be to me that you can't hike."

I looked into the distance and back at Drew. "If you need an answer today because you don't want to waste time, then that answer is no. But if you're willing to give *me* time, if you could agree that it wouldn't be *wasted* time, then…."

I looked up again, across the churning water, its depth unknowable, the color deep blue and intense. "If you're willing to give me time, I'm willing to see what happens."

I looked back at Drew.

"Will you do something for me?" he asked. I shrugged. "Would you kneel down beside the chair for a minute? Either side."

Odd. But I did, on his left. "As close as you can get." I moved closer. What was this? Was he going to show me his legs? Have me feel his abs? What the fuck?

He reached out his right hand and curled it behind my neck. In the several seconds when he held me like that, I thought, *Is he going to try and kiss me? No way!* I got ready to hold my neck firm and pull away if necessary.

But he didn't. Even so—or maybe because he didn't—I felt fingers of flames shoot through my chest. It was as though I *wanted* him to kiss me.

He smiled, his eyes as gentle as I'd ever seen them. "I'll give you time, Nathan Bartlett. I ask only that you tell me when you've had enough time to know what you want."

We were still in that position, me kneeling on the ground beside Drew's chair, his hand holding our faces close together, when a man and woman with a young child passed behind us. I might not have noticed them if the woman hadn't spoken.

"That's disgusting." Her voice was so quiet I almost couldn't hear the words. But I did.

I pulled away from Drew and stood. To the woman's back I shouted, "Lady, you don't want to know what I think about *you* right now." I glared at the back of her head. She didn't turn around.

In the few seconds before I heard Drew's chair turn on the gravel, I felt a powerful surge of something like daring boldness rise through me. It wasn't a feeling I'd never had, but I think it was the first time I had felt it around this aspect of my life. That is, being gay. It felt fabulous.

For several seconds we watched the retreating group. "I'm sorry if that bothered you," I told Drew. "I know you said you generally ignore people like that."

He shook his head. "That wasn't about the chair. That was about us as a couple. And that," he looked up at me and grinned, "is an entirely different matter. Let's get 'em!"

And he was off. I ran beside him, and as we approached the group I heard Drew shout, "Coming in hot!"

They scurried out of our way. Laughing while running is a challenge, but I couldn't help trying.

Drew and I didn't go anywhere for lunch. Instead, we chatted at the opened back of his van like a couple of trail buddies.

"What I'm hoping," he said, "is that you'll spend some of that upcoming time I promised you thinking of things you want to know about my life in the chair, and what those things might mean for you. Is that something you'd be willing to do?"

"So I should make a list?"

"However you'd like to do it. I don't want to rush you, but how about if you come—alone, and I'll invite you and Margot another night—to my place for dinner. Just to get the discussion started. Say, Thursday? Is that too soon?"

"No. No, Thursday's fine. Can I bring anything?"

"Just you're gorgeous self, and the list." One side of his mouth lifted in a salacious grin. "Just so you know, this will be dinner. Nothing else. And, Nathan, no question is off limits."

I did my best to stifle a slightly embarrassed grin.

"If we do this again," he said before rolling into the back of his van, "let's consider Day Mountain. It has a carriage road ascent. There are some steep sections where I'll need to go kind of slow, but it's a rewarding hike for a small mountain."

By the time I drove out of the parking area I had already started my list, at least mentally.

Number one: *How would we fuck? That is, who could do what to whom?*

Number two: *Where would we fuck? Not in the chair, certainly, but would it be limited to a bed?*

Number three: *Does fucking cause you pain?*

Number four: *How many wheelchairs do you have, anyway?*

Within half a mile, a few more questions occurred. *What do your legs look like? Exactly what was the injury? Other than hiking real mountains, what did you used to do that you regret not being able to do anymore? Do you feel any resentment for people like me who don't have to live in a chair?*

I thought back to that asshole who'd tripped over Drew's chair at the Lompoc, and more questions occurred. *How often does something like that happen? Do some people treat you as if you were helpless or stupid or deaf (besides ATM thieves, that is)? What's traveling like for you? Can you take your chair onto an airplane? Where would you like to travel to, and can you see that happening?*

And then the really tough ones: *How much pain are you in most of the time? Are you in recovery, or were you never addicted to opioids? Is your disability going to limit your lifespan?*

When he'd suggested making a list, I'd thought maybe I'd come up with five or six questions. I had already lost count. And even after all those, I was beginning to think there would be more.

And suddenly the most important one of all hit me: *What the fuck am I doing?*

Sunday evening, I went into my bedroom to call Nina. On my way home from the Kalalau, after feeling that powerful connection with Gram and Neil, I'd vowed I wouldn't waste the time I had with Nina.

"Hey little brother," she opened, and a hot pang went through me. That had been Neil's pet name for me; Nina had never used it.

"Hey." I wanted to say "big sister," but it wouldn't come out. "I waited until Fashion Week was over to call. Did it go well?"

"Hard to tell. At least I didn't do anything to mess things up, so I'm calling it good."

"Are you sleeping late every morning now?"

She laughed. "Not yet. We're still busy with output from the Milan show, but the pressure's off."

I waited for her to say something about Luc. When she didn't, I said, "Luc is over there now, I assume."

"Yeah."

Hmmmm. That was a very flat "yeah." Fine; I had plenty to talk about. In fact, all day I had been reflecting back on my "hike" with Drew and my assignment, and it had begun to feel a little too deliberate. Even contrived. It had occurred to me that I could just blow the whole thing off and send regrets for Thursday. That would give him the answer he needed.

I just wasn't entirely sure it was the answer I wanted to give him.

Nina had been a source of pragmatism and (sometimes) brutal honesty for me since Neil had died. And she was as far from sentimental as a normal person could probably be. So she seemed like the logical sounding board for the Drew issue. I expected she'd say "skip the dinner."

"Okay," I said to Nina, "enough about you. Can I pass something by you?"

She laughed. "Shoot."

I described as much about Drew as I could without taking forever. I'd just finished saying that we'd gone around Eagle Lake when she interrupted me.

"So how do you feel about him, Nathan?"

"I—well, I'm not sure."

"The chair bothers you."

"I never said that!"

119

"Please. How could it not? You, the vigorous, competitive young mountain man?"

"Drew's a mountain man, too, y'know. That's how come he was on the Precipice Trail and knew how to save that kid's life."

"Oh, he's obviously self-sacrificing, no doubt. But what would you two ever find to do together?"

"He's got a special chair, the one he used yesterday, that can climb over rocky trails and tree roots."

"Really. But could he hike—oh, I don't know, Katahdin with you?"

"I could hike Katahdin by myself."

"But don't you see him as weak? He's disabled, Nathan."

"He can climb straight up rock climbing walls at his gym! I've never done that, and I have four limbs to work with."

"Isn't he disfigured?"

"What do you—well, I mean, I haven't seen his legs yet. He's had jeans or slacks on."

"And otherwise, what does he look like?"

I pictured Drew's face, his longish brown hair, his gentle brown eyes, his nicely trimmed mustache and beard, and (here's something I hadn't focused on before) his full lips, which stood out in stark relief against the facial hair. I summarized all that as well as I could for Nina.

"So he's attractive. He must have a hell of a lot of upper body strength. He must have money, to buy himself specialized chairs. He's polite. He's got a sense of humor. He plans to stay as active outdoors as he can. He thinks you're adorable. What are you waiting for?"

It hit me suddenly what Nina had done. Jennifer had done it to get that hyper-Christian girl to talk, deliberately misquoting scripture. I had done it to reach Emmett, saying stuff he understood intuitively but couldn't afford to talk about.

And just now, Nina had played a kind of devil's advocate.

"Why are you doing this?"

"Doing what, Nathan?"

"Making his case for him."

She paused for a few seconds. "So I'm right. You need a case made. He likes you, and you think you like him, but there's this chair in the way. Let me ask you something. How does he make you feel?"

"What are you talking about?" Was she asking if he turned me on?

"I'm not necessarily talking about sex, though those feelings should be in there too. I'm talking about how you feel as a person when you think of him. Like, does he make you feel special. Or does he give you the sense that he'd change you, that you're not quite good enough yet. Does he pressure you or manipulate you. Do you feel as though you could tell him anything, or are you walking on eggshells about the chair or anything else. Does he make you feel like you, Nathan Bartlett, are exactly who and what you should be." She took a breath. "That's what I'm talking about."

My head spun. I didn't have a clue what to say.

"I guess what I'm saying, Nathan, is that I think we fall in love—even in friendship, but certainly in romance—with the way someone makes us feel. There's a saying that goes something like this: A man might admire a woman for her wit, her charm, her beauty, her wisdom; but he falls in love with her because of the way she puts on her galoshes."

"That's—" I didn't know what that was. I stopped talking.

"Crazy? Were you going to say crazy? Because it's not. Why do you think some people fall in love with someone who treats them badly? I'm thinking it's because they somehow believe that's how they *should* be treated, and so it makes them feel safe in a way that might not make any sense to someone else."

"I—He asked me to make a list of questions about life using a wheelchair."

"He what?" She sounded dumbfounded.

"No subject's off limit. That's what he said. I'm supposed to have dinner at his house Thursday to talk about it."

I heard an odd, choking laugh from Nina's end of the line. "Nathan? Do you like him at all?"

"Well, yeah, I kind of do." Even as I said that, I knew it was an understatement. "But I might not go. I'm not sure I want to get into a relationship—"

She interrupted me again. "With a wheelchair?" Again, I heard that choked laugh. "Nathan, you owe it to yourself—never mind to that brave, attractive, open-hearted man—to find out what this thing is. What this thing might be. Maybe it won't work. But I'd bet you anything that if you don't give it a chance, if you don't explore what this might be, you'll regret it the rest of your life."

Nina's voice had taken on an odd sound, a character that in someone else I would suspect meant they were about to cry. I couldn't picture Nina crying, except at the deaths of family members.

"Nina? Are you okay?"

She took a few seconds to respond. "I'll be fine. I just have a tough decision to make. I'm—well, it's already made. I'm moving out."

"You're leaving Luc?" The line from that Karla Bonoff song came to me: *I hope I'll know him if he's ever near.*

"Yeah."

"Um…. How does he make you feel?"

Her laugh this time was more of a bark. "Squeezed. Pressured. And, somehow, less than."

"Less than what?"

"Less than him, professionally. He's the big star, the photographer. He has groupies, fans, hangers-on."

"You're, what, ten years younger than he is? You might

be even bigger soon, in your field. And—why pressured?"

"He wants to get married."

This confused the heck out of me. My idea had been that she loved him more than he loved her. Something in my mind slipped sideways. I didn't know what to say.

"I've already put a deposit down on my own loft. One with lots of space, an open floor plan, with room to design clothes and test styling options and—I need space, Nathan. My space."

"Luc wouldn't give that to you?"

"He uses the word 'someday' way too often."

"Wow." That one word stopped me from saying anything stupid. Maybe someday I'd ask her if there had been anyone before Luc, someone that Karla Bonoff song would apply to. "Does he know?"

"Not yet."

Not yet. So he'd come home from Milan to the woman he wanted to marry, and she'd be—what, packing? Already gone?

As for my own issues, I had some thinking to do. Was Nina right? If I didn't give this thing with Drew a chance, would I always regret it?

Monday, Emmett showed up for the teen session. He assumed that same melted posture I'd seen before. I did my best to ignore him without seeming to ignore him, even though he kept staring at me.

As the session ended, I tried to get a sense of whether he'd approach me, but it seemed unlikely. I walked down the hall toward the front slowly, as one member after another passed me. When Emmett passed me, he was moving more quickly than anyone else, almost as if something was chasing him.

Another session without a connection. Well, Jennifer had said this would take time.

Wednesday was an exciting day, and not in a good way. A clinic member in his twenties, a big, hulking guy with long, scraggly hair and baggy clothes, missed his nine o'clock dose of methadone. He showed up just before eleven with something heavy, and he banged several times on the side door to the med clinic. Katie and I looked up at each other.

Juan appeared suddenly. He shut and locked the front door. "Don't let Leo in," he said, his tone heavy with concern. "I've called the police."

Less than a minute later, Leo had worked his way around to the front of the building. He must have figured someone from this part of the facility would hear him, and he wasn't getting any satisfaction banging on the clinic door.

At first he limited himself to hitting the side of the building. Katie peered out of the window near her desk. "He's got a tire iron!" she told me, her whisper hoarse and laced with excitement.

A sudden crash, accompanied by an animal yell from Leo, brought a small scream from Katie as glass splintered onto the floor. She jumped farther into the room, toward my desk.

"Now I know," I said as calmly as possible, "why there are bars on the windows."

From outside, we heard Juan's voice. He had approached Leo, keeping his distance but getting close enough to talk.

"Leo, you need to stop. This isn't helping you."

Leo raised the tire iron over his shoulder, threatening Juan. "Give me my meds!"

"You missed your time. You know what that means. Put that thing down, and we can talk."

Leo raised the tire iron over his shoulder and made a dash at Juan, who stepped gracefully to the side. He grabbed the tire iron and twisted it in a way that made Leo let go. Leo charged Juan again, weaponless this time, and again Juan avoided him.

An approaching siren made Leo raise his head, looking for all the world like some wild thing realizing that the sound he was hearing did not bode well for him. He wheeled and ran down the street in the opposite direction. Juan stood watching him, looking like he was contemplating giving chase. A police car whizzed past him, and he turned and walked back toward the clinic.

Jennifer had come into the office at some point; my attention had been outside. "I've unlocked the front door. Is everyone all right?" she asked.

Katie looked a little shaken, but maybe she was just excited. "Oh, yeah," she said. "Happens all the time." She gave a nervous laugh.

"Katie, would you call about getting the window fixed? I'll get someone here to cover it in case there's rain in the meantime."

Within five minutes, Juan was back. He cleaned up the broken glass and then hammered a piece of plywood over the opening. He had to do this on the inside, because from the outside the bars would be in the way.

His job complete, he turned to Katie. "You all right?" He waited for her to smile and nod. "I mean, after last time…." Juan turned toward me. "Katie tell you about that?"

"She did not. What happened?"

"It was a guy named Brian. When he saw the clinic was closed, he didn't yell or bang things. He came into the office here with a knife and threatened Katie." He shrugged. "I took care of it."

He took care of it. Whatever that meant. His tone was flat, matter-of-fact, not bragging at all. It seemed like Juan was a good person to have on your team. I said, "I saw you out there with Leo. You've got some impressive moves."

Juan came over to my desk and half-sat on the corner. He held his left forearm toward me and poked at a spot with his right forefinger.

"See that?" There was a hard, white-ish lump under the skin. "Speedball. Heroin and cocaine, together. Four years ago. I don't really know what's in the lump now, but something happened, and this lump has been there ever since."

Okay. Non sequitur. I nodded, doing my best to look knowing. "How long have you been in recovery?"

"Three years, five months, twenty-seven days."

"Were you a client here before becoming a counselor?"

"Portland." He lifted himself off my desk. "You guys let me know if Leo shows up here." And he left.

# CHAPTER EIGHT

The night before dinner with Drew, I was in a very peculiar mood. State of mind. Whatever. Nina's warning about the regret I'd feel if I didn't at least take Drew up on this one invitation fought in my head with a childish, even irrational feeling that I didn't want to go. It didn't help that Emmett had shown up at the teen session that afternoon and had proceeded to ignore me. He was beginning to piss me off, which I knew to be profoundly unprofessional, and which I blamed on my apprehension over Drew's dinner.

Anyway, instead of sleeping Wednesday night, I lay restlessly in the darkness, imagining what the dinner would be like.

Drew so obviously wanted me, and I wasn't sure how I felt about that. I mean, don't get me wrong, I was hardly inexperienced. What was new to me was someone who wanted me not just as a friend, and not just as someone to sleep with. Drew wanted *me*.

Once before, someone had wanted me. Alden. And look how that had ended.

I didn't yet know whether I could even get to a place where I wanted Drew the way I'd wanted a man in the past. Sure, he was attractive, and charismatic, and even a little sultry. He had been willing to risk his life for someone else's kid, and he'd suffered for it. He'd tried to help Johnny Crosby. And, sure, I'd felt turned on more than once in his company. But wanting Drew meant dealing with someone I didn't understand in a very important way. Dealing with Drew was also dealing with his chair and all that came with it. And if things went the way Drew seemed to hope they might, I would be involved with someone who wasn't physically whole. At least, he wasn't physically whole according to my idea of what that meant.

Did he see himself as essentially the same person he'd been before he'd fallen? Was all the bravado, the climbing of rock walls, the fancy expensive equipment—was that just denial?

If he was not in denial, if he was as sure of himself as he seemed, I'd have a lot of catching up to do in terms of what being with him would mean. I'd have a lot of adjustments to make. If he was in denial, then this whole thing was doomed anyway, because it would mean he was fighting with himself. And it was likely that he was somewhere in between.

I decided the first step was to figure out, as best I could, how he saw himself. He'd said he liked intense honesty.

He was going to get it.

Carrying a bag that contained some Strong Black Velvet Stout, I walked from my car toward Drew's house, thinking that this was something Drew could no longer do.

A two-bay garage, doors closed, faced the driveway where I parked. The house was positioned behind and to the left of the garage, softly-weathered cedar shingles with pale, sage green wooden trim. There were no trees close to the house, but the land on either side of the building was wooded. The house itself was tastefully surrounded by various kinds of plantings. Drew evidently had a landscaper.

A ramp toward the left side of the house led up from the paved sidewalk to a small porch. As I got close to the house I saw that the land sloped down behind it, and I caught a glimpse of water. Somes Sound.

The door had a few glass panels in it, and I could see that there was a small foyer inside. I rang the bell and then watched, expecting to see the top of Drew's head appear. Instead—well, I nearly dropped the beer.

An upright Drew rolled into view, fully standing, his head now about eight inches higher than mine. He grinned at me as he opened the door. I could hear light jazz in the background, not unlike what I'd played for him.

"Welcome to my abode," he said, rolling out of the way to let me enter. Standard protocol would have me look around admiringly and comment on what a lovely place he had. But I couldn't take my eyes off of him.

He laughed, a good-natured laugh, no doubt at the expression on my face. I dropped my eyes to the base of the—well, the wheelchair, for lack of a better term. "Isn't this the same one you used when you came for dinner?"

"It is. It's a versatile thing. Officially, it's a standing chair." He touched a control attached to the side of the right armrest and moved into a large open room, polished wooden floors everywhere, no rugs. A wonderful food aroma wafted toward me as I followed him. I took a silent guess at something with beef and really interesting spices.

The space served as a very modern combination of large kitchen, spacious dining area, and expansive living room. On the far wall was a wood stove beside glass sliders that led onto the deck, which I could see through the glass. Beyond the deck was water.

There was an abundance of seating for someone who didn't need a wheelchair, and there were spaces all around where a wheelchair could settle as part of a social group.

"Pardon my boldness," Drew said, pointing to the bag I was still holding, "but is that for me?"

"Um, yeah. It's the stout you had at the Lompoc."

"Excellent. Could you put it in the fridge? And get out that bottle of champagne while you're in there."

Champagne. As though I had said the word aloud, complete with the guarded tone I heard in my own head, Drew said, "Not to worry. It's not that I'm anticipating a celebration. I'm just inordinately fond of the stuff, and it'll go well with the appetizers."

He reached into a cabinet and pulled two champagne glasses from a shelf high enough that I might not have been able to reach it. He twisted the wire cage off the champagne bottle, covered the cork with a towel, and very gradually turned his hand to ease the cork out.

"I hate it when the bottle pops too much. It lets some of the fizz out. And sometimes it even lets out some of this nectar as well." He handed me the bottle. "There's an ice bucket stand in the living room. Could you push this down into it? And then sit wherever you'd like."

I looked around as I moved toward the couch and the fascinating chairs facing it, which were covered in a material of dark beige with a flecked pattern. The term "architectural" came to mind. I don't know how else to describe the chairs. I had to try one. I loved it.

Drew rolled into the room with the glasses held in his left hand. With his right he touched the control again, and the chair lowered itself into the shape I'd seen before, a true chair. Drew poured champagne into a glass and handed it to me. I waited, wondering if he'd want to toast.

He did. His glass poured, he held it aloft. "To honesty." Each of us took a sip. "Help yourself to anything here, Nathan."

On a long, low coffee table there were two kinds of cheese, thin pale crackers, little pinwheels of smoked salmon twisted with something white and sprinkled with—I don't know, chopped chives? A bowl of mixed nuts balanced the rest of it.

Drew's invitation on Saturday had seemed so natural, so normal, that at the time it hadn't occurred to me to wonder what kind of meals it was possible to prepare from a wheelchair. It would have done me no good to wonder; I'd never have guessed at this.

Finally, I looked around. "Sorry if this seems mundane," I said, slowly waving my hand with the glass in it, "but I have to say it. This place is gorgeous."

"I know," Drew said, grinning. "But I love to hear it."

"First question?" I asked, and Drew nodded. "How do you get upstairs?" I glanced toward the far side of the room, where a staircase led to an upper floor.

"As you can see, there's a wall beside the staircase, but beyond that there's more space. On the other side of the wall is an elevator."

Good God, but the man must be loaded.

"My bedroom is up there," he said, "and a spare bedroom, and also my study, where I do most of my writing. But sometimes I work down here. There's a dumbwaiter beside the elevator that lets me send stuff up or down as I need to if I don't want to carry it."

I was quiet, still looking around, imagining him alone here.

"After my accident," he told me, "I made a lot of changes. I was on my own. My parents had died a couple of years before. So I needed to make some accommodations."

"I can see that."

"You're probably thinking about how much money I've put into those accommodations."

"It looks like a lot, I'll grant you. I can't help wondering how someone without money would manage, if they had to use a wheelchair."

He nodded. "I'm extremely fortunate. The money came from my folks, so it's not like I earned it. But I give a good chunk every year to a charity that helps people with disabilities get equipment they need."

Drew, who had positioned himself strategically near the coffee table, reached for a plate and piled food onto it. "I can tell you've been brought up with manners. You're waiting for me to start."

I laughed. "Sure, I'll let you think I'm polite. But if I'm not, it's not the fault of my Gram."

Mention of her led to a number of questions from Drew, and I spent more time than I had intended describing my family. I told him more about the highway accident that had killed my parents and my grandfather when I was all of one year old. I told him about how Gram had taken in her three grandchildren and raised us. I talked about Nina, her sardonic nature, her huge, soft heart that she showed rarely and to almost no one. And then I talked about Neil.

Drew listened, obviously interested, honestly empathetic. When I finally took a break, he said, "So Neil was your father surrogate, really. He sounds like an amazing person."

I repeated to Drew something I'd said at Neil's funeral. "Neil wasn't perfect. But he was the perfect brother for me."

"It sounds like you figuratively placed your own feet into his boots and carried his baton up as many mountains as you could."

I chuckled. "Yeah. That's a pretty accurate description."

Drew poured more champagne into our glasses. "Did hiking mean the same thing to him as it does to you? I mean, based on what you told me at the Lompoc?"

"What I told you was almost exactly what Neil had said to me."

He smiled. "I like that. Because when you said it, I knew you meant every word. Was there anything else he did that you picked up?"

I laughed. "He loved downhill skiing. I didn't. I don't know if I would ever have been good at it, and Neil was very competitive. So I took up Nordic, which he dismissed as baby stuff. But I showed him."

I took a sip of champagne and held Drew's gaze. "I challenged him to ski with me. And I took him to a place where you have to bushwhack all the way up a significant hill through the woods. No trail. And then you have to be really skillful to ski back down without crashing into trees, rocks, logs, whatever." I laughed out loud. "You should have seen him! He acquitted himself well, but he was way behind me,

132

going up and coming down, and when he emerged he was covered head to toe in snow, he'd fallen so many times. He never made fun of my skiing after that."

Drew laughed with me, his deep voice pulling at something in my chest. He said, "When we get snow here, which isn't as often as it used to be, you can take your Nordic skis almost anywhere. The carriage roads are great, though I'd be surprised if they're not too tame for the likes of you." He raised his glass as if to toast me.

He looked down at his hands. "I used to ski. Like you, Nordic." He looked up at me. "I'm still trying to come up with a good way to do it without my legs. For downhill, I've tried the mono ski with the seat and the modified ski poles. The poles have mini-skis instead of points, so you control your descent not only by leaning your body, but also with the poles. But that's only for downhill. Going uphill is the problem, so Nordic is out for me."

He set his empty glass down decisively, like that was the end of that discussion. "Ready for dinner?"

He had me carry a large, steaming pot, kind of like a soup tureen, to the table. It was a stew, full of chunks of beef, big pieces of carrot, pearl onions, peas, pieces of potato, and a mysteriously fragrant sauce.

Drew set a board with a bread knife and a baguette on the table beside a tub of butter. "I have salad, but let's do that after the stew, before dessert."

The last thing he brought to the table was a carafe of red wine. "I poured this earlier so it could breathe. It's a Pauillac that I think goes especially well with this stew." He said that as if of course I would know what that meant. I had no idea.

Once I had taken a sip from the tall, light-as-a-feather wine glass, I knew it was a wine I hoped I would have again, and again, and again. I glanced over to where the bottle stood on the counter, hoping to get a good look at it and commit it to memory.

Drew spooned stew into big, white bowls and had me take one. Once we were both served, he was ready for business.

"I hope you have more questions for me now." He smiled and lifted his wine glass.

Maybe it was the champagne (we'd gone through half the bottle), or the red wine (my glass already had room for more), or perhaps Drew had managed to put me so at ease that I wasn't nervous about my list. It helped that when he spoke about his disability, he was forthright and unhesitant. But I wasn't going to open with the first question that had occurred to me on Saturday.

"Okay, here goes. What's the sign for? The one you had at the Precipice Trail?"

"What do you know about my accident?"

"My college roommate—he's in grad school in Orono, and I visited with him and his wife after I saw you that first time—told me you fell when you pushed a child away from the edge. You saved his life, sounds like."

"I've climbed that trail several times," he said. "I really enjoyed it. But no one should take children on it. The only people who should climb that thing are experienced hikers who have a good sense of balance and no fear of heights. There are metal rungs and ladders embedded into sheer rock faces, and narrow tracks with nothing but death on the other side—in other words, obstacles no child should have to navigate."

He closed his eyes, opened them, and went on. "That day I found myself behind this family, a man and woman and an eleven-year-old boy. I almost passed them a number of times. But something held me back. Something told me to wait. At one point, Darren—the boy—was part of the way up a metal ladder that was embedded into a rock face that went straight up. The rungs were too far apart for him to climb well, and he was slipping and struggling. His mother was already up, and his father was behind him. Darren fumbled a

134

few times, and each time his father caught him. But then…."

Drew took a sip of wine, and then another. "I'm not sure what happened. But Darren's body came flying through the air. His father reached desperately for him, and he almost caught him. But the boy came hurtling toward me. The ledge below that ladder was narrow, and the drop beyond it was sheer. I tried to brace myself against the trunk of a small tree that had taken root in a crevice of the rock, thinking I could catch the boy. But his body was coming too hard, too fast. At the last second, I realized that if I caught him, his inertia would take us both over. So instead, I thrust my arms at him to push him back onto the ledge."

He took a deep breath. "I'm not an idiot. And I'm not a martyr. I still thought I could use that tree to catch my own fall. But it gave way. And I fell. It seemed like slow motion. I know you hear that a lot, but it's true. I fell through the branches of a couple of trees and landed on my back, on a pile of rocks."

Another sip of wine. "I'm lucky to be alive. Anyway, to answer your question, I don't ever want to see kids go up that trail. So every once in a while, I go there to hang out, my sign at the ready. I don't hold the sign up unless I see someone approaching with a child. I've talked several families out of taking children up. Perhaps I've saved some lives."

"You, um, you held it up to me."

Drew swallowed the mouthful of stew he'd taken, his eyes watching me with a teasing, sideways glance. "Oh, well, you. Yes. I wanted to get your attention."

"Why?"

He chuckled. "Are you kidding? Nathan, you are— God, I don't know where to start. Your posture said you're confident and powerful. Your outfit that day said you know what you're doing. Your face," he closed his eyes as if to see it again, at the trailhead. "Your face was full of light. There was an openness, a genuine honesty, something I'll call hopefulness. No, wait. Trust. There's a trust in you that means you know, I mean you *know* your place in the world, and you let others have their place."

I almost laughed. "You saw all that in one quick glance?"

"I did. And I see it now. It comes and goes, to be truthful. You've been guarded with me on and off." One side of his mouth lifted in a half-smile. "My favorite moment with you, before tonight, was when you yelled at that woman on the carriage road, and then we chased off after them and passed them at full tilt. That was fucking wonderful." Then he said, "Next question."

It came quickly. "Are you in pain?"

"Sometimes. I do have meds, but I try not to take them often. There's kind of a constant discomfort, partly because of all the sitting. But the standing chair helps, and when I do things like climb walls, it makes me feel powerful again. It also helps to keep my circulation healthy."

I took a mouthful of stew to give myself some time to get up the guts to ask my next question. I was determined not to have a repeat of Alden. Was I willing to be with someone in recovery? Possibly, but not if they weren't up front with me about it.

I took a sip of wine, swallowed, and looked directly at Drew. "So you've never abused the meds? I know that's a really personal question...."

"I told you, nothing's off limits. I came close, I'll admit. But, no."

I believed him. I took a little more wine, relieved to have that issue off the table. "Do you resent people who aren't disabled?"

"Sometimes. Yes." He left it at that, and I wasn't sure what more to ask about it. So I went on with my next question.

"Do ever dream about not being disabled?"

"All the time." Again, he offered nothing else.

"How often do people say stupid things, like that guy at

the Lompoc who tripped over your chair?"

"Oh, my God, where to start? First, the answer is a lot. And it's not just what people say. It's also what they don't think about. Here's an example. I think I told you I try to go into the bank branch rather than use the outdoor ATM. I hadn't been in my chair very long, maybe a month, when I had to go into the branch. The door has one of those blue symbols with the line drawing of a person in a wheelchair. So I could have opened the door. But to get to the door, I had to go up four steps."

He shook his head, remembering a scene. "I sat there on the sidewalk and yelled and yelled and yelled until someone came out. I told them if they hadn't done something by the next time I had to come, I'd sue them."

"How did you get inside that day?"

He laughed. "You know, I don't remember!" He shook his head. "But they did put in a ramp. I could write a book about it. Hey, I write books! Maybe I will. Anyway, there's no shortage of idiots."

I waited while he finished a piece of buttered bread. "What else would you put in that book?"

"Okay, well, here's one. Sometimes someone will grab the back of my chair. Maybe they're trying to help, maybe they see me as being in their way, I don't know. But it's like they've taken hold of my body. For a while, I had a sign on the back: TOUCH THIS CHAIR AT YOUR PERIL."

I knew there was more. I waited.

"I've had unsolicited comments like, 'I'm sure you'll walk again. Don't give up.' Or, 'So-and-so uses a wheelchair. Do you know her?' Or they'll talk about all the research that's being done for, you know, people like me." Drew's voice grew harsh and louder. "One person saw me getting out of my van at the supermarket and said how nice it must be to get such great parking reserved for me. I've had drunk women ask if they could sit on my lap. I've had people tell me I'm too young to be in a wheelchair, or I don't look like I need it.

Shall I go on?"

As he spoke I watched his face change from his typical partially amused look to something dark and thunderous. I knew he wasn't mad at me. But I knew he was mad. I knew he was furious.

"No need. But I'm sure you have more for that book."

He dropped his head for a few seconds. "Sorry about that."

"I asked. You told me. That's fair."

He poured more wine as he said, "On a calmer note, I hope you'll learn to use the term 'people with disabilities' rather than 'disabled people.' On the whole, people like it best when they're recognized as people first. Now, I know that we say 'gay man' or 'bi man' rather than 'man who is gay.' Even so, please keep it in mind."

"Got it." I took a sip of wine, remembering Ellie's friend Laura, and how seeing Laura had made me realize I didn't know how to see the person rather than their disability. Drew was teaching me.

I added, "You know, I'd like to say that I'd never do or say any of those offensive things. I hope I wouldn't. I can't swear to it. At least, not before you listed them. But I have a better chance of avoiding it now."

"Yeah. I keep telling myself people don't mean to offend. Most of them, anyway. But, damn it, they seem so thoughtless." He started to chuckle. "Before my fall, God— who knows? Maybe I was one of those thoughtless people. Fuck me dead."

My jaw dropped.

"What? What did I say?" Drew looked honestly concerned.

"My roommate says that. I never heard anyone else say it."

"Margot? *Margot* says that?"

The idea of Margot saying that made me laugh so hard I had trouble stopping. Finally I managed. "No. Not Margot. I mean my college roommate. I don't know why I still call him that. We roomed for four years. He's like a brother to me."

"He's the one who told you about me?"

"Right."

"You hiked together?"

"Sometimes." And this reminded me of something else from my list of questions. "So, other than hiking mountains like Mont Blanc, are there things you used to do that you regret not being able to do anymore?"

Drew's face grew thoughtful, his eyes on me but not in an intense way. "Yes. Many things. But I think what I miss the most is knowing that if I meet someone I really like, and they seem to like me... I'll just say there didn't used to be anything unusual in the way; it either worked or it didn't, on its own. But now that I'm disabled, someone I'm interested in is usually stymied by misgivings. They get stuck on what our life together would be like. Especially about sex. About who could do what to whom. About how much prep is necessary, and even whether it would be possible at all."

Now his gaze intensified. "I have to believe you have those questions, Nathan. So I'll give you some information up front. Unlike the case with some men who have spinal cord injuries, my injuries are such that I still have functional genitals. I can get an erection and hold it as well as I ever did. I can fuck you, I can be fucked. I can give head and take it. Sure, there are some positional considerations, but they're not intrusive. Some of them are even fun."

He let out a noisy breath through his nose. "I know you have those questions. But you haven't asked them. I really hope it's not because you've already decided the point is moot."

I held his gaze, determined to respect his courage and not side-step.

"I almost didn't come here tonight," I said. "But my sister asked enough questions about you in a very clever way, kind of playing devil's advocate, forcing me to defend you and admit that I'm attracted to you. So although I'm still thinking about things, the subject is not moot."

I dropped my eyes, organizing my thoughts, and Drew waited. When I looked up at him, I was ready.

"You said you wanted honesty."

"I can't deal with anything else. Without it, things go in circles. I hate that."

I nodded. "You seem so determined not to let the chair get in your way. You have all these accommodations that cost a fortune. You have—what, three chairs? One of those chairs lets you leave me in the dust, at least on a smooth, level surface. Another lets you stand. You climb rock walls using only your hands and arms."

I paused, but Drew said nothing.

"It's almost like you're in denial."

That surprised him. "Denial?"

"Like you're not really disabled."

He was not happy with me. "So you'd prefer it if I whined and begged for people to help me and had a long list of things I wouldn't try because I'm so helpless?"

"Of course not."

"So what the fuck, Nathan?"

"Who are you now, compared to who you were before you fell?"

Drew heaved an exasperated sigh. "For God's sake, Nathan. I don't know what you want from me. I'm still the same person. I just have to live differently from how I used to live. This chair—whichever chair I'm in—isn't me. It's just the way I get around. Am I disabled? Yeah, I am. Am I helpless? No fucking way. Do I want a relationship with someone who pities me?" He glared at me and took a few harsh breaths. "Is that you? Do you pity me?"

I wasn't exactly calm and relaxed, myself. My tone had an edge to it. "If I did, I wouldn't in a million years ask you all these questions. And I wouldn't be here." It wasn't until I said those words aloud that I realized they were true. Maybe there was pity when I picked up his money, and maybe again when I let him buy me a beer. But I did not pity Drew. Not anymore. Not at all.

He closed his eyes and relaxed, but only a little. When he looked at me again, his face was softer.

"Nathan, I want you. I want to be with you. At least I want to see where things might go with us. Maybe they won't go anywhere. Maybe there are reasons other than this chair that would get in our way. But I want to try, and I'm too impatient to wait for you to approach me. If I've put too much onto you, if you feel pressured, I'm sorry. But like I said, I don't like wasting time, and I don't like going in circles."

We watched each other's faces over our empty bowls. Then he reached into a pocket and pulled out his phone. The jazz stopped, and another song started playing.

It wasn't a sad song, but there was a feeling of patient resignation in the music and the lyrics. I was pretty sure the singer was Molly Tuttle, the singer he'd admired at the Lompoc that first time. She sang about how she would be there "when you're ready." She sang that line several times. When it ended, Drew touched his phone again, and no more music played. The room was silent.

Something stirred in me. It wasn't an unfamiliar feeling, but there was something new, something fresh in it, even unpredictable. It took me two seconds, if that long, to realize what it was. This man excited me. This man was everything I wanted in a partner—at least, in every way but that chair. I had to know what I'd be in for.

I said, "So how would you make love to me?"

Drew drained his wine glass and sat back in his chair a little. He didn't smile. "Let me count the ways."

He looked at me closely for a few seconds, and a smile spread across his face. "Unless I miss my guess, you're vers. I like that. Because I enjoy getting as much as I enjoy giving. And as for head, well… I'll just say yes. Am I on the right track so far?"

I'm sure I blushed, but I don't know why. I'm not shy about sex, I'm not a prude, and he was right about all of it. "You are."

He nodded slowly, said "Then for now, I will choose what we do." He closed his eyes.

"First I would stand as close to you as I could. I would take your face between my hands and hold it until I was sure you wanted to kiss me as much as I wanted to kiss you. Then I would bring our faces close enough for me to run my tongue slowly over the tender insides of your lips. I would do that until your response told me you wanted more. And then," he opened his eyes, "I would pull away."

As I'd watched his face, as I'd become aroused by his description, I hadn't realized what he was doing. Not, that is, until those last four words. Because I hadn't expected them. And opening his eyes on me at exactly that unpredictable moment caused something urgent to shoot through me. I knew then that he'd manipulated me. And I didn't care.

"I would take your hand, and we would go upstairs together. I would lower my chair and remove two things from under my bed and set them into position on the floor. For now I'm not going to say what they are. I would stand again and watch you watch me as I removed my shirt. I think you already know what you'd see there. And I don't mean the nest of brown curls over my sternum. I mean the muscle, clearly defined under my skin, muscle that comes as Margot said not just from using my manual chair."

He paused as if to let me appreciate the hyper-masculine image.

"Then I would move close enough to you to remove your shirt. I would adjust the chair to bring my head to where I could place my hands on either side of your spine and pull you toward me, your back arched, and I would run my mouth over everything it could reach. And then," he inhaled deeply, "I would make my way slowly to one of your tits, and I would lick it and suck it as I pulled you as close as possible. When I heard you groan, maybe the second time, I would move to the other side and lick and suck again."

I tried to keep my breathing normal. I knew I failed, and I knew Drew could see that.

"This is the point at which I'd lower the chair even more and undo your pants. I'd push them down to your knees. No farther. I want you helpless. By now your dick is high and full, and your balls are tender. I would grab your ass with both hands and tease that sweet dick with my tongue, making him bounce and slip and ache with unspent pleasure."

He closed his eyes, his own breathing far from normal, and his mouth fell open, his jaw in a forward position as though my dick were right there, ready for entry. Then he smiled and opened his eyes again.

"The next part I'll leave a mystery for now. I'll just tell you that I'm not in this chair any longer. But I'm in a seated position. We're both completely naked. There is a condom on my hard dick and as much lube as you want, anywhere you want it. And you, Nathan," he closed those eyes again briefly, "you are on your back, your knees bent over my shoulders, your hands clenched and gripping hard onto something over your head. Your dick is pointing straight up at me, and mine…."

He inhaled and exhaled loudly. "Oh, God." Another breath. "Mine is deep inside you. I have teased your ass until it opened for me, until it screamed for me, until you shouted 'Fuck me! Fuck me now!' Your chin is pointing to the ceiling, your eyes are clenched, you're barely breathing. I can see the strain in your neck and jaw."

I swallowed hard, for maybe the fourth time, and he smiled again. "Now the real fun begins."

My stomach contracted so sharply that a loud puff of air exploded from my mouth. Porn. He was giving me porn. And I was loving it.

"Now, Nathan, my hands hold your legs, which are still bent over my shoulders, and I begin to rock, back and forth.

Slowly at first, while I test how far I can pull back and push forward. Out, almost to the tip, and in, gently but deeply. And again. I find your prostate and work it. A little faster, now. Faster still. Harder and faster." His words sped up with the action he described. "One of my hands is on your dick now, pulling and pushing with the rocking motion. Harder. And harder. Your balls are nearly crushed with each thrust."

It was everything I could do not to grip the edges of the table.

"Finally your prostate can't stand the ecstatic pain any longer. I hold your dick against my chest as you release that salty, spicy milk of pleasure. Then, and only then, do I release myself inside you."

He closed his eyes again, briefly. "I help you lower your legs until they wrap around my hips, and I pull you up toward me. We're so close there's barely room for our sated dicks. With your head against my chest, we allow our breathing to quiet."

He paused and waited until he knew I was calmer.

"Then we kiss. Our mouths are a little sticky from panting, but they're warm. With our tongues we explore the insides of each other's mouth, our lips working together. You will feel my mustache and beard against your face, and its masculinity will excite you, but not so much as to ruin the afterglow. We will stay like that as long as we can. Then I will lower you back down, rock gently away, my dick falling away from you in a silent gasp."

I closed my eyes.

"We will be on the bed now. I'm on my back, your body curled against my side, and I caress your skin with my fingertips. Every once in a while, we kiss. And then we sleep. It's a warm, gentle, sweet sleep."

He paused and waited until I opened my eyes. "When we wake, everything will have changed."

I drained my wine glass, trying to re-establish a feeling close to normal, close to who I'd been before I'd asked my last question. I couldn't.

First, I said, "I'd almost forgotten that you're a writer." That made him smile. And then I said, "Everything has changed already."

He nodded. Then he did something on his phone, and once more there was music in the room. This time it was solo guitar, gentle but with an interesting rhythm.

He said, "Are you ready for desert?"

"I think I just had it."

He laughed and pushed away from the table. "We'll skip salad, if that's okay. Help me get these dishes over to the sink."

Desert was dark, rich, fudgy brownies with a scoop of vanilla ice cream, and huge brandy glasses with a large splash of something in them Drew named but which I can't remember. Whatever it was, it was heavenly. We spoke little and gazed at each other a lot.


In his standing chair, Drew went to the door with me as I was about to leave for home. I turned to him, not quite knowing what to do next. Drew did know. Positioned beside me, he lowered his chair just enough to bring our faces to the same height, pushed the chair arm up and out of the way like he would have in an airplane seat, and wrapped his arm around my neck.

The kiss—our first, if you don't count the porn scene— was long and sweet. When it ended I looked into those warm brown eyes. "I'm not used to being pursued."

He shook his head as if in disbelief. Then he said, "Get used to it."

# CHAPTER NINE

In my car, it took me a minute to adjust my jeans before I started the engine. I pulled away from Drew's house, fully aware that he had not said anything about getting together again. Not for dinner, not for hiking, not for more porn, not at all. Either he was letting me wonder, or—more likely— waiting until I contacted him, despite his pursuit of me. He wanted to know I wanted him.

Had I felt turned on during his porn show? I had. But was I turned on to him, or just turned on?

And it wasn't just a question of sex—the sex we hadn't actually had, the sex it almost felt like we'd had. Nina's question was important: *How does he make you feel?*

Something warm expanded from my chest all the way up to the top my head and brought tears to my eyes.

Wanted. Desired. Desirable. Incredibly turned on. Excited. And like I was seeing the world in a whole new light.

Then—fear. Where was that coming from? I pushed it aside.

One of the most important things Neil had done for me was to make me feel like I belonged. That feeling had disappeared with Neil's death, an aching empty space all that remained where it had been. I wasn't always aware of it, and for sure it had seemed a little less dark after the Kalalau. But I had felt it again in New York, and something about young Emmett and the pain he was in had given it new life.

When I thought about how Drew made me feel, I couldn't locate that darkness. Even so, as I tried to concentrate on the road, I told myself the emptiness would be back. Neil would still be dead, our family was almost all gone, and (thanks a bunch, Margot) hiking had not filled that emptiness.

"Neither can Drew." My voice broke the silence in the car.

Another voice, in my head, said, *Maybe not. But he could sure make you feel it less.*

Without any conscious intent on my part, my right hand banged hard enough on the steering wheel to be painful.

"What the fuck do I want?"

By the time I pulled into a parking spot at home, I was no longer feeling the warm expansiveness that had been with me at the start of the drive. Clinging to the top of the steering wheel, I leaned my head on my hands and squeezed my eyes tight to stop the tears forming in them.

Here was the fear. *What if I let Drew into my life and we fall in love, and then something happens? What if I can't handle his disabled state and all the requirements that go with it? Maybe his health will fail. Maybe he'll fall out of love with me. Maybe my career will take me far away from him.*

On one hand, I'd be no worse off than I was already. On the other, I'd be in for a shitload of hurt, and I'd be no further ahead, emotionally, than before. No closer to that feeling of belonging, and maybe even further away from it. Because how much worse would it be if he gave me that feeling, and then we had to split for one or more of any number of reasons?

*Well, dickhead,* that other voice said, *where else are you gonna find that good feeling you want so badly? Isn't it gonna have to be with someone like Drew?*

What I'd learned up to this point in my studies about addiction included descriptions of the struggles and conflicts people go through as they're trying to get clean. They can become so familiar with a life of addiction, and so convinced that it's the life they're destined to lead, that just the idea of trying to live without addiction feels like taking a massive risk.

For me, saying "yes" to Drew was like saying "no" a life where I'd become familiar with a kind of emptiness, or at least to the conviction that it was my lot in life. It would mean leaving something that might not be great but was at least familiar, something I knew how to manage. Saying "yes" to Drew was taking a giant leap of faith. It would take courage I wasn't convinced I had. It would take trust greater than anything Drew could have seen in my face. It was like jumping off a cliff.

Or a precipice.

I leaned back and pounded the steering wheel again, this time with both hands, this time deliberately.

I just couldn't get past that *chair*.


"So? How did it go?"

I was barely inside the door. Margot was curled on the couch, and the television was on but muted. She sat up and patted the couch cushion beside her.

I glared at her.

"Not pushing," she said. "Just interested."

I considered my options. She had a certain wisdom, and I had no one else to talk to about this, at least not at the moment. It was after ten and too late to call someone. The only question in my mind was whether I wanted to talk at all.

"Fine," I said, "but I'm not going into detail."

"Fair enough."

I sat, one knee bent on the cushion under me so I could face Margot. "He's a good cook. Likes wine and brandy. The house is even nicer inside than out. He has an elevator to take him between floors."

"And you know this how?"

"Stop. We did not go upstairs." Not really, anyway. "Remember that powered chair he was in when he came here?" Margot nodded. "It has a feature he didn't show us that night. It allows him to stand."

"What? Are you serious?"

"There's a brace that goes around his waist, and these pads that brace his knees. There's a kind of joy stick that unbends the seat and brings him up. He can stop it anywhere in the process."

"That's huge! So he uses it when he cooks?"

"He does. And he wouldn't even let me help wash dishes."

I thought she'd ask what we'd had for dinner, but she wanted meatier information. I had already told her his agenda; that is, I was to come prepared to ask about his life. "Did you ask him all the questions you had?"

"I think so."

"You think so?"

I looked at the silent figures moving around on the TV screen, then down at the floor, giving myself time to decide how much to tell her.

What the fuck.

"I got a little distracted after he pushed me to ask about sex."

Margot's jaw dropped. "What does that mean, he pushed you?"

"He said he knew I would have questions about that, but I hadn't asked them. So he told me."

"He told you."

My chuckle was almost a giggle. "Yeah. But I'm not telling you."

She looked at me a little sideways. "How much do you like him now? Is the chair still in the way?" I didn't answer. Just rubbed my face. "You're afraid to let yourself go, aren't you?"

I exhaled loudly. "It's just—so many things could go wrong."

"That would be true of anyone."

I let my head fall back. I needed to think. She let me.

Maybe half a minute later, I landed on this: "I haven't come close to having the kind of relationship Drew wants. Not since freshman year in college. That one did not start as a romance. At first, we just fucked. It developed into more. But it ended very badly."

"You were, what, all of seventeen? Eighteen at the most?"

"Not the point."

"Then what's the point?"

Indeed, what was the point? My frantic brain landed on the last thing Drew had said to me. "I've never been pursued."

Margot threw her head back and laughed. "Well, hell, Nathan. Don't you think it's about time you were?"

I tried not to grin and, mostly, failed. "It scares the shit out of me."

"Why? Don't you think you're worth it?"

There it was again. Was I worthy? Of what, though? Because this time it wasn't a question of being worthy of Neil. I tried changing the word a little. "He wants so much. I'm not sure I'd be enough for him."

She smiled. "Oh, Nathan, you're enough. You're more than enough."


*Enough.* That word followed me to bed that night. Somehow it seemed bigger than whether I was "worth it." The two concepts were similar, but there was a difference. They both lived in that darkness, that gaping hole. And it seemed unlikely that my feelings for Drew, and his feelings for me, and all the feelings in the world would ever be enough to fill it.

And if he and I together couldn't fill it, the world of hurt I'd been worried about would come for both of us.

By noon on Friday, Katie had noticed I wasn't my usual efficient self.

"What's bugging you, Nathan? You okay?"

I sat back in my chair. "Yeah. Just trying to figure out how to proceed on something."

She swiveled her chair in my direction. "Anything to do with Drew Madden?"

Christ, how many women in my life wanted to know about my relationships? "Why do you ask?"

"Just a hunch. He hasn't been here since Johnny died. Then you show up, and then he shows up and leaves a note for you."

I turned back to my computer. "I'll let you know when I figure it out."

By lunchtime, I had accomplished very little work, but I had made a big decision regarding my love life. It would not include Drew Madden.

Was he a great guy? Yeah, he did seem to be. Was I attracted to him? Sure. Did I want someone who wanted me enough to pursue me? That question still gave me pause, but whether it was a plus or a minus, I was sure it wasn't what carried the most weight in my decision.

In an odd way, it was almost because he seemed like such a great fit for me in almost every way that I decided to call a halt. I didn't know where my career would take me. I was on this island for a year, and that was it. The idea of him leaving his home seemed ridiculous. And even if he did, who's to say how many career changes, how many geographical changes I would make? What was he going to do, renovate every house we lived in to accommodate his chair? Chairs? Whatever.

He'd agreed to give me time. I'd taken some time, and I had done what Nina had said I should—that is, to at least give him a chance. I figured I'd done that. So the next decision was how to let him know. Just leaving him in limbo seemed all wrong, and he'd specifically asked me not to do that. Telling him via text seemed wrong as well, but it was a place to start.

*I've taken all the time I need. Can we meet someplace?*

His reply came about an hour later. *Will I like what you have to say?*

Maybe he did want to know by text. *Don't think so.*

Maybe ten minutes went by. *No need to meet.*

So that was that. What a relief.

Why did I feel like shit?


I was in bad shape the rest of the afternoon. I got work done, but I came close to making Katie mad at me, I was such a misery guts. That is, when I wasn't feeling pissed off. I had hit on one reason I was pissed. Drew hadn't even tried to talk me out of my decision. Pursue me? He wasn't fucking pursuing me. He was willing to let me go with a text. It was very much like when I'd left him sitting at the Lompoc that first time. I'd walked away. He hadn't called my name. Just let me go. This felt very much like that. If nothing else convinced me I'd made the right decision, this second dismissal did.

Around four o'clock, the office had a visitor. Or, rather, I had a visitor. Emmett Chaplin.

You hear the expression, "He stormed into the room." I don't think I'd ever before witnessed what that would look like. But that's exactly how it felt. Emmett headed for my desk, and for a second I thought he was going to upend it by force. But he just glared at me. I say "just," but that glare held a power that sent me rolling back in my wheeled chair.

"You!" Emmett shouted at me. "What are you doing with that cock-sucking bastard?"

In my peripheral vision I saw Katie pick up her phone as unobtrusively as possible, no doubt calling for help.

The only way to respond to Emmett, I felt certain, was more or less in the same way I'd responded to him in the past. "I've known quite a few cock-sucking bastards in my time. Which one are you referring to?"

For a couple of seconds, I thought Emmett would storm out of the room as violently as he'd stormed in. But then he nearly spat the name, "Drew Madden!"

My stomach clenched. But I couldn't back down. "Then your description confuses me. The only Drew Madden I know is kind of a nice guy."

"If he ever comes back here, I'm out. D'you feel me?"

I was about to explain to Emmett that I had little or no control over where Drew Madden appeared, but suddenly Juan Diego was in the room, no doubt in answer to Katie's call.

Juan's voice was low and heavy with meaning. "Emmett, you need to turn around and leave."

Emmett did turn, but only to confront Juan. "This is none of your fucking business!"

"You are threatening a clinic employee. That makes it my business."

Emmett's body was nearly shuddering. Frustration? Fury? Both?

"Then you keep that bastard away from here. D'you hear me? Or else I'm history. You choose." His body wasn't as solid as Juan's, but he was taller. He nearly pushed Juan aside as he… well, as he stormed out again. Juan went to the window to make sure Emmett was leaving the area. He was still staring out the window when I found my voice.

"Um, can anyone tell me what that was all about?"

Juan faced me, a half smile on his face. "You should ask your friend Drew. All I'll say is that it bothers Emmett because he likes you." He paused at the doorway. "And while you're at it, tell Drew to stay away, at least for a while." And he was gone.

My mouth flapped open and shut a couple of times as I

debated whether to follow after Juan and assure him I wouldn't be delivering any messages to Drew. I sat where I was.

I turned to Katie. She said, "So you want to know what that was about."

"Well, yeah."

"I told you a little about Johnny Crosby, who used to be a member here. Drew's family had been friends with his folks, so he and Drew knew each other. A couple of years ago, Johnny was hurt in a car accident, and that's what put him in the chair. Even though Drew sort of took him under his wing, Johnny got hooked on meds. So Drew brought him here."

"How long ago was this?"

"Maybe eighteen months. Anyway, Johnny got clean, but then he had a relapse. His dealer had been arrested, but Johnny knew Emmett used. Emmett sent him to his own dealer, and the heroin Johnny got was laced with fentanyl."

"Jesus." I knew what that could mean.

"After Johnny died, Drew—well, he kind of fell to bits. He waited for Emmett to leave school one day, tied him up, drove him over here and dumped him on our doorstep."

In my mind I recreated the image of Drew tossing the two would-be thieves onto the ground. Even so.... "From his wheelchair? Are you kidding?"

Katie gave me an odd look. "I don't think there's much Drew Madden couldn't do, wheelchair or no. Anyway, Emmett didn't join the program then. But he came back nearly a year later." She shrugged. "My guess is that Emmett is still pissed off about the kidnapping and probably feels guilty about what happened to Johnny. He associates all that with Drew."

"So—was Drew arrested?"

"Emmett's parents are a waste of oxygen. They didn't pursue anything. And Drew didn't hurt the kid, and he didn't keep him any longer than it took to bring him over here. So,

154

no."

That explained a lot. But there was still something bugging me. "So how did Emmett know I've even met Drew?"

Katie shrugged. "It's a small town. Probably a lot of people know. And Drew is well known. He has a lot of friends, but he also has a lot of—I'll say detractors.

"What? Why?"

"His parents had money, and they were generous with it. They supported a number of local causes. After they died, Drew reduced how much he gave, though he still supports this clinic. Now folks wonder if he's just hanging onto the rest."

"I don't know how much support he offers, but he does give to organizations that help people with disabilities." I gave myself a virtual pat on the back for remembering to say that right. "They probably aren't local, so maybe no one here knows about those contributions."

"That's nice, but you know there aren't a lot of disabled people here on the island."

"Okay, but it's a big world out there. There are people with disabilities everywhere. And, you know, a lot of them have to buy expensive things to make life livable. They have to pay for services you and I can do for ourselves."

"That's true."

"Just because people here don't know what charities he supports doesn't mean he's keeping it all for himself." Why the fuck was I defending Drew Madden?

Katie shrugged again and turned to her computer as if to say, *Conversation over*.

But I had another question. "So how does Juan know that I know Drew?"

"He's Emmett's counselor."

I forced my mind away from Drew and onto Emmett. So Emmett liked me. Well, well, well.

Saturday morning over a late breakfast, I let Margot know that Drew and I were not going to be an item.

She sounded both sad and annoyed. "But why?"

"Look, I've gone over this and over this in my head. I don't want to talk about it anymore."

"The decision is yours, obviously, but I'm not sure you should be making it in a vacuum."

"Margot." My tone made her freeze. "I don't have to explain myself to you."

The rest of the meal was not fun. If it hadn't been for the music I played, the room would have been entirely silent.


After breakfast cleanup, Margot and I went to the mainland to find her some furniture, including a bed, with delivery promised for tomorrow afternoon. It felt like a kind of make-up session after our tense breakfast. On the drive home we decided, rather spur-of-the-moment, to do a short hike; it was already two thirty, but one of the benefits of small mountains is that they don't take long to climb.

After just a little research we selected Beech Mountain, which promised to be a relatively short hike with a combination of gratifying elevation and excellent views. This would be our first hike together since the Kalalau, and her first on the island.

We took our time, refraining from pushing hard; we had nothing to prove. So conversation was easy.

We were not far from the deserted fire tower at the summit when Margot surprised the hell out of me. There was an opening on the right a little off the trail, exposed granite overlooking Long Pond, and she stepped out onto it. We stood side by side to admire the bright blue water and the patchwork of color in the trees on its other side.

"Erik is coming for a visit."

I struggled to recall who Erik might be, and finally it

registered. "Erik Buxton? From the Kalalau?"

"Yup."

I waited for more information, but it didn't seem to be forthcoming. This alone was intriguing. "Okay, and is he coming to see the sights, or is he particularly coming to see you?" I looked at her rather than at the view. She kept her gaze on the water.

"I, uh… me, I think."

"You think?" I put one hand on a hip. "How long has this been in the works?"

Margot moved a little forward and sat down on the warm stone. I sat beside her.

"Margot, spill."

Her fingers toyed with little pieces of grit on the granite in front of her crossed legs. "He's not as old as you might think."

"Did I say anything about that?"

"He's just turned thirty-eight. He does a lot of sailing when he's not flying, so his eyes have that squint-line look. And his hair's thinning, so that makes him look older, too."

"Margot, enough about his age. You've said you liked him. So do I, but clearly not in the same way. How do you feel about this visit?"

She tilted her head and grinned at me, looking slightly shy or embarrassed or both. "I don't just, you know, like him, Nathan. I *really* like him."

"Have you felt that way since you met him?"

She lifted a shoulder and dropped it. "There was a pull right from the start. But it never occurred to me that he'd noticed me. So after he sent me that first e-card, I wasn't sure whether to reply. I didn't want him to think I was expecting something."

"Margot, *he* reached out to *you*. So he's obviously been thinking about you. You've been writing since?"

"And he's called me a few times."

"*A few times?*" Just how far up my own butt had my

head been that I hadn't noticed any of this? Then I started to laugh. "Is this visit what inspired you to go and get a bed all of a sudden?"

"What? No! He's not staying with us. I told him about the place where you stayed in Bar Harbor, but he found something in Southwest Harbor."

"How long will he be here?"

"He's flying into Boston and driving up from there. He'll be here at least a week, maybe longer."

"Longer, depending on how things go?"

"I guess."

I shook my head and grinned. "I suppose your room will look better with a real bed in it, and I'm sure he'll see the place. And then, of course, there's always the chance...."

"Nathan, will you stop?"

"I will not. You're the one who was so sure Drew and I should get together, and here you are acting all coy about Erik." I looked at her and waited until she returned my gaze. "I think this is marvelous. He seemed like a terrific guy. When will he get here?"

"This weekend. Well, Friday. So we can spend the weekend hiking, and then we'll see."

"You seem reluctant to talk about this, but I'm telling you right now, if you need the place to yourself I will make myself scarce."

She gave me the kind of look that told me she wanted to say something she wasn't going to say. She scrambled to her feet. "Let's go find this fire tower."

# CHAPTER TEN

When I left the clinic Monday, there was someone leaning against my car, doing his best to appear casual and failing. Emmett Chaplin.

He didn't move as I approached. "Emmett. Can I help you with something?"

"Why are you here?"

"This is my car."

"You know what the fuck I mean. You've never used. You don't know anything about what we're going through here. Are you just a gawker, or what?"

"What makes you think I've never used?"

"Don't fuck with me. I can tell."

I watched his face for a few seconds and then turned away, tilting my head to get him to follow me as I headed for a wooden beam that lay on the ground, separating the road from the clinic's land. I sat with my back to the road, and Emmett sat a few feet away.

"I'm going to tell you something I haven't told very many people. At least, not in as much detail. When I was a college freshman, I fell madly in love with someone, and although he never said as much, I'm pretty sure he fell for me as well. One day I told him about someone I knew who'd started using fentanyl. He froze, practically solid. I had no idea at the time that he was in recovery." I laughed without humor. "I was so green."

I picked up a small stone and tossed it into the grass in front of us.

"He was from St. Louis, and I was from New Hampshire. At Christmas break, each of us went home. After the break, in January, he didn't come back, and he wouldn't

159

answer my calls or texts. So I hitchhiked off campus out to the house he'd been living in at school. He wasn't there."

I looked briefly at Emmett. His eyes were on the blades of grass in front of his black high-top sneakers.

"There was someone there, though. His mother. She was very nice to me. Told me my friend had gone back into rehab. That was bad enough, in terms of a shock to me. But then she said he didn't want—or wasn't allowed, I can't remember now—to stay connected to anything or anyone. Like, you know, me."

I tossed another pebble. Emmett was barely breathing.

I looked at him. "I loved that man, Emmett. But he didn't tell me he was having trouble in recovery. When it got bad, he left me in the dust. Didn't even tell me that he was going back into rehab. That left me feeling that his relationship with fentanyl—the way it had made him feel, the way he wanted it to make him feel again—had meant more to him than me."

Emmett was as still as stone.

"Now I know that it wasn't about me. I know his relapse was back into something that he wasn't choosing over me. And maybe I don't know what it's like to use. But I know this. My friend was in pain. I never got a chance to find out where that was coming from, but it was clear he'd found a dangerous way to help him avoid it, to make him feel like he was okay after all, to fill some black hole he felt like he'd fall into without the drug."

Still nothing from Emmett.

"I know that it felt to him as though fentanyl was the only thing keeping him alive." I changed from talking about Alden to talking about Emmett. "Whatever you're using, to you it's hope in a hopeless situation. Giving it up feels like letting go of the tree root you're clinging to as your feet dangle and thrash in the air hundreds of feet above jagged rocks. Just the idea makes your desperate need feel even more desperate."

Emmett stood suddenly and paced back and forth a few times between the clinic building and me. Finally he came to a stop a few feet from me.

"How do you know that, man? How the fuck do you *know* that?

I shrugged. "Does it really matter? It's true I don't feel it the way you do. But many people are addicted to something. Some people are addicted to food. Some to sleep. Some to sex. Those things aren't as immediately dangerous as drugs, but the addiction is just as real."

I stood and looked directly into his eyes. "You do not have a corner on suffering. That doesn't diminish it. But I know the knots we tie ourselves into. I know the screaming frustration of not being able to change something about ourselves we think we want to change, because we can't really believe in what's on the other side of that change, and maybe because we can't really believe we can do it."

*Oh, really?* that voice in my head said. *You mean, like how you can't trust the kind of life Drew's offering you?*

We glared at each other, each from his own painful place.

Very quietly, gently, I said, "Does that answer your question?"

Emmett's eyes filled with tears. Before any could fall, he turned and ran. I watched his retreating form chase the setting sun around a curve in the road, wanting so much to follow him, wanting to hold him and let him cry, knowing that would be the wrong thing to do. Instead, I went back into the clinic, found Jennifer, and told her about the exchange.

"He's bonding to you, Nathan." She watched my face. "Are you prepared for that?"

"I hope so. I want to be."

She picked up her phone and dialed a number. "Juan? Can you join me in my office?" She hung up and said, "I love that Emmett is looking to you. But in your position, you can't interact with him on your own to any great extent."

As soon as Jennifer finished telling Juan about my encounter with Emmet, he said, "I'm not surprised about this. Like I told you, Emmett likes you." He grinned. "That was a gutsy thing to say. Not having a corner on suffering."

I shrugged. "He seems to like it when I say gutsy things."

Jennifer chuckled. "He does, doesn't he? So here's an idea. Juan, maybe you could ask him to go into town with you and Nathan one afternoon and get a snack. That would give the three of you a chance to talk in a casual atmosphere."

"Fine with me," Juan said, and looked at me.

"Sure, I'll even treat. But doesn't it seem a little contrived?"

"I understand what you're saying," Jennifer agreed. "But we need to avoid putting you in the position of being alone with Emmett. If he approaches you again, which is obviously unpredictable, it would be even more awkward for you to say, 'Hold that thought while I see if Juan can join us.' And if Juan couldn't join you, you'd have to shut him down. Do you see?"

I didn't know what to say. Jennifer was right, of course. But…. "What if he won't agree to this idea?"

"I know it's a risk. But Nathan, you do understand why this approach is necessary, yes?"

I nodded. "I do. I just wish it didn't mean limiting Emmett."

As I drove home, it hit me how very much I wanted what I'd said to Jennifer to be true. I really did want to help Emmett. It meant more to me than I would have expected to think that he was bonding to me.

I felt something in me soften. I couldn't have said what it was, but the feeling was clear.

Margot was excited/anxious/excited/anxious about Erik's arrival, still scheduled for late Friday afternoon. Tuesday I asked if she wanted me to be somewhere else when he arrived.

"Oh! No, I think it would be better if you were here."

"Why?"

"Just—just because. And anyway, where would you go?" I listened between the lines and heard, *...now that you've been stupid enough to let Drew go.*

"Well, I could stay in Erik's room."

"Be serious!"

"Don't worry about me. I could even go visit El Speed for the weekend."

Then on Wednesday morning, it was, "Nathan? Can I change my mind? About Saturday night, at least? You know, just in case...."

"You may. Consider it changed." I texted El Speed to ask him if that night at his house was an option. He responded, *Absolutely.*

All week I had trouble focusing on work, on conversations with Margot, on anything. My mind kept going to Drew. I began looking forward almost desperately to getting off the island, even for one overnight.

I was gazing sightlessly at my computer screen after lunch on Wednesday when I heard the sound of heavy rain.

"Shit." I gazed through the bars of the recently-repaired window at the heavy downpour.

"What?" Katie wanted to know.

"I was really hoping for a short hike after work. I need to stretch my legs in a big way."

She followed my gaze to the wet window and then looked back at me. "Maybe you could leave a little early and pacify yourself at Cadillac Mountain Sports. They close at five-thirty today. Is there any equipment you could treat yourself to?"

I'd told Katie, in one of the many friendly conversations we'd had in our shared space, about my love of hiking. And damn if she hadn't just hit on a great idea.

"Katie? Will you marry me?"

She laughed her deep chortle. "You're not my type, Nathan. And, while we're at it, that's for more than one reason."

I felt my eyes widen. "Are you shitting me? All this time you knew I was gay, and you never said 'Me too'?"

She threw me a flirtatious look. "How else do you think I've been able to resist you?"

So I got permission to leave at four. Just before I shut down my computer I got an email from Juan, who was in an office upstairs.

*It's a go with E. Tomorrow after teen session. Says he has questions for you.*

More questions. Well, at least he'd agreed to go. That had to be a good thing.

I headed for my car and drove into town. I'd been meaning to visit the store anyway, and I already had something in mind. Crag gloves. I wasn't sure when I would hike the Precipice, but I was sure I would. And I'd really liked the look of those gloves I'd seen on the YouTube hikers.

I picked out a pair that were medium grey synthetic leather on the palms and fingers. The index finger and thumb had darker grey reinforcement, probably because they'd get the most wear. The back was a bright blue stretchy material that also padded the knuckles well. I got the style with no fingertips rather than the full glove; I figured I might need the extra dexterity, and I wasn't getting these for warmth.

I looked around the store while I was there, really loving how in touch with the outdoors the place made me feel. It was cathartic, even though it made me itch to get back on the trail again. After I paid for the gloves, it was an effort to force myself to leave them in the bag and not wear them home.

As I dashed back to my car through the rain, I noticed a grey van on the other side of the street. My feet stopped moving. Was that Drew's?

Fuck it, what did I care? But once I was safely behind the wheel of my car, I craned my neck to see the van better. I couldn't be sure.

I really didn't care, I told myself. I really didn't. I was purged of the feelings from the temptation Drew had teased me with.

Purged or not, I was still a little preoccupied Thursday, at least until the afternoon teen session. There I was able to focus, but only because of Emmett. He was there. He was dressed better than I'd ever seen him, even if still giving off an air of "fuck everyone." But he was not melting in his chair. He sat up. He listened when other people spoke, even though he still said nothing. But he looked at me several times, and once he almost smiled.

Juan drove us in his car into town, Emmett in the front seat. What went through my mind was this: *I've been feeling—maybe even acting—like a little kid lately. Maybe even a sulky, poor-me little kid. But right now, I have to be the adult. No more "poor me."*

It was scary. And it was exhilarating.

Emmett turned as far sideways as the seatbelt would allow, and the questions began. "What do you do for fun?"

That was not the line of questioning I had anticipated. I decided to keep it simple. "I hike."

"Mountains?"

"Yup." I opted against adding, *What else?*

"Where?"

"Anywhere. New Hampshire. Hawai'i. Here."

He gave that some space. Then, out of the blue: "So

what's your addiction?"

In the rear view mirror, I saw Juan's eyes dart toward me and back to the road. A few beats went by as I considered how to answer. "It's complicated. Not as straightforward as drugs or alcohol. Why do you want to know?"

"We're all spilling our guts in there. Even Jennifer. She's told us what it was like for her."

"Well, actually, you're not spilling *your* guts. I haven't heard you say anything about yourself at all."

He turned back toward the front, so I added, "Here's an idea. Once we get where we're going, I'll tell you how my addiction feels, and if you want you can tell me how yours feels."

I got no response; we'd have to see how things went.

Emmett chose the place where I'd had my first meal on the island. As soon as he sat down, he looked at Juan and asked, "You buying?"

Juan looked at me, and I said, "My treat."

"Can I have anything I want?"

I grinned. "Anything but booze."

Emmett ordered two burgers, fries, a cola, and a chocolate milkshake. Juan ordered a burger, fries, and a ginger ale. I ordered a burger and an iced tea.

Emmett looked at me. "You on a diet?"

I laughed. "Hardly. This is a snack for me. My roommate is a fabulous cook, so I need to save myself for dinner."

Emmett looked at me, waiting for something. Finally he said, "Talk."

"What? Oh, my addiction. Right." I leaned back in the chair. Emmett had been right. If I was going to listen to everyone's innermost troubles, it was only fair to share mine—at least with Emmett. It would mean nothing to him that I wasn't supposed to participate during the sessions. So if I wanted Emmett to open up to me, I had to get his trust. Whatever I said, it had to be authentic. It was an effort not to glance at Juan; I was pretty sure anything I said would be treated with confidence, but I'd have to ask him later to be sure.

"Okay, here's my thing. It's very hard for me to believe that I'll ever again feel the way I felt before my brother died. He was five years older than me, and our parents died when I was all of a year old. So he was my dad. He made me feel safe, secure, whole. Then *he* died. And now I don't know where I'll find those feelings again. In fact, I'm kind of afraid to look. I can manage the shit I feel. Letting go of that for something promising but unknown, unfamiliar, scares the hell out of me. Like I'm not good enough for anything better than what I have."

Our food arrived, and the waiter left.

"Your turn." I took a sip of my tea.

He wrapped a hand around his drink, but he didn't lift it. He stared at the dark liquid as if it held some secret he needed to discern.

When he raised his eyes to me, the look was intense. "I hate my life."

"Why?"

From the corner of my eye I saw Juan glance at me. Was I being gutsy again? I had to trust that he would step in if he thought I was going in a direction I shouldn't.

"My parents hate me. My sister hates me." He threw a hand in the air, an impotent gesture. "Drew Madden hates me. You should hate me."

That took me by surprise. "Why should I hate you?"

He gulped half his drink. "I ain't exactly been nice to you. I yelled at you. I called you a fucking secretary. I told you that you don't know a fucking thing."

I nodded. "True. But I choose to believe that was your anger talking. And I don't really think I'm the target of it."

"Why not?"

"Because I'm not the cause of it."

He threw himself back against his chair. "How come

you're such a fucking know-it-all?"

I think it was at this point that I realized I was going to have to draw on everything I'd learned studying psychology in my four years of undergraduate work. I also realized that although Juan was there, this conversation was between Emmett and me. I asked, "How come you keep trying to make me mad at you?"

The waiter set our plates down and disappeared quickly.

I went on. "If you can make me mad at you, that validates your idea that no one cares about you. The more people who hate you, the more right you are. Something like that?"

He just stared at me.

"Why are you angry with Drew Madden?"

"That cock-sucker."

This again. I did glance just for a second at Juan before I said, "Emmett, I'm a cock-sucker. So you won't tarnish his image to me by using that term. Why are you mad at him?" If Juan hadn't known before that I was gay, he knew now.

Emmett didn't care about anyone else coming out of any closet. Right now, everything was all about him. It had to be. "He kidnapped me! He tied me up!"

People at tables nearby were beginning to look our way. Somehow I knew pointing that out to Emmett would only make matters worse.

"And he could have beaten you to a pulp."

"Could not!"

I shrugged. "According to what I saw him do to a couple of hoodlums who attacked him at an ATM, I think he could."

Emmett's eyes shot into mine, and it hit me that he'd been one of those hoodlums. I *knew* I'd seen him before. I did my best to give him a knowing look as I took a sip of my iced tea.

"And the day he kidnapped you," I went on, "he had a

reason why mauling you would have been tempting. But he didn't do that. Instead he left you someplace he hoped you could get some help."

Emmett shoved a few fries into his mouth.

I said, "Seems to me Drew has a reason to be mad at *you*, not the other way around."

"How do you know?" It wasn't a denial.

"I know about Johnny. I knew Drew really cared about him, and I know your part in what happened to him." I felt rather than saw Juan stiffen.

"See? You hate me too."

I poured a pool of ketchup onto my burger. "I don't hate you. I doubt that Drew hates you. Because although we might have some idea what your life is like, we know it's challenging in ways we've never experienced."

Emmett grabbed the ketchup as though I'd been keeping it from him. I took a large bite of my burger and watched him smother everything on his plate with the gloppy red stuff. It was as if he were bleeding all over his plate.

We ate in silence for a while. I was kind of hoping Juan would say something, but he seemed to be leaving it all up to me. I wasn't sure that's what Jennifer had in mind, but there wasn't much I could do about it.

Emmett had finished one burger and was half way through the other before he spoke. "How do you know Drew doesn't hate me? You sucking his cock?"

Juan made a very slight choking sound. I almost smiled. "Not ever. But I know him well enough to believe he feels about you the same way I do."

"You feel sorry for me."

"That's not quite right, no. I do think you're looking for a path you're having trouble finding, and because you're having trouble, you're angry, and you don't care who knows it. It isn't pity. But if I can do something to help, or even just something to make you feel a little less angry, that's what I'd like to do."

169

"Why?"

"I told you about my friend who got lost. I don't want that to happen to other people."

"So I could be anybody."

I smiled at him. "No, Emmett, you couldn't be anybody but you."

He didn't say much of anything else after that. Neither did I. Neither did Juan. But when we got back to the clinic, he said, "See you," before he headed off down the road.

I turned to Juan. "You're a man of few words, aren't you?"

"Yup."

"I thought the idea was that this was a team effort."

He grinned at me. "Seemed like you were doing just fine on your own." As he turned toward the clinic, he added, "He's been clean for almost six months. That's a big deal."

I'd barely settled at my desk the next morning when Juan and Ken stepped into the front office.

In his usual no-nonsense way, Juan announced, "Emmett wants to go hiking with you."

"He—what?"

"I don't hike. But Ken does."

I looked from Juan to Ken. "So the idea is that Ken and I would take him?"

"Right."

A rush of excitement shot through me. But I had to ask, "How does Jennifer feel about this?"

Ken said, "We wanted to check with you first. We'll talk with her as soon as she gets in."

"Does he have any equipment?"

Ken shook his head. "I'm sure he doesn't. That's an issue."

I sat in my chair and gave myself a few seconds to think, while Ken and Juan watched me. I definitely had the money to buy Emmett some equipment. How far into this thing did I want to go? And how much of a prick would I be if I just stepped in and took over buying everything for him? "Let me know what Jennifer says."

I didn't have much time to think. Right after they left, I saw Jennifer come in; she waved as she passed the office. Fifteen minutes later, she called me from her office and asked me to join her there. Juan and Ken were already in the room, sitting in the only two guest chairs, so I stood.

"Ken," Jennifer said, "please tell Nathan what you just told me."

Ken stood and moved to where he could see everyone in the room. "I told her hiking helped me get clean. Now, it helps me *stay* clean. It was a huge step for me, hiking a mountain, accomplishing something on my own that no one could, you know, belittle. No one could take away from me. Something about the physical effort made me feel alive again. So I'm thinking that maybe it could do that for Emmett. Especially since he asked."

I said, "It helped you that much?"

He nodded. "Now, on weekends in the summer, I work for an organization that takes kids with developmental issues hiking. I love seeing them light up when they realize they've done something they didn't know they could do."

Once more wondering how much to butt in about it, I said, "Well, he'd need some equipment."

Ken nodded. "That almost stopped me before I even started hiking. Not having any equipment, I mean. But a friend of my dad's bought me some gear. It was huge, knowing someone was willing to do that for me. To trust me to see it through, you know?"

Jennifer looked at me. "With Ken's experience, he'd be the effective leader. Are you willing to go?"

"Absolutely."

"Excellent. I'll leave the three of you to talk, and you can decide whether you can go forward." She left the room, closing the door behind her.

Ken was obviously very enthusiastic about this plan. "I have a spare day pack he could use. Actually, I could just give it to him."

Juan stood and leaned against the desk. "Like I said, I don't hike. But I could lend him a water bottle and a first aid kit. That something he'd need?"

"It is," said Ken. "Nathan?"

I looked at each of the others in turn. "I think Emmett is taller than anyone here. I have a spare anorak he could have, but I think it will be too small for him. And then there's the question of footwear."

The room was quiet until I asked, "Where would we start? Hiking, I mean."

Ken had obviously thought of that. "I'd suggest Day Mountain. It's got great views, and in case he's not quite as up for this as he thinks, it's not a huge hike."

I struggled to maintain a neutral facial expression, but I felt a bit of a flush at the mention of the mountain Drew had said he and I should tackle "next time." I had already looked it up on my map.

Juan asked, "So could he wear his sneakers?"

"For Day, probably," Ken said. "But if he decides to hike for real, sneakers won't do it. I don't think anything Nathan or I have would fit him. But we might be able to find him some used boots."

Here was my opportunity. "I'm thinking if he had a decent pair of boots he could wear them up Day to start breaking them in. Then if he wanted a bigger hike, he'd have them."

Ken said, "You mean, new ones?"

"Yeah. I think he'd feel more special if he had his own, new, bought just for him. So I'm gonna go out on a limb, here. I'll buy him a pair of boots."

They both turned to stare at me. Ken said, "You realize that even a pair of hiking *shoes* is likely to cost over a hundred bucks. Full boots that support the ankle are more."

"I do know. Yeah. But, see, my grandmother left me some money earlier this year. And I'd really like to do this for Emmett." I looked right into Ken's eyes. "If hiking helped you so much, and if it helps those kids in the summer, I would love to see it help Emmett. And I don't see how it can do that if he sticks to trails he can hike in sneakers. Day Mountain is a great place to start, I agree. But it's only—what, six hundred feet at the summit? And there's a carriage road you can bike up. In my book, it's not a real hiking experience if you don't get above a tree line that's closer to at least a thousand feet. And I don't want to see bikes, cars, or baby carriages at the top."

Juan shrugged, but I knew Ken felt the same way I did. I said, "You told us what it meant that someone bought stuff for you. I'd like to do this for Emmett."

Ken picked up a pen and a note pad from Jennifer's desk. "All right, then. I'll make a list."

Ken and I took Emmett on a buying spree that afternoon. It was fun to see how hard Emmett worked to make it look like this was just another day on the planet for him rather than a really exciting experience.

I ended up getting him a good pair of boots, a few pairs of socks and liners, spare laces, and a blister treatment in case the new boots gave his feet any grief in the beginning. I decided to get him an anorak as well; I knew mine wouldn't fit him.

Afterward, Ken bought us each an ice cream, and we sat on a bench to enjoy it. Ken checked the forecast. "Saturday's not looking great for our hike, but Sunday might be good. Everyone up for that?"

Emmett nodded and took another mouthful of ice cream.

"I'll be in Orono overnight Saturday," I said, "but I

could be back in time for an afternoon hike."

Emmett surprised me by asking, "What's in Orono?"

"Spending the night at my college roommate's place there."

"He your boyfriend?"

"No, Emmett, he isn't. Not that it's any of your business."

Ken's head turned sharply toward me, but he said nothing. Emmett just shrugged and polished off his cone.

Emmett didn't want Ken to drive him home.

"But you need to drop all this stuff off there," Ken told him.

Emmett shook his head. "You keep it. It'll be safe that way."

Safe from what? I didn't want to think too hard about it.

# CHAPTER ELEVEN

"You look terrific, Margot. Don't change again."

"But I'm not sure about this top."

"Sweetie, he isn't going to be critiquing your clothes. That's my job. Why do you think you have a gay roommate? And I'm telling you, stop. You're perfect."

It had taken me some time to talk her down from her original outfit, which had been way over the top—overdressed and trying too hard.

She ran to the window overlooking the parking area. "I wish I'd asked what kind of car he'd rented."

Erik had called Margot from the road and said he expected to be here around four. It was now ten minutes after four, and Margot was figuratively dancing on a razor's edge.

She turned from the window, her face contorted with panic. "Should I have put my hair up? What do you think?" and then "Oh!" as the buzzer rang. She looked frozen, so I went to the intercom.

I heard, "G'day, mate."

I laughed. "Isn't that Australian, you Kiwi?"

"You yanks don't know the difference."

I grinned at Margot as I pressed the buzzer to let him into the lobby. "He hasn't changed, has he?"

She grinned and shook her head.

I pointed to the fireplace. "Go stand over there and try to look like you aren't about to face a firing squad."

I stood in the open door as Erik approached, a broad grin on his handsome, weathered face. He reached out his right hand to shake, but as I took it he wrapped me in a warm hug, patting my back like any proud, straight guy might do. Then he walked past me, paused when he saw Margot, and

175

his smile changed from excitement to tenderness. I loved seeing it.

She smiled and came to him, offering both of her hands. He took them and said, "You are a vision of loveliness."

Margot blushed charmingly, and I thought they looked for all the world like something out of a Victorian romance.

The three of us spent the evening reminiscing about our trip down the Kalalau Trail. I had expected to feel like a third wheel and was staying only because Margot had decided she wanted me there, but it was more like three friends getting together than anything else.

Margot had felt a little sorry for Owen Palmer, the guy Erik had kept in his place with his quiet, acerbic barbs. Over our dinner that night, she brought him up.

"I wonder what Owen is doing now." She looked at Eric. "He did finish with the rest of the group, didn't he?"

"Yup. Complaining all the way. I thought he might have been a little subdued after you fell, especially given that it was his pack cover—that he hadn't fastened well enough— that went flying into your face and took you over the edge. But he didn't change his spots."

I gave a humorless snort. "I seem to remember that he begrudged letting Margot use one of his trekking poles after hers threw itself into oblivion. Conroy had told us to bring only one, anyway."

Margot was more generous. "Well, but he said they were expensive. And I was turning back. He wasn't. I did send it back to him."

Erik smiled at her. "That sounds like you. But he could afford them. He struck me as one of those asshats who think they deserve the best and want everyone to know they have it, but who still pinch every penny just to hear it scream."

"And," I added, "Conroy was right about using only

one. Can you imagine trying to use two poles on that trail? In places, with the rock going straight up on one side and a five-hundred-foot sheer drop on the other, we barely had room for our feet. We were lucky if we could find a place to plant the pole on the ocean side of the trail to brace against falling. Using a pole on the rock side would have sent us right over the edge."

"Hard out."

"Hard out?" I asked.

"Kiwi term. Would right-o be more understandable?"

Margot and I laughed.

Her smile at Erik was unabashedly fond. "I do love those wacky expressions of yours."

"Wacky, are they? You should hear some of yours with fresh ears."

"Like what?"

The two of them launched into silly banter about colloquialisms while I watched. I had always liked Erik. I was extremely fond of Margot. I sat quietly and allowed myself a secret joy at seeing them get together.


Driving off the island the next morning, I felt something lift off of me. It was like when I'd been hiking and wearing a forty-pound pack, and I'd gotten so used to the pack that its weight didn't register. But when I stopped to take a breather and removed the pack, it was almost like floating off the ground for a few minutes.

It wasn't that I didn't like being on the island. I did. I loved the environment, the salty fresh air, the smell of pine woods. Margot and I were getting along really well. I liked my work at the clinic and the people there, and earning Emmett's trust was a heady combination of apprehension and exhilaration.

So the weight must have been Drew. His expectations. He'd tried to make me believe he had no expectations, but if he believed that he was kidding himself.

El Speed was the same old El Speed, which was just what I needed—like putting on a well-worn, favorite shirt and sinking into the feeling that it was okay just to be. Ellie seemed like she was glad to see me, which I hadn't been entirely sure about.

There was an addition to the front of the house: a ramp built onto the opposite side of the porch from the steps. I stopped to examine it.

El Speed stood beside me. "Laura and Tim were here a couple of weeks ago. They couldn't stay with us overnight. We can't accommodate Laura for that. But there's a place nearby where they stayed. We hope they'll be here again."

So they'd had this ramp built just so their friend could get into the house.

They both looked delighted by the portable lamp I'd brought for their patio. "Something to light your meals with until it's too cold to sit outside," I said as Ellie held it up, smiling at it.

I hadn't decided whether to mention Drew to them or not. On my last visit, I'd denied to Ellie that I was seeing anyone, even though I'd already started to have feelings for Drew. This time I could be more definitive. So sitting around the fireplace after dinner, I had more to tell her.

"You know that guy, Drew, who sits at the Precipice with his sign?"

El Speed said, "Sure."

"We, uh, that is, I got to know him a little."

Ellie wanted to know, "Meaning?"

"Meaning we saw each other a few times."

"Saw, as in dated?"

I shrugged. "I guess you could use that word."

"So you're seeing him?"

"Well, no. We—that is, I decided it wasn't a great fit

after all."

Ellie's face told me she was dying to ask more questions, like why not, and what happened, and maybe even couldn't I deal with the wheelchair. But she said nothing.

El Speed was prepared to be philosophical. "Sometimes it just isn't meant to be. Good to figure that out early on."

There were maybe two minutes of silence and then Ellie gave in. "It's okay if you want to talk about it, Nathan."

I let out a long breath.

Before I could say thanks but I didn't feel the need, she said, "He's a nice guy, though. Right?"

I nodded. Clearly, she was the one who wanted to talk about it. "He is. He's a really nice guy. It's just…." I let that hang in the air.

El Speed was with me. "Yeah."

Ellie, I guess, couldn't help herself. "Nathan I—look, I'm just curious. Because, you know, my fried Laura uses a chair. Um, how much of it had to do with that? With Drew's disability?"

I shook my head. "That wasn't really it. He's unbelievably independent. Even has a powered chair that raises him to a standing position. And he has another one designed for off-road trails. He drives this van that opens in the back and has a ramp he can lower with a remote. He rolls into the back, and then he transfers to the driver's seat. It's pretty amazing."

More silence. We watched the fire until El Speed asked, "Could he have a full relationship? It's just that sometimes, with a spinal injury…."

I grinned at my friend. "I didn't get a chance to check that out, but he says he could." I shifted my position in the corduroy-covered chair. "Plus, you know, I'm going to be in school next year. I won't be on the island."

Ellie thought otherwise. "You could be. It's not that long a drive from Orono."

"I don't know yet whether I'll get in here."

Ellie bit her lip like she wasn't quite sure whether to say what was on her mind. She gave in to temptation. "I think that if you want something to come into your life, you have to make space for it."

Something about that shocked me into silence. I barely heard El Speed, in his gentle but unequivocal way, repeat what he'd already said. "Sometimes it's just not meant to be."

Lying in that narrow bed later, in the cozy room under the eaves, it took me a while to get to sleep. Something about the space had an intimate feel that was both comfortable and confining. My mind didn't race, but it was definitely not ready to settle.

I'd told Ellie it wasn't Drew's chair that was the problem. I'd leaned, at least a little, on the fact that I was on the island only temporarily.

And something in me knew I'd been blowing smoke.

The real question was whether I was kidding myself that I wanted a relationship. With anyone.

*If you want something to come into your life, you have to make space for it.*

My whole body twitched, and I shifted position under the covers.

Maybe I should try to answer a related question: What did I want in a partner?

I wanted someone who wanted to be with me as much as I wanted to be with him. Someone who would be there for the long haul, as in marriage. As in as permanent as things get in this life. Someone with whom I could enjoy sex without making the relationship about that. Someone I wanted to wake up next to, for years and years. Someone who wouldn't be afraid or ashamed to cry and who wouldn't think less of me if I cried. Someone who cared about other people enough to reach out and help them. Someone who was open to new ideas but also wasn't bored with contentment.

I sat bolt upright and nearly hit my head on the slanted ceiling above the bed.

I had just described Drew Madden.

Just as driving off the island had lifted a weight, driving back dropped it onto my shoulders again. I had to go through Somesville and very close to Drew's house to get to Southwest Harbor. The closer I got, the heavier that weight felt.

To take my mind off of Drew, I focused on today's hike. It still felt surprising to me that Emmett had suggested this activity. I couldn't help getting a rush out of the idea that it was because of what I had told him I do for fun.

Ken and Emmett were already at the clinic, where we'd agreed to meet, when I got there at half past one. They were sitting on that wooden beam where Emmett and I had sat when I'd told him about Alden. Emmett was already in his new boots and doing his best to act like it was no big deal.

Ken drove us in his Jeep to the parking area off of Route 3. I sat in the back so Emmett could take everything in. When we got out of the car, I waited for Ken to lead the way and indicated to Emmett to go ahead of me. Emmett needed to know who was in charge, and I felt the need to be the sweep—a kind of co-leader position in the back to make sure no one is having trouble.

Once we were on the trail, pretty immediately it went steeply up over a rocky section. I watched as Emmett struggled a little to figure out where and how to plant his feet, but pretty soon I saw he was watching Ken, imitating his choices. I took that as a good sign.

The trail wasn't especially challenging after that initial section, but even so, Ken didn't set a fast pace. He stopped frequently for water and to admire the view and, I was sure, to assess Emmett's condition.

For his part, Emmett was doing really well. It seemed

to me that his face had lost most of that "fuck you" expression, and he was starting to look like he might be enjoying himself just a little.

For the final stretch of trail up to the summit, Ken picked up the pace quite a bit. Emmett stayed right with him, even looking like he might want to overtake Ken.

We sat together at the summit, where a chilly breeze came to us from over the water. The sun poked in and out between large patches of clouds, some white and some grey, all moving quickly across the blue sky. Ken and I had each brought some gorp that we pooled together, and Emmett ate quite a bit of it.

As Emmett tipped his water bottle over his mouth to catch the last drops, I realized Ken had let him drink however much he'd wanted during breaks. Running out of water is the best way to learn that you must ration what you have, and also to decide how much water to bring on your next hike.

I handed Emmett my bottle. He nodded as he took it. He didn't take much, which I thought was another good sign; he was considering others.

We didn't talk much. I wasn't sure whether Ken was letting Emmett decide whether to speak, or if Ken was a quiet hiker. I liked the silence.

After our descent, as we approached the parking lot, I noticed Emmett favoring his right foot.

"Blister?" I asked.

"Maybe. But I think my knee's tired."

Ken had Emmett sit on the open back of the Jeep. "I'm going to test your knee. That okay?"

Emmett nodded, and Ken massaged Emmett's right thigh just above the knee. He said, "Descending a steep trail can do a number on the muscles right here. If you want, later I'll show you an exercise you can do to strengthen them. Now take your boots and socks off and we can check for hot spots."

Based on an examination of Emmett's feet, Ken put

blister treatment on the backs of both heels. Then he said, "If you're up for it, we can drive to the summit of Cadillac and walk around a little. What do you think?"

Emmett shrugged, so I said to him, "I'm up for that if you are."


I'd never been to the summit of Cadillac Mountain, though I'd known there was a road up to it. Emmet said little as he walked from spot to spot, but it seemed like he was getting a kick out of the views.

At one point, out of Emmet's hearing, I said to Ken, "This was a great idea, coming up here. He's seeing what things look like from this high up, and it might make him want to try a bigger climb next time."

"Right. And I didn't want to come here first, or Day Mountain would have seemed like not much of an accomplishment."

When we got back to the clinic, Emmett grabbed his sneakers and his battered leather jacket from the back of the Jeep. He took off his boots and the anorak, which he handed to Ken, along with the day pack. Then he said, "Thanks," and headed off.

I had to ask. "Do you know why he doesn't want to take these things home?"

"I don't know for sure, but I think his sister is still using. I think he's afraid she'd sell anything she could get money for."

"Jesus."

Ken nodded. "It's a testament to Emmett's determination that he's been able to stay sober, given his family situation. Dad's a drunk, Mom sleeps around. No wonder he started using."

"And maybe in a certain way, no wonder he stopped."

Margot and Erik were putting the final touches on dinner. I'd told them I could eat elsewhere if they wanted to be alone, but Erik had insisted that I join them. Even so, when I went into the condo they were—well, they were in the kitchen, but it wasn't just dinner that was heating up. I didn't mean to interrupt a close embrace and a passionate kiss, but that's what happened.

"Carry on," I called as I headed for my bedroom.

"Nah, mate," Erik said. "We're done here. Done with this, anyway." And he gave Margot a quick kiss. "For now."

When I'd met Erik, as much as I'd liked him, there had been something dark hanging over him. At one point during the hike he'd told me his wife had died of cancer the previous year. He'd looked like he was still mourning. If Margot could bring him back to life, back to joy, I was all for that. And if he could be the kind of man her family had never shown her, I was all for that, too.

I hung out with them in the living room after dinner. Each of us had a glass of my Glenfiddich single malt as we chatted. I talked a little about Emmett (anonymously) and about my trip to Orono, and then Erik opened another line of conversation.

"I hope it wasn't out of line for Margot to tell me about your friend Drew."

A quick glance at Margot, who dropped her eyes, told me she'd spilled everything.

"Not much to tell."

He tilted head slightly and watched me as he took a sip of scotch. His movements were slow as though he were contemplating something. "You and Conroy. On the hike, you weren't a thing anymore, eh?"

I felt my back stiffen. "Anymore" implied that we had been a thing. I'd thought Conroy and I had been very discreet on the hike. We hadn't seen each other for weeks before that, and once we were on the trail I figured I looked like just another hiker. Or so I'd thought. But after turning back with

Margot, I'd found out that she had sussed us out. Now, it seems, Erik had, too.

My voice a little edgy, I asked, "Did Margot tell you that, too?"

"Nah, mate. No one needed to tell me that."

I gave up on my righteous indignation. "No. We weren't a thing anymore."

He took another slow sip. "That seemed like a good thing to me at the time. I figured you could do better than Conroy. You deserved better than Conroy."

He emptied his glass, gazed at it for a second, and set it down. "Maybe I was wrong."

Stunned, I sat where I was and watched as Margot went to the door with Erik; evidently he was going back to his hotel. They stepped outside the door briefly. By the time Margot came in again, I was already in my room with the door shut.


During Monday's teen session, I noticed that Emmett had put on his hiking boots. He must have gotten to the clinic early so he could fetch them from Ken's office. And something else was noteworthy: He spoke.

"It's just one more thing I can't do right."

I did my best to imitate Jennifer, who was doing really well at not looking surprised. I barely saw her touch the screen on her phone.

Jennifer asked, "What else can't you do right, Emmett?"

"Anything. Like, finish homework. I can start it, but I can't finish it."

"Does something make you stop? An interruption? A feeling?"

He glared at her. "Like you don't know." She waited, and he spoke again. "It. It pushes itself into my brain. I can't even read a paragraph, and suddenly it's right there."

"What does it feel like to deny it?"

I could see his jaw grinding, as though there were words he wanted to shout but also wanted to swallow. The shout won. "It hurts, okay?"

Jennifer opened her mouth, about to say something else, but Emmett was up and out of the room faster than she could speak. I looked at her, the question *Should I go after him* in my eyes. She shook her head, tiny motions, but enough to communicate.

After the session Jennifer asked me to come into her office.

"I didn't want you to follow Emmett," she said, "because I'd signaled Juan to be ready in case he bolted."

"How did you know he would?"

"I didn't know it would be today. But Juan has told me that Emmett is developing a trust for you he hasn't shown for anyone else. When this happens with a client, it can be very frightening for them, and especially for the teens. They start to open up, and they realize they're making themselves vulnerable. They know that at some point they're going to have to choose between that trust and their addiction. And they bolt, in one way or another. So Juan has been on the alert for about a week now."

"But why shouldn't I have followed him?"

She took a slow breath. "You are doing wonderful things with him, Nathan. You've made friends with him. I hope that can continue. But you're not a counsellor. I can't put you in the position of dealing with a client in crisis, and I can't put the client in your care, either."

"So—I have to wait for him to come to me?"

She smiled. "Hasn't he been doing that?"

I didn't get a lot more work done that afternoon. I was thinking about Emmett, about what he'd said, and about whether I had anything in my non-counselor bag of tricks that might help him. What Jennifer had said had stung a little, but I knew she was right. Even so, I'd already had some kind of effect on him—a good one, to all appearances—and I wanted to deepen the connection. After all, wasn't connection said to be the opposite of addiction? It was on that poster in the front hall, and since I'd been here at the clinic, I'd heard the same thing, or something very like it, said a number of times. And, as Jennifer had said, someone in crisis might go toward trust or toward the addiction, but they wouldn't sit still for long.

So sitting at my desk, and driving home that night, and alone at home (with Margot and Erik out on the town someplace), I thought about addiction, about what it meant, about what it felt like, and about how to lessen its hold.

Between my undergraduate work and my own research, I had learned a few things. If someone in addiction can figure out what they want to change about their life—the way they think of themselves, how they treat other people, what their life could be like without the addiction—just figuring those things out is a good place to start.

Change, though, brings up the pain and the fear of not having whatever you're addicted to in your life anymore.

So many addicts believe they are worthless. And they feel like they can't trust anything or anyone—and that no one trusts them, and probably shouldn't. This is an extremely painful place to be. To avoid that pain, they try to replace it with something external; if they're good for nothing, then good must be something outside of them. At the very least, good can be a feeling they get from what they're addicted to, and if it's powerful enough it blocks out the feelings of worthlessness. Temporarily.

Once they're addicted, the addiction itself becomes the only thing they trust. And the realization that they're addicts deepens—confirms—their sense of guilt and self-loathing.

Like I'd said to Emmett once, addiction might come from different things for different people. Anyone can be an addict to *something*. But the truth that addicts need to see is that we can't be better within ourselves by reaching out to grasp something outside of ourselves: drugs, alcohol, sex, food, whatever. I'd told Jennifer that addiction was a substitution. It was second-best rather than what the addict really wants.

El Speed used to play this song by David Wilcox. One line in it stuck in my head: "You can get what's second-best, but it's hard to get enough."

The way I saw it, that was the essence of addiction.

So what would be something Emmett could reach for inside himself rather that outside himself? Could climbing mountains give him enough confidence in himself, in his own ability to accomplish something, to point at least one of his feet toward recovery?

Margot wasn't home yet by the time I went to bed. I heard her come in later, because I was still awake—all those issues and questions bouncing around in my head.

It made a change from obsessing on Drew.


All that week, it seemed that every time I went anywhere other than work or home, I saw Drew, or I saw his van. Sometimes I was sure he saw me. Sometimes I was pretty sure he hadn't. We didn't even nod to each other, let alone speak. Every time, Erik's words stung me yet again. Those words carried an implication: If I didn't deserve better than Conroy, then Drew deserved better than me. And every time, the wound those words had made went deeper.

By Thursday morning, to avoid the pain of that wound, I forced myself to think about hiking. Like any other addict, I was using something that gave me pleasure to block negative feelings about myself.

Hiking was, at least, a healthy addiction. Being on the trail had always been a solace to me, even at times when I hadn't felt the need to bind a wound. And I realized that I'd had an image in the back of my mind for a while: my hands, snugly inside my crag gloves, fingers curled around the edge of a granite boulder as I prepared to pull myself up and over the rock formation. From the YouTube images, probably shot from a GoPro on the climber's head, all you could see of him was the hands and forearms. So it was easy to picture myself in the place of that climber working his way up the Precipice Trail. Sitting in teen session Thursday, no Emmett in sight, I decided that Saturday, come hell or high water (well, barring an ice storm or a nor'easter), I would climb that trail. Maybe Drew would be there with his sign. Maybe he wouldn't. Didn't matter. That hike would be mine.

At the teen session that afternoon, Emmett was once again wearing decent clothes and his new boots. But he looked sulky, and he said nothing.

It wasn't great hiking weather on Saturday. It was cold, and windy, and there was the threat of light rain or drizzle.

I didn't care.

Margot did care. She tried to talk me out of it, even as Erik (who hadn't left the island yet) pulled open her laptop to watch a YouTube vid of the ascent. As I drove to the trailhead, I put Margot's parting words aside: "If you die, can I have your hiking gear?"

"And my car," I'd called out as I'd left the condo.

There was only one other vehicle in the parking lot. A grey van. And over near the trailhead was a guy in a wheelchair. Deja vu all over again.

I turned the ringer on my phone off; this was a dangerous trail, and I didn't want a message or a call to distract me. I had a light pack: just water, a couple of power bars, a waterproof windbreaker, a wool sweater, spare socks, a first-aid kit, my phone, and a whistle. Before closing the back hatch of the car, I pulled on my crag gloves and shrugged into the pack.

Determined not to be influenced by Drew, I walked with easy strides toward the trail. I looked at him as I got close. He was watching me. I smiled and nodded. He didn't. He looked worried.

Climbing that starting flight of granite steps, I wondered what he was even doing here. Surely, no one would take kids up today. Maybe Drew thought the weather was bad enough that no one should hike, child or adult. But he hadn't tried to stop me. Hadn't lifted his sign. Not like that first time, when he'd wanted to get my attention.

I'd passed a couple of general warning signs already, but as the trail grew steep I passed a few more.

Before long there wasn't much of what most people would think of as a trail. Rectangles of blue paint led me up a steep incline of huge, tumbled boulders, skinny trees—beeches and birches mostly—poking up from where they'd managed to find enough dirt to send down roots. The boulders got bigger, and the grade grew steeper. I was breathing hard, and the pounding of my boots on the granite and my heart in my chest were the only sounds I heard. There was some wind, but I couldn't hear it unless I stood still, sniffing in through my nose as exertion caused my sinuses to run.

Soon I encountered the first iron rungs, plunged deep into vertical granite by some mysterious process I couldn't imagine. The rungs seemed to have been placed far enough apart from each other as to make it impossible—or nearly impossible, at least—for a child to scale up and over onto the top of the rock. It was like the rungs were saying, *Now would be a good time for you to turn around.*

I came to a stop at the bottom of what must have been a massive rock slide. It was literally a field of large boulders, as though some gargantuan being had dropped a cartload of them onto the hillside. Hands on hips to allow my chest to expand fully, I let my breathing slow almost to normal before tackling this next obstacle.

Once past that boulder field, I found myself walking along ledges narrow enough to compete with the Kalalau, steep granite going straight up on my left, steep granite going straight down on my right and into an abyss, and usually with nothing to hold on to. Some ledges ended at a metal ladder, or at another set of iron rungs, themselves seeming to cling to the rock for dear life.

Occasionally there were wooden planks set as a walkway or a rudimentary bridge, dangling above a cavernous drop, with nothing but a narrow iron rail between me and certain death. Even though I knew the name of the man who had designed and worked on this trail, I had to wonder, *What kind of guy would build this thing? Who was the genius/idiot who determined where to climb this cliff, where to place the rungs,* how *to place the rungs, and why this was the best route up?*

I might have asked why anyone would climb this trail at all, but I knew. Because here I was.

I passed the turnoff to the Orange and Black Trail, the blue slashes of the Precipice leading me through a very narrow gap between a huge boulder on the right and, on the left, another slab that must once have been part of the larger piece, broken off in some cataclysmic event.

After that, the trail went nearly straight up over rungs and ladders on sheer, exposed cliffs. It went on and on. And it was the sort of thing that could kill a person. I found myself wondering how far up the trail the young Darren and his parents had made it before Drew had sacrificed himself to save the boy.

There were precious few places where I could just walk, and very few where I didn't use hands and arms, either to support my balance or to help pull me up over boulders— with or without rungs and ladders. I was very glad of my gloves—not only because they protected my hands from the sharp, gritty rock surfaces, but also because the exertion made me sweat everywhere, and there's no way I'd want a slippery grip on those iron bars.

At one point, after scrambling up a long set of rungs, I stood on a narrow section of rock and looked off into the distance as the wind cooled my face. The tops of trees I had passed moments ago were many feet below me. Over the water, I could see storm clouds whipping around, curtains of what must be rain falling miles away. A sudden gust of wind pushed me backward against the rock face, and I grabbed for the lowest rung on the next ladder I'd have to climb.

I looked hard at that rung and asked, aloud, "Does someone climb this trail every once in a while to be sure all these rungs are secure?" Because, seriously, if that one rung had been wobbly, might I have gone over the edge to end up like Drew?

I'd been climbing for maybe forty minutes, pushing myself hard and stopping seldom, so I was glad to get to an area that the video had shown was not far from the summit of Champlain. I walked across exposed granite ledges, led by a combination of blue paint on the stone and small cairns that I would have been needed if there'd been snow on the rock.

I had been feeling pretty drained of energy just before coming out onto this open part of the mountain. Getting above tree line had always made me feel exhilarated and energized, and I picked up my pace.

Suddenly I stopped, a very particular cairn in front of me. About eighteen inches high, it was shaped almost like a stone person. Memories crashed into my brain. They were memories of a smaller, carved stone: Inuit art, an inukshuk, placed conspicuously in the living room of Alden's college apartment. There were also memories of another inukshuk, in the living room of the house Conroy had stayed in last year. And here was another. These things were following me around.

What was that about?

The inukshuk is a practical thing. Typically as tall as a human, these piles of stone were placed strategically by people living in the Arctic, where a thick layer of snow would render one section of tundra indistinguishable from another. Inukshuks might have led the way to settlements, or food storage, or anywhere you might need to go. Their job was to make sure you didn't get lost. Otherwise, you'd die.

Was there a message for me here? Was I in need of guidance to keep me from getting lost? Was the inukshuk trying to save my life in some way?

Another gust of wind shoved me sideways. I shook myself off and moved onward, leaning forward to avoid being shoved again.

As I stepped up over the last edge of granite, I noticed a carving I'd expected to see:

EH May 9 1904

REB

TIN

When I'd looked up information about this trail, I'd discovered that the trail, opened in 1904, had been built by one Rudolph Brunnow. So REB was him. No one seemed to know what EH or TIN stood for, but there they were, so they must have been important to REB. Had they helped him build this trail, perhaps? Had they funded the effort?

I knew I'd reached the summit when I saw a large pile of stones around a wooden stake, with pointed pieces of board nailed to it, directing hikers to trails whose names were engraved on the boards. Hunching against the wind, I looked back to the southeast. The rain curtain was closer, and the dark clouds were nearly overhead. I could barely see the bits of land, green and brown, that poked out into the ocean. The water was an ominous grey, punctuated by churning whitecaps.

I had two choices, now. I could either go back down the way I'd come up, which was not recommended but which would be faster, or I could follow another trail down to where it intersected with a trail that would lead to the parking lot. That would take longer, but it would go through more wooded areas, and I wouldn't have to lower myself down iron rungs and ladders, buffeted by winds, with rain making the metal slippery despite my gloves.

I chose the safer route. I'm not an idiot. And faster might mean falling. That would be faster, all right.


It was pouring rain, driven nearly sideways by the wind, when I approached the parking lot. Aloud I said, "Light rain or drizzle, was it?"

I stepped out onto the tarmac of the parking lot and stopped short. Drew was still there. He had covered himself in a dark green hooded rain poncho that draped over both himself and the chair, making him look for all the world like some mountain troll waiting to ambush unwary wanderers.

He must have taken his sign to the van and come back to resume this post, because the sign wasn't beside him, and there was no room for it under the poncho. But why was he still here? His mission here was to use the sign to get people to talk to him so he could convince them to abandon their climbing plans. Without the sign, why was he here?

As soon as he saw me, he lifted the edges of the poncho and started to wheel over to his van. I ran after him.

I had to shout over the wind. "What are you doing here?"

"What do you think?"

I shook my head.

He said, "I wasn't leaving here until I knew you'd made it down safely."

He stared up at me, rainwater rolling down his face like Nature's tears. I was transfixed. I didn't move. He didn't move.

This storm didn't come with thunder and lightning. Even so, a bolt of something electric struck my brain and then my heart.

Was Drew my inukshuk?

Every trail marker I'd seen had pointed toward Drew. His name was carved onto every piece of figurative wood fastened to every post I had come across for weeks. Had I been an idiot to ignore them? To pretend they didn't matter?

Once, hiking alone, I'd gotten completely lost. I'd decided to follow a trail that I knew hadn't been used for years, partially because I was so full of myself I was sure I wouldn't be misled. My attitude was that I could find any trail, or I'd make my own.

This trail had a few markers at the start, but soon it was more like I was following the path of least resistance, finding only the occasional paint splash in the underbrush.

About half-way up the mountain, I'd come to a thickly wooded section that leveled out, not going up or down. I strode into it confidently, but before long I realized there was no clear way through it. So I started scouring the ground for paint splashes on rocks, or on exposed granite, or on anything at all. At one point I looked up and realized that I no longer knew which direction I had come from.

At first I looked for signs of broken twigs, torn leaves, anything to show me where I'd been. But I'd circled a large enough area thoroughly enough, trying to find a marker, that these signs were everywhere.

I began to panic. And in my panic I turned around and around, nearly making myself dizzy. Finally I stopped, found a low boulder and sat on it, closed my eyes, and waited until I calmed myself down. Before I opened my eyes, I told myself that whatever direction I was facing, that's the way I would go.

I opened my eyes, stood, and walked forward. Within a couple of minutes, I realized I had reversed direction and was now walking back down the way I had come up.

With this memory in my mind, I decided that going in circles had to stop. I had to go forward, whatever direction that turned out to be. It no longer felt like the opposite direction from Drew was the right one. But if toward Drew turned out to be the wrong direction, at least I wouldn't be making myself dizzy. At least I would know.

Drew was still watching my face, as though he knew what was going through my mind. None of my reasons for passing up the potential of this man's love meant anything. None of them held rainwater. They melted away as if made of salt.

I blinked hard. My breath caught in my throat, so that my words sounded strangled. "Can we try again?"

He backed the chair away from me a little and stopped. "Come to me tomorrow. Mid-afternoon. We'll see what happens."

I stepped away from the van so he could lower the ramp and wheel himself in. He lifted the poncho off. I reached in, took it, and shook it off as best I could given that the rain was still pelting. I tossed it onto the floor of the van as he went through the process of moving into the driver's seat. The ramp withdrew, the back of the van closed, and as Drew drove away I watched sheets of rain enveloped him.

My hair was drenched. Water leaked in at my neck and found its way down the middle of my back. I shivered with cold.

And I felt ridiculously happy.


I threw my pack into the back of my car and fished my phone out. I tossed the anorak in and dashed for the protection of the front seat. On my phone were four messages from Margot, sounding successively more frantic.

I was just about to call her when I saw her little red Honda pull into the parking lot, Erik beside her in the front seat. She pulled in beside me as I placed the call rather than open a window in this storm.

"What the hell, Nathan? Are you out of our mind?"

"I know, I know. But I didn't come down the Precipice. I went around."

"You're still an idiot!"

"*I'm* an idiot? Well, maybe, but just what did you think *you* were going to do once you got here?"

She had no response to that. "Why didn't you answer your phone?"

I started to explain but changed my mind. "Can we talk at home? I'm drenched and freezing."

Erik's drawl came over the line. "And it serves you right."

As I pulled the car around to head back to the road, I looked up into the woods at the trailhead. That gate was open. I wondered whether it was ever closed for weather, or just for falcons. Seemed like it should be closed now so idiots wouldn't attempt the climb. I smiled at that gate. Maybe I was an idiot. But I was a happy idiot.

Happy or not, I drove myself crazy all Saturday night, barely sleeping. "Come to me tomorrow." That's what Drew had said. But what did that mean? Sure, okay, it meant maybe there was a chance for a relationship. But this had been the strangest lead-up to being with a guy I'd ever heard about, let alone experienced. Usually there's this dance, part verbal and part physical, and eventually someone says something directly related to getting together. Or maybe two bodies just get really close, and something happens. But to have someone come right out and say *I want you let's see what we can be together* was—well, it just wasn't done. Or, it wasn't how it happened. Or—fuck, I didn't know what I meant.

I threw the covers off at around two and went outside to sit on the deck, a blanket wrapped around me, a glass of scotch in one hand and my phone beside me. At first I just stared out at the ocean past the harbor. But my mind wouldn't stop.

*When you're ready.* The first time I'd gone to Drew's house, he had played that song for me. I'd had no doubt at the time that it was directed at me, and I was still sure about that. I looked up the lyrics online.

The singer is talking to someone who's trying to convince themselves of something, but the singer knows it isn't quite true. That other person is keeping his distance, trying to carry too much weight alone, and taking "the long way to come around." But the singer says she'll be there, waiting for the call. Her door is open. "When you're ready."

Circles. Fucking circles. I'd been torturing myself for weeks, going round and round with questions I couldn't answer, questions I barely understood. Were the questions themselves the weight I was carrying around, the weight I didn't need to carry alone?

Suddenly a line from that song Cotton played at Neil's funeral came to me. The song was *Live It*. After the shock of finding out it had been his favorite song, I'd downloaded a copy of it. And one line from it seemed especially applicable right now.

"The knots that tie us down are tangled by ourselves."

And that's what I'd been doing. Tying myself down with knots. Knots made from turning in useless, unproductive, entangling circles. It was up to me to untangle them.

So here was the important question: Was I ready to find out what it meant to share my weight with Drew and help him with his? Yes or no? I was ready to stop going in circles, to move forward. That much, I knew.

So, yes. I was ready.

# CHAPTER TWELVE

Sunday dawned bright and fresh, chilly but not cold. I took Margot and Erik out for a late breakfast, despite knowing that she was almost obnoxiously ecstatic about my giving this thing with Drew another go. To be honest, it was more like I needed to distract myself than anything else.

Driving to Drew's in the afternoon, after texting him that I was on my way, the mood I was in wasn't the same as it had been the last time I'd driven here, and yet there were similarities. As before, I didn't really know what Drew had in mind, and again I felt in the dark. Was he thinking we'd make that porn scene a reality? Or was he angry with me for calling things off? Both? Neither?

It wasn't until I turned into his driveway at around half-past two that it occurred to me I should have come up with some intentions of my own. Once again, I was allowing myself to be in the position of following someone else's lead. And I had promised myself I wouldn't do that again.

But for now, I was here. I pulled alongside the van in Drew's driveway, the back of it standing open, the ramp already down. He was in his trail chair, the blue handles and spokes brilliant in the afternoon sun, his face turned to catch what warmth the rays could offer.

He opened his eyes and smiled as I approached. "Hey, Nathan."

"Hey." I felt awkward. What should I say? How should I act?

Drew solved that, of course. "Hop in." A push or two on the handles brought the chair into position for rolling in. I climbed into the passenger seat and watched his smooth motions as he maneuvered himself behind the wheel.

Clearly we were not going to be jumping each other's bones in the house. I had to admit that the idea had its appeal, and it had been—Christ, over three months—since I'd had sex with anyone other than myself. But Drew was in control.

Resigned to my follower role for the moment, I asked, "Where are we going?"

"Day Mountain. The one I told you about during our tour of Eagle Lake."

He pulled onto the road, and immediately I felt torn. Should I tell him I'd already climbed it? Ridiculously, I was put in mind of when a couple agree to see a movie together, and then one of them goes without the other. I hadn't made a decision about revealing my "betrayal" before Drew broke the silence.

"Did you enjoy your hike yesterday?"

It took me a couple of seconds to adjust; he wasn't referring to Day. He was referring to the Precipice. "I did. I like it when I don't see other hikers."

He let a few beats go by. Then, "Why did you do that hike yesterday, of all days?"

"It was time. I don't know what else to say. I'd been thinking about it all week." I chuckled nervously. "Maybe if I were still in school, I would have skipped classes to go on a better day during the week. But now that I'm a working stiff, my options are more limited."

Silence.

"And besides," I added, "the prediction wasn't for a rainstorm. Not like that."

"The ocean makes its own weather."

Where had I heard that before? Oh, yeah. "My brother used to say that about mountains."

"He was right."

As he drove, Drew pointed out landmarks and locations that we passed, or that we could see in the distance.

During a pause, I asked, "Could you ever see yourself living someplace else?"

"Depends."

"On?"

He glanced at me briefly and smiled. "A number of things."

It took nearly half an hour, what with driving around the north end of the Sound and not being able to drive straight through the park. And then Drew turned off the road in a place I hadn't expected. I knew the parking area was off of Route 3. But Drew pulled off that road at Seal Harbor and drove north to Wildwood Stables.

"Are we riding horses?" I asked.

"Nope."

"Because isn't the parking area for Day over there someplace?" I pointed more or less south.

"It is." He pulled into a space and started the process of getting himself out of the van and onto his trail chair.

It occurred to me that although this was still interesting to me, at some point it would no longer be interesting. Just necessary. There would be many things about being with Drew that would take longer because of his disability. He had no choice about that. I did. If I went into this relationship, it would need to be with my eyes open.

I was almost annoyed at his brief, unhelpful responses. "So you want to be mysterious and not tell me what we're doing. Is that it?" He closed the back of the van and grinned at me but said nothing. So I told him, "As it happens, I've climbed Day Mountain."

He blinked. "You have? When?" I think he was just surprised, not pissed.

"Last Sunday. I hiked it with Ken, one of the clinic counselors. And with one of the members who's been doing really well."

"So you went up the trail, then? We're going up the carriage road."

"Don't both of them start at the same place?"

"From the Route 3 parking area, the access to the Day

Mountain carriage road goes up an extremely steep slope. I don't think there's a person alive who could get up it in any kind of wheelchair. So I have to start from here."

It was everything I could do not to tell him, *Why didn't you just say so?* But I figured I was kind of on trial today. I kept my mouth shut. And besides, I'd seen that slope. I'd climbed it on my own two feet. If I'd given any thought to Drew's disability, I'd have realized that no wheelchair could make it up.

Shame on me.

"You ready? Let's head out." And he pushed on those blue handles and rolled away.

From the stables, we had to go up a pretty steep incline to get to the carriage road. Drew struggled a bit, but he made it.

"I'm sorry I didn't think about the Route 3 access," I told Drew. "I should have realized there was no way a chair could go up there."

Drew nodded and half-smiled. It wasn't much in the way of forgiveness, but I'd take it.

Once we were on the carriage road, I opened a subject I wanted to hear Drew talk about in his own words. Emmett Chaplin.

"I'd like to ask you about something that happened at the clinic a couple of weeks ago. It concerns Emmett Chaplin."

Drew's pace slowed and he looked at me, apparently confused. But then he nodded and picked up his pace again.

I had no trouble keeping up with him here; in fact, it felt slow-going for me. The road was a little washboard-like, which made it harder in a wheelchair, and it was steep enough that Drew had to work.

Finally he said, "To be honest, I'd rather not talk until we're up. This is a real workout for me."

"Got it."

So I had time to admire the views, which got better and

better as we ascended. The road followed along a ridge overlooking the ocean. We would come down the same way we went up; it was not a loop, like Eagle Lake had been.

Drew worked harder and harder, slowing down for the steeper sections. I slowed with him, even though the pace often seemed snail-like. Small groups of cyclists whizzed past us from time to time. Other people, on foot, also made better progress than Drew and I were making.

At one point, Drew stopped at a spot with a broad ocean vista. Between panted breaths, he said, "Need a water break. Plus," and he held his arm out toward the sea, "there's all this."

I stood beside him in silent admiration for what this climb took out of him, for what an effort it was. I was pretty sure he wouldn't want me to say that out loud.

We stopped a few more times before we reached the summit, where I sat on the ground a few feet from the side of his chair. It was rather nice, sitting there with him and not talking, just being. There was a bit of a chilly breeze, but we were dressed for it.

Drew broke the silence. "So you want to know about Emmett."

"Please."

"I don't think he's a bad kid. His parents are, as my mother used to say, not good people. That's not his fault, but it seems to have affected his view of life. I assume you've encountered him at the clinic."

"Yeah."

"I'd known the father of another kid, Johnny Crosby, for a while. Johnny was injured in a car accident when he was nine. Had to use a chair after that, and he hated it. Eventually he started using drugs, probably at least in part due to chronic pain. His father begged me to talk to the kid, and we started going on outings together. I was trying to help him handle being in the chair and everything that means."

He stopped for a drink of water. I didn't interrupt.

"I managed to convince him to join the clinic, and he was doing okay but not great. And for some reason," He stopped, and I turned to look at him. His face was twisted, but whether it was anger or pain I couldn't tell. "I feel like I should have seen it coming. But I didn't. For some reason he gave in and decided to use again, which I guess happens a lot with people in recovery. His old dealer had been arrested. He knew Emmett was using, so he went to him. And Emmett put him in touch with a really bad guy. The heroin he sold Johnny was laced with fentanyl."

Drew's voice grew a little hoarse, here; I think he was trying not to cry. "Johnny died." He took a deep breath. "I'd met Emmett once or twice, because the boys had been friends when they were younger. So I did a very stupid thing. I grabbed the kid one day as he was leaving school. Had to tie his hands and ankles together, he fought so hard, understandably. Dumped him at the clinic doorstep. I wasn't thinking straight, but I guess it wasn't a completely stupid thing to do. Because eventually, Emmett went there on his own."

After a respectful silence, I asked, "Have you seen Emmett since?"

Drew let out a short, barking laugh. "He was one of the kids who tried to rob me the day you and I met."

So I'd guessed right, that day Juan and I had taken Emmett for burgers.

We gazed across the water for bit, and then Drew had a question. "What was it that happened at the clinic? You didn't say."

I wasn't sure how much I should reveal about a clinic member, even to someone who knew Emmett was there. It even seemed questionable to let Drew know that it had been Emmett I'd climbed this mountain with, that it had been Emmett who'd been doing so well in the program. I said as little as possible. "He told me to tell you to stay away from the clinic, or he'd stop coming."

"Interesting. I'm not sure why he associates you with me. I certainly haven't said anything to anyone about us, although Margot might have known something."

I opted against picking up on that last comment. "Katie says it's a small town. And there was that day you came by to leave the note."

Drew took another swig of water and nodded. "So I guess I'll stay away, then. I don't know if he meant it, but it's not worth the risk." He looked at me sideways, part teasing, part something else. "Besides, there's no need for notes, now." He smiled. "I have other ways to reach you."

It surprised me that these words, that smile, that fond look from this man brought back that warm feeling in my chest that I'd felt in the first part of my drive home after dinner at his house.

"You seem to have reached him somehow." Drew seemed genuinely interested, but I still felt limited in what I could say.

I decided I could repeat what I had said, because it was about me, not Emmett.. "I thought it was important to let him know that I had at least a superficial idea of how addiction can play out in someone's life. So I told him about my first boyfriend, freshman year in college. How he had disappeared suddenly because he had to go back into rehab. And how even though I know it wasn't a reasonable comparison, it had felt like he'd valued his relationship with fentanyl more than his relationship with me."

Once upon a time, telling someone—anyone—about how I'd felt when Alden disappeared would have brought up painful feelings. But since being here on the island I'd talked about it a few times. Each time it had brought on a little less pain. Telling Drew now made me feel a little sad, but that was all.

Drew watched my face but said nothing. So I kept talking. Maybe, like when I'd wanted Emmett to understand, I now wanted Drew to understand as well. He'd told me he'd come close to addiction. So I told him what I know about how fentanyl makes you feel. About how the first time is the greatest high you'll ever have, and even using again can't get you back there, because that first time raised the bar for what would feel good. But you keep trying, desperate for that great feeling once more.

I gave him my description of what it feels like even to consider leaving your addiction behind—that hanging-from-tree-roots-over-jagged-rocks feeling. And then I glanced at Drew; I hadn't intended to draw a picture so close to what had actually happened to him.

We stared out over the ocean for a couple of minutes. And then I heard, "The first time we met, when you told me what you wanted to do, I didn't respond very well." He turned toward me, and I glanced at him. He said, "I'm thinking now that I was wrong."

"And I was wrong, thinking I didn't want to see where things might go with us." It felt good to see Drew smile. "So maybe," I added, "we can put 'wrong' behind us."

On impulse, I moved to sit closer to him. He reached out and stroked my hair. "I love the color of your hair," he told me.

What was there to love? It was just straight, black hair. But I took the compliment gladly.

"What's the Asian part of your heritage?"

I chuckled. "Wow. Most people think they know right away."

"Well I don't. I mean, your coloring is common to people from a number of Asian countries."

"My maternal great grandmother was Chinese. After that, all the marriages involved people with dark hair. My grandmother looked almost native Chinese, for some reason." I brought my knees to my chest and hugged them. "My sister Nina is gorgeously exotic. She's in the fashion industry, and she knows how to make the most of her natural good looks."

Drew's fingers caressed my ear. It felt so good. The

shivers that raised goose bumps were not coming from the chilly wind.

He said, "I'd be willing to bet that if she were to describe you to me, she'd say, 'Oh, yeah, Nathan's hyper attractive. Clear skin, black hair styled in a way that really suits him. He has a body to die for, muscled and slender at the same time. His nose is adorable, and his mouth—if I weren't his sister—"

I pulled away from the chair and stood up, blushing and laughing. "All right, that's quite enough. I doubt she'd say anything like that." I grinned at him. "But I like that you did."

"How would you describe me to her? And, yeah, I'm fishing for compliments."

My hands flew into the air and landed on my hips, and I laughed again. But then I regarded Drew carefully. He was squinting a little from the bright light, his head tilted slightly as he gazed up at me.

"Okay, fine. I would say that you have rich brown hair, a little longer than I usually like but it suits you. It almost but not quite looks like you don't care how it's cut, but a closer look says that you do. It's a studied casual look, if you like. Your features are a compelling combination of classic and interesting. Your nose looks like it might once have been broken, and that adds to the character. Your eyes...." Here I paused to search for the best words. "Your eyes have an immense capacity to be hard to the point of virtual destruction of what they observe and yet so gentle they'd make a baby coo. And your mouth—defined by the facial hair surrounding it, your mouth looks like it's waiting for something."

I stopped, and Drew said, "Waiting to be kissed, perhaps?"

"Perhaps." But that wasn't quite it. I shook my head. "No. It looks like it's waiting to kiss."

"Tell me what the difference is."

I gave him as unemotional a look as I could. "One is pursued. The other pursues." I gazed into the distance for a few seconds. This was getting a little intense, and I felt the need for a breather. "Let's go back, yeah?" And I turned toward the road.

We didn't say much on the way down. Drew was working to control his chair's speed of descent, perhaps lost in his own thoughts, perhaps not really thinking about anything. I was thinking. Hard.

Although I'd had a respectable number of sexual encounters with other men by this point in my life, only three relationships had been meaningful. One of those, Daniel, hadn't even been sexual. And in each of those three relationships, the other person had been decidedly in control.

After nearly a year of that on-again, off-again fuck buddy relationship I'd had with Conroy, I had decided that what I wanted was a partner—someone who didn't control me, someone I didn't control. And although I couldn't quite put my finger on it, when it came to Drew I was feeling a little controlled. Perhaps it had to do with his approach. That is, not wasting time, being so up-front about what he wanted. I'm not sure I would have been entirely comfortable with that, even if he weren't in a wheelchair, and if that was true then any reluctance I felt wasn't something I could blame on the chair. But I needed to be sure. I wouldn't be controlled any more.

We were nearly at the intersection at the bottom of the mountain, where one road led back to the parking lot and the other led to more of the carriage road, around the base of the mountain. I stopped. Drew was a little past me when he realized I wasn't with him. He stopped, and I moved forward slowly.

"I, uh, I don't know what else you have in mind for the afternoon." I paused, and he started to speak, but I held a hand up, and he stopped. "But there's something I need to say, and something I need to hear from you, before we decide about that."

I had his full attention. His face looked open, expectant,

willing to hear whatever it was I had to say. That was a very good start.

But then I wasn't sure what to say next. I looked into the distance at nothing, my hands clasped just for a second behind my head before I turned back to Drew.

"Look," I said, "you've told me you want honesty. So do I. So here's some honesty. I haven't yet had a meaningful relationship with a man where I didn't end up feeling controlled. I need to be sure that isn't happening again." I paused to see what he'd say.

"I don't want to control you, Nathan. In fact, I don't think I could. I'm not going to tell you that I can't live without you. If we try this and it doesn't work, I'll be just fine. I'll be sad for a while, because right now I think we would be amazing together. But my happiness doesn't depend on you, and I know yours doesn't depend on me."

"So when you waited at the trailhead yesterday, in the pouring rain, watching for me, was there something there besides what you said? Were you hoping I'd feel guilty or obliged or something?"

Drew fell back against his chair. It took him several seconds to speak. "You don't know me very well yet, so I'm going to—I don't know what I'm going to do. Fuck."

He closed his eyes for a second. "No. The answer is no. There was no hidden agenda. There was nothing I was trying to make you feel." I heard him exhale through his nose. "Have you forgotten what happened to me on that trail? I was *worried* about you, you idiot! If I'd gone home, knowing you were up there in that weather, I would have been a basket case."

He chuckled. Actually chuckled. "It wasn't about you, silly. It was about me. About my—I don't know, some might call it PTSD, though I think that's giving it too much credit. I can't tell you for sure that I would have done the same if you had been someone I didn't even know, but it's very possible I would have. Does that answer your question?"

So it wasn't a way to control me. "Yes, thanks. It does. But you have to admit that you've kind of led the way where we're concerned. You've been in the lead, and I've been following. I—" *Should I say it? Fuck; why not?* "I want a partner, not a leader."

His eyes softened, and he smiled. "So do I." He shook his head, obviously amused. "The reason I've been leading is probably because I'm the one who sees where this might go. You've been hesitant. Even reluctant. But I haven't forced you into anything. I haven't tried to manipulate you. Can *you* admit *that?*"

A memory made me smile. "No? What about that porn scene you gave me, the night I came for dinner?"

He threw back his head and laughed. "Busted! Okay, maybe there was a little manipulation in that. But my intention was to make you understand that I can do for you what any man could do. I needed you to know you wouldn't be giving anything up in the bedroom department. And," his smile was wry, "I'm pretty sure you enjoyed it."

"I did."

"Oh, whew. To be honest, I was more than a little afraid that I'd gone too far."

I tried to stop my smile and failed. "That was some description."

I walked over to the side of the road and sat on one of the rectangular granite slabs that lined the edge. Drew followed me. He waited for me to speak.

I shook my head, kind of in disbelief. "You know, I don't think I've ever talked about a relationship as much as this, even when I was in the middle of one. And we aren't even in the middle of one."

"Not yet."

I nodded. "Not yet."

"Is there hope? I'm not asking for a decision, just a direction."

Looking into his eyes, I couldn't help wondering

whether his ability to change their expression was conscious. Right now, they looked like some combination of hope and doubt and pain.

Mentally, I pushed the chair out of the way so I could consider just the person. In front of me, wanting me, was a man who risked his life to save a stranger's son, who cared so much about a damaged kid that he risked arrest, who was brave enough to fight for the rights of the disabled and put his money where his mouth was, who was so determined not to lose sight of who he'd been that he'd climb rock walls with just his hands and arms, and—this was huge—who'd come closer to the edge of opioid addiction than I ever would, and had pulled himself back. This was exactly the kind of man I wanted as a partner. And did he turn me on? Did he excite me?

Hell yes.

I stepped up to the front of his chair and placed my feet on opposite sides of his legs, as close to the chair's seat as I could get. I leaned forward until I could reach the back frame of the chair with my hands, where I could support my weight. I leaned farther forward until our faces were so close I could feel his beard.

"Yes." And I kissed him. It was a gentle, sweet, loving kiss. He returned it without intensifying anything, maybe by way of not taking away from me the control I'd just exerted.

I pulled away in time to see a male cyclist pass close by us.

"Queer."

Feeling again that surge of power, I shouted, "And proud of it!"

Drew said, "Kiss me again, you courageous queer man."

I did, and this one was more intense, more insistent, and more—well, arousing. When I pushed myself away from the chair, I was laughing. I squatted down beside Drew. "So. What now? Around the mountain? Or a trip up your

211

elevator?"

He was surprised, I could tell. And delighted. "No contest. I'll race you."

And he was off toward the stables.


During the drive back, the more road that passed under the wheels, the more ready I felt for what was about to happen. And the more curious I felt about whatever the contraption was that would allow him to fuck me the way he'd described over dinner, and that is what I wanted.

Drew pulled the van into the garage, and he traded the trail chair for the standing chair that he'd left waiting in there. I followed him into the house, and immediately he positioned the braces and raised himself up. He held out a hand, I took it, and together we went up the elevator to his bedroom.

The bed itself was huge, a massive four-poster of dark wood. The bedspread was a deep maroon, and there were what looked like silk ropes, a dark gold color, tied in various ways around the posts. But one look at what Drew was setting up between us and the bed told me I wasn't likely to find out today what the ropes were for.

There were two things, a chair and a horizontal rectangular frame, each with what looked like smooth, black, leather-like material slung onto the frames, where someone might sit or lie. The setup was both intriguing and a little frightening, maybe even kinkier than the ropes implied. This was going to be an adventure for me—an adventure I hoped I was ready for.

"I'm going to let you undress me," he said. Will you do that?"

"I might need some guidance."

"Not a problem."

By the time I was done, Drew was still in his standing chair, naked, ready for me. I'd deliberately avoided staring at his legs. And, of course, my eyes went to his dick anyway, which was hard and dark with blood and as large as his hands would have led me to expect. I moved my gaze to his stomach, the abdominal muscles clearly defined. He seemed to be giving me time to take everything in, allowing me to admire him. And there was much to admire. His upper chest fanned out to his shoulders and then upper arms, all of it thick with lean muscle. It wasn't bulging. It was dense, but it was sleek. My eyes traveled up his neck to his mouth and then to his eyes.

Drew lowered his chair. "I'm going to move onto that chair now." His voice was slightly hoarse with what I knew was desire.

I watched his transfer process as I stripped, a little surprised that my own dick was only at half-mast. But I knew that would change.

When he was fully settled, he grinned at me and, moving slowly at first and gradually faster, he rocked the chair forward and back, toward and away from the narrower end of the rectangular frame in front of him. The demonstration was clear enough. Then he stopped and held out his hand. I moved forward to take it.

"Let's start with you on my lap, just sitting. That okay?" I nodded, and he guided me so that my legs were positioned on either side of his thighs. He nearly lifted me into the perfect position, and our balls were close to touching. As I wrapped my arms around his neck, I noticed that he smelled like salty air and wet moss.

"If anything makes you uncomfortable," he whispered, "say wait, or stop. I will stop."

I nodded, and suddenly we were kissing. I felt his hands explore every inch of my back, my shoulders, my upper arms, my lower back, and finally they cradled my ass as he started to rock, so gently.

It was intoxicating. The motion caused our bodies to touch and shift and touch and shift almost like ocean waves. I felt my dick grow fuller, and soon there was precum lubricating where our groins met.

Drew pulled back, and lifting me with his hands under my ass he reached for my left tit with his mouth. My feet were on the floor, now, and I was able to press against him in ways that made everything even better. I groaned.

Just as he had described, he moved to the other side of my chest. This time he sucked and licked and rubbed his mustache against me until I was ready to scream. I clutched his hair in my hands and held out as long as possible before nearly yelling, "Now! Fuck me!"

Drew released me, and I nearly fell back onto the platform. I don't know where the condom came from, but I heard the packet rip. I lay back and gripped the sides of the frame over my head, my neck stretching back hard. I heard the snap of the lube as it opened and felt the cool smoothness as Drew painted me with it, fingers gently probing into me. He must have spread some on himself, but I couldn't see and almost didn't care.

Drew positioned my legs so my knees were on his shoulders. I felt the end of his dick, teasing, tantalizing. He barely poked at me some number of times I lost track of, and then he pushed in, just a little. He was out. He was in farther, and out again. And then— "Ah!" I yelled. "Oh, God!"

He pumped in and out of me as he rocked, holding my legs with a vise-like grip I barely felt for the sensations in my ass. I was familiar with this sensation. I was hardly new to it. But never had it felt so smooth, so full, so completely overwhelming.

I felt one of Drew's hands on my dick, adding lube, and as he rocked he pulled and pushed. I held onto all the sensations as long as I could, sending my mind from one to another and round again. But finally the sum of it was more than I could contain.

My jaw flew open and I uttered a sound I'd never heard from myself before. It was an animal cry, somewhere between pain and ecstasy, and it was completely involuntary.

I felt my legs shake and my toes curl. As I came, Drew captured the cum in his hand and held my dick as he continued to rock. Finally he pushed harder than ever and yelled. It was another animal cry, but it sounded more like triumph than anything else.

I lay panting as he cradled my dick against his soaked chest, and inside me I could feel his dick shudder a few times and then lie still.

We stayed like that for maybe a full minute, pressing together to maintain the connection. My head throbbed. My feet throbbed. My dick throbbed. My ass—my ass would never be the same.

He rocked back just enough for his dick to slide out of me, and he lowered my legs to his hips. My eyes were closed. I heard his panted relief almost as loudly as I heard mine.

I think it was at least another minute before I could move. I brought my arms down and rubbed my face, and Drew captured them and pulled me upright, on his lap once more. My head fell forward onto his shoulder, and we held onto each other until we were nearly nodding off.

Drew held my arms and gently pushed me away from him. "I need to lie down. Come with me."

We lay on the bed, just as he had described. He was on his back, and I curled against him on my side, inhaling that mossy smell that was now edged with sweat and sex. I drifted off.

# CHAPTER THIRTEEN

Drew shifted his position a little, and I woke up. He turned his head to look at me. I felt more at home at that moment than I could remember feeling anywhere. Any time.

I said, "Everything has changed."

He kissed me, softly, tenderly. "Yes."

I rolled onto my back, loving the feel of his hip touching mine and his hand on my thigh. And then I giggled.

His tone teasing, Drew said, "Explain yourself, young man."

"I don't know why this never occurred to me before, but in college I played a character in a play, a character whose name was Drew."

"Anything like me?"

I shook my head. "Nothing like you." I lifted myself up and sat straddled on Drew's hips. "There is nothing and no one like you anywhere else in the universe." He grinned. "And when do I find out what all these ropes are for?"

"All in good time, my sweet man. Though to be honest, they're mostly for me to lift and turn myself."

"We'll see about that." I sank my tongue deep into his mouth.

When I came up for air, he said, "I think we are both very much in need of a shower. And then let's have dinner. Here, or would you rather go out someplace?"

"Shower, yes, fine. And I think I do want to go out, if that's okay."

"Can you help me on with my underwear so I don't sully my chair with my bare ass? It'll go quicker if you help."

As I did that, I took a good look at his legs for the first time. They were pale under the brown hair, and there was very little muscle mass. It made me feel deeply tender, seeing them, knowing what a profound contrast they were to the upper half of his body—and to what they must have been before.

We showered together, so I got a chance to see what that activity was like for him. There was a special chair, and the large tiled area was surrounded by strong supports that he could use to help him move around and wash everywhere. I confess I took some pleasure in helping with that—and even more pleasure as he lathered my body in various places.

We talked about nothing in particular the whole time, as though it were the most normal thing in the world. And I was beginning to feel as though it could be.

At one point he told me, "I want you to know that the intimate rider is new. No one else has been on it."

"Intimate rider?"

"Sorry. That's the product name. The chair and platform."

I nodded, trying not to laugh. "Good to know. I'm assuming you had one before, though."

He grinned. "An older one, not nearly as nice."


We went to a new place for me, Cafe This Way. While we waited for our order, I had a topic I wanted to broach, and this seemed like a good time. "I'd like to ask you about that previous rider, if that's okay with you."

"Rider?"

"Ned."

"Ah." There was an odd sound to his voice. I couldn't place it. "What do you want to know?"

"When you came to dinner with Margot and me, you mentioned that you'd been hoping to marry him. I'm obviously nowhere near ready to consider that with anyone, and neither are you right now, I expect. So this isn't about us. But I'm curious if you still think you'd like to be married one day, if you're headed in that direction."

He looked at me thoughtfully. "So it isn't Ned per se you want to know about."

I shook my head. "Sorry. I did lead you in that direction. No, I don't need to know anything about him you don't want me to know."

His eyes closed for a few seconds, and he sighed. "Good. Because that was part of the reason we split. He wanted to know about everyone I talked to, everyone I encountered. He was jealous of Lonnie, the waiter at Lompoc, for Christ's sake. He watched me carefully when there was a woman he thought I might be attracted to. It was like everyone was potential competition for him. I would be so—I want to emphasize that—*so* disappointed, right now, if you turned out to be the jealous type."

I grinned. "I'm not. At least, I've never been in the past."

"Okay, well, about me, then. Yes. I would like to be married. I know that the way I have to live, the limitations I have to face with everything I do from the moment I wake up until the moment I fall asleep, are going to affect my spouse, not just me."

He waited for our waiter to place dishes before us and leave before he went on.

"That tempts me to get right to the point, as I did with you when we met, and that's how someone feels about this chair I live in. I hope I never again fall in love with someone who decides it's too much, though I have to face the fact that that could happen. Easily. Possibly even with you."

I wasn't ready to make any promises, and I was glad he knew that. "That's not why Ned left, though?"

"No. But it's why Lorraine left."

I felt my eyebrows lift. "She was before Ned?"

"She was. We didn't get as far as an engagement, but I think we both felt we were on the brink of it. She told me she'd had concerns about my—um, change in mobility, let's say—for a few months before we broke up, hoping she'd get over them. But she couldn't." He waved a hand in the air. "It wasn't fair to her. We'd been together for several months when I had my accident. She saw me through that, and through part of the recovery and adaptation, and she thought she could handle it. I don't blame her."

Drew swirled the beer in his glass thoughtfully. Then, "This might be a good time for me to say something. I really appreciated that Lorraine was honest with me. The last thing I would have wanted would have been for her, or for anyone else, to stay with me for any reason other than they wanted to stay with me. I've already told you I don't want pity. Even more than that, though, if there's anything you wanted to do, and you didn't do it because I couldn't, you should leave."

Our eyes locked. I said, "You mean like hiking."

"Yes. Or anything else, but hiking is a perfect example. And if it bothers you too much that I can't scale peaks with you, that's another reason you should leave. I will not be the cause of diminishing anyone else's life."

"I understand." In my head, I heard Nina's voice: *Holy crap. Can this guy get any more amazing?*

We took a few mouthfuls of our meal, and then I sat back and looked at Drew. He'd already had two really close relationships, both of which had gone south for him. Yet here he was, ready to start another one. I asked, "How old are you?"

"Twenty-nine. You?"

"Twenty-two."

"Why do you ask?"

"It's just—you know, I haven't come close to having the kind of relationship you've had two of already."

"What about you, then, Nathan Bartlett? What kind of partner do you want?"

I turned my fork over and, stalling for time, distractedly watched the tines poke into the various items in my salad. Among the lettuce leaves there were bits of something that looked like pea plants, thinly shaved pieces of lightly-fried red potato, shreds of crisped prosciutto, sliced briny olives—

"Nathan?"

I looked up at him. "I know what I want to want."

He shook his head gently, obviously puzzled.

I set the fork down. "I want what you want. I've had enough of short flings and fuck buddies. I want to commit myself to someone who'll commit himself to me. I want someone I can build a life with, someone I like and love and respect and want sexually, someone who feels like that about me."

He waited, and when I said nothing else, he said, "I hear a 'but' in there. Almost like you're not sure."

"What I'm not sure of is that it would be real. That it's possible. I'm not sure I could trust it."

"You don't trust yourself. Is that it?"

That put me on the defensive. Over Drew's shoulder I saw our waiter approach, no doubt to ask if everything was satisfactory. I shook my head and he went in a slightly different direction. "Doesn't it feel a little weird that we're talking about this kind of thing at this point? I mean, we met all of—what, four-plus weeks ago? We've fucked only once—"

"We made love once. So far. I think there's a big difference."

He was right. Conroy and I had fucked. Drew had made love to me. I gave him a brief smile. "Granted. But the point is, we're sitting here talking about marriage."

Drew laughed. "Simmer down, you young whipper snapper. I haven't even asked you to the prom, let alone to go steady. And I don't think it's too early to be clear with each other about what we'd like our lives to be. If all you want is a fall fling, I'm not your man. You've said you're ready for more. Great. But if there are major barriers in the way for us that we know about now, I'd really like them to be out in the open. Wouldn't you?"

Good point. Otherwise, why the hell was I torturing myself over what the wheelchair meant to me?

"Touché." I sighed and poked at my plate again. "I know I started this, but can we change the subject?"

"We can. But at some future time, I'd like to come back to it."

I searched my brain for something else to say. "This is a little out of the blue, but Margot has an admirer."

We spent the rest of the meal talking about things that were interesting, or funny, or anything that floated on the surface, anything that didn't reach down into the pain I'd felt ever since Drew had said I didn't trust myself.


Emmett came to the Monday session, still in the boots but back in his grunge wardrobe, back to slouching half off the chair, still into silence. I looked his way often enough to know that he didn't look toward me at all. It made me sad.

I was glad when Drew left me pretty much alone the next week, giving me space, not crowding me or controlling me. He did send a text on Wednesday:

*I dreamt about you last night. Movies don't have a rating high enough for it.*

I replied, *That kind of talk will get me exactly what I want. You too, I think.*

Emmett was there again for Thursday afternoon's session, booted but grungy again, silent again. Afterward I didn't realize he hadn't left with the other clients until he appeared in the doorway to the reception office. He leaned against the door frame and waited for me to look up.

"Emmett? S'up?"

"I need to talk to you."

It was a chilly, rainy day, so I didn't want to sit outside. And I knew that even though Jennifer wanted me to be Emmett's friend, I'd get into trouble if I didn't involve Juan.

"Okay," I said. "Just so you know, in my role as a—you

know, fucking secretary—I need to ask Juan to join us." I watched his face as I reached for my desk phone.

"I don't care one way or the other about that. I have questions for you, not him."

I nodded and called Juan's office.

He was there. He said, "Meet me in the upstairs conference room."

Juna was seated at one end of the oblong table. I sat on one side of him. Emmett chose a chair across from me. I folded my hands on the table and waited. As I'd expected, Juan said nothing.

Emmett fidgeted, shifting his position in the chair, seeming to have trouble figuring out what to do with his hands. Finally he imitated my posture.

I opened. "What would you like to talk about?"

It took him a few seconds to speak. I wasn't sure whether he hadn't known what he wanted to say, or if he just didn't know how to start.

Finally, looking down at his twitching fingers, he asked, "What did your brother do to make you feel whole?"

Whole. Was that one of the words I had used? Must have been. It wasn't likely Emmett would come up with it on his own.

It was so tempting to play therapist and turn it back to him with *What would make you feel whole?* Or, *What's making you feel like you aren't whole?*

But I wasn't his counselor. I was his friend. So instead, I just gave him my truth.

"My parents died when I was one. I was raised by my grandmother. She was a wonderful person, very loving, very supportive. But I grew up with no parents who were actually parents. This is true for lots of kids, but that makes no difference to any one kid who grows up like that."

It was a good start, I figured, but Emmett's face told me

it had just scratched the surface.

"I needed someone to show me the way. Someone to help me grow into a man. And that didn't mean telling me when I'd done something wrong." I took a breath. "My brother showed me what I should be like by being the kind of person I knew I wanted to be. I can't tell you how he did it, or how he knew what to do. He was only six when our parents died, so it wasn't like he was a lot further along than I was."

I shrugged and waved a hand. "He wasn't perfect. He was a kid, too. Sometimes I made him mad, or he made me mad. But the most important thing was that even when we were mad, he was still there for me. I never wondered whether he cared about me."

I had Emmett's attention, but he wasn't looking ready to speak. So I told him something very personal.

"I realized I was gay when I was in my mid-teens. I didn't tell anybody right away. No friends, no family members, no teachers, no one. I was terrified of people finding out. I don't think it was at all clear to me what would happen if they knew, but I was sure it was bad. And then one day I told Neil."

I rubbed my face. "Here's what he said to me. He told me that I needed to be who I was. He told me to be the best version of myself I could be. In other words, he helped me understand that being gay was only one part of who I was, and that it was okay. And that made me feel loved. It made me feel whole."

Emmett got up suddenly and walked to the side of the room, to a window that looked out at trees growing along the side of the building. I waited.

Maybe it was a minute, maybe it was two, before he said, "I ain't got no brother."

His back was still toward me. From what I'd heard about his family, I knew better than to refer to them. I said, "I didn't have a father. Neil was a kind of substitute. Do you have anyone who can be a substitute for the brother you don't have?"

He turned slowly, head down a little, eyes gazing at me from under his eyebrows. "I got no one. Why do you think I'm talking to you?"

Juan spoke up. "You have all of us here, Emmett. We all care about you. We're all here to help you."

"That ain't the same thing!" He glared at Juan and turned back to me.

I said, "Well, I don't pretend I can be a substitute brother, but I think you already know I care about you. What do you think would help make you feel whole?"

He nearly threw himself into his chair and gave me a look that said, *Fuck you and the horse you rode in on.* His posture was defiant. His eyes were full of pain.

I tried a different approach. "What's your favorite thing to do, other than get high?"

He pushed the sides of his mouth down. "Nothin'."

"Do you have a bicycle?"

"Nope."

"Rollerblades?" It hit me that Drew had asked me this as we'd traveled around Eagle Lake.

"Nope."

"Do you ski?"

He gave an ugly snort. "Are you out of your fucking mind?"

I ignored the attitude. "Do you sing? Play an instrument? He just glared at me. "So there's nothing in your life, nothing you've done, that gives you anything like a feeling of accomplishment?"

"Have you been fucking asleep?"

"Did you enjoy hiking?" He folded his arms across his chest and said nothing. I decided against pursing that right now. "So you feel worthless. Is that it?" It was a risk. It was a risk, because it was true. It would hit him hard.

His sharp intake of breath was audible. I saw Juan's body jerk ever so slightly, but he didn't interrupt.

I wondered if anyone had ever talked to Emmett like this. Juan had called it gutsy. And yet Emmett kept coming back to me.

Emmett's jaw ground.

"You feel shattered," I said, "like you're in pieces, and you don't know how to put them together. You don't even know if you can find all the parts of yourself. Have I got that right?"

"Who the fuck do you think you are?"

"I think I'm someone who cares about you, who'll be honest with you. I think I'm someone you want to talk to, even if I don't have all the answers. And it's true, I don't have all the answers. But I do want to know what your questions are. And I think you know that."

I barely saw Juan's head nod once. I took it as approval, or at least not as disapproval.

We stared at each other, Emmett's eyes shooting flames, and mine—I hoped—calm and receptive.

When he stood this time it was with a force that knocked the chair over. He started toward the door but then turned back. "Just who am I supposed to do all that shit *with*, exactly? Huh?" He threw the word "Hiking," at me as though it were a knife he flung into the ground at my feet, and he left.

It was like I'd failed him somehow, but for the life of me I didn't know what else I should have said. What else I could have done.

I felt like shit. To Juan, I said, "I hope I didn't go too far."

He let out a long breath. "You do take risks, man. Sometimes they'll backfire, sometimes they'll pay off. But you aren't seeking Emmett out. He comes looking for you. I think the bond that's forming is a good thing. But maybe, if he comes to you again, you should not be so blunt. You okay with that?"

"Yeah. I hear you." And I did. I just hoped I'd be able to rein myself in.

Nina. How long had it been since I'd talked to her? Three weeks? She was leaving Luc, she'd said. Milan's Fashion Week had ended a week after I'd talked with her. Luc must know by now that his hopes for marriage had been dashed. Had she already moved out?

When I phoned Wednesday evening, she answered on the fourth ring. "I've been meaning to call you," she said. She sounded a little breathless.

"You busy?"

"Unpacking. I'm in my new place. I'll text you the address."

"Sounds like a lot has happened in the last few weeks."

"You could say that."

"Did Luc take it well?"

"He took it like Luc. Calmly, with the kind of resignation only the French have mastered. It helped me understand I'd made the right choice."

"You know, when I was staying with you, I got the impression you were really in love with him."

I heard a kind of surprised snort come over the line. "What gave you that idea?"

I didn't want to admit I'd noticed her playing that song, "If he's ever near." I said, "Not sure at this point. Obviously I was wrong."

Silence for several seconds. Then, "And you? Were you wrong about your friend Drew?"

I gave her a brief rundown of how things had unfolded, balancing on a fine line of honesty and not making myself look like the fool I'd almost been.

"So here's an idea," she said when I stopped talking. "How about if I come up there for Thanksgiving? You can show me around, and I can meet this guy." She chuckled. "Sounds like each of you got put on the earth just for the other."

Nina always was smarter than me.

Emmett showed up on Thursday, sloppy, slouchy, silent. No boots. That hurt. I wracked my brain through the whole session about how I could help him and came up empty.

Drew called me after dinner. "What say we take a trip to Orono on Sunday? I'd love to impress you with my climbing skills, and that's where my climbing wall place is."

"Orono? Really? That's where El Speed lives."

"What's an El Speed?"

I laughed. "My college roommate." I explained where the nickname came from.

"So your sister gave him that name?"

"Yeah. And, uh, well, she's coming up here for Thanksgiving."

Drew sighed dramatically. "Assuming you're okay with me meeting all these people, I'm feeling decidedly pauper-ish in terms of family. I have no family I can introduce you to."

"El Speed's not family."

"You said he was like a brother."

"Okay, yes I did. And he is. In any case, I definitely want you to meet him."

"Great. So why don't you plan to stay here Saturday night, and we can drive up to Orono Sunday? You can impress me with your friends, and then I can impress you with my amazing power."

I grinned. "You do have amazing powers. Sounds like a plan."

So then I had to call El Speed. Ellie answered.

"Hey, Nathan. Coming up for another visit?" She actually sounded like she thought it was a good idea. "Hang on. I'll put you on speaker. Larry's right here."

Even though I felt a little sheepish admitting to them that I'd been all wrong about Drew, that he and I were now in a relationship, and that we'd be driving up on Sunday, I came clean.

"Both of you should come for lunch!" Ellie said. "This will be fun."

El Speed spoke up. "Besides, it will give me a chance to prove to my dad that there was more than one reason for him to help me build that ramp."


Margot missed Erik. She talked about him practically non-stop (okay; slight exaggeration) when she and I were together, which was every evening that week. And he missed her, too. He called almost every night our time, wherever his job as a pilot had taken him, whatever time zone he was in.

Over dinner on Friday she said to me, "If someone not from New Zealand marries a New Zealand citizen within three months of getting there, the immigration process is fairly simple."

I stopped chewing my mouthful of the best mac and cheese I'd ever had. Margaret's own recipe, of course. "What did you say?"

She grinned. "I think you heard me."

"Okay, so has either of you asked the other to get married?"

She shrugged as if to say it wasn't a big deal, but of course it was. "We've talked about it. That's all. It's not something that would happen right away."

I stopped short of saying that was a good thing. "Oh, well, then, I don't know why you're even bothering to research the immigration laws."

"Sarcasm is not a good color on you, Nathan."

"That wasn't sarcasm. That was incredulity. You barely know each other!"

Another shrug.

"So have you also looked up what it would mean if *he* moved *here?*"

She shook her head. "I don't give a damn about my

family. His parents are both still alive. And he has a younger sister. So, no. I'd go there."

"What about your career?"

She sighed. "Yeah, that's a consideration. It would mean recertification, possibly more education. Certainly, I'll stay where I am through the spring. I owe the clinic that much."

"And he's a pilot, Margot. How much time would he spend at home?"

"He's planning to stop. He's had an offer to become an instructor, starting in November. It won't mean as much money, but he's on pretty sound financial footing already. He, um, he offered to pay for me to visit him there, over Christmas."

I sat back, my head shaking slowly side to side. "Wow. Just wow."

We stared at each other for several seconds.

"Tell me you don't think this is a terrible idea, Nathan. Please."

I smiled at her. "Look, I'm in no position to advise you. I mean, I really like the guy. But, seriously, be sure about this, Margot. Take a little time. I mean, a completely different country. A guy who seems great, but you haven't known him very long." She seemed to be searching my face for encouragement I hadn't exactly offered. So I added, "I'd have someplace to stay when I go hiking there. Right?"

She jumped out of her chair and ran to my side of the table, nearly wringing my neck with a hug.


I spent Friday night at home. Drew invited me over, but I'd gotten little sleep all week (mostly thinking about Drew through the wee hours). But Saturday Drew and I spent the day together. We walked in a leisurely fashion (most of the time) along a couple of the park's shorter carriage roads, going back to his house so he could change from the trail chair to his powered chair. We drove to Northeast Harbor for lunch and then browsed through a few shops there. I did my best to pretend no one was staring at us because of Drew's chair, but I came close to delivering short-tempered comments to a few people who seemed to think he was causing them some inconvenience.

In one shop he found a sweater he wanted—intricate pattern, gorgeous colors. When he placed it on the counter, the woman at the cash register looked at him, then looked at me, and said, "Does he want to charge this?"

I felt Drew's hand on my arm, which stopped me from saying something coarse. He fastened the belt of his chair around himself and placed the knee braces, and I watched the face of the astonished sales clerk as Drew rose to a standing height, his head now above both me and her.

He kept his eyes on her as he pulled out his wallet.

"I use a wheelchair," he told her as he handed her a credit card. "I'm not deaf. And I'm not mute."

Out on the sidewalk, I said, "Man. That wasn't even in any of the scenes you told me about."

He chuckled. "Y'know, it's almost worth using the chair to be able to shock people like that woman. I bet if she has another customer in a chair, she'll think before she speaks."

Drew drove us in the van to various places around the island I hadn't been to yet, giving me a better idea what the communities were like for people who lived there year-round.

The last thing we did before dinner was drive up Cadillac Mountain to watch the sunset. He parked the van and we wandered round the summit, which had quite a bit of paved area as well as some grassy sections. His powered chair managed all of it.

I was on guard for people who stared impolitely or said stupid things, but no one seemed to care that there was a guy in a wheelchair rolling all over the place.

We decided to watch the sun set. I stood behind the

chair on a slab of open granite, my hands over Drew's shoulders and holding one of his hands in each of mine. The wind had picked up, and the temperature was probably around fifty degrees. We watched silently as the bright red-orange sun sank behind the mainland's hills, the brilliant light reflecting off the water that separated bits of land along the coast.

I could hear the occasional comment of someone else nearby as they spoke to the person they were with, but all my attention—or, anything that wasn't admiring the view—was on how wonderful it felt to be here with this man. His hands in mine were warm and solid, and from somewhere deep inside me there was a glow that would have kept me warm in temperatures much colder than the chilly air where we stood right now.


Back at Drew's house, we worked together to construct a casserole of potatoes, ham, and a whole lot of cheese. He played some contemporary popular music with lively rhythms, and I pulled a few fancy moves across the floor.

Drew smiled and said, "Are you big on dancing?"

I laughed and shook my head. "Can't you tell what a rank amateur I am? No. I can't remember the last time I went anyplace there was dancing."

"Whew. 'Cause, y'know, that ain't something I've got a special chair for."

I danced my way over to where he stood at the counter, placed my hands on either side of his beautiful face, and stood on my toes so I could plant a kiss on his mouth.


This was to be our reverse night. That is, the reverse of had happened last Sunday. I wasn't at all sure how we'd arrange things; the intimate rider didn't seem like the right configuration when I wasn't the bottom. But I knew Drew had done this before. I knew he would know just what to do, and he would not be shy about getting it done.

He played soft jazz after dinner, saxophone this time. It was sultry, romantic, and perfect. We sat in the living room for a bit, drinking that exquisite brandy he'd served me before.

I got up to examine the bottle. The name on the label was too much for me. "How do you say this?"

"Trockenbeerenauslese," Drew said as though it were the most natural thing in the world to pronounce. "German name, though that one you're holding was made in Austria."

I tried the name, mangled it, and set the bottle down. Drew laughed. "Come over here."

He patted the couch cushion beside his chair. I had wondered why there was no arm on this end of the sofa, but once I had sat there it became obvious. It was so Drew and—well, whoever, but me, now—could be physically close. "You don't have to be able to pronounce it to enjoy it. But if you want, I'll help you with that. Some other time."

He took a sip from his glass and leaned toward me. It took me a few seconds to realize he was holding the nectar in his mouth and was planning to feed it to me. I leaned toward him and made a seal on his mouth with mine. He transferred just enough of the stuff to me for me to taste.

My god. Why was that simple act so fucking erotic?

It affected him, too. "Let's take this upstairs with us," he said. "And let's get up there immediately."

I had been right about the intimate rider. It wasn't in the picture tonight. All the action took place on the bed.

I left trails of the brandy all over Drew's body, licking it off his lips, his eyebrows, his throat, his tits, and his belly, stopping just above his dick.

"You can spread my legs apart."

I positioned myself between them so I could take that warm, throbbing shaft into my hand and tease the end with my teeth. Drew gasped. I stopped.

"No! It's good! Do it again!"

I did. I teased the tip and then took the whole thing into my mouth while I cradled his balls. I nearly giggled as it occurred to me I could now tell Emmett that I had, indeed, sucked Drew's cock.

I reached beneath Drew with one hand to grab his ass as I worked his dick. He wasn't moving his hips the way I would have done, the way any man whose dick I'd sucked before had done. He couldn't. But he was sure able to come. And he was able to yell, a kind of groaning scream that sent all the right kinds of shivers up my spine.

I held the cum in my mouth as I released his dick and followed back up his chest, leaving a new kind of trail as I went, making sure I still had enough to share with a deep kiss.

"I want you on your belly," I told him. "Now."

He grabbed a pillow I hadn't seen before. I helped push him over onto his stomach, the pillow beneath his hips so that his ass was accessible. His hands clenched the sheets as he breathed hard into them.

There was one bad moment when I saw the scar. It was an ugly, reddish-brown gash along his spine above his waist, no doubt where surgeons had attempted to repair the damage to his back. I nearly lost my erection, but I forced my eyes up to where I could see the side of Drew's face, a little slack from the pleasure I'd already given him. Time to give him some more.

"Nathan."

"Yes?"

"Not too hard."

"Got it."

I pried his cheeks apart with my lubed fingers and stroked that tender spot between balls and asshole, back and forth and then in circles, until Drew groaned. I pushed a finger in, then another, then a third as he panted and clenched the sheet harder.

Lubed condom in place, I took him. I'd done this

before, many times, and it had always been a nearly athletic exercise. This time it was an exercise in restraint, and in exploration. I moved inside him carefully, feeling everything as well as I could. I knew I'd found his prostate when he gave a kind of animal cry, wordless, wild. I worked it until he seemed ready to faint, until I was ready to explode. And when I finally did, I heard my own explosive cry of triumph and rapture.

I fell against his back, panting, spent, and my dick slipped out of him. We lay like that for a few minutes. When I was able to lift myself off of him, I looked at the scar again. I ran my finger along it and felt Drew's shoulders shudder. He said nothing, though, so I leaned toward it and kissed it, all along the several inches, as tenderly as if the magic of my kisses could erase it.

When I helped Drew turn onto his back, he was weeping quietly.

My knees on either side of his hips, I stroked his face. "What is it?" I asked. "Did I do something wrong?"

He shook his head. "No one has ever done that before."

"What?"

"Kissed me there."

"Give me a little time," I told him, "and there will be no place on you I haven't kissed."

Drew drifted off before I did. As I lay there, seeing the scar in my mind's eye, I remembered a similar experience. Alden.

The teenaged Alden had once asked another boy out— to a dance, I think it was. Either the boy hadn't been gay, or he'd been terrified of being discovered. In either case, he and a bunch of his buddies had dragged Alden into the woods and beat him with branches. He'd had to be hospitalized.

Once, after making love with Alden, I had kissed the crisscrossed scars on his back.

In one way or another, we are all scarred.

234

# CHAPTER FOURTEEN

In the morning, Drew made coffee while I scrambled some eggs and made toast. He had music playing. It wasn't Molly Tuttle this time; it was another female singer, and the style went all the way into bluegrass.

When I asked about it, he said, "That's the first album Alison Kraus put out. Her later style is a little less bluegrass, but she didn't veer very far away from it."

Bluegrass. There it was again. I couldn't seem to escape it. "Why do you like bluegrass?"

"You don't?"

I set our plates down on the table. "It's just—there were a few things I never knew about Neil, things I didn't find out about until after he died. Like, I didn't know he loved bluegrass."

"How did you find out?"

"First thing was when his girlfriend played what she said was his favorite song at his funeral reception. By Cherryholmes."

"Great band. I was sorry when they stopped recording."

Surprised that he knew who they were, I gave him a glance that I'm sure he couldn't interpret. "And then, after Gram died, this line got into my head: 'Gravestones cheer the living, dear. They're no use to the dead.' I couldn't remember where I'd heard it, so I searched the internet."

"'Buy For Me the Rain.' Nitty Gritty Dirt Band."

"How do you know this shit?"

He laughed. "I love a good banjo. And I think cowboy poetry is a gas."

"Cowboy poetry?"

"'She put him out like the burnin' end of a midnight

cigarette.'"

My voice dripping sarcasm, I drawled, "Okay."

"'Gone is the sweet love, tried but untrue.' 'Sitting beside you in the dark is like holding a box of kittens I can't touch.' 'You take the high road, and I'll take mine.'"

I kind of liked that last one. Even so, I said, "Okay, okay! Stop."

"'We are just common threads trying to be a stitch.'"

That time my face turned suddenly and sharply toward him. He said, "What is it?"

"That was in the song. The song from Neil's funeral. His favorite song." My voice cracked a little with emotion. "And I never even knew he liked bluegrass."

Alison Kraus was wailing away about the winter of a broken heart.

"It's just—it made me feel like I hadn't known my brother very well."

Drew watched me for several seconds as I stared down at my buttered toast. Softly, he asked, "Do you want me to play something else?"

I shook my head. "No. Maybe hearing it here, with you, will take the sting out of it."

He wrapped his hand around mine and squeezed before letting go. "So many of these songs speak to me. They express feelings I understand. I guess the songs reflect my life back to me. Maybe that's why I like them so much. They're honest. They're real."


We pulled into El Speed's driveway at around twelve-thirty. Both El Speed and Ellie came out to the van despite a light drizzle with a few snowflakes mixed in.

"I gotta see this," El Speed said to me as the van's ramp lowered. All three of us watched as Drew maneuvered himself out of the driver's seat and into his powered chair. As the chair moved smoothly down the ramp and onto the driveway, El Speed, said, "How cool is that?"

Ellie and El Speed had rearranged their kitchen just enough to accommodate a wheelchair, not only so Drew could pull up to the table, but also to leave a clear path to the bathroom. I sent a silent thank-you to Laura.

El Speed, in his new role as sous chef to Ellie, had made a pumpkin soup with bacon and bits of potato and green peas. There was freshly-baked bread and a salad, and a warm drink of weak tea and cranberry juice. The kitchen smelled as wonderful as everything tasted, and I was trying not to glow too much with pride at my friends.

I'd been afraid the conversation would go immediately to Drew's misadventure on the Precipice, but instead, because I'd let him know about the ramp and the reason for it, he asked about Laura.

"She and Tim ended up moving to Boston," Ellie told us. "It's kind of far away, but we're hoping they'll visit a few times this year."

El Speed, knowing Drew had done some serious hiking, asked him about some of his earlier adventures, most of which I'd heard before. At one point I got up to go to the bathroom, and when I got back the subject had changed.

As I walked into the room, I heard Ellie say, "…the worst turbulence! Can you imagine being over the Pacific and thinking you might plunge into it?"

Was she talking about me? Because that had happened on my way back from Kaua'i. I had told Ellie and El Speed about that the last time I'd been here.

"And then they lost cabin pressure," Ellie went on. She waved her hands in front of her face by way of demonstration. "Those face things on the tubes all dropped. Nathan had a little girl next to him. Her mother was in the row behind them with two other kids. So Nathan helped the little girl."

"Theresa." I was trying to buy a little time to see if another topic came to me, but I failed.

"Anyway, she clung to him like he was her savior."

"I wouldn't put it like that," I said, hoping to downplay Ellie's enthusiasm a little. But she went on, and as she did I wondered if she was trying to match Drew's heroism on the trail with mine in the air.

"And then there were all these people who got disoriented, and they didn't put their masks on. Some of them were falling into the aisle. So Nathan and another passenger went around with the flight crew, holding their breath, picking people up and putting them back into their seats so they could get the masks on them."

Ellie, across from me, sat back in her chair, finally at the end of her story, a satisfied look on her face as she gazed at Drew, who was on my left.

Drew looked at me and said, "It doesn't surprise me that he'd do that." I looked down at my empty soup bowl, but I could tell he was smiling.

El Speed jumped onto the bandwagon. "Yeah, it's like Nathan's trip was all about helping people. Because all that was right after he'd rescued a girl who'd fallen off the trail in Hawai'i."

Drew's smile turned to El Speed. "And now she's his roommate. I adore Margot." He looked at me. "So glad you managed to save her."

I heard the slight tease in his tone. He knew I wasn't any more comfortable hearing my exploits described than he would have been hearing his. I will say, though, that if I'd had any doubts about whether Ellie liked me, they were gone. I figured part of it was probably to encourage Drew.

I took over. "That's quite enough of that. Let me tell you what Drew and I are going to do this afternoon."

As I described the climbing wall and how Drew was capable of using it, it was gratifying to see the expressions on my friends' faces, their eyes wide, their jaws dropped.

Ellie's face changed quickly to something like flirtation. "Maybe that's not such a surprise. I mean, right through your sweater I can see there's muscle in your arms and shoulders."

Drew blushed. I wouldn't have thought it was possible to make this man blush. The cheeks above his beard grew quite pink, and even his forehead grew rosy. Amused, I wondered if Ellie might be just earthy enough for Drew to feel an attraction. She looked a little like Margot, but strawberry blond hair and freckles aside, the two women were quite different.

No matter how many times I might end up seeing Drew climb one of these walls, I will always be in awe. Just describing it could stretch credibility.

He suggested I have my lesson before he climbed, which ended up meaning that I wasn't so intimidated by his prowess that I didn't want to try. My trainer was Bruce, a tall, powerful guy. He was trained in working with paraplegics, so he would also be Drew's spotter.

It was hard as shit. I think they make all those handholds and footholds in bright colors to keep your spirits up. I made it to the top, but only because I had that harness around me, attached to a safety rope that went up to a pulley and back down to a harness that Bruce wore, so that every time I lost my grip I didn't fall—just had to swing my way back to the wall and try again.

When it was Drew's turn, he wheeled his chair over that bouncy material they pad the floor with. Bruce helped Drew get into the harness, and then he helped to position Drew at the base of the wall, bracing him until Drew grabbed firmly onto handholds. Then he stepped back as Drew started to climb, taking up the slack in the rope as Drew went higher.

Up and up he went, faltering only a little bit once or twice, pulling his own weight with his hands and arms all the way up the wall. He looked as natural as a spider. I barely noticed his legs dangling beneath him; I was as impressed with his grace as I was with his power.

When we left the gym, Drew was standing, moving beside me, holding my hand.

We decided to stop for dinner in Bar Harbor. It was nearly dark when we got to the edge of town. We'd been discussing our options when Drew stopped speaking in mid-sentence. He slowed the van as we approached the parking lot of a restaurant that had gone out of business.

"What the fuck?" he said.

I followed his gaze and saw that there was a group of four boys, teens, in one corner, huddled around something on the ground. There was just enough light left for me to see that the boys were on rollerblades. My guess was that they were on the high school's Nordic ski team, because they had poles, so they were probably out Nordic blading for pre-season ski training. But that training did not include standing around and stabbing at the ground. Or, stabbing at something on the ground, which they seemed to find hysterically funny, but in a demonic way.

Drew had just put on his turn signal to pull into the lot when I saw another boy, not wearing blades. He was streaking toward the group, looking for all the world like a dog about to attack—head low, not growling, not barking, not warning. Just attacking.

It was Emmett.

"Holy shit!" I said.

"Yeah." So Drew had recognized Emmett as well.

I had my seatbelt off and was out of the van before it stopped moving, no clue what was happenings but knowing that Emmett did, and that he was going to be in trouble. I knew Drew would be behind me as soon as he could get his chair out of the van.

Emmett was in the thick of everything, arms flailing, pushing and shoving the skiers. It was almost comical; on rollers, they couldn't take a solid stand and very well, and a couple of them fell over. But it didn't take long for them to step out of the rollerblades and fight back. They were surprised when I ran into the group, giving me a momentary advantage. I pulled a couple of them off of Emmett and yelled, "That's enough! Knock it off!"

They ignored me, and as Emmett and I did our best to hold them off, I barely noticed a body on the ground, curled into fetal position, arms folded protectively over his head. That was what the boys had been stabbing.

If the boys had been surprised when I joined the fray, imagine their shock when Drew came barreling into the group, his powered chair going full tilt. Just like he'd once thrown Emmett, Drew now threw first one boy and then another. When the shock wore off, they regrouped and circled around the three of us.

Drew's growl was deep and frightening. "Just try it."

It was four to three, but Emmett and I collected the rollerblades and poles into a pile behind Drew, and we picked up one pole each and held them like weapons.

The boys moved off a little way in a group and stood watching us, obviously undecided about what to do. Keeping his eyes on them, Drew pulled a phone from his pocket.

"Dialing 9-1-1," he said loudly. "Get gone or get into more shit than you're already in."

One of them, probably some kind of leader, took a tentative step forward. "We need our blades."

"You need shit. These are going to the school. If you get them back, it will be from someone there who knows how you've used them. Now, git!"

Someone must have picked up on the other end on the phone line, and Drew explained what was going on and asked for an ambulance. While he was talking, the boys turned and started a halting, slow progress away from us. I wondered how they'd get wherever they needed to go; it would have been much easier to get here on rollerblades than it would now be to get back on foot. Maybe they'd call a friend for a ride.

When we were sure they weren't coming back, Emmett and I turned to the kid on the ground, who was still in a tight ball, shaking and sobbing.

I asked Emmett, "Do you know him?"

He nodded. "He's a kid from the clinic."

I took another look and recognized Andy Green. "Shit."

"Yeah."

I picked up one of the poles. The tip wasn't metal, and it wasn't sharp, so maybe Andy wouldn't be badly wounded.

I sat on the ground behind Andy. He wore a dark jacket, and I couldn't see any blood. "Hey, Andy." I kept my voice soft as I rested a hand on his shoulder. "It's Nathan Bartlett. From the clinic."

I waited as he rolled slowly in my direction.

"Are you badly hurt?" I asked, but he didn't respond. "Someone will be here soon to make sure you're okay. We'll wait together. All right?"

He nodded, but then he resumed his fetal position. The sobbing slowed gradually.

I looked at Emmett. "You're bleeding," I said.

He lifted a hand to his nose. "Caught a good one. I'll live."

Emmett rode in the ambulance with Andy, and Drew and I followed in the van, a police cruiser close behind. From the hospital, the admitting nurse called Andy's parents, and we all stayed with him until they got there. Mrs. Green was very grateful. She gave Emmett and me a hug each, careful not to touch Emmett's bloody face. Mr. Green offered Drew his hand.

A nurse checked Emmett's nose. He winced as she cleaned the blood away. "It's not broken," she told him, "but you're going to have a nasty bruise for a while."

"It'll just add to my rakish good looks."

I blinked in surprise; that did not sound like the Emmett I knew.

We all walked out of the hospital together and came to a halt at the sidewalk. We stared at each other while trying not to stare. As Emmett stepped toward me, I noticed his footwear for the first time that night: the hiking boots.

I was so shocked when he wrapped me in a hug that I nearly neglected to return the embrace. It was over in about two seconds, and in another few seconds Emmett had nearly disappeared from sight.

Drew looked at me, puzzled. I told him, "I'll explain that over dinner. Where are we going? I'm starved."

We opted for the Lompoc, even though there was no patio service that night. After that ordeal, we wanted something familiar, a known quantity.

Plates of warm, delicious food and glasses of good beer in front of us, Drew opened the discussion about Emmett. "I was about to tell him he'd done a really good thing. Didn't exactly get a chance to do that."

I nodded. "I'm not sure it would been well-received, anyway."

"Praising him is a *bad* thing?"

"Depends."

"On what?"

I waved a hand. "Give me a minute, here. This is a little complicated."

I took a sip of beer and a mouthful of food. Then, "Okay, here's the thing. Complimenting someone who's struggling with recovery by saying there's something good about them will go one of two ways, partially depending on their recovery progress. Either it will give them a warm glow that gives them a boost—and something they can return to later—or it will send them deeper into their feeling of worthlessness. See, they know for a fact," and I did air quotes around fact, "that they are worthless, and here's somebody lying to them about it. Even addicts who wish they weren't addicts often recoil in terror at the prospect of losing their addiction. It's almost like they're addicted to the addiction itself. And worthlessness is part of what they can't let go of."

Drew did not sound any more patient than before. "So you're telling me I should have insulted him?"

"I'm telling you there was no way you could have known what the best thing would have been to say to him."

Drew sat back and rubbed his face. "I guess I have a lot to learn about this addiction stuff."

I nodded. "We all do."

# CHAPTER FIFTEEN

Monday morning, the Columbus Day holiday, dawned bright, glorious, and chilly. Perfect hiking weather. The view from Drew's deck, across the Sound, was everything autumn in New England was meant to be.

Over breakfast, Drew asked, "So where are you and Margot hiking today?"

I swallowed my mouthful of English muffin, silky with butter and sweetened with strawberry jam. "No idea. She's going to surprise me."

He chuckled. "If you don't have other plans, how about if you both come here for dinner? We can eat on the deck. I've got outdoor heaters."

"Sounds great. I'm sure she'd love that."


Margot did surprise me, but not in a good way.

She was lying on the couch when I got to the condo, her head propped up on bed pillows she'd brought from her room, a thick, cream-colored Irish throw covering her from chin to toes. Beside her on the coffee table were all the items she might want in the next four hours or so to pamper the cold she was evidently suffering from.

"I'm sorry, Nathan. I almost texted you yesterday when this hit, but I didn't want to spoil your time with Drew and El Speed."

I was bummed, actually. For whatever reason, I felt full of energy and ready to hit the trail. Still, I didn't blame Margot.

"Not to worry. Is there anything I can get you?"

"I have a feeling I'm going to need some cough syrup.

It hasn't hit me yet, but I'm sure it will. Maybe later? Why don't you go hiking on your own today?"

I glanced out the front window at the harbor before turning back to her. "It is a really great hiking day. I'm sorry you don't feel up to it."

"You go. Seriously. I don't need tending, just time."

"Drew invited us both to dinner tonight. Do you think you'll feel up to it?"

She made a sad face.

"Let's see how you are when I get back." I blew her a kiss and went into my room to prepare my hiking gear. As I ran through possible hikes in my head, I had a brilliant idea. I would get a bottle of Trockenbeerenauslese to take to Drew's tonight. Then I'd find someplace to hike that wouldn't take all day.

First I changed into hiking gear, and then I called the liquor store in Southwest Harbor to see if they carried what I was looking for. I was a little surprised that the clerk even knew what I was talking about, because I mangled the name so badly, but he figured it out. However, they didn't have it in the store.

"That's kind of a specialty item," the clerk told me. "I'm not sure you'll find it on the island."

And, in fact, I made a number of calls, and I ended up having to go all the way into Bar Harbor. It hadn't occurred to me to ask about the price, which turned out to be nearly a hundred dollars for a bottle about half the size of a normal wine bottle. But it was the same label as the one Drew had, so I bought it.

I had just settled back into my car, hadn't even started the engine, when my phone rang. The caller ID said it was Emmett.

"Emmett?" Mentally, I went through the steps of what I'd have to do to reach Juan today if Emmett was in trouble.

"Great day for a hike."

Odd. I played along. "Sure is."

"That's what I'm doing. Thought you might wanna join me."

Christ! It wasn't Juan I'd have to reach. It was Ken. Maybe both.

"It's, um, a little late notice. Let me see if I can get Ken in on this."

"Don't want Ken."

Shit. "Why not?"

"Just don't, that's all."

My mind raced. What was I supposed to do? Maybe I could get to him after reaching somebody from the clinic. "Where are you right now?"

"At the trailhead."

It was everything I could do not to shout. "What trailhead?"

"The one Drew Madden couldn't handle."

My heart lurched in my chest. This time I did kind of shout. "The Precipice? Emmett, that's an expert trail. It's dangerous."

"No shit. I can see the signs. Why do you think I wanna climb it?"

*Should I call Drew? He's always talking people out of going up that trail. But no; Emmett hates him.*

I was on my own.

"You coming or not? 'Cause I'm starting up."

"Emmett! Wait! I'm on my way."

"See if you can catch up to me."

Jesus Fucking Christ! There was nothing for it. All I could do was head that way. I had Juan's and Ken's office numbers stored in my contacts. As I drove, I tried Ken first.

"You've reached Ken's desk. I'm in Canada for the holiday weekend. I'll be back first thing Monday. Have a positive day!"

Juan's automated answer was less wordy but equally useless. He wasn't on the island, either. Should I call Jennifer?

I did. She had her home number on her office message, so I tried that.

"Nathan? What's wrong?"

"I can't reach Ken or Juan. Emmett's already started climbing the Precipice Trail. He told me to catch up to him. I'm headed there now. I don't know what else to do. But he can't hike that trail alone!"

"No. You're right. Crap." She paused to think, and I listened to the silence on the line. Then, "How experienced are you as a hiker?"

"Very. And I've done the Precipice. But I've never led a hike, like Ken has."

There was a brief silence. Then, "Nathan, I can't ask you to do this. It's not your job."

"You're not asking me. Emmett is. And I don't see any other option."

"I'm going to call the park service."

"Fine. But by the time they get to the trailhead, Emmett and I will be at the summit." Probably not true, but there wasn't much they'd be able to do in any case, barring the need for a helicopter rescue. And I couldn't quite see how that would work on this trail, anyway.

Jennifer let out an exasperated breath. "I don't suppose it would do any good for me to tell you not to go."

I gave a nervous laugh. "It's not a work day. My boss can't tell me where I can go hiking."

"Still…. All right, so I'll drive over to the parking lot there and wait. Call my cell when you catch up to Emmett, assuming you do, and let me know what's happening. I'll need to know whether we need emergency services."

"K. I'll be at the trailhead in a few minutes."

"And Nathan? If I don't hear from you in the next forty-five minutes, I'll be making those calls."

I drove as fast as I thought I could get away with; I couldn't afford the time it would take to be stopped for speeding.

When I got to the parking lot, there were five other cars there. So I knew Emmett wasn't alone on the trail, which was some relief. I wondered how he'd gotten here. I couldn't have said whether I was glad or sorry that Drew was not at his post. I pulled on my crag gloves as I ran for the trailhead.

I don't think I've ever hiked so fast. I set a pace for myself that might have been manageable if I hadn't been so worried about Emmett. At one point I had to stop and gasp for air, finally calming myself down enough to manage the pace better.

There are many places on that trail where there's no way to pass the person in front of you. Between those spots I managed to get ahead of three other parties: a man and a woman about my age; two women maybe in their thirties; and a trio that included a man, a woman, and a young girl, who was maybe twelve. As soon as I passed that third party, I stopped in the trail ahead of them at a point narrow enough that they couldn't pass me, so they came to a halt. By that point on the trail, there had been only two sets of embedded rails, neither of them very long.

The man, who was leading the trio, looked up at me where I stood higher on the slope. "What?" he said, his breath coming in slow pants.

"Are you aware that this is an extremely dangerous trail?"

"I saw the signs." He seemed arrogant.

"Have you been up the trail before?"

"Who the hell are you?"

I looked down at his shoes. "Running shoes are not appropriate for this trail. Not for you, not for the girl, not for anyone."

"Just get out of our way."

"There are metal rungs farther up that are much more challenging than the ones you've seen so far. There are metal ladders several feet high. There are ledges with rock face on one side and oblivion on the other. Are you sure you want your daughter to try and navigate all that?"

The woman was looking concerned. "Henry, maybe we should go back."

The man turned his head to look at her. Loudly enough to be sure she heard me, I sad, "If you're going to turn back, you should do it right now. If you go very much farther, turning back will not be an option. No one goes down this trail." Maybe someone would, but they'd be an idiot.

Henry turned back to me. "You some kind of expert?"

"Yes. I am. And I'm telling you this is not a trail for anyone who isn't a very experienced hiker. And it's not a trail for anyone who isn't dressed for it. And you're not."

The woman had heard enough. "That's it. I told you this was a mistake. Monica, turn around. We're going back."

"Mom!"

"Come on. No one in my family is dying today."

Henry glared at me as his wife (I supposed) and daughter turned around carefully on the narrow trail and started what would be a perilous trek down. But it would be less perilous, I was certain, than continuing up.

Henry said, "I don't know who the hell you think you are."

"I've told you. I'm an expert. And I know this trail. I also know of a young boy who would have died on this trail if a friend of mine hadn't saved his life."

I didn't wait to see what Henry was going to do. I had to find Emmett.


I had reached the place where one of the wooden bridges crosses from one edge of granite to another, spanning a gulf into certain death, when I saw Emmett. We were not quite two thirds of the way up the trail. Emmett, wearing his hand-me-down daypack, stood at the near end of the two planks he'd have to cross, holding onto a small tree by the side of the trail, staring down into the gulf. The planks before him were maybe eight feet long.

Softly, I said, "Emmett?"

He didn't turn around. It was as though he hadn't heard me. So I said his name louder as I moved toward him. Slowly he released the tree with one hand and pointed down.

When I was very close to him, his shaky voice said, "I can't do that."

Part of me panicked. I knew he could, but if *he* didn't believe it, then—in truth—he couldn't.

When I'd told Henry's family they'd gone almost too far to turn back, I'd been right. Emmett and I were way, way past that point now. The only way was forward. And if Emmett couldn't come to a place where he trusted me— scratch that—where he trusted *himself* enough to cross, the worst could happen. He might fall. And while I didn't go to a place in my head where that would be my fault, I knew it would feel like that.

I looked around for any resource that might help, wishing uselessly that I'd brought something like the rope Conroy had carried on the Kalalau. He'd tied knots into it, and he'd held one end while I held the other, and he'd thrown the loop down to Margot. She'd wrapped it around herself as he'd instructed, and we'd pulled as she gripped the knots and walked herself up.

My kingdom for a rope! I wasn't sure how I would have used it, but damn, I wished I had one. Or something.

But I saw nothing anywhere around me that I could use. So it was up to me.

I let out a long breath. "I happen to know that you can."

He shook his head.

I wracked my brain. And I came up with something that worked, though I can't say why it did. "Emmett, do you know the expression 'riding the tiger?'"

He looked at me, his eyes wide with fright, and shook his head.

"You have to be very brave to get onto the back of a

251

tiger. And once you do, you can't get off. If you try, the tiger will devour you. So you just hang on and keep going."

I paused a minute to let that sink in. Then, "We're on a tiger right now, you and I. This is not a trail we can get off of by doing anything other than going forward."

I couldn't read his reaction to that. So I added, "You know, before Drew fell, he'd climbed this trail a number of times. I've climbed this trail before. So I know that you can cross that bridge, because I know what it takes to cross it. And Emmett, you've got what it takes."

He looked at the other side of the bridge, but he didn't move. I gritted my teeth. He had no choice. We had no choice! Except one. I have him that one choice.

I asked, "Do you want to go first, or do you want me to go first?"

"You."

"Okay."

Before starting across, on an impulse I pulled off my gloves. "See if these fit you at all," I told him.

"What are they?"

"Crag gloves. They help keep your hands from slipping on the metal rungs, and they're great for when you have to grab the edge of a boulder. They're made for a trail like this one."

He reached for them and pulled one on. Maybe because I'd opted for the style with no fingertips, he got it on. He was about to put the other one on, but he hesitated.

"What about you?"

"I've done this trail before. I'll be fine."

"So this is the only pair?"

"Well, yeah."

He held the other glove toward me. "You wear this one."

On his face I saw something that told me to do as he asked. *People in recovery begin to consider the needs of others.*

252

"Thanks." I put it on and stepped forward and around him.

There was a skinny metal handrail on one side of the two planks. I wrapped my hand loosely around it. A couple of feet onto the bridge, I said, "This is just to help me keep my balance. It's not really a support."

When I got to the other side I turned. Emmett was watching me intently.

"Ready? I'll be right here. Look at me, not at your feet."

He did it. His body was stiff, and his movements slow and a little ragged, but he made it. When he was safely on the other side, he looked back at what he'd done as though he couldn't quite believe it. I called Jennifer, without saying her name, so Emmett wouldn't know who I was talking to. It was an effort to keep my voice steady, there was so much adrenaline pounding through my veins.

"We're more than half way up," I said. "All's well. I'll call again at the summit." As soon as she acknowledged that she'd heard, I rang off.

"Okay, then," I said to Emmett, hoping to sound as casual and normal as possible. "How are the boots holding up?"

He nodded. "Good."

I took off my pack. "Water break." He did the same.

It surprised me that he'd had that moment of panic. I wondered how he'd do on the rest of the trail, but all we could do was go forward.


It was not a hike I hope to repeat. Emmett had several moments of hesitation, and I got to see the whites of his eyes more times than I would have liked, but we made it. We stood side by side and looked out at the view. The sun was fully out, almost no clouds now. The breeze was stiff and crisp, wicking sweat away from our bodies quickly.

After about five minutes, Emmett turned to me. "I did it."

I grinned and reached out my right hand. "You did." We shook. It was not going to be my place to chastise him for doing something so foolish, so reckless. That would fall to Jennifer, to Juan, maybe also to Ken. I saw my job as affirming his courage, his determination, and—most of all—his accomplishment.

I turned and pointed across the granite expanse toward the signpost with trail names on it, some distance away. "Let's head that way."

"So we don't go down this trail?"

I laughed. "We're off the tiger, kid. I ain't gettin' back on, and neither are you."

I let him get several feet ahead before I called Jennifer. "We made it to the summit. We'll be coming down by another route, through the woods."

"Thank God. I was almost ready to call for help. I added the park service number to my contacts."

I gave her a rough time estimate and rang off.

We sailed past the cairns until we got to the one that looked like an inukshuk.

Emmett stood still and pointed down at it. "This is a weird one."

"Yeah. It's kind of like an inukshuk."

"A what?"

So I gave him the story of these markers as they were used in the Arctic.

"Cool." And he was off again. He seemed to have fully recovered from any fear, any hesitation.

I'm glad he was looking around and not at me, because I couldn't stop a huge grin from spreading across my face: Maybe I was an inukshuk for Emmett. After all, inukshuks don't make the journey for you. They just point the way. You might need several of them to reach your destination, and I would be proud to be one of his.

The trip down was literally a walk in the woods—steep at times, but never dangerous.

We didn't speak much at first. I wanted Emmett to experience what it was like just to be, and nothing else. That is, just to exist in a place where his own strength had brought him. I wanted him to feel the burn in the muscles he'd never used for this kind of achievement. I wanted him to understand that he had accomplished something big—something he could accomplish again if he chose.

Finally I brought up something I'd wanted to ask him, about what had happened last night. "Are you and Andy good friends?"

Emmett looked at me as though I had three heads before turning his gaze back to the trail. "He's a twerp."

I had not seen that coming. "So—but weren't you with him last night? Isn't that how you knew he was in trouble?"

Emmett shook his head. "No way. I was just—you know, hanging out."

I stopped myself before asking if he'd been looking to score, which would have ruined his current streak of good tests.

He went on. "I saw those assholes from school blading around town like they own the place. They piss me off. They all went for the corner of the lot and started laughing. Then I heard this scream, like. And someone crying. I didn't know it was Andy until I got over there."

"Got it. So you just knew someone was in trouble, those guys were the cause, and you—what, you didn't care what happened to you?"

"Don't you think I've been on the receiving end of bullshit like those guys were doing to Andy?"

*Was he being bullied at school? Or abused at home?* "Has that happened recently?"

"No one fucks with me anymore."

I waited to see if he'd say more, but he didn't. My mind

went to what Emmett had done last night. I had assumed he'd raced into that swarm of delinquents to rescue a friend. Now it looked like a combination of hating the privileged guys on the ski team and something else I doubt he would have admitted: He'd wanted to help someone who was in trouble.

This was huge. This was massive. Like when he'd given me one of my gloves back, it told me he was ready for the phase of recovery where doing something for someone else became a major source of self-worth.

I decided to take a risk. "Are you going to tell Juan about what happened last night?"

He shrugged. "Hadn't thought about it."

"I hope you do."

He glanced at me. "Why?"

"I think Juan would like to know what a great thing you did." Like I'd told Drew, compliments were a risk. But this felt like a good time to take that risk.

He shrugged again. "Maybe. I mean, I don't need his approval." Then, a few steps later, "I'll think about it."

We were silent for about ten minutes, and then he asked, "This the biggest mountain you've been up?"

"Well, no. Not really."

"What is?"

I knew it was important not to diminish his accomplishment. "I've hiked a lot in New Hampshire. Most of the mountains there are higher than Champlain. That's the mountain the Precipice Trail is on, the one we're on right now."

"So you're some kind of mountain man."

I could have hugged him. Of course, I didn't. "I guess I take after my brother."

"The one who died."

"Yeah."

Maybe five minutes later I heard, "I'm gonna do that one day."

What it was he would do "one day" wasn't entirely

clear to me or, I suspected, to him. Even so, it sounded like a positive goal.


Jennifer was in the parking lot, leaning against the side of her car and hugging her arms to her body for warmth, when Emmett and I emerged from the woods. I'd have bet she had been working on her poker face—not too angry, not too relieved, not too worried, but a little of each. If Emmett was surprised to see her, he didn't give himself away.

"Hello, Emmett," she opened. "Have a good climb?"

He nodded. "Yeah."

She pushed away from the car and indicated for us to follow her over to where we could sit on a few boulders lining the parking area.

"First, Emmett, I'm delighted that you've decided you enjoy hiking. Being outdoors, relying on yourself to push through challenges, achieving summits—that's all good." She smiled at him before she continued.

"But what you did today was irresponsible." She pointed to one of the warning signs. "That information was meant for you. I hope you become an experienced hiker. I hope that very soon you'll be able to read those signs and know for certain that they don't apply to you. But right now, they do. And by ignoring them, you put yourself at risk. You also didn't consider that Nathan might have had other plans for today. But because he *is* an experienced hiker, he knew he needed to put everything else aside and come find you. He did that because he cares about you. And I'm here because *I* care about you. I really want you to love the mountains, Emmett. But you need to approach them responsibly. You need to think before you act."

Emmett sat quietly, his long legs allowing him to plant his feet on the ground, his hands dangling between his knees, his head down but not in a way that looked especially contrite. He was silent.

"I need to know you heard me, Emmett. And that you understand."

He looked up at her, his expression an odd mix of hurt feelings and defiance. "So what should I have done?"

"Next time you want to hike, let Ken or Nathan know. Then you can decide together where and when to hike. If you keep hiking, soon you'll be in a position to decide for yourself. You'll know you can handle a trail like this one." And she pointed straight up.

"I handled it just fine."

Jennifer looked at me. I was barely out of Emmett's line of vision, and I gave my head two or three very tiny shakes.

Jennifer said, "You managed it with Nathan's help. I'm sure you know that." She heaved a sigh. "Emmett, this is a wonderful thing for you. You just need to approach it more carefully. Do you understand?"

He lifted a shoulder and dropped it, which was probably all the assent he was going to give.

I asked, "Emmett, do you have any questions?" I liked that better than "do you understand," which can feel confrontational.

He looked at me. "Where do we go next time?"

I grinned at him. "Someplace with a little more challenge to it than Day Mountain. Let's talk to Ken about it tomorrow. He knows the island really well. And by the way," I said, pointing to his jeans, "those might not be the worst pants to hike in, but they're close. We need to get you something better for hiking."

Jennifer smiled at me and said, "Okay, Emmett, let's get you home."

As we approached the cars I asked, "Emmett, how did you get your boots?"

"Whaddya mean?"

"Weren't they in Ken's office?"

He shook his head. "I been wearing 'em all the time.

258

Gotta make sure they're broke in."

I decided against asking about the day pack, which was also with him today. The administration part of the clinic was closed and locked until tomorrow. Maybe he'd found a better hiding place.

I called Margot before heading back to see what she wanted by way of cough syrup. When I got home with it, she was sound asleep. I left the syrup on the dining table, texted Drew with Margot's regrets, and headed for the shower.

Drew was surprised when I handed him the bottle of brandy. "So you remembered how to say it?" he teased.

I shrugged. "Well enough, I guess."

He thanked me with a very nice kiss and then had me help him bring a few appetizers and, again, champagne out to the deck, where three heaters were already working.

Drew asked after Margot's health, and then we sat silently for a few minutes, admiring what we could see of the water and the few lights glowing on the far side of it. He reached for my hand.

"So Margot didn't go hiking with you," he opened. "What did you end up doing?"

I looked at him and grinned. "I had a really amazing day." I'd been looking forward, the whole drive over here, to describing what had happened. Despite Emmett's lack of good judgement, I saw today as a major step forward for him.

"Did you hike alone?"

"Nope." I took a sip of my drink, teasing him with suspense.

He chuckled. "Okay, wise guy, spill."

I set my glass down on a side table, reclaimed the hand he'd been holding, and sat forward in my chair. I knew Drew would understand completely why getting the kid to hike was such a big deal. And I wanted to let him know I'd talked that family down from the Precipice, as it were.

I said, "So, you know how I've told you that people with substance addictions lack self-confidence?" I waited for him to nod. "They feel like they've failed at life, and when they realize they're addicted, their self-image takes a total plunge. So something that helps them feel positive about themselves is major."

"That all makes sense. So….?"

"Last night, when Emmett charged into that gang of kids, I thought he knew Andy was the one they were attacking. He recognized Andy, and I thought maybe they'd been hanging out together. Turns out Emmett didn't even know who it was those kids where assaulting. He just charged in."

As I reached for my glass, Drew asked, "What's this got to do with your amazing day?"

I sipped and set the glass down again. "Getting to that. So another thing that really helps addicts is if they can do something for someone else. Help others. And that's what Emmett did last night. He could have been hurt. He could have gotten into trouble. I mean, two substance abusers against a privileged ski team? And he hadn't even known who it was, on the ground, being stabbed. I figured, you know, maybe he was ready for the next step, but I didn't know what that would be. Anyway, when Margot said she couldn't hike, I decided to find that bottle of—whatever it is—and then hike on my own. But right after I bought the bottle, Emmett called me."

"Emmett? Is he supposed to do that?"

I shrugged. "Don't really know what his rules are. I don't call him, of course. Ken and I took him up Day, like I told you, and after that we walked around the summit of Cadillac. And I guess Emmett got bitten by the bug. Because today he headed for the Precipice."

"He what?" Drew's body went stiff. He was so still that

he might have been a mannequin. Or a corpse.

"I tried to reach Ken or Juan—"

"What the fuck, Nathan? *That's* where you went hiking? *With Emmett?*"

It was like he hadn't heard me. "I—It wasn't like that. Let me tell you—"

I didn't see him touch his remote, but the chair moved back suddenly and almost collided with one of the heaters. He moved from one heater to the next, turning each one off, and then headed into the house. I followed, totally confused.

Drew had stopped in the middle of the room, his back to me. As I started to go around and stand in front of him, he turned the chair so that he wasn't facing me.

"Drew, what the hell? Will you tell me what's going on?"

"Get out."

"What?"

"Get out!"

Had I heard him right? Of course I had; he'd said it twice, the second time very loudly. I felt like I couldn't catch my breath. My knees felt weak.

My voice sounded forced and broken to my own ears. "I'm not going anywhere until you talk to me."

He moved away from me. I was about to run in front of him when he wheeled to face me. His voice was harsh and angry but icy cold at the same time.

"How could you do that? How could you take an inexperienced *child*," he leaned hard on that word, "up that dangerous trail, a child who for all you knew could have been high on something?"

"He wasn't on anything. And I didn't *take* him. He was half-way—"

"You don't know that! And does it mean nothing to you that I've spent hours—*hours,* Nathan, many many hours—sitting in the cold, in the rain, in the *snow* even, to stop people from doing exactly what you did?"

261

"But—"

The ice was gone from his voice. It was all fire now. "Does it mean nothing to you that one misstep might kill a person or land them in a fucking wheelchair for the rest of their life? Does it mean nothing to you that this happened *to me?*"

"Drew, of course—"

"Are you so insensitive that you would not only do such a thing, but that you would present it to me like some kind of *accomplishment?*"

"Okay, stop!" He was tearing me a new one without even waiting for me to explain! "My turn to talk. This was Emmett's idea, not mine. And anyway, what I did for him today was exactly like what you once described. Those wheelchair users who pulled the plane? Remember that?"

He blinked.

"Remember? You told Margot and me about it the first time you met her. It was for that charity that teaches people with disabilities," (would I get credit for using that phrase correctly, I wondered?). "how to fly friggin' *planes. That's* not dangerous? Of course it is. But it gives them a sense of accomplishment. It gives them back some self-confidence. Emmett loved hiking. He *loved* it. He wants to go again. He's reaching out in a huge way. This is a milestone for him!"

I stopped to catch my breath. I was about as angry as I'd ever been in my life. I couldn't stop myself from referring to something that might hurt him.

"You told me you'd come close to abusing your meds." I saw him wince. "But you never developed an addiction. So maybe you can't understand what happened for Emmett, last night and then today. But it's huge. Huge!"

Drew's voice was so quiet I could barely hear him. "And maybe *you* can't understand what it means to lose the use of your legs. To have people think of you as not quite human anymore. To assume that you're useless. To relegate you to the outer edges of society."

"That's not the point!"

"Of course it's the point! It hurts me so much, Nathan, so much, that you would take that trail, the trail that changed my life so completely…" he took a quick, rasping breath, "…that you'd take it so lightly that you'd climb it alone, in the rain, and then—" he closed his eyes for a few seconds, "and then risk Emmett's life there. I don't think you care about that boy, and I don't think you care about me."

*He was still hung up on my solo climb?* "You've got this all wrong!"

We stared at each other, a virtual canyon between us.

Then he said, "Do I? I once told you that you weren't hiking to prove anything. You told me I was wrong. I *was* wrong. Now I see that it's all about you."

I'd had enough. I barely remembered to grab my jacket as I ran for the door. He said nothing else. Didn't try to stop me. Didn't call my name.

Gravel sprayed behind my car as I wheeled out of Drew's driveway. Turning left would have led me south toward home. I turned right.

I sped through the dark, miraculously not being stopped by police. Without thinking about it, I headed like a homing pigeon for the tallest mountain I could get to: Cadillac. As I drove—too fast, by far—up the auto road, I nearly collided with a car on its way down.

There were only two other cars at the summit. I parked well away from them, got out, and wandered vaguely around. My chest hurt. My head hurt. My throat hurt. I could barely see what was in front of me, blinded as much by pain as by darkness. At one point I found myself standing where Drew and I had been, the day we'd been to Northeast Harbor. That night we'd had sex—made love—for the second time. I'd kissed Drew's scars, and he'd cried.

I landed in a heap on the granite. My head fell forward. I clenched my jaw to stop the tears. It didn't help. I didn't care whether anyone was still on the summit or not. I sobbed. I cried for the loss of Drew, and I cried for the fury and frustration of being completely misunderstood and unfairly accused.

Gradually the sobbing quieted. I lay back on the granite, my breath still catching a little. It was cold. *I* was cold. I didn't care.

The sky was clear. The moon, if it was going to appear later, was not yet visible. Part of the black sky was awash with a soft, pale streak of greyish white, as if someone had dipped a brush into dull glitter and swiped it across part of the black bowl overhead: the Milky Way. Many stars were distinct and bright, pinpricks in that darkness, tiny diamonds on black velvet.

A thin streak shot across the sky, and my eyes followed it. A meteor? A shooting star? There was another. I let my mind go blank as I watched for more streaks.

The cold granite had soaked up any heat from the anger I'd felt, and I realized I was shivering. Aching, stiff, I got up and went to sit in my car. I stared out over the lights of the town of Bar Harbor, and my mind bounced around from one thought to another, finally landing on one.

I'd known this would happen! Hadn't I predicted it, on my drive home the night I'd gone to Drew for the first time? The night he'd tempted me with porn? I'd told myself then that this was a bad idea. I'd known—somehow I'd known—that this was going to end badly. If only I'd listened to my gut.

Some inukshuk Drew turned out to be. What he pointed the way toward was misunderstanding. And rejection. And pain.

I took a couple of shaky breaths. Why the fuck was Drew like this? Why had he jumped to the conclusion that I had done something wrong? Christ! For all he knew, I had saved Emmett's life! And how could he think I didn't care about him?

He'd put so much effort into getting this relationship started. Pursuing me, he'd said. Get used to that, he'd said. All that trouble, just to fly into a rage and throw me out of his house. Out of his life.

It made no sense. I'd wanted to help Emmett. That had nothing to do with Drew. And yet he'd made it all about him, even as he'd accused me of making everything be all about me.

See, bluegrass was just a bad omen. Somehow I'd known that, too.

Suddenly one of the lines Drew had quoted came to me. He'd said he liked what he called "cowboy poetry" because it was real. It was honest. And he'd spouted a few lines at me.

I fished out my phone and texted to him, *You take the high road. I'll take mine.*

I turned off my phone.

# CHAPTER SIXTEEN

By Tuesday morning, Margot was feeling well enough to go to work. Over breakfast she told me I looked like death warmed over and asked what was wrong.

"Tell you later," I said, not sure when "later" would be. But she cornered me for lunch and pulled it out of me. In truth, I didn't put up much of a fight. I needed confirmation that I'd done nothing wrong.

For her part, although Margot was supportive and loyal to me as her friend and roommate, she was too generous to be completely harsh toward Drew. She mourned with me, and she mourned for Drew, as well.

"I totally get that this was really something wonderful for Emmett," she said.

"It seems wrong that Drew just assumed the worst," she said.

"How unfair, not to let you tell him what actually happened," she said.

But....

"It's likely that Drew has unresolved issues about his accident," she said.

"I wonder if he's shown you ways he's adapted but hasn't let you see how much emotional pain he feels because of his disability," she said.

And her most interesting comment: "It might be that he feels some kind of jealousy that you can go climbing with the teenager he holds responsible for Johnny's death, and you can't go climbing with him. And maybe he's ashamed of that jealousy. Shame often makes people lash out at the wrong person, or at the wrong time, or both."

Ken, Juan, and I had a short conference with Jennifer in the afternoon. She filled them in on what had happened, and I described a little about the hike. Ken and I agreed on Gorham for Emmett's next climb; I'd been up it, so my familiarity would be helpful, and it was a significant enough step up from Day to (we hoped) satisfy Emmett. Juan said he'd see if Saturday was good for Emmett, weather permitting.

During dinner wash-up on Wednesday, Margot asked, "Do you love Drew?"

That stopped me in my tracks. Because even before that fight, I hadn't said to myself that I loved him, let alone said it to him. And after the fight, I'd assumed everything was over between us, that there was no place for love in that picture. But Margot asked the question in the present tense; that is, not "*did* you love him," but "*do* you love him."

Love. Other than family, the only man I'd ever loved was Alden. Did I love Drew? I had wanted to love Drew. I'd wanted him to love me. I had wanted to get to that point. How close had we come?

"I don't know," I told Margot. "Maybe." I said right after that. "No," I said, finally. "I don't. So why does this hurt so much?"

Margot smiled her sweet smile at me, her eyes soft and fond. "You gave him your trust."

Drew's words about his first impression of me flew into my head: *Your face was full of light. There was an openness, a genuine honesty, something I'll call hopefulness. No, wait. Trust.*

I shook my head at Margot. "I'm not a trusting person. I've always been guarded. I hide the parts of me that feel vulnerable. Just look how long it took for me to agree to give him a chance!"

She nodded. "And once you did, you went for it whole

hog. Lock, stock, and barrel. Whatever metaphor seems best. You go all in, Nathan. Once you start, all of you goes. You're not good at compartmentalizing. So right now, the pain you feel isn't just from getting parts of yourself unfairly rejected. *All* of you feels rejected."

Thursday, at the teen meeting, Emmett showed up wearing his boots. I risked giving him a smile. He acknowledged that with a nod. He didn't speak during the session, but he sat up in his chair, and he seemed to be listening to what others said.

It was just past nine that night when I got a phone call from Jennifer.

"Nathan, can you get to the hospital emergency room right away?"

A shivering feeling came over me. It took only seconds for my breathing to grow shallow and quick. "I can," I said, closing my laptop. "What's happened?"

"Emmett needs you."

"Is he okay?"

"Physically." She hung up.

When I told Margot where I was going, she said, "I'm coming with you."

My heart was pounding as we ran into the building, my head full of the scenarios I'd imagined during the twenty minutes it took to get there.

I found Jennifer and stepped breathlessly into the emergency room bay. There was a body on a gurney, the face covered with a sheet. Bending over it, weeping, was Andy Green's mother. Behind her was Mr. Green, in obvious misery, his face contorted and wet with tears. I felt the blood drain from my head, and took a step back to maintain my balance.

Margot moved around the bed to stand with Mr. Green.

I looked at Jennifer. "Emmett?"

She handed me a small piece of paper, torn from something. The scrawled writing on it read, "Tell Emmett I'm sorry."

Andy wrote that to Emmett? Had Emmett understated the connection between them?

"Where is he?"

Jennifer guided me away from the gurney into an open area. "Not long ago, Andy reached out to Emmett. He'd seen that Emmett was doing better in session, and he was desperate for help."

"But—did anyone else know Andy was in trouble?"

"Yes. But we can't follow these kids around twenty-four-by-seven."

"Emmett told me they weren't friends."

"There was something between them, more than Emmett would ever have admitted. He's a loner, and Andy is—was—a needy young man. But for some reason Andy responded to Emmett, and Emmett was trying to help him stay clean." She took a deep breath and rubbed her face. "And it seems he failed. Andy went out to score tonight, evidently with the specific intention of overdosing. To die, if that note is any indication. Emmett tried to reach him by phone, just to check in, and when he couldn't he went to look for him in the same place he was attacked Sunday."

Jennifer turned away for a few seconds, evidently trying to gain emotional control. She turned only half-way back to me. "Emmett found Andy's body. And he found the note."

My eyes were filling with tears I knew I couldn't release. My voice sounding strangled, I asked, "Where is Emmett now?"

"He rode in the ambulance and stayed with Andy's body until the Greens showed up. Then he turned and ran. He's barricaded himself in a closet. I'm told there are no drugs in there, so I stopped Security from breaking in and then called Juan. He's there now, talking to Emmett through the door. But the only thing Emmett has said so far is that he wants you."

"Show me."

As we walked, she told me that when Andy's parents arrived at the hospital and found Emmett in the ER bay, quite unsettled, they'd called her for help with him. She'd phoned Juan, who was both Emmett's and Andy's counselor.

When we got to the closet, I saw Juan sitting on the floor, his back to the wall. His head rested against the wall, and his eyes were closed. I could hear him saying, "Nathan's on his way. I promise."

I ran to the door. Juan stood, and something about the pain in his face made me reach out and hug him. He'd lost one of his kids today, and another was struggling.

"Emmett? It's me. Nathan. I know what happened. Can I come in?"

The three of us stared at the door for a good twenty seconds before we heard scraping sounds coming from inside. Then Emmett's voice: "Only Nathan. No one else." There was more scraping, and the door opened a tiny crack. I stood where he could see me and waited. He was just inside, the hum of overhead fluorescent lights the only sound. He backed away from the door and I went in, closing the door behind me. Emmett dropped to the floor and huddled with his back against a set of shelves that held what looked like towels and gowns. He pulled his knees to his chest and hugged them. He didn't look at me.

I sat on the floor beside him, not too close. I turned my phone off and waited. I wanted him to speak first, and I was prepared for this to go on for a while.

It had been maybe five minutes when he said, "I tried to help him."

"I know. And it sounds like he wanted you to help him. But it also seems like he might have already been beyond help."

"I knew what he was feeling."

"I believe you."

"Yeah, but you don't *know*."

"You're right." There was no point in pretending. And in the several minutes of silence that followed, it hit me hard that for all my images of hanging from tree roots, for all my talk about being terrified of letting go of the only thing keeping you alive, for all the pain I'd felt when I'd told myself I'd been addicted to the feeling Neil had given me, I knew fuck all. I knew shit.

The boy on that gurney was dead. *Dead.* He'd seen death as the only escape from his pain. He'd wanted there to be no more him, no more time with his family, no more familiar sights and smells of home. No more thrill at seeing winter's first delicate snowflakes descend. No more fresh breezes through bright, spring-green leaves. No more brilliant autumn trees, dropping leaves through crisp, pine-scented air. No more figuring out what life was all about. He knew what life was about, at least for him. It was about pain and nothing else.

Andy had used drugs not just as a source of hope in a hopeless situation. He'd given up on hope. Drugs were no longer just a relief from pain. They were an escape from life, because life was pain.

I leaned my arms on my bent knees and lowered my head. I let the tears fall to the floor, watching as they left dark spots on the grey tiles.

And then I heard Emmett sob.

I lifted my head to look at him. His head, too, was on his folded arms, and his shoulders shook violently. I laid a hand gently on his arm, but he pulled away. So I waited some more, slowly getting my own emotions under control, feeling the most profound frustration. Because it had looked like Andy's life wasn't that bad. It looked like his parents loved him, cared about him. He had people doing their best to help. He even had a knight in shining armor in the form of Emmett.

It hadn't been enough.

So what the fuck was the source of this pain? What had made Alden start to use in the first place?

My head jerked up. Alden. I'd replaced Andy's name with his in my mind. And, in fact, that question had plagued me years ago, when Alden had disappeared from my life. It had plagued his parents, too—parents who loved and cared for him, parents who had accepted that he was gay. His mother had been warm and generous to me when I'd showed up, the night she was cleaning out his apartment. She had given me something of high value, not just monetarily, but also meaningful to Alden and to me, something that had inspired me to follow in Neil's bootsteps: the Sarah Warren tapestry.

For all I knew, Alden, too, was dead. I felt overwhelmed with an urge to know, but it would have to wait. For now, I was here for Emmett and no one else. Not for me, not for Juan or Jennifer. Not even for Andy. For Emmett.

Emmett's sobbing lessened gradually, but he didn't lift his head. I shifted my legs and sat cross-legged, determined to wait him out, hoping Juan and Jennifer would not do anything to interrupt. I closed my eyes.

Emmett's body slumped against my shoulder, his head hanging, his arms limp. I lifted my arm and draped it behind his head over his shoulders. He pressed his face into my shoulder, sniffling occasionally.

I was tempted to tell Emmett again that he'd been right, that I couldn't possibly imagine how Andy had felt, how Emmet felt. But that might have been like a wedge between us, a difference that didn't matter right now. This wasn't the time for true confessions from me. This wasn't about me at all.

Emmett surprised the hell out of me. He sat up, sniffled loudly, and said, "This happened to you."

I had no idea what he meant. "What?"

"That guy you were in love with. He disappeared. You

weren't enough for him. I wasn't enough for Andy."

Again, I said, "You're right." I let out a long breath. "Maybe no one person is enough for any other person. Maybe we have to be enough within ourselves."

"That's the hardest part."

"Yes."

He turned a tear-streaked face to me. "So how can we help someone else?"

"I guess all we can do is be there for each other, and be clear that we *want* someone to be enough within themselves. Help them see that we believe they are. That's what I want for you."

He watched my eyes for several seconds. "That's what I want for you, too."

I nodded and closed my eyes. I opened them on him and said, "Thank you."

Margot had said that once I was in, I was in all the way. It looked as though Emmett was like this, too. Maybe anyone working their way through recovery is like that. And maybe, in one way or another, we're all working our way through recovery.

We sat side by side, the shelf behind us, legs crossed on the floor, hands limp in our laps. Finally Emmett said, "Okay."

As we stood he faced me and, for the second time in only a few days, hugged me. It was a longer hug this time.

I nodded at him, and he returned the nod. I went to the door. "Coming out," I called.

When I stepped out of the room, I saw Juan and I saw Jennifer, and just a little way down the hall from them I saw Drew. *What the fuck?* I looked away from him quickly.

A voice in my head said, *You don't have time for him right now. This is about Emmett.*

No one said anything stupid, like asking Emmett if he was all right. Everyone there knew that in some ways he was all right, and in some ways he wasn't.

273

Emmett looked at Juan and asked, "What happens now? I ain't going home."

Juan looked at Jennifer and then at Drew. Jennifer smiled at Emmett.

She said, "Someone else has offered you let you stay with him, at least for a while, if you're willing. Then we can see what will happen."

Emmett looked at me. But I knew who it was. I looked at Drew.

Drew touched his remote to move the chair forward.

"You?" Emmett's voice had more of confusion than anything else in it.

Drew said, "I'm a registered foster parent. Johnny's parents asked me to do that in case there came a time we thought it would be better for him."

Jennifer said, "I knew that. And Emmett, I know how challenging your home life is. So I called Drew and asked him to be here. Just as an option."

Drew waited to give Emmett and me time to adjust our faces. Then he said, "Emmett, if you'd like, I have a spare room you can call your own while we figure out the next steps. This doesn't mean you have to stay with me if you don't want to. But it would mean the only reason to go home tonight would be to collect a few things."

Everyone looked at Emmett. Jennifer asked, "What do you think, Emmett?"

He shrugged. "Better than nothin', I guess. For now." Then he looked at me. "Will you be there?"

Drew saved me from awkward stammering. "Nathan has a home of his own, Emmett, but if he'd like to stay with us tonight, he's welcome."

Welcome. I'd be welcome to stay with Drew. Would that be on his couch? Or in his bed? And did I even want to do that?

Emmett looked at me, naked anticipation on that face that was usually so guarded against expressing anything.

*This isn't about you, Nathan.*

I looked at Drew. "Your couch is big enough for me, right?"

I couldn't read the expression on his face. "It is."


I left my car for Margot so she could get home after whatever time she spent with Andy's parents. Which meant that I rode with Drew and Emmett to the Chaplin home, behind the car Jennifer and Juan were in.

Emmett's parents weren't home. Jennifer wrote a note for them, Emmett shoved a few things into a trash bag, and we left.

There was no way the scene at Drew's would be anything but awkward. I followed behind them as Drew gave Emmett a tour, showed him the spare room with its own private bathroom, showed him how to use the elevator if he wanted it, and in the kitchen he told Emmett he could have anything other than alcohol.

"Not my thing, anyway," Emmett mumbled.

"Have you had dinner?" Drew asked.

"I could eat."

As I helped Drew put something together for Emmett, I took care that we didn't touch in any way. At one point Drew said, "Nathan, can you finish here? I need to fetch you a blanket and pillow."

Emmett devoured the tuna salad sandwich and veggie chips, nearly chugging the ginger ale I poured for him. Drew, back downstairs, got some cookies out and gave those to him, and he ate quite a few of them.

By this time Emmett was nearly falling over with exhaustion. Once he'd headed upstairs, I went into the living room to examine my bed for tonight. Drew followed with a beer for each of us.

His voice low, he said, "When I went upstairs I put my meds into a locked cabinet I keep up there. I don't lock them away usually, but with Emmett in the house...."

I nodded and took the beer more automatically than out of any feeling of wanting it. I stood in the middle of the room, wondering when he was going to leave. I felt dead tired.

Drew said, "We need to talk."

"Do we?"

"Well, I need to talk. I need to tell you how sorry I am about my behavior Monday night."

"And how sorry is that?" And how much would it matter?

He lowered the chair and gestured toward the couch. He really did want to talk. Fine. But I sat in one of those amazing architectural chairs instead.

"I said some terrible things to you. Things that weren't really meant for you. Things that were coming from a part of me that has nothing to do with you."

"Like?"

But instead of answering that question, he said, "You were absolutely right to want to help Emmett. I still think taking him up the Precipice was ill-advised, but my reaction was way out of proportion. I don't offer an excuse. But there is a reason."

"Yeah. Your own fall." I saw the slightest flinch. "You never let me finish, you know. You're wrong. I didn't take Emmett anywhere."

"What do you mean?"

"You jumped down my throat every time I tried to speak, so you don't even know that I had no choice. Emmett called me to say he was at the trail, heading up, and if I wanted to I should catch up to him. I called Ken. I called Juan. Both were out of town. So I called Jennifer. We agreed that I had no choice but to go after him, and she drove to the trailhead herself. I got there first and started up."

I took a breath. Drew waited, a pained look on his face.

"I passed two parties on the trail. They seemed like they knew what they were doing. Then," I glared at Drew here and did my best to keep my voice low in the hopes that Emmett wouldn't hear, "I caught up to a family. Parents. Young girl. I talked them into going back down. It was almost too late. They were almost too far up. But *I talked them down*."

Drew closed his eyes briefly and swallowed.

"When I caught up with Emmett, he was at that long-ish plank bridge, the one with the thin handrail, maybe two-thirds of the way up. He was terrified. I had to convince him he could do it. And he did. He finished the whole fucking climb, Drew. He was so proud of himself!" I had to stop and take a couple of breaths; tears had come to my eyes. "Do you know how massive that is?"

"I'm so sorry."

"Yeah. You said that." I was breathing hard, furious all over again.

We watched each other's faces, his looking sad almost to the point of tears, mine no doubt contorted with fury.

He rubbed his forehead. Then, "All I can say is that it was my own experience on that trail that caused me to jump to conclusions. Have you ever had an experience that was traumatic enough to bring you close to death?"

I couldn't tell whether he was assuming I'd say no, or if it was a genuine inquiry. I told him, "Yes."

It looked like he was surprised and trying not to show it. "How did it happen?"

So I told him about my very first hike. I told him how I'd followed Daniel, an experienced but ill-prepared and irresponsible climber, up a mountain in March, through a snowstorm, missing the cabin near the summit because Daniel hadn't investigated the climb and didn't quite know where the cabin was—especially in the middle of a snowstorm.

I described my state—poorly shod, badly clothed for the climb, wearing a too-large, borrowed frame pack that was more my enemy than my friend. I told Drew how my watch had frozen, how Daniel and I had been forced to set up a make-shift camp using my sleeping bag as a roof. I described the painful shivering that turned into convulsions and how my wet feet grew colder and colder until the tissue in them began to freeze.

I said that I had been nearly comatose in the morning and almost couldn't wake up, and that it had taken over an hour to get up and repack, a chore that should have taken no more than twenty minutes; I was so cold I could barely move. I told him about trudging through snow again, with my boots now ill-fitting because my feet were too swollen to go all the way in. I described finding the cabin, now useless to us, and I told him how Daniel had started to descend on the wrong trail, which would have landed us in the middle of nowhere, at night, where we would certainly not have survived. I told him how I had insisted on the correct direction, how Daniel had finally followed me, how we had crossed a river tumbling through a ravine by crawling across a fallen tree with limbs and stubs poking every which way, interfering with our progress and nearly causing us to fall.

And I told Drew about my feet, which were badly frostbitten, my feet that became so swollen I couldn't see my ankle bones, feet I couldn't walk on for two weeks.

Then I told him how I'd gone back up that same mountain a few months later, alone, after Neil had died, and how I'd been inspired to take up my brother's challenge of climbing all the four-thousand-foot-plus peaks in the White Mountains.

The last thing I said was, "My feet will never be the same. I can never hike for more than a few hours in winter again. I have to baby them from September through April, because they get painfully cold very easily and can't warm themselves up. So, yeah, I do have a life-threatening trauma behind me, complete with a constant reminder."

He sat quietly and listened to my story without comment until I had finished. Then he said, "I can't go back up my mountain."

I stared at him, not sure this was the right thing to say

but I said it anyway. "Maybe adjusting to your life in a wheelchair is your way of doing that."

Drew clenched his eyes shut again, as though forcing tears to stay put. His voice was ragged. "This is what I mean about you. You have a way of seeing things most people don't." He wiped at his eyes. Then, "Do you know what it is about you that makes Emmett trust you?"

With a nod of thanks to Margot, I told him, "I think so. I think he senses that when I commit to something, I commit completely. I'm either in it, or I'm not. And I managed to convince him that I care about him, and that recovery from addiction means that I want him to recover himself." There was a roaring silence for about five seconds before I added, "I guess I didn't manage to convince you. You don't see me as someone who goes all in."

Drew pinched the bridge of his nose, his eyes tight shut. Then he said, "That's where you're wrong."

I didn't hear what he meant. All I heard was an accusation. "Yeah, well, that's the trouble, isn't it? You seem to think I'm wrong about a lot of things."

He shook his head. "No. I mean you have convinced me."

I waited a couple of beats before saying, "And what good is that now?"

He let out a long breath. "I'm not sure we're going to be able to talk about this tonight. There's too much else going on."

"Do we have something more to talk about?"

"Oh, God, Nathan. I hope so."

"Because, you know," and I quoted him another of his cowboy poetry lines: "You put me out like the burnin' end of a midnight cigarette."

He looked ready to cry. "You're determined to hurt me. I hurt you, and you're striking back."

I stood. "I'm not striking back, Drew. I'm struggling to recover from what you did to me. You spent weeks trying to get me to see that we could have a relationship, and almost as soon as I committed to that idea you sent me packing because you were so sure—so wrong, but so sure—I had done something wrong. What the fuck am I supposed to make of that? You think it's enough to say you're sorry?" I waited. He said nothing. So I said, "It isn't. I'm staying here tonight for Emmett's sake, not for yours. And I'll thank you to go upstairs and let me try like hell to fall asleep here on the couch."

The look on his face was beyond sad. It was miserable. Wretched. He backed his chair away slowly, turned, and headed for the elevator.

In the morning, after about three hours of broken sleep, I wrote a note to Emmett saying I'd see him soon. I left the house before anyone else was downstairs. From the driveway, I called Margot and woke her up.

"Come get me."

The next several days were a blur. Somehow I managed to go through enough necessary motions at work to meet my job requirements. Katie tried to talk to me but—as politely as possible—I refused to engage. Perhaps she assumed I was upset about Andy. That was true, but I was more upset about Drew.

His image haunted my days and intruded on my dreams. The picture I saw most often was his face and the near-desperate look on it when I'd told him to go upstairs and leave me to sleep on his couch.

It had been four weeks since Drew and I had gone around Eagle Lake, a little over two weeks since I'd texted Drew to say things with us wouldn't work, a week and a half since I'd asked him if we could try again. That was a month of me obsessing on Drew: on Drew and me together, on me alone, on Drew and me together again. Now I was back to me alone. So why did it feel like he was still with me?

Margot did her best to get me to talk things out, but every time I considered that, I felt like crying. So I kept putting her off.

Emmett knew something was up, but he was wise enough not to refer to it in any way. His parents said they didn't care where he went, so he stayed with Drew that whole week. But in an interesting turn of events the Greens asked if they could be his foster parents. They offered to take in his sister as well, who was thirteen, but she told them in no uncertain terms to fuck off.

"Maybe she'll change her mind," Mrs. Green told Margot. "We'll leave the offer open."

Emmett, however, agreed. The legal process was started, and he was to move in with them on Sunday morning.

Saturday, a chilly and overcast day, I drove to Drew's to meet Ken and Emmett for our hike. I was deliberately a few minutes late, hoping to avoid Drew. I left my car, and Ken drove us to Cadillac Mountain Sports to get Emmett an appropriate pair of hiking pants—wicking fabric, with zippers above the knees to convert them into shorts— and his own pair of crag gloves. We made another stop for a packed lunch, and then we hit the trail.

I was pretty quiet all day, but that gave Ken and Emmett a chance to get to know each other a little. It did seem to me as though Emmett was opening up in a way I hadn't allowed myself to expect.

After the hike, driving back to Drew's place, rain began—a near deluge, actually. As we pulled into the driveway I saw that Drew was outside, right in front of the garage, in his manual chair, a dark green poncho covering everything from his head to his wheels. His beard dripped water. Even his eyebrows dripped water.

Emmett gave me a significant look, grabbed his pack, and ran for the door.

Ken stared at Drew and asked me, "What's he doing?"

I had a pretty good idea. But what I said to Ken was,

"It's fine. Thanks for driving. See you Monday." I got out of the car and waited for Ken to leave. Then I walked through the rain to stand in front of Drew.

He was sitting there drenched with rain for a reason. I had no idea how long he'd been waiting, but I knew he'd been waiting for me. And I knew the rain was meaningful.

As I stood in front of him, I thought back to the first time this had happened. When I'd come out of the woods after hiking the Precipice alone, drenched with rain, he'd been waiting. He'd wheeled himself over to his van and I had followed, and we'd regarded each other, a mixture of grief and pain and hope flowing between us. And here we were again.

As before, water worked its way under my collar and down my back. It was much colder today, though, and it made me shiver. That's when Drew spoke.

"Can we try again?"

"Come to me tomorrow. Two o'clock. On the Eagle Lake carriage road, where I yelled at that woman. We'll see what happens."

I turned and dashed to my car, not waiting for an answer.


I barely slept, awake most of the night wracking my brain, going back over everything that had happened between Drew and me. I'd misjudged him in a number of ways. And he had misjudged me, too.

Initially, I'd seen his disability as a weakness. In some ways, of course, that was true. But the way he'd presented himself had looked anything but weak. I'd even wondered—and had had the gall to ask him—if he was in denial, by which I'd meant was he denying that there was any weakness about him in this new way of life. But as I'd gotten to know him, I'd seen a courage and a confidence that had nothing to do with weakness or denial.

On the other hand, when he'd reacted so powerfully—and with such a wrong-headed assumption—to my hiking the Precipice with Emmett, he'd revealed a true weakness. Because when it came to how his disability affected his life, there were areas in which he could be completely irrational. So maybe he wasn't in denial. But it sure seemed like he was still adjusting, still working to understand himself as a person with a disability.

If what had happened to him had happened to me, I don't know that I'd ever be able to adjust. It was to his credit that he'd managed it as well as he had.

Even so, one thing that I knew from my study of psychology, and something I'd seen played out at the clinic, was that strength is true strength only when you acknowledge vulnerability rather than deny it. Trying to hide it is cowardly; admitting it, letting others see it, is courageous. I felt sure Drew had some growing to do in this area of his life. And if he wouldn't see that, I needed to know.

Of course, I had not exactly been perfect, either. I'd known I had a problem seeing the person rather than the disability, and yet when I'd decided we wouldn't work as a couple I'd refused to see what was really in the way. I'd been guilty of my own brand of denial. *Oh, no, it's not the chair that bothers me. Not at all.*

Bullshit.

By the time I got up, groggy and sleep-deprived, I had some clarity. I'd made some decisions about what I needed to know before I answered Drew's question.


I was at the spot by one-thirty, deliberately ahead of Drew. It was even colder today than yesterday, and tiny specks of snow fell around me, making occasional tinkling sounds as they hit the nylon of my anorak. There weren't very many of them; it was more like snow drizzle than anything else. It reminded me of the light, almost musical crystals that had been falling the day Daniel and I had started our hike. They hadn't seemed like much at the time, but before we'd gotten half way up the mountain, struggling through many inches of snow that had fallen earlier in the season, it had begun to snow in earnest. I almost hoped that would happen today. Soon. Before Drew arrived.

I was gazing across the lake when I saw him approach, pushing the bright blue handles of his trail chair. He wore a black knit hat, grey gloves, and a puffy navy parka that had obviously been altered to fit precisely around his body where he sat in the chair. His legs were covered with navy pants that matched the parka and were almost as puffy, no doubt because he wouldn't even know if his legs got cold, and he couldn't afford to risk that happening.

His eyes on mine, he pushed himself toward me steadily, slowing only when he was very close.

He spoke first. "You have a marvelous sense of the dramatic." His smile was tentative. Good; he wasn't sure what would happen.

Neither was I.

But I did know what I was going to say. "That night at your house you really hurt me. I know you've already apologized. Now I want to know two things. One, what was behind how you treated me? And two, if I spend more time with you, how likely is it that something like that will happen again?"

"Can I answer the second question first?"

I lifted an arm, hand open, as permission.

"I don't remember ever creating a scene like that before. Maybe when I was a child, but certainly not since. This tells me that my misunderstanding—just hearing that you'd been back there under any circumstances with someone who shouldn't hike that trail—pressed a button I didn't even know I had. It's also likely that no one but you could have pressed it so hard. And that—" He took a breath and let it out slowly. "That is because I love you."

I crossed my arms. I hadn't been ready for that, and I didn't want to show my surprise. I also didn't want it to get to me, to make his job today any easier.

When I said nothing, he lowered his head for a second, and when he raised it he said, "Now that I know how powerful your effect is on me, I can tell you this. I will do everything I can to make sure nothing like that ever happens again."

He paused, so I said, "And the first question?"

"That's harder. Sure, you pressed buttons. Hard. I didn't take the time to consider that you hadn't even known they were there, let alone that you hadn't intended to push them. But that was part of the pain. I had expected that you *would* know they were there."

Again he paused. I asked, "And why do you think I didn't know? Maybe because up to that point you'd taken great care to appear invulnerable? Maybe because we hadn't known each other long enough for me to have a snowball's chance in hell to see the pain you're still carrying?"

He opened his mouth, but no words came out, just a strangled sound as though he'd hoped letting a little breath out would bring words with it.

"And here's another possibility. Was there something in you that made you jealous because I was hiking with Emmett and not you?"

His "Yes" was barely audible as his face crumpled into what I could only call naked pain. Tears formed in his eyes and spilled over onto his cheeks and ran into the tangle of his beard. He was holding his breath, and when he nodded a sob escaped his mouth. He caught it back in with a sudden intake of breath, but the next one came quickly, and then another, and then he was weeping.

As if in concert with his tears, the snow grew heavier. Everything in me wanted to kneel beside him as I'd done the last time we were here. Almost everything. Something held me back. I turned my attention inward, trying to identify the source of that hesitation. And I found it. It was a mixture of pride and fear. Pride, because he'd hurt me, rejected me, betrayed me. Fear, because if I gave in to the impulse to hold him, kiss him, be with him again, this might not be the last time he would hurt me.

It might not be the last time I'd hurt him.

But wasn't that part of what relationships are all about? And as that thought settled into my mind, I made a connection I hope I never forget. I'd told Drew that climbing a mountain was a metaphor for life, with all the details you have to navigate your way through eventually leading you to a rewarding summit. And I'd told him we needed reminding about that, because there were always more details, more things that could trip us up, and that we had to learn to keep going through the areas that might be painful or difficult or boring because there was a summit waiting.

What hit me at that moment was that relationships are like that, too. So the question I had to answer for myself was whether I had what it took to work through the challenging details of a relationship. Because if I didn't, I didn't deserve a relationship. I didn't deserve Drew.

I knelt beside the chair, one knee settling painfully on a small stone. I left it there. Snowflakes settled in a thickening layer on his thighs. I removed the glove from one hand and reached up through the falling flakes. His sad brown eyes held mine as I wiped tears from his face. The sobbing gave way to an occasional catch of his breath. He was barely able to say, "Can we try again?"

I nodded. "Yes. But no more hiding. No more pretending we aren't scarred and damaged. No more angry reactions to expectations we haven't expressed."

He swiped across his face with one hand while fishing with the other for a handkerchief. I shifted my knee painfully off of the pebble but stayed where I was as he blew his nose and snuffled.

We stayed like that, frozen in place, an artist's image of

two damaged men in the snow, until Drew said, "Kiss me?"

It wasn't a great kiss. But it was a kiss. Then he said, "Is it too soon to invite you to stay the night?"

I chuckled and shook my head. "You always did want to move forward quickly. No patience for waiting. No wasting time."

He smiled a wobbly smile. "Maybe that's because I feel like I've been waiting for you all my life."


We got takeout for dinner. Drew opened a bottle of wine, and we sat at his kitchen table. Classical guitar music played in the background.

I was half-way through my mushroom risotto with parmesan crusted chicken when, in a quiet moment, Drew and I looked at each other and smiled. It was not a sexy smile. It was a contented smile.

Drew broke the silence. "Emmett really enjoys hiking with you."

I took this for the peace offering I believed it was. "He's a great companion. Doesn't complain. Barely talks. Seems to be up for anything."

"And I'll bet it's giving him the feeling of accomplishment you want for him."

I nodded. "Hope so. One of the counselors at the clinic said hiking helped him during his recovery. I'll hike with Emmett again. You need to know that."

I looked up at Drew's face, open and soft, ready to hear whatever I had to say, and it occurred to me that I'd told Emmett more about me than I'd told Drew, at least in terms of my own vulnerabilities. Was this a good time to venture into that area?

I said, "I was pretty hard on you this afternoon."

His voice teasing, he said, "And not in a good way." We both laughed. Then he added, "I deserved it."

"Okay, well, where I was going with that was to admit

to a few of my own weak spots."

"Only if you're ready."

"I hear Molly Tuttle's voice suddenly."

He laughed at that. "You remember!"

"I do." I grinned at him. "So…. I hit a bit of a brick wall the night Andy died. That is, in terms of my understanding of addiction recovery. Here I'd been telling Emmett that okay, maybe I didn't use, but I had some idea what it was like to be afraid to let go of something that really wasn't good for you. But that night—" I paused. Then, "Shit. Andy fucking *died!* He was caught between being desperate to end his addiction and desperate to end the pain. The only way out was to end himself."

Drew and I gave that some space. Then I said, "I realized I didn't know shit. I mean, I've never been in that much pain. I can't even imagine being in that much pain." And then I said something I hadn't intended to say. All I'd intended to do was admit to Drew that I wasn't the cracker-jack, addiction-ending expert I'd thought I was getting to be. But instead, maybe because of how emotional the past several days had been, this is what I said next: "Except maybe once."

As a delaying tactic, maybe to come up with a way to change the subject, maybe hoping that we'd both forget I'd said that, I toyed with my fork, pushing food around on my plate. Drew didn't speak. Finally I couldn't stop myself. It all came spilling out.

I said, "I think I was kind of addicted to Neil. To the way he made me feel, anyway. And when he died—" I closed my eyes and leaned my head back. "Jesus."

Still, Drew waited.

"You weren't wrong when you said Neil had essentially been my father. He was. He gave me all the security a really good father gives his child. I felt loved unconditionally. Cherished. Protected. Perfect, just the way I was. Hell—*I belonged.* He was the first person I came out to, and he was— God, he was amazing. Just wanted me to be true to myself."

I set my fork down and dropped my hands into my lap. "After he died—" I swallowed hard. My throat tightened and my voice sounded choked. "I wouldn't exactly say those feelings disappeared. But a huge part of it went away." I looked up at Drew's gentle eyes. "I want it back."

It took Drew maybe half a minute to speak, and when he did, it contained a warning. "I feel the urge to say something that—well, you probably won't like it. And it might even hurt. Should I go ahead?"

"Why do you think you need to say it?"

"Because of how much you mean to me."

I closed my eyes briefly. "Say it."

"I think that sense of being perfectly yourself, of belonging, is something that exists inside you. It sounds like Neil showed you it was there. He primed the pump, and God bless him for that. But, Nathan," Drew's eyes actually watered here, "all of that—that sense of peace, that security—is inside you. That's where you have to go to find it. If I've learned nothing else in the past few years, I've learned that. I can't give it to you. No one can give it to you. Not even Neil."

Neither of us said anything for maybe two minutes. I sat there, staring in the general direction of my plate, struggling with the most tangled up, mangled mess of feelings I'd known in a long time. There was pain, deep and terrifying. There was anger—at Neil for dying, and at Drew for—God, so many reasons. For nearly ending this relationship before it really got started. For saying Neil hadn't given me what I'd always believed he had, for saying he couldn't have given it to me, that I was wrong to think he had. For telling me I wouldn't find it anywhere else I looked, not even here in this house. For laying the burden of finding it on me. And, somewhere at the bottom of that Pandora's box—yes, the same one I'd told Emmett about—was love. Because despite our recent conflict, I knew that Drew would never say something like that to me except from a place of love, and respect, and deep concern.

My brain bounced from one side of my skull to the other, yelling painful questions and painful truths at me, sending me back into those dizzying circles of indecision and doubt I thought I'd found my way out of.

*Am I worth the good feelings I got from Neil? Do I deserve them? Did the best part of me die with him?*

*Drew just fed me the same line counselors feed addicts, the same thing I'd just told Emmett. And it has shocked me. Why? Because this time it was said to* me *rather than* by *me?*

*I'd told Emmett what giving up an addiction feels like—dangling over jagged rocks, clinging for dear life to fragile tree roots. That metaphor wasn't Emmett's. It was mine.*

*What Drew just said to me was almost the exact same thing I told Emmett, in the hospital linen closet. I* know *this. Why can't I get there myself?*

*How can I help anyone else? Why would anyone who needs help listen to anything I have to say? I don't understand fucking anything.*

It felt like my whole life was thrown suddenly into question. Everything I'd believed, everything I'd wanted, everything I'd thought I could contribute was now in doubt.

I barely heard Drew's voice. "You okay?"

I shook my head.

Drew rolled away from the table and came to me. He took my hand as he raised his chair.

"Come with me."

I pulled my hand away, angry. "I don't want sex right now! Christ."

"Neither do I." He held his hand toward me again. I looked up at his face, and something I saw there pulled me to my feet.

We went up to his bedroom, where he undressed me and then himself. We lay in his bed, his arm around my shoulders, my face buried against his chest. Tears bled slowly from my closed eyes until I fell asleep.

I heard screaming. It seemed to go on and on. It wouldn't stop.

"Nathan! Nathan, wake up! It's okay. It's only a dream."

Someone pulled me against his body and held me. I started to sob, and the screams stopped. At some point I realized it was Drew holding me. He had managed to get himself into a sitting position, and he had pulled me up beside him. He held me gently, saying nothing, letting me cry.

Slowly the sobbing subsided and I pulled away.

"There's a tissue box on the table beside you."

I groped and found it, blowing my nose again and again, taking in shattered breaths. Finally, exhausted, I lay back against the pillows.

My breathing was still unsteady, but I managed, "I've never told anyone what I'm about to tell you." I sniffled a few times and blew my nose again.

My voice was steady enough when I started talking. It didn't last.

"The last hike Neil went on was with his friend Jeremy. They were in Virginia, in the Priest Wilderness. Extremely remote. They bought a satellite phone to take with them. No cell reception there."

I paused to snuffle a few times.

"Neil was always very well prepared. He'd told the forest service where they were going, using geographic coordinates. He and Jeremy were staying in a rustic cabin, hiking out from there during the days. There were fires in the area, but nothing very close to them. Even so, they bought a two-man, portable fire shelter. I was at home—"

I felt Drew stiffen; he had some idea what was coming, and he knew it was bad.

I had to stop. I had to stop talking. I had to stop breathing. More tears squeezed their way from under my clenched eyelids. I took a gasping breath, and I felt Drew's hand take mine.

"It was mid-morning. Gram was out grocery shopping, and I was alone in the house. My phone rang. When I answered it—"

I pulled away from Drew and sat forward, knees up, hands clenching my hair. "It was Neil. The noise was terrible. Like a rushing train that just kept coming. He told me to tell Gram he loved her. He told me to tell Jeremy's mom the same thing. I know he was going to say he loved me and Nina, but that's when the screams started."

The room was totally silent for several seconds.

"They screamed and screamed, both of them. I shouted Neil's name, over and over. Then, nothing. I heard Neil die. I heard Jeremy die."

Silence. Then I took a couple of shaky breaths.

"Gram came home. I told her what Neil had said." I shifted in the bed to look at Drew, or as much of him as I could see in the dark. "I never told her about the screams. I never told anyone."

"You've told me."

"Yes."

He held me for a long time.

Monday evening after dinner I told Margot I had something private to do, and I went into my bedroom and closed the door. This was something I had thought about so many times over the last few years, something that I was determined to do and yet terrified of doing.

After last night, with Drew, I was feeling a lot of different things. I felt fragile, because of that screaming dream and how completely shattered it had left me. But I realized that the reason the pain in that dream had surfaced— buried for three and half years—was that something in my subconscious knew that being with Drew was a safe place to be.

Safe. That was the key. And I think that's what made me realize it was time, at last, to bring some closure to another painful time. Alden.

Although I hadn't known his parents' first names, I knew that his mother was a surgeon and that his father owned a dealership for exotic cars. I knew they lived in St. Louis, which was behind me by an hour in terms of time zones. It was now just past nine here.

A little searching yielded quite a few Armstrongs in St. Louis, none named Alden. I made note of the addresses and looked all of them up on an online map. Only five of them seemed to be in the kind of neighborhood where I expected Alden's wealthy parents would live. Only two of these were listed as doctors, and only one was a woman's first name. Leona.

I stared at the name. I took a deep breath, and then another.

Holy shit. Was I really going to do this?

Yes. I was.

I moved to sit in an upholstered chair that had been in my house in Concord, an unattractive green and brown tweed that Neil had been fond of, which I had moved into my room here rather than have it in the condo's living room. I held up my phone, and I touched the numbers.

The line rang five times. I was about to cut the call off when someone answered. "Nathan?"

It was her. Only Alden's mother would have recognized the name that showed up on her phone.

"Yes. This is Nathan. I, uh, I'm sorry to intrude. It's just that I've been thinking a lot lately about Alden." I paused, but she said nothing. She also didn't hang up, though, so I said, "I'm not trying to get in touch with him. I was just hoping to find out how he is."

The line was silent so long, that I said, "Hello?"

"Yes. Yes, I'm here." Her voice sounded odd. "I'm sorry to tell you, but—well, Alden died last year. December."

Now the line was quiet on both ends.

It had been in December when he'd relapsed before, when he'd disappeared from my life.

I didn't need to ask how it had happened. I swallowed a couple of times and finally managed, "I also wanted to thank you for how kind you were to me that night I showed up at the house in Dover. The tapestry you gave me has been a huge inspiration for me."

"Tapestry?"

I looked up at it as I spoke. "The one on the front wall? With the fall colors on mountains? And the lake?"

"I'm sorry, Nathan. I remember you, certainly, but I don't remember the tapestry."

"It—never mind. It's been important to me, that's all. I'm so sorry about Alden. Thanks for telling me. I'll let you go now."

"Nathan?"

"Yes?"

"I'm glad you and Alden knew each other. I—maybe you knew, and maybe you didn't. But he loved you."

Not enough. I didn't say that. It would have been profoundly unfair. Instead I told her, "I loved him, too."

After we hung up, I sat in that chair for nearly half an hour. I expected that at any moment I would cry. My eyes did well up a few times, but that was all. My heart felt sore but not broken.

As sad as this news had been, it helped me. It brought a kind of closure to a very troubling chapter of my life. And it answered a question that had haunted me: Had Alden loved me? And now, I knew.


The rest of that week was a little like the week after Drew and I had had sex the first time. As then, he sent me short texts that made me almost wish we hadn't agreed to wait until Friday night to get together again.

I got the sense from Emmett that the move to the Greens' had been a success. I asked him at one point how things were going there, and he said, "Good enough." From him, that was high praise. Then he said, "When do we hike again?"

"I'll look into the weather forecast and we can talk to Ken."

A few seconds went by. Then he said, "You're better."

"Better?"

"Back with Drew?"

What a kid. I smiled and nodded.

# CHAPTER SEVENTEEN

Friday evening couldn't come soon enough. Katie had grinned at me on and off all day, and as I was leaving I took one more glance at her.

Katie sucked in her cheeks. I gave her a mock-dirty look, and she raised her hands in the air. "Not sayin' nothin'. Not sayin' nothin' about you and that handsome hunk gettin' together again."

"Katie!"

"I said, not sayin' nothin.'"


Drew had made dinner. Coq au vin. "I've been on my feet all day!" he whined facetiously as soon as I came in the door.

We talked little over dinner, and that was just fine. Because we smiled at each other a lot. Dessert was something I'd never had before: profiteroles.

"I've been really spoiled," I told him. "Margot's a fabulous cook. You're a fabulous cook. At this rate, I don't know when I'll learn how to feed myself."

"Two things," Drew said. "One, I'd be glad to teach you a few recipes. And two, if you play your cards right, maybe you'll never have to learn." I gave him a stern look. He raised a hand in protest. "Not saying anything specific, here. Not pushing. Not being impatient. Just planting a seed."

"A seed."

"A seed. And, you know, it's gettin' on toward winter. So it might be a while before we know whether it will sprout."

I swear there was something of an aphrodisiac in those scrumptious little balls of eggy dough filled with silky vanilla ice cream and covered with warm fudge sauce. The glasses of the Trockenbeerenauslese I'd bought only added to my libido. But when I got up from the table to help clear, I realized I was so full I could barely more.

Drew looked ready for love. "Let's leave the dishes for tomorrow. Come with me." He raised his chair and held out his hand.

"Maybe we should clean up first. I'm not sure I can make it upstairs with all this food inside me. It's making me feel tired."

Drew laughed. "Leave everything to me. And prepare to have something else inside you."

That did it. "An offer I can't refuse."

He had me lie on the bed, naked, and close my eyes while he leaned against the headboard and did something mysterious that I wasn't allowed to see. My eyes flew open, though, when I realized that in one swift move, Drew had wrapped loops around both my hands and pulled on something so that I couldn't move my arms beyond bending my elbows a little.

"What the fuck?"

He grinned at me. "You said you were tired."

"Yeah. Tired, not tied!"

"What's a letter r between friends?"

"Missing! It's missing!" I wasn't sure whether to protest or not. "Do I get a safe word?"

He had moved to the foot of the bed. I couldn't see how he did it. "If you'd like. But you won't need it."

"How do you know?" I nearly winced as he secured just one of my ankles with another silken loop.

"I won't be doing anything to you that you won't love."

"Potato." Ridiculous word. No idea where it came from. I had wanted to say profiterole.

He laughed. "Fine. Potato, it is."

I never said it. I could not have predicted how well he could pull me, push me, flip me over, all so he could do spectacular things that made me nearly weep with pleasure. I came twice. At least, I think it was only twice. I was a helpless mess by the time he untied me.

I slept really, really well.

By the time I woke up in the morning, Drew wasn't in the room. I could hear noises coming from downstairs; sounded like he was dealing with last night's dishes.

I went to the top of the stairs. "Drew?"

He called, "About time you got up, lazy bones. Go take a shower and come down. We're going out right after breakfast."

"Where?"

"Surprise."

As I showered and dressed, a lot of thoughts went through my head. I'd needed to know whether Drew could face his vulnerabilities. He'd shown me that he could. But that didn't mean everything was going to be lollipops and roses from here out. I had no doubt there would be other scenes like the one that caused me to leave. The good news was that they would almost certainly not be as disruptive, that no one would walk out, that although they would be painful we would be able to work through them. It meant that Drew wasn't perfect, but who is?

Not me. Nothing perfect, here. So why would I want—and how could I expect—a partner who was? And what would that even mean?

I paused at the top of the stairs, about to join my boyfriend—yes; my boyfriend!—for breakfast when a feeling like my heart smiling came over me. Maybe Drew, who wasn't perfect, was nonetheless the perfect man for me.

Breakfast was blueberry pancakes with rich maple syrup, bacon, coffee, and orange juice. "I'm going to get fat."

"I'll still love you."

His tone was part jest, but there was more in it. This was the second time he'd told me he loved me. And I hadn't said it back. The difference now, this second time, was that I knew how to respond.

I rested my wrists on the edge of the table and smiled at him. He looked back at me, his half-smile holding some combination of anxiety and anticipation. I said, "I'll still love you, too."

As I watched, his body relaxed. A tension that had been barely noticeable had lifted. The joy that bloomed in my chest told me I'd spoken the truth. It felt so fucking good.

I picked up my fork and let it hover over my plate. "Where are we going after this?"

"All right, I'll tell you. I'm buying you a present. A mountain bike. So you can keep up with me."

I couldn't help it. I laughed.

Drew had queued up some music. He was about to start it playing, when I interrupted him.

"How about if I play you some music that I really love?"

"Sure." As we did the Bluetooth dance to get my phone connected to his system, he asked, "What kind of music is it?"

"Hawai'ian slack key guitar." I queued up Keola Beamer's "Tales from the Dream Guitar."

Drew listened for a couple of minutes. "It's very evocative. Palm trees. Gentle breezes. Sandy beaches. Soft ocean waves. Hang on a minute…. Didn't you tell me you'd hiked in Hawai'i?"

"Yes. Kaua'i. The north shore. The Kalalau Trail." I repeated something Conroy had once said: "If I were a god I would live there."

"Why?"

I scrunched my face briefly in an effort to mitigate

some of the intensity of what I was about to say. "This will sound—I don't know, corny, or hokey, or something like that. It's not a feeling I've had at any other time or in any other place. But I swear to you, it was real. It was almost palpable."

He grinned. "Don't keep me in suspense, here."

"Okay." I took a long breath to create some space for the importance of what I was about to say. "What I felt there was that I'd found a place where the physical and the spiritual meet. There is no bridge between the secular world and the sacred, because no bridge is needed. They exist together, right there, in some kind of nexus. And I was in the middle of it."

I paused and watched Drew's face. There was a softness about it, as though what I'd said had affected him deeply.

I asked, "D'you think I'm out of my mind?"

"Yes. I hope so. There are times and places where we need to leave our intellect behind and just be. It sounds like you found one of them."

We ate in silence for a few minutes. Then Drew surprised the hell out of me. "It would mean so much to me if we could go there together sometime. Would you be into that?"

I'd told Ellie that it was unlikely that I'd go back, afraid the experience wouldn't be as special. But with Drew, there would be a different kind of specialness. So I hesitated for a nanosecond because of that, but also because I had no idea what it would be like for Drew to travel. Or for me to travel with him. But—so what? It would be just one more way of experiencing life with him.

"I would. Yes."

Drew made a fresh pot of coffee and we let Keola's album play out, and then Drew reclaimed his connection to the sound system. "I thought you might like to hear just a few cuts from an older album by Molly Tuttle," he said. "You're so good at remembering those snatches of cowboy poetry."

I glanced at him, alert for a dig, but one side of his

mouth was lifted in a teasing grin.

The first song that played was something called "Good enough." It's what Emmett had said about his new home, which I knew had meant it was working out really well. Mollie's lyrics referred to something more along the lines of a romantic relationship, although they were equally understated.

In the song, she said the warmth of her lover pushes away thoughts of doubt and dread. She's learning how to let some doors stay shut. There are things about the past she'll never figure out. There will be times she's not okay, but she'll be with her love. And now, "There comes a time to say, 'That's good enough.'"

Good enough? Pretty damn good, actually.

I heard guitar. I heard banjo. I heard fiddle.

Maybe bluegrass isn't so bad after all.

The End

# ACKNOWLEDGMENTS

Years ago, I realized that the maxim "Write what you know" is woefully inadequate for the kind of writing I want to do. So sometimes my characters find themselves in situations requiring expertise or knowledge I don't have. When this happens, I rely on someone who knows more about the situation than I do.

*On the Precipice* features a central character, Drew Madden, who uses a wheelchair. While I have experienced injuries in my life, I have never doubted that I could get up, walk across the room, descend the stairs to my garage, get in my standard-issue automobile, and get wherever I needed to go.

Drew Madden lost the ability to take these things for granted. Everything he does requires planning and logistics that mean he needs more time and money than I do to accomplish absolutely anything.

To represent Drew as accurately and as sensitively as possible, I asked for help. Stevie M. Jonak, a wheelchair user herself, guided me as I wrote sections of this story that involve Drew. She provided a foreword that I hope will help non-disabled individuals see the disabled community with new eyes and new understanding.

Most importantly, Stevie provided a wonderful example of what it looks like when someone with disabilities refuses to sit in a corner and feel sorry for herself. Stevie lives alone. She acquaints herself with the ins and outs of medical insurance, she understands the arcane rules of the Social Security Administration (no small feat) as they relate to her, and she

302

locates other resources available to her. She travels frequently. She learns skills like archery. She is applying for college courses. She visits family and friends and participates joyfully in their gatherings. She speaks up continually for the rights of people with disabilities. She takes on the responsibility of having a cat live with her. In short, there is no stopping Stevie.

I am profoundly grateful both for her practical support and advice and for the ways in which she has inspired and enlightened me.

A Reading Group Guide

ON THE PRECIPICE
(Trailblazer Series, Book 3)


Robin Reardon


ABOUT THIS GUIDE


The suggested questions are included to enhance your group's reading of Robin Reardon's novel, *ON THE PRECIPICE* , Book 3 of the *TRAILBLAZER* series.

# DISCUSSION QUESTIONS

Note: The questions in this guide contain spoiler information. It is recommended that you finish the book before reading through the questions.

1.  When Nathan meets Luc, his sister's boyfriend, he believes that Nina loves Luc more than the other way around. Why does he have this impression? How does it make you feel about Nina? When he finally figures out that he was wrong, does your impression of Nina change? If so, how? Do you like Nina?

2.  The first time Nathan sees Drew Madden, he draws conclusions about Drew because he's in a wheelchair. He assumes Drew is inadequate as a mountaineer. What else does Nathan assume because of the chair? When you see someone you don't know who's in a wheelchair, what goes through your mind? How do you think of that person? How do you treat them?

3.  Drew's ability to thwart a robbery attempt impresses Nathan. Even so, when Drew suggests they go for a beer, Nathan is reluctant. Why? And why does he end up going, even though his inclination had been to decline?

4.  Nathan and Drew have an intense, fascinating conversation over dinner right after they meet. During that conversation, do you think Nathan manages to forget that Drew has a disability? If so, might that be part of the reason for Nathan's reaction when Drew asks him for his impressions about it? Drew essentially pushes the chair into the conversation, pushing it—in a way—between him and Nathan. Do you think Nathan's irritation comes from almost having forgotten about the chair and then being forced to acknowledge and respond

to it? Or is it more likely Nathan is reacting to his own sense of guilt?

5. When Jennifer asks Nathan where he came up with his Pandora's box response to Emmett, he tells her he couldn't respond to Emmett's racist comment. So he responded to Emmett's pain. Do you think that at this point in the story, Nathan has a fairly good idea what Emmett's pain is like? If not, what is he missing?

6. After Drew has dinner at the condo with Margot and Nathan, Drew invites Nathan to walk to his van with him. Drew tells Nathan he's attracted to him and would like to see him again. Nathan is very unsure of himself, unsure of Drew, unsure of the wheelchair. But when he stands beside the van and sees Drew in the driver's seat, Drew looks perfectly "normal" to him. Drew's disability isn't evident, and he's a very attractive man. How do you see this juxtaposition playing out as the relationship between them progresses?

7. Drew invites Nathan to make a list of any question he might have about Drew's life and about his disability. He wants to see if there's the chance of a relationship, and he doesn't want to waste time. If Nathan has reservations, Drew wants them out in the open so they can be discussed. If you are able-bodied, can you imagine yourself being romantically attracted to someone like Drew—someone with an obvious disability? How do you think you would respond to an invitation to talk openly with that person about any reservations you might have?

8. Despite really enjoying his evening at Drew's house, Nathan decides to tell Drew it won't work. What reasons does Nathan give himself for this decision? Do you understand them? Do you agree with them?

9. Were you surprised that Drew waited in the rain at the Precipice Trail parking lot until Nathan was safely off the trail? Do you believe Drew when he says he was there for his own peace of mind rather than as a way to make Nathan feel guilty?

10. Part of the way up the Precipice Trail, Emmett freezes at the sight of a set of narrow wooden planks that span a deep crevice. Nathan knows that if Emmett can't trust himself enough, he won't be able to cross it. How is this concept apparent in Nathan's own life?

11. When Drew misconstrues the situation in which Nathan and Emmett hike the Precipice, Drew's reaction nearly destroys their relationship. Later, Drew admits that his reaction was inappropriate, even selfish. In fact, it seems to have surprised Drew, himself. He tells Nathan he will do his best never to repeat that kind of scene. Nathan contemplates this promise in light of his belief that they are bound to have more bumps in the road, that they are likely to hurt each other again. He accepts that this is part of what relationships are all about. Do you agree?

12. What do you think will happen to Emmett?

13. At one point Drew tells Nathan that the feelings he believes he got from Neil—the powerful sense of belonging, of security—don't actually come from outside of himself. Drew says no one can give him that peace, not even Neil; it must come from within. Nathan has no trouble with this concept in the physical world; when he didn't have a rope or any other external resources to help Emmett cross a rickety bridge, he came up with the solution from within himself. And, in fact, he had just said almost the exact same thing to Emmett after Andy Green died. Yet he balks at Drew's words. Why?

14. Since his college freshman year, Nathan had felt haunted by the ghost of Alden Armstrong. Toward the end of *On The Precipice*, Nathan contacts Mrs. Armstrong to ask about Alden. Her response, though the news is tragic, gives Nathan some closure. Do you think you could ever be with someone who was in recovery, if they were honest about it, as Alden was not?

# PLAYLIST FOR
# ON THE PRECIPICE

Every time I write a story, I'm influenced—and sometimes haunted—by some number of musical pieces. *On The Precipice* was no exception.

I've included a playlist for anyone interested in exploring the music that influenced my writing of *Precipice*.

- "If he's ever near" (Karla Bonoff)
- "When You're Ready" (Molly Tuttle)
- "The High Road" (Molly Tuttle)
- "Good Enough" (Molly Tuttle)
- "Live It" (Cherryholmes)
- "It's Over" (Alison Kraus)
- "Box of Kittens" (The Audreys)
- "Whiskey Lullaby" (Alison Kraus)
- "Hurricane" (David Wilcox)
- "Buy for Me the Rain" (Nitty Gritty Dirt Band)

If you enjoyed this book, please consider posting a review on the online sites of your choice. This is the best way to ensure that more titles by this author will become available.

If you would like to be notified when new titles are released, you can sign up for Robin's mailing list at robinreardon.com/contact.

# ABOUT THE AUTHOR

Robin Reardon is an inveterate observer of human nature, and her primary writing goal is to create stories about all kinds of people whose destinies should not be determined solely by their sexual orientation or gender identity. Her secondary writing goal is to introduce readers to concepts or information they might not know very much about.

Robin's motto is this: The only thing wrong with being gay is how some people treat you when they find out.

Interests outside of writing include singing, nature photography, and the study of comparative religions. Robin writes in a butter yellow study with a view of the Boston, Massachusetts skyline.

Robin blogs (And now, this) about various subjects that influence her writing, as well as about the writing process itself, on her website.

# OTHER WORKS BY ROBIN REARDON

**Novels**
ON CHOCORUA (Book 1 of the Trailblazer series)
ON THE KALALAU TRAIL (Book 2 of the Trailblazer series)
AND IF I FALL
WAITING FOR WALKER
THROWING STONES
(Published by IAM Books )
EDUCATING SIMON
THE EVOLUTION OF ETHAN POE
A QUESTION OF MANHOOD
THINKING STRAIGHT
A SECRET EDGE
(Published by Kensington Publishing Corp.)

\* \* \*

**Short Stories**
GIUSEPPE AND ME
A LINE IN THE SAND
(Published by IAM Books )
\* \* \*

**Essay**
THE CASE FOR ACCEPTANCE: AN OPEN LETTER TO
HUMANITY
(Published by IAM Books )

www.ingramcontent.com/pod-product-compliance
Lightning Source LLC
Chambersburg PA
CBHW071531110726
47908CB00007B/1838